The British seaman had his left arm around Conchita's waist encircling her arms. She wore only a plain cotton shift which was rucked and pulled tight across her belly, leaving her legs bare. Williams's right fist held the long blade of his deckknife to her throat. Dunbar knew the edge to be as keen as a razor, for he had seen how easily it sliced manila fibres. Under the slight prick of the knife blade, Conchita had pulled her head back upon her captor's shoulder. Her eyes were huge with terror.

'Ah, Foggy,' Williams said as he caught sight of Dunbar and Hawkshawe in the doorway, '*you* won't want me to hurt this little chicken, will you?'

RICHARD WOODMAN

Waterfront

WARNER BOOKS

A *Warner* Book

First published in Great Britain in 1995
by Little, Brown and Company
This edition published by Warner Books in 1996

Copyright © Richard Woodman 1995

The moral right of the author has been asserted

*All characters in this publication are fictitious
and any resemblance to real persons, living or dead,
is purely coincidental.*

A CIP catalogue record for this book
is available from the British Library.

ISBN 0 7515 0466 1

Typeset by Palimpsest Book Production Limited,
Polmont, Stirlingshire

Printed and bound in Great Britain by Clays Ltd, St Ives plc

Warner Books
A Division of
Little, Brown and Company (UK)
Brettenham House
Lancaster Place
London WC2E 7EN

PROLOGUE

His earliest memory was of his father's church in late afternoon, with brilliant shafts of light piercing the green glass of the clerestory and given substance by the myriad floating motes of holy dust. The sunbeams failed to warm the deathly chill which, even at the height of summer, radiated from the hallowed stones. This eternal cold and the aqueous tint of the glass, suggested the tall and narrow nave was underwater.

Through the west window the sunlight fell dramatically upon a huge silk ensign. Generations of the village's children had been christened in the Norman font beneath its almost motionless scarlet folds. The additional blue and white of the Union nestled high up, in its upper and half-concealed canton. To him, the awesome symbol of secular power in that hallowed place far outweighed in fascination the worn oak of the holy rood at the opposite end of the nave, and the consecrated and gleaming adornments of the altar beyond.

It was this potent and contrary image that he always unconsciously called to mind whenever he thought of 'home'; not the cosy warmth of the rambling and untidy rectory next door, not even the warmth of his mother's arms; but this cold, sub-marine church with its memorial banner licking upwards, it seemed to his childhood fancy, like a great, rebellious red flame to join the yellow sunshine slanting through the perpendicular windows.

Partly concealed behind the red ensign and set in the damp plaster, a marble tablet commemorated a once famous vice-admiral of the British navy's red squadron. It was in his immortal honour that the huge, decaying oriflamme hung in the parish church of St Nicholas, patron saint of sailors. The memorial, spelling out the hero's glory, was set beneath a classical pediment and surrounded by a carved rope cable which terminated at the bottom in a fouled anchor; the anchor's shank crossed the barrel of a dismounted cannon. Above these nautical embellishments, a dusty bas-relief of men-of-war under sail and exchanging broadsides, delineated the triumphant moment of the vice-admiral's apotheosis 147 years earlier. The year, 1757, in Roman numerals, recorded the date for posterity.

No other monument, tomb or hatchment in that ancient place of worship made the least impression upon him. No other event in the church's familiar history, no other treasure held in his father's vestry, such as the breech bible or rare Saxon chalice, had any power over him. Not even the dessicated pieces of skin, said to date from the ninth century and to have been flayed from the bodies of two marauding Vikings, gripped his imagination like that vast flag and its accompanying tablet. Thus when at the age of eight, in answer to an aunt's question as to which service he most liked, he had answered, 'the sacrament of baptism'.

The charmed and simpering enquirer was deeply shocked by the candour of his next reply: because, he explained when asked why, it was the only way he could see the red ensign without having to turn round.

'But', his aunt had remonstrated somewhat illogically,

'you should never turn from the cross upon which Christ was crucified for you.'

The boy had frowned, then shrugged his shoulders and run off, while the prescient aunt took the matter up with her sister-in-law.

'You will have trouble with James, my dear,' she had said, 'he is far too fond of this world.'

His mother, caught in the act of baking, had dusted the flour from her hands and exchanged glances with Mrs Broom, the cook, then gone to the window and watched her eldest son's retreating figure crowned by its mop of dark brown hair, dodging away under the trees.

'He will not make a priest, if that is what you mean, Gwendolyn,' she said without turning from the window.

'That is not what I mean, Anne dear. I mean he is over-fond of,' Gwendolyn Dunbar paused, seeking a word which would encompass the possibility of damnation without shocking; 'of diversion.' She uttered the word with a profound and distasteful emphasis.

Mrs Broom kneaded the next basin of cake mix-ture with renewed vigour and awaited her mistress's response.

'He is only nine . . .'

''Tis too late,' the older woman declared with the conviction of superior knowledge. 'Well past the age of correction!'

'This is not a Jesuit house, Gwendolyn.'

'More's the pity, perhaps! But mark my words!' And the aunt swept from the room, her sombre bombazine hem making a faint, rasping noise upon the flagstones.

'What nonsense!' Mrs Broom said, wiping her hands and bending to withdraw the first batch of cakes from the oven.

'Nevertheless,' Anne Dunbar said, spooning the new

3

mixture into the browned cake moulds, 'I sometimes worry about what will become of him.'

James was sensible of this disapproval from an early age, for it came not only from his Aunt Gwendolyn, but was conveyed to him by scores of glances from the parish women who found his behaviour in church unacceptable. His fidgeting was no worse than that of their own children, but it was inexcusable in the rector's eldest son. It was, moreover, thrown into sharp contrast by the demeanour of his younger twin brothers, whose light curls, blue eyes and identical beauty seduced their maternal sensibilities.

James's dark restlessness was seen as an improper rebelliousness in a county in which the fair predominated, and possessed withal a tendency to dullness. Only Jenny Broom was his partisan, and her support was suspect, for she was 'Mrs' only by the courtesy and charity of the Reverend Dunbar, who had made the young woman his household's cook when he first became incumbent of the parish of St Nicholas, Clayton Dobbs, in the County of Suffolk. He had also discreetly arranged for her bastard daughter to be adopted by a couple in Ipswich.

James became aware of this vague hostility only gradually. At first it was to be found in the severe glances of his father's parishioners, and then in the contrasting and exclusive delight which greeted the arrival of the twins, David and Michael, whose adoration by the peering village women he was compelled to endure at the wheel of their perambulator. It seemed at these bleak moments that even his mother had cruelly deserted him.

Later, when he attended the village school, he was isolated as 'the parson's son', shunned or poked fun at, only to be adopted as a chum if there was some advantage

4

to be gained, or prior to his being set up for some planned humiliation. This situation was only made bearable by a fight he had when one of the boys declared Jenny Broom to have been a harlot.

The word had gained a currency from having been read out in an Old Testament lesson at matins the previous Sunday, and James resented his father's implicit conspiracy in the mortification of being thrown into a ditch. Nevertheless, though he had not gained a victory, his stalwart defence of Mrs Broom's good name earned him a grudging respect, until the time came for him to be sent away to a preparatory school near Ipswich.

Thereafter his visits to the village became rarer, and when he did come home he drifted in search of amusement, or perhaps diversion, two miles away from Clayton Dobbs, to the narrow estuarial hamlet of Clayton Wick, where black-tarred clapboard cottages huddled behind the shingle banks through which the River Clay forced itself eastwards into the North Sea.

Here he made friends with the stow-boaters who let him make himself useful about the decks of their smacks as they lay against the slime-covered staithing.

His father found it incomprehensible that he should wish to spend time in the company of such men and their families.

'James, you will not pass your examinations without some study during the holidays,' the rector said obliquely, adding by way of a barb, 'for there is precious little evidence that you do much at school.'

'I loathe school, Father, and I do not wish to go to Rugby,' he said defiantly, challenging his father's wishes.

'There appears to be no chance of that either,' his father retorted, dissembling conscientiously, for he could not afford the fees that, without a scholarship, would prevent James from following in his footsteps.

'David and Michael will not disappoint you there,' his son said.

'But my dear boy,' the Reverend Dunbar replied, 'what on earth are we to do with *you*?'

'You may send me to sea, Father.'

'To sea?' The rector could not hide his dismay. 'But the entrance examination for Dartmouth—'

'Oh, damn Dartmouth!'

'James!' The rector rose from behind his desk. 'Mind your language! You see what comes of keeping bad company.'

'What bad company?'

'Those blessed fishermen,' his father spluttered, unconscious of his own irony.

'I thought the disciples were fishermen.'

'Don't add blasphemy to the catalogue of your wickedness.'

James had fled from his father's sudden and unreasonable rage, and gone at once to Clayton Wick where he had found the *Eliza Maude* ready for sea and a hand short.

'Young Nattie Matthews be sick, Jim. Will 'ee ship out with us?'

And he had gone aboard without a second thought, to spend his first night at sea in the clothes he stood up in.

Matters had come to a head when he came back a week later, on the eve of his return to school. His father had taken him to his bedroom and thrashed him 'for the anxiety he had caused his mother'. He learned later that Jenny Broom had heard he had gone off with Skipper

6

Hopton and reassured his parents that 'no 'arm'll come of the lad's waywardness'.

'He'll be safe enough,' she had said to her mistress, though privately reserving to herself a wonder that the rector's faith in the mercy of God was not stronger.

But this event convinced the Reverend Dunbar that his wilful son required the rein of discipline and, whilst he could not afford Rugby, he discovered he could muster the premium of £120 to bind his son apprentice to a firm of Swansea shipowners. This welcome news resulted from a visit to Clayton Hall where Colonel Hugh Scrope-Davies lived in some state, mourning the death of his own elder son in the Boer War. The Scrope-Davies family had an interest in the shipping company and he assured the rector a place could be found for James.

'Least I could do, Dunbar, after the service you did my family,' Scrope-Davies said, brushing aside the rector's gratitude and alluding to the affair of Jenny's unwanted pregnancy. 'Boys will be boys and my first-born paid the price for his moment of pleasure.'

'He made the supreme sacrifice, Colonel,' the rector said sanctimoniously. '*Dulce et decorum est . . .*'

'*Pro patria mori*, eh? That's a damned humbug, Rector, and you know it! There was nothing sweet and honourable about the crossing of the Tugela; lot of bloody incompetence on our side, by all accounts, though not on the enemy's. They tell me the damned Boers had the water filled with barbed wire.'

'Sometimes it is a consolation . . .'

'Huh! Anyway, I was about to say your lad is welcome to what I can do for him. Settles the score, wouldn't you say?'

'Indeed, and I am most grateful.'

7

'Send the boy up to see me before he goes. I've a pair of Jack's field glasses he might find useful.'

And so, in the late summer of 1904, James Dunbar went to sea under the red ensign.

PART ONE

The Hotel Paradiso

CHAPTER ONE

The Eve of Arrival

Apprentice Dunbar shook the grubby ensign, secured its toggle and eye to the halliards and hoisted it to the truck of the ensign staff. In the warm breeze caused by the forward motion of the ship, the flag lifted, then settled down to wave languidly over the stern of the SS *Kohinoor*.

James Dunbar stared at the ensign, shading his eyes from the brassy glare of the sun, thought briefly of the magnificent standard which had hung in St Nicholas's church and felt a faint, ineluctable sense of profound disappointment. Then he shrugged it off and leant on the rail, watching the wake boil out from underneath the counter-stern where, hidden in the blue depths, the *Kohinoor*'s propeller spun, thrusting the laden hull northwards, parallel to the coast of Mexico. He tried but failed to catch some of the cool freshness that the thrashing screw churned up from the depths of the ocean as it turned the sea to a seething froth. The heat was as oppressive as the chill in his father's church had been eternal, and it seemed to hem them in, confining their small circle of visible sea by a haze.

'It's a sign of the land,' Mr Mitchell had said a few minutes earlier when Dunbar remarked upon it. 'You can still see about four miles, but it prevents us from taking sights by obscuring the horizon.' The second mate was a serious exponent of his profession and generously undertook the instructing of the young and eager Dunbar. Mitchell had handed him the ensign and bid him go aft and hoist it. The significance of the unceremonious little ritual he had just carried out was not lost on Dunbar. It meant they were nearing the land, closing with it, in seaman's argot, coming to the end of their long passage which, but for a short, twelve-hour break in Rio de Janeiro, had brought them from South Wales, through the Strait of Magellan, to the coast of Mexico.

The sea was unruffled, flat beneath the tropic sun, its surface dull and seemingly heavy as lead, jealously holding fast to the boon of its coolness. Dunbar had by now seen the ocean in all weather and attributed to it a moodiness which, he had discovered, he responded to himself. In his first gale he had felt no sickness, only a wild and reckless joy, but this present leaden flatness was sullen and enervating. He felt there was no hurry to return to the bridge, that his contribution to the safe navigation of the ship was minimal and he might linger idly here for a moment or two longer.

Dunbar watched the wake kink slightly as the helmsman, Able Seaman Daffyd Idris Williams, perhaps affected by the same *ennui* as himself, corrected the ship's course a trifle. A bosun bird, its long central tail-feather twisting to stabilise its flight, flew over the imperfect wake, quartering their progress in search of food. A natural opportunist, Dunbar thought, just like Able Seaman Williams.

Idris Williams had become Dunbar's sea-daddy, his mentor and instructor. Apprentices in the British merchant marine occupied an ambiguous status, particularly in tramp ships owned by hard-nosed Welsh shipowners. For all the panoply of their uniform, or company livery as it was properly termed, and which they wore only occasionally, there was little to suggest in their daily toil they were aspiring officers.

They were generally acknowledged to be a source of cheap labour, cheaper even than the poorly paid seamen and stokers who manned the *Kohinoor*, for their allowances came from the premium their parents had lodged with their employers, who in turn banked the sum and drew its interest, instructing their shipmasters to dole out a few pounds as and when necessary. These shipowners also empowered their masters to deduct from this pittance any expenses over and above food, which they generously consented to provide in order to keep body and soul together. They were, after all, permitting the apprentice the privilege of learning the art and mystery of navigation – if he put his mind to it. If he did not, it was no matter; either his family rescued him and found him a clerk's job ashore, or he lost face and crossed the boundary of class, to become a seaman himself, an imperial hobo, an embarrassment to the reputation of the British and the scourge of vice-consuls and merchant shipmasters the world over. Such men were, nevertheless, a most necessary evil if ships were to carry British manufactures across the globe and return with the raw materials for national aggrandisement.

Williams had occasionally intimated some such fall from grace had happened to him. The able seaman hinted sometimes about other aspects of his past; he had spoken of the temptations open to the youth of his own generation, when the goldfields of Ballarat had beckoned and more than one apprentice had abandoned the study of haversines and the traverse, to seek sudden wealth. Everyone had heard of someone finding the rich and elusive lode, though few had actually met the lucky ones. They were said to quit for Melbourne or Sydney and then London, decked out in new suiting and sporting gold watch-chains, with a bevy of the most beautiful women New South Wales or Victoria could find for their pleasuring.

But, two days earlier as they sat on deck splicing, Williams had assured the new apprentice things had changed these days.

'It's a new century and a new world. You'll not find goldfields in New South Wales that aren't sewn up by the big companies, nor up in Californio neither.' And he jerked his head at the ship's bow, indicating California lay somewhere beyond the forecastle. 'They were there once, of course, ripe for the picking, like plums in the vicar's orchard, but not any more.'

Dunbar ignored the gentle jibe at his ecclesiastical origins. He had learned that such guying was an acceptable part of the world of men, not to be taken seriously. It required no such defence as would be called for in the playground.

'What's Puerto San Martin like then?' he asked as he wrestled with the harsh manila hemp.

'Well, it's not California proper, that's in the US of A; it's in what the Mexies call Baja California.' (Williams pronounced the word 'badger'.) 'There are plenty of women all right, but no gold – oh dear me, no, unless you count fool's gold, and there's a lot of that.' He chuckled at his own joke and deftly twisted his lignum vitae fid into the thick rope across his lap. Opening up the lay of the heavy warp, he thrust a single strand through the aperture thus forced, removed the fid and let the twisted fibre close naturally upon itself. Dunbar watched in admiration, acknowledging the power in the weatherbeaten wrist and strong fingers. He had learned to splice ropes aboard the *Eliza Maude*, but they had been mere string compared with these ten-inch-diameter mooring warps.

'Fool's gold?' Dunbar frowned, bending again to his task, and forcing his own fid into another rope's end.

'Copper, mate. Tons and bloody tons of copper. That's what we're going there for. That and to deliver all that steel and whatnot in the 'tween-decks.'

'The conveyor belt system,' Dunbar said, unconsciously admitting his superior status. He had heard the cargo being discussed by Mitchell and Sanders, the third mate. 'You've been there before then?'

Williams nodded. 'Oh yes. So've most of us that shipped out of Swansea or Barry in the little copperbarques a few years back. You'll still see plenty of sailing vessels hereabouts.'

Dunbar's interest had picked up. He had seen several barques during the passage, including the monstrous five-master *Potosi* storming up the South Atlantic from the Horn, all sail set to her royals and bound from the Chilean port of Iquique to Hamburg, her holds laden with nitrate for German industry. It had come as something of a surprise to see not the red ensign of Great Britain, but the black, white and red of Imperial Germany flying from the upper gaff on the huge barque's after jigger mast. She was not bound for the inside passage, through the Strait of Magellan. *She* had come round the Horn, doubled Cape Stiff both ways, eastbound against the headwind westerlies, and westbound with her heavy cargo.

'That Cap'n Hilgendorf never takes nothing off her but the royals,' Williams had advised him at the time.

'How d'you know his name's Hilger . . . ?'

'Hilgendorf? *Everybody* knows that,' Williams had said, staring at the great ship, and Dunbar had thought of the sleeping shire he had left behind, and the farm labourers who knew nothing of such things. Even his father, who quoted Homer in Greek and Ovid in Latin and had been, to his son's intimidation, a polymath of enormous stature, was ignorant of this fact. Dunbar had learned too, during that memorable forenoon, that in order to make the grade as a real sailor he must undertake at least one passage in sail. His father's placing him with a steamship company seemed now to have been something of a disservice, a palming off, a quittance of a parental obligation.

'Well, it's understandable, on account of being so much cheaper, see?' Williams had explained later. 'It'd have cost your papa three hundred or so to take out indentures with a pukkah sailing outfit like Devitt and Moore. But don't worry about it. Once you've finished your time, ship out for a round voyage to Australia before you sit for your second mate's ticket. You won't get sea time for a sailing certificate, but you'll be able to tell a yarn or two.'

This advice had irritated Dunbar. He was bound by his indentures to serve his present employers for four years, and the time stretched ahead of him like a gaol sentence. Besides, it seemed that even now his father's genteel poverty, if not his disinterest, had blighted him, condemning him to second best. He felt again both resentment and disillusion, and fell silent, bending to his task.

Williams was not thinking of the past; his mind was on the immediate future and, having made his last tuck, he beat the splice with his fid and sighed with the contentment of anticipation. 'Puerto San Martin . . .

16

Paradiso . . . A place where even a poor sailor can fool himself into thinking he's a man of substance.'

Dunbar looked up from his struggle with spike and strand, saw the gleam in Williams's eye and frowned. He knew the older man wanted to expand but waited to be prompted.

'Why d'you say that?' he asked dutifully.

'Because there are women so poor there, they'll do anything for a dollar.'

'What d'you mean *anything*?' Dunbar was moved by a prurient curiosity which he knew to be sinful, but which out here, on the heaving ocean in the salt-laden fresh air, seemed robbed of its wickedness.

'Anything,' Williams had repeated without enlargement, though he looked for a moment at the boy and seemed to consider saying more. 'You'll see.' And having baited his protégé, the elderly able seaman left Dunbar to the warmed excesses of his adolescent imagination.

Dunbar had been thinking of this conversation as he gazed astern. He was recalled to the present by the imperious blast of Mitchell's whistle, which called him back to the bridge. He turned and was engulfed by a cloud of smoke carried across the after decks by some caprice of the turbulent air abaft the ship's funnel. Choking from the sulphurous fumes, he staggered forward while the off-duty Chinese firemen who lived beneath the poop and sat sunning themselves round a low wooden table covered with their empty rice bowls, laughed at his choking retreat.

The long peninsula of Baja California came in sight that

evening as they passed inside Cap San Lucas and entered the long Gulf of California, which some called the Sea of Cortez. The haze had gone and the arid summits of the Sierra de San Lázaro stood out against the afterglow of sunset.

'What a damnable coast,' remarked Captain Steele from the port bridge-wing to the chief mate, Mr Rayner, pointing out the distant peak of Santa Genoveva. The two men stood side by side in silence, both anticipating their arrival at Puerto San Martin the following evening.

'I hope they can take us alongside straight away,' remarked Mr Rayner, the mate.

'No doubt about it,' Captain Steele replied with his customary certainty. He was a Welshman of medium height whose stockiness made him appear shorter than he really was. Iron grey hair and sparkling blue eyes made his heavy features handsome, in a middle-aged way. 'They want this machinery urgently,' he went on, 'and will get it out of the ship as soon as we arrive.'

Rayner sniffed doubtfully. He was a man for whom optimism was a rare luxury. As far as he was concerned, the reality of life at sea was one of incessant problems and he made heavy weather of them all. Thorough and reliable, he was senior to his commander in years, but the ship's owners had denied him promotion to master on the pragmatic grounds that he was a better chief mate, a fuss-pot who missed no detail in caring for the ship and, more important, her cargo.

Nor was his judgement on this occasion that of an habitual prejudice. They were approaching a port engaged in a sailing-ship trade: coal and patent fuel outwards and copper homewards, bound for Germany or Britain, carried via Cape Horn, a long and tedious voyage, not yet invaded by the regular steamship. Speed was not yet a criterion in the world, but the mining company had recently purchased a new, static steam engine and miles of sectional steel tracking to form a long delivery system. The conveyor belt was intended to be cheaper to run than the railway hitherto used to carry the *boleos* of copper from the mines to Puerto San Martin. They had, therefore, shipped this huge contrivance aboard the *Kohinoor* for prompt delivery, hence the steamship's invasion of this Pacific backwater.

'It'll speed up the loading time,' said Rayner, referring to the contents of their 'tween-decks, '*then* they'll want regular shipments and we'll find ourselves steaming up this Godforsaken arsehole on a regular liner trade.'

'That's progress,' said Steele sententiously. 'Everyone knows the sailing ship has had her day, except for a few old fools and romantics.'

'And a load of university wallahs. I met Paddy McLaughlin when we were in dry dock and he'd just come off the old bald-header *Corryvreckan*. Paddy said they had one doctor of philosophy and three undergraduates in the half-deck, all wanting to experience what they called the romance of sail!' Rayner's tone was richly contemptuous.

'Bloody fools!' Steele scoffed. Both he and Rayner had obtained their certificates of competency in sail, each spending more than twenty years in square-rig before taking to steam. 'They'll be writing bloody books about it all, you mark my words! Telling a pack of lies about poor bloody sailormen.'

They were silent for a moment, then Rayner said, 'I hope you'll order us off to the anchorage once we've discharged the conveyor gear.' Both men knew the rest of their holds were filled with best Welsh steam-coal and the compacted briquettes of patent fuel.

19

'I thought you *wanted* to be alongside,' remarked Steele, looking askance at Rayner.

'I do right enough, to get the conveyor gear out of her. God knows that'll take long enough. But I want to haul off to an anchor and lighter that bloody coal ashore.'

'Why?'

'Because staying alongside that hell-hole means trouble with the crew.'

'Trouble with women, you mean,' said Steele, laughing in the dusk with a secret quickening of his heart.

'Exactly that, Captain,' said Rayner with an air of finality. 'Have you been here before?'

'No.'

'There's a bordello called the Paradiso. The place is trouble.'

'I've heard of it.'

'Well, believe me, you can expect trouble with the men.'

'Not with the crew of *my* ship, mister.'

'Don't you be too sure, Captain Steele. They'll kick the traces over at the first opportunity.'

'Not if I have anything to do with it,' Steele announced firmly.

'Well,' Rayner said resignedly, 'I just hope you're right, that's all.'

'Of course I'm right, mister, and if any of 'em misbehave, I'll stop their shore leave and log 'em a day's pay for every misdemeanour they commit.'

'On their money that'll not stop 'em,' Rayner remarked sourly, foreseeing the burden of extra labour that would fall upon a chief mate's shoulders.

'Maybe not, but Jack-the-lad doesn't like being brought up with a round turn when it comes to shore leave,' snapped Steele tartly. 'Take away a seaman's access to drink and a woman, and he's like putty in the hands.'

Rayner remained silent, frowning in the gathering darkness. The Old Man was in a damned funny mood.

'Anyway, I'm looking forward to it,' Steele said, as though his emphatic use of the personal pronoun removed all Rayner's miserable objections.

The mate had practical doubts about confining anyone to the *Kohinoor*, based on long experience of the ways of determined seamen, but he said no more. Whatever the coming weeks brought, he thought to himself, Rayner only hoped the Old Man did not himself cultivate an appetite for the women of Puerto San Martin. Where chief mates had a great deal to do in port, masters had very little and he hoped the devil would not make work for Captain Steele's idle hands, for he certainly seemed to have recovered from the loss of his wife.

Captain Steele had not merely recovered from the recent death of his wife, he rejoiced in it. Moreover, he intended to revel in it. He possessed the energy and the expectancy of the reborn; God had given him a second chance and Captain Steele, armed with the experience of more than forty years, was determined to make the most of it. He, like his newest apprentice (though he would have disdained the comparison), had been reared in the fearful shadow of religion. For Captain Steele it had not been the confident, authoritarian Anglican tradition that had scarred his young mind, but the retributive, demagogical flame of Welsh non-conformism. As a youth he had been unsubtly coerced to link sin and sexuality in a misguided attempt by his elders and betters to redeem him from the rot of licence. Steele was intended to belong to a generation who would purify the imperial race. This inextricable union of sex, wrong-doing and imperial mission had blighted his young life and led him, as it did so many others, into a precipitate, unsuitable and unhappy marriage.

When the intemperance of a passion founded entirely upon his own expectations had burned itself out, he realised he had married a shrew. What the lady expected, or afterwards discovered about the sacramental institution of matrimony, he did not trouble himself to find out. To be fair, the imperial demands of trade paid for by his long absences at sea and short periods ashore, left little time for either the development of intimacy, or the sustaining of a relationship based upon an initial and mutual attraction. But as well as possessing a sense of national vocation, Arthur Steele belonged to a generation of males confident in what it held to be its legitimate birthright: he could never understand why his wife resented falling into step behind him. Her spirited resistance made her, at least in his eyes, a termagant nag.

Despite this apparent heartlessness, Captain Steele had, withal, been faithful to his wife; but time belied the poet and failed to heal; time excoriated and corroded; time banked the interest of contempt to fan the flames of hatred that flared in accusations of wasted life, of useless and unappreciated sacrifice. Time proved, as ever, the true and triumphant enemy.

So, when his wife succumbed to a tumour, Steele was apt in his innermost heart to regard it as a fatal retribution for her foolish rebellion against the natural order of the world. That her death returned to him the freedom men first eagerly throw away and subsequently hold most dear, seemed merely to confirm his secret opinion.

What existence in the interim had taught him, was that

young men make fools of themselves and older men waste their opportunities. Armed with this acquired wisdom and a small unencumbered fund of money, Captain Steele had every intention of altering the course of his life by a deliberate and considered act, and the thought thrilled him. In short Steele had reached that age of indiscretion which men take to signify maturity and the mastery of their own destiny. At this goatish age Steele's fading powers sharpened his desire and refined his tastes; they made him less fastidious, but no less eager.

He had high hopes of Puerto San Martin, hopes far beyond the discharging of his cargo of conveyor belts and coal, for he had heard stories of the Hotel Paradiso and they engendered hopes that he might engineer for himself, and entirely on his own stringent terms, the highest and most perfect happiness. It would be a commercial transaction, of course, based upon the ineluctable laws of supply and demand found in any marketplace, *soukh* or bazaar, but it would confer upon the lucky girl the obligation of gratitude. From this would arise the most perfect bliss.

And in this exalted anticipation he dismissed all his chief mate's mundane apprehensions.

Able Seaman Williams nurtured a similar, though simpler desire. Life had in many ways been unkind to him, though he had enjoyed moments of disreputable and improper revenge upon it. It suited him to foster in the young and impressionable Dunbar the false assumption that he had fallen from social grace through no fault of his own. In part the oblique claim, never explicitly uttered, was true. In fact Williams had never pretended to the rank of aspirant, though an indulgent and lonely chief mate

23

of the first ship to which the orphanage had sent him had seen promise in the boy and would have groomed him for the part, had not a wave carried the elderly man over the side of the barque *Earl of Balcarres* as she ran her easting down in the southern Indian Ocean. The boy had been orphaned a second time.

Williams had, however, demonstrated the ultimate soundness of the old man's judgement, and after years of obscure rootless ocean wandering, had turned up in Cardiff and become a steady employee of the South Wales Steam Navigation Company.

His past, however, provided him with a fund of anecdotes which most of his shipmates discounted as mere boastful, wishful thinking, for they contained elements of inconsistent evidence that suggested he made most of them up. He had, he said, sailed under the stars and stripes alongside the famous novelist and great American liar, Herman Melville, whose stories were largely plagiarised from his own adventurous life. For, so Williams alleged, among his footloose years he had spent several months living with the natives of the Marquesas and many more aboard a Nantucket whaler, seeing with his own eyes a white sperm whale and a shipmaster with one artificial leg of whale ivory.

Nevertheless, Williams's yarns possessed incidental details which, despite the contradiction of common sense and logic, survived to inhabit the imaginations, and afterwards the memories, of his listeners. Consequently while at the time they dismissed them as fabrications of 'Williams the Lie', they afterwards recounted them with some pride as 'having occurred to an old seaman I once knew'.

This alone would have ensured Williams a kind of immortality among the nautical confraternity at large, but immortality was not something he sought, even as a by-product of life. Whatever his pretensions, his had been a life of unremitting toil, at the beck and call of others placed always in a superior position to his own. His labours had gained him little: a few dollars, a passable suit, shirt and a pair of shoes for shoregoing. In this he was typical of thousands of freebooting seamen who owned no real nationality beyond claims upon the red ensign of Great Britain at the sterns of their ships. He could stuff the accumulation of a lifetime into a single ditty-bag.

He had only one long-term expectation of existence, and that was a persistent one which the early patronage of the chief mate of the *Earl of Balcarres* had raised forever in his psyche; the desire to have friends. As a young man it had led him into bad company, company the like of which the Reverend Dunbar, chiding his son for his association with fisherfolk, could not imagine. That Williams had freed himself from the influence of such dominance was to his credit, but it had been at a cost. Advancing years had left him less susceptible to older men and he courted now the young, finding in the admiration of the apprentices some solace for his own wretched life. His stock of yarns was the currency with which he purchased their indulgence, and occasionally he sought a shy domination of his own.

In the short term, however, there were other pleasures. For Williams, Puerto San Martin held the allure of a watering hole to a thirsty traveller, and life had taught him never to pass up the opportunity to grasp those amusements it laid fleetingly before him.

These, Williams was capable of seizing with a practised and primitive savagery.

* * *

It may be supposed that all of the crew of the SS *Kohinoor* nursed some dream of an earthly paradise at the end of their long passage. It was in the nature of their harsh lifestyle. Not all were profligate; the steady married men like Rayner, the mate, and the chief and second engineers, wanted only a little light amusement, a drink ashore, a walk, the chance to post a letter home; perhaps – though not seriously expected – a letter *from* home. For these officers, however, time for even a walk would be hard come by.

Mr Mitchell looked forward to collecting some botanical specimens which he dried and meticulously reproduced on paper with his Rowney watercolours. Those inclined to jeer at this pursuit as unmanly, were tactfully reminded of how, at a notorious bar in Rio de Janeiro, the mild Sid Mitchell had rescued six of his overpowered and beaten shipmates from the clutches of a gang of cutpurses intent upon their robbery by way of murder.

This mood of sharpened anticipation closed about the *Kohinoor* on her last night at sea. Among those restless with its infection was young James Dunbar. For him all was a tumble of confusion. He was at once disappointed and excited by his new life, betrayed and satisfied, full of lust and yet full of holiness.

Home, the red ensign hanging in the church of St Nicholas, without which was the rectory and the sprawling village of Clayton Dobbs, seemed further off in time than ever it was in distance. He felt the very act of coming to sea as an act of irreversible parturition; it had wrenched his life around so great a corner that he could never look directly back upon the past, for there would always be that cranked view, like the kink in the *Kohinoor*'s wake; fading and insubstantial, but nevertheless there.

When he had told his father he would not go to

Dartmouth he had reacted instinctively, out of a deep-rooted conviction. He could not see how the Royal Navy with its guns and torpedoes was a moral force for good. He had developed similar misgivings about the established church, misgivings which the power of the huge scarlet flag had provoked and sustained. James had developed a naive but strong aversion to killing, even in the service of the British Empire. Knowing the treason of his thoughts, he kept them to himself. His father, unwitting inseminator of these ideas, completely misunderstood his son's refusal to try for a commission in the Royal Navy.

The rector's presumption was not only wrong, it was unkind. He had misguidedly told his wife he did not think the boy 'fitted to undertake the discipline and rigour of becoming a naval officer'.

But James nursed a romantic affection for that great red banner and would not, *could* not countenance sailing under any other. This was no quixoticism; the flag's symbolism was a potent and ineluctable influence. The faint and very occasional sussurations of its silk folds whispered of great deeds which, because they were in the past, were beyond the taint of moral dubiety. Yet, James thought privately, providence had played its part in this matter of his life; for although the flag glowed with the gules of heraldry rather than the post-office scarlet of the red duster, it had become that lesser thing, eclipsed by the white ensign flown by Nelson at Trafalgar when the naval hero of neighbouring Norfolk had received a far greater apotheosis than the vice-admiral who had once lived in Clayton Hall. The British Admiralty had decided, not forty years earlier, just within his own father's lifetime, to abandon squadronal colours. Consequently Britain's oldest sea flag was left for the humble mercantile marine, the business of trade, and the dreams of young men like James Dunbar.

Thus a sort of pacifism and an adolescent fancy had combined with his father's misjudgement and a decision by a dead Admiralty Board, to set him on his lonely course and bind him hand, foot and finger to the owners of the SS *Kohinoor*.

There had seemed a certain romance in the name of the ship to which he was sent. The export of coal, the 'black diamonds' of the South Wales mines, had inspired the owners of the steam navigation company to name their vessels after more lustrous products of carbon. In a copy of *Lloyd's List* consulted in Ipswich, he and his mother had found others of the line: the SS *Orloff*, the SS *Florentine*, the *Pitt* and the *Star of the South*.

'Here it is,' his mother had said, pointing a gloved finger.

'Here *she* is, Mother,' he had murmured, his voice betraying a wonder that he was soon to be associated with a world which meant inclusion in a newspaper. He had read the entry: *Arrived Swansea from Takoradi, 24th, SS* Kohinoor, *South Wales S.N.Co, now lying in dry dock. Shortly loading coal, patent fuel and industrial plant for Puerto San Martin*.

Takoradi . . . Puerto San Martin . . . the foreign names breathed freedom far beyond the horizon of the North Sea which, even from the deck of the little *Eliza Maude* had seemed limitless with possibilities! When he had found the two places in his father's atlas, his heart thundered at the adventure of his enterprise.

But, alongside a coal staithe in the King's Dock at Swansea, reality gave his eager heart a lurch of a different kind. He had seen the King's men-of-war at anchor in Great Yarmouth Roads, but the *Kohinoor* bore no resemblance to their stern grey magnificence. His sensibilities were to cost him prestige, he realised, if his father's wrinkled face was anything to go by.

The ship had been dwarfed by the tall structure of a coal hoist which took uncoupled railway trucks and, upending them, shot their contents of best Welsh steam-coal into the tramp ship's capacious holds. This act was accompanied by the clatter and crash of the free-wheeling trucks which were released from their laden fellows in a raised siding and pushed by a couple of men down an incline and onto a platform. Here their flight was abruptly arrested, the platform was detached from the rails, lifted and, by an ingenious system of wires and pulleys, tipped, releasing the truck's contents to cascade into the waiting hold of the ship. Thereafter the platform was returned to the horizontal, switching the empty truck to a second, exit track, and gravity pulled it down to a lower siding where, with another crash, it joined those that had preceded it.

A black and hellish dust accompanied each discharge, rising in clouds that subsided to lie thickly over everything. James and his father stood and breathed in its sulphurous stink as they observed the process of loading.

The *Kohinoor* herself had been practically painted for this practical trade. Her hull, with its three islands of forecastle, centrecastle and poop, was black with a brick-red boot-topping. The superstructure of bridge and engine casing, which housed the ship's officers and engineers, was stone-buff. The tall funnel was also black, though one third of its height from the top was girded with a row of painted white diamonds.

The rector, garbed himself in black and white (though the irony escaped him), held his hat against the wind,

clucked his tongue and, having found the rickety gangway, bore his son aboard during a brief interlude between
emptying trucks. Captain Steele, they learned, had not yet
come aboard, but Mr Rayner seemed a steady fellow,
older than the rector himself. As the rector told his wife
afterwards, he had not detected 'the slightest trace of
strong drink upon him, nor evidence of a bottle in his
cabin which was rather tastefully curtained in chintz and
possessed rather splendidly polished portholes'.

These observations assuaged any guilt the rector might
have felt at consigning his son to such a thing. (He could
not say place, for the ship was strangely impermanent, a
philosophical consideration the Reverend Dunbar withheld
from his wife.) His jollity served to postpone Anne
Dunbar's anxiety to the small hours of the night, and she
had lain awake frequently, worrying about her eldest son.
Now he had left home she missed him, acknowledging
that his silences and long periods of absence might be a
reproach, evidence of her failure as a mother. Perhaps she
had favoured the twins. But the labour of having children
simultaneously was a disproportionate burden and few
could understand the strain it imposed. Her husband,
bless him, had had his head in his heavenly clouds.

So, when some weeks later an early autumn gale rustled
the yew trees in the adjacent graveyard, she fretted enough
to wake her husband.

'His ship will have gone days ago,' consoled the rector
irritably, but he was wrong. The loading of the long
sections of steel conveyor track had succeeded the coal
and had been far slower than the rector imagined. The
Kohinoor spent that very night pitching heavily, thirty
miles to the south and west of Lundy Island.

After the tedious and humiliating drudgery of loading,
in which the stowage of the captain's personal stores had

30

chiefly occupied the two apprentices, that gale-torn night proved a sublime justification. A high, full moon rode in and out of the racing scud and the strong spring tide which ebbed into the Atlantic from the Bristol Channel sharpened the peaks of the waves as it forced the sea against the westerly gale. Posted as lookout on the bridge, draped in black oilskins and sou'wester bonnet, Dunbar had clung to the awning stanchions and stared blithely into the screaming night. There was even a moment or two when, almost unconsciously, he had begun to sing: 'Loud roared the tempest o'er the deep . . .'

They had heard him in the wheelhouse where Mr Mitchell and Captain Steele stood the middle watch.

'Is that young Dunbar?' Steele had asked, noticing the new apprentice properly for the first time.

'Yes, sir.'

'That's a hymn he's singing, isn't it?'

'He's a vicar's son, sir.'

'No wonder we've got a bloody gale on our hands then!' Steele had said, voicing an old superstition. The captain thrust his head through the wheelhouse door. 'Dunbar!'

'Sir?'

'Is that a hymn you're singing?'

'Singing . . . ? Oh, yes . . . Yes it was, sir.'

'When I want a church service, I'll ask for one, d'ye hear me?'

'Yes, sir, sorry, sir.'

Steele slammed the door shut. 'Yes, sir, sorry, sir,' he mimicked.

'I suppose we all started off like that,' Mitchell said reasonably, liking the new boy and mildly disapproving of the master's unkindness.

'I bloody didn't!' Steele staggered as the *Kohinoor*

31

plunged over a heavy sea and drove her bow into the advancing face of the next wave. Both men watched as water, silver-grey in the moonlight, poured over the forecastle and cascaded down onto the forward well-deck. They felt the ship shudder at this sudden burden, felt her innate buoyancy assert itself and then heave her upwards with a creaking of her riveted hull. Then the next wave passed under her so that her black bow lifted, lifted and climbed beyond the crest, until she tipped, shuddered as the supporting sea fell away, and plunged downwards again.

'Vicar's son, eh? Well, well. We'll have to have church on Sunday then, Mr Mitchell.'

'Church, sir,' Mitchell frowned in the darkness. 'Oh, yes, church . . .'

'We all started off like *that*.'

And so, shortly after breakfast on the first Sunday of the voyage as they headed south and west on a great circle track down the length of the Atlantic, James Dunbar found himself the butt of a practical joke. He was sent down to the saloon where the officers took their meals 'to find the hymnbooks for the church service' which, he was told, the Old Man habitually held at nine sharp.

Captain Steele and Mr Rayner had been lingering over their own breakfasts, the former in anticipation of the jape, the latter because he had been up since four o'clock and was enjoying his coffee. Under the master's eye, Dunbar's search was assiduous.

'Are you looking for something?' asked Captain Steele in a solicitous tone of voice which would have registered as untypical, had Dunbar known the captain longer.

'Er, yes, sir, the hymnbooks.' Dunbar had stood

awkwardly irresolute, trying to balance himself against the easy roll of the ship, and feeling uncomfortably queasy after having his head in the musty lockers.

'Now let me think,' ruminated the captain. 'I expect we moved them while the ship was in port. Yes, that's right, we did, don't you remember, Mr Rayner?'

The mate had grunted. With a stomach full of porridge, eggs and bacon, he was feeling sleepy.

'I think,' said Captain Steele, drawing the verb out in earnest of his concern, 'I think young Humphries must have stowed them away in the fog-locker. Go and ask him, Dunbar.'

So Dunbar had toiled his way up to the bridge to ask his fellow apprentice whether or not he had stowed the hymnbooks in the fog-locker.

Edgar Humphries had been aboard the *Kohinoor* for two years. The departure of another apprentice and arrival of Dunbar had elevated him from the lowest form of animal life aboard the tramp, to the puissant position of senior cadet officer. He had been quick to recognise the obligations of rank, and sent Dunbar to the bosun in quest of the key to the fog-locker, which he confessed he had not got. The bosun had in turn despatched Dunbar to the chief steward who, he had explained, had borrowed the key to pack away some bottles of communion wine, and whilst Dunbar had thought this circumstance odd, he lacked the confidence to call the bluff of these men. The chief steward, who had happened by then to have been taking a cup of coffee with Captain Steele and Mr Rayner, said he had passed it to the chief engineer who had wanted to oil the spare foghorn. When he finally located that worthy inspecting the steering gear, the chief engineer had told him to 'bugger off and stop wasting my time'.

Disconsolate and wretched, Dunbar had been left on

deck, wondering what to do next. Beyond the rail the horizon heaved as the ship rolled and pitched in a ceaseless motion that had already lost its thrill. This grim, grey Atlantic with its grim, grey sky of a slightly lighter tone, was a harsh reminder of his loneliness. This was a Sunday, he had reflected, thinking of home, the cold church and the great red flag. Humiliation at the failure of his quest, confusion and homesickness had made him vomit over the rail. As he had leaned, sweating and miserable, on the cold steel, he was aware of someone next to him. He looked round. An old seaman Dunbar had seen on the bridge as helmsman during his own watch put a kindly hand on his shoulder.

'You all right, son?' The man smiled. 'What the hell are you doing here?'

Dunbar had swallowed and straightened up. 'I'm looking for something, actually.'

'Well, what is it you're *actually* looking for?'

'The key of the fog-locker.'

Able Seaman Williams had stared momentarily at the pallid and unhappy face. Then he had grinned. 'Your name Dunbar, is it?'

'Yes.' Dunbar had felt awkward at this revelation. He had felt sure he ought to maintain a distance between himself and this man, but then he had relaxed. The man reminded him a little of Skipper Hopton.

'I'm Daffyd Idris Williams,' the able seaman had introduced himself. 'I'm on the same watch as you are.' He had smiled again and held his hand out.

'Yes, I know. I'm pleased to meet you, Mr Williams.'

'You'd better not let the Old Man hear you calling me that. Call me Id.'

This had sounded even more impractical to Dunbar, but he nodded as Williams went on. 'They're after making a fool of you, see. Now the question is, what are you going to do about it?'

'You mean there isn't such a thing as the fog-locker?' Dunbar voiced the suspicion already forming in his mind.

'No. Not at all.'

'Oh.'

'Nor any hymnbooks, neither.'

'Oh.'

'But we could invent one.'

'What, a fog-locker?'

'Yes. Go and tell the Old Man that you've looked in the fog-locker but there are no hymnbooks in there. Then tell him Able Seaman Williams said the chief engineer sold them to the Bethesda Chapel in the back of Port Tennant.'

'The Bethesda Chapel in the back of Port Tennant,' Dunbar repeated obediently.

'And the chief engineer sold them.'

'All right.'

'You're a vicar's son, aren't you?'

'Well, a rector's son actually.'

'Right, well, you call the Old Man's bluff by saying this doesn't matter, because you know the words by heart and if he'll preach, you'll sing the hymns.'

Dunbar hesitated, staring at the seaman, wary now that he was to be made a double dupe by Williams. Besides, he could recognise insolence and the ploy stunk of it. Captain Steele did not look like a man to trifle with. He shook his head. 'No . . . No, I couldn't do that.'

'Scared of him, are you?' asked Williams sharply, the line of his mouth hardening and a cold gleam suddenly showing in his eyes. 'Well don't be,' he said softening

35

again. 'He can take a joke, see. Come on, go and tell him like I said.'

Dunbar had shuffled forward, aware that this was the first test of his adult life. He had thrashed the loudmouth who had called Jenny Broom, *his* Jenny, a harlot; how much more satisfying to call Captain Steele's bluff, even if he did, as before, come off the loser. The thought of Jenny made him resolute.

It was only afterwards that he thought of the *lèse-majesté* inherent in this course of action. But wayward-ness had ever been part of his character, and Steele had ordered him *not* to sing hymns, which seemed as illogical a thing as his father telling him not to keep the company of honest fisherfolk. Emboldened, he returned to the saloon.

'Find 'em?' asked Captain Steele impatiently.

'No, sir, they're not on board.' He stood at what, on the rolling deck and with an imperfect knowledge of military matters, he considered to be attention.

'Not on board, d'you say. How so?'

'Because, sir,' Dunbar had said, fighting a nausea only partly due to the ship's motion and aware that all three adults were now looking at him with renewed interest, 'the chief engineer has sold them to the Bethesda Chapel at the back of Port Tennant.'

'Has he by damn!'

Rayner and the chief steward turned away to conceal their laughter, but the captain's eyes blazed with a sudden apparent fury, and Dunbar plunged on quickly, committed now and not caring what became of him, in an effort to acquit himself at least in Williams's eyes.

'But I know most of the hymns, sir, and if you will preach, I will do my best to encourage the ship's crew to sing!'

Rayner and the chief steward exchanged glances and then looked at Steele. The expression on the captain's face was preposterous; the ridicule intended for the initiate rebounded upon himself. Rayner disapproved of such practical jokes; they were unfair, intended to humiliate, to confirm the ignorant in their ignorance and mark clearly the hierarchy of the ship. Had the joke been played by the second and third mates, it would have been tolerable. That it should have been initiated by the ship's master was, in Rayner's opinion, a diminution of the captain's dignity. Rayner did not approve, for it undermined his own status.

But Rayner was not so misanthropic that, in the captain's discomfiture, he could not see amusement. Moreover, the boy seemed to be capable of handling it well, standing there with his thumbs aligned with the seams of his reefer suit trousers as Captain Steele stood up.

'No, boy! *You* can preach the sermon, Mr Dunbar! Number 24 of the Rule of the Road at Sea, on the bridge, by noon.'

And Captain Steele had looked down at his two colleagues and roared with immoderate laughter before stalking imperiously past Dunbar and into the alleyway beyond.

Chuckling, Rayner had looked at the new apprentice. 'I think you may pay for that later, young fellow,' he had said. 'Now cut along and start learning Rule 24.'

When Dunbar had disappeared, the chief steward, referring to the captain, asked, 'Did you know his wife passed over a while ago? That's why he was late joining the ship.'

'What? Steele's missus?' The mate had been astonished. 'No, I'd heard nothing.'

'Aye,' the chief steward leaned forward on his elbows.

'An' I wouldna' say he's particularly grievin', would you?'

Rayner made a non-committal face, but said nothing.

'He doesn't look like a man over grieving, does he?' the chief steward persisted. 'They didna get on, I'm thinking.'

In the heat and the excitement of imminent arrival, Dunbar could not sleep. He lay waiting for Edgar Humphries to call him to be relieved at midnight. It was funny, Dunbar thought now, how in remembering what had happened on that first Sunday at sea he could also recall what he had remembered at the time.

Specifically, it was funny how he had recalled Jenny Broom in that moment of discomfiture, drawing on his memory of her to brace himself against the captain. *His* Jenny, he always thought of her; a most private, arrogant and entirely unjustified conceit. And yet, had he been older, or just bolder, she might have been truly his; his in the full, biblical and carnal sense.

Perhaps he had dozed a little and confused Williams's apparently limitless promise: *they will do ANYTHING*, but it was odd how here, on the broad bosom of the ocean with no women within a hundred, perhaps five hundred miles, one thought so much about them. He was sure Williams would have an opinion upon the matter and, remembering the look the able seaman had had in his eye the day they had been splicing, kicked himself for not having prompted him further. Williams needed a nudge to bend, that much Dunbar had learned, for he had known some of the old fishermen of Clayton Wick to be reticent, and thought it a characteristic of men long used to their own company.

But now he thought of Jenny, and it was a most urgent and intense reminiscence.

She was not so *very* much older than himself, he supposed; a little over thirty perhaps. She would have been about seventeen when he first remembered her, not long after she joined the rector's family, when he had been about three years old. She had red-blonde hair and a broad, handsome face with a crop of freckles that he had found fascinating, though her skin turned russet on the cheeks in the summer. Freckles dusted her chest and, when she bent over the large kitchen table, he could see they spread down over her big breasts.

His isolation had made him something of a solitary, but occasionally he would talk to Jenny, catching her in an idle moment, sitting on the old bench outside the kitchen door, drinking tea. It was inconsequential talk most of it, but now and then they had touched on more serious subjects. He liked talking to her, for she never brushed him aside, and while she was sometimes guarded in her answers to his often gauche and frank questions, she always answered. But he had learned from her the trick of patience, of coaxing, then waiting for the relaxing of inhibition, a skill he had used on Williams quite subconsciously. Manifesting itself as consideration, it conferred on him a charm for which other lonely people fell. He seemed, sometimes, one of those fey children who possess an ancient wisdom without a shred of precocity, and in him both Jenny and Williams recognised a fellow-feeling for the outcast.

When he was about twelve and she was rolling out pastry he had come into the kitchen hot and dusty in search of a drink. As he had assuaged his thirst he had noticed her breasts and she had looked up and seen his eyes upon her. Smiling, she bent and resumed her work.

He had stood until his awkwardness could tolerate no more, then fled and was not seen until his mother called him in to dinner.

Later that same year he had been helping her gather apples in the orchard. Her threadbare pinafore had become so overladen with windfalls that it split and spilled her load on the long grass.

'Oh, botheration!' she had said, exasperated.

'I'll get a basket, Jenny,' he had offered, eager to court her good opinion, since, apart from his mother, for whom he conceived it to be a matter of duty, Jenny seemed the only person who genuinely cared for him.

'No, don't worry, Jim. If your ma don't see and you don't tell, Oi'll use my skirt.'

And James had joyously filled her skirt, feasting his eyes upon her calves and ankles, while they both laughed and he felt buck-high and happy.

Later, when school took him away from home, he returned for the holidays anxious to see Jenny. There were more elegant women in Ipswich; there were even girls of his own age, the sisters of his fellow pupils who turned his head, but none occupied his imaginings quite like Jenny Broom.

Times changed; he was no longer a boy, but a young man with dark hair on his upper lip, and his absence at school bespoke the social gulf between them. He found opportunities to talk to her no longer existed and, for her part, Jenny called him 'Master James', or 'Master Jim', and once, at Christmas, bobbed him a curtsey.

He had hated it.

One summer evening shortly before he finally left home and after he had run away with Skipper Hopton, he and Jenny had been alone in the house. His father was out visiting a sick farm labourer, his mother had taken the twins to see the doctor in Woodbridge, driven into town in Colonel Scrope-Davies's car.

Dunbar had dined alone, off a game pie and salad eaten, at his insistence, at the kitchen table. Jenny had refused his invitation to join him. She had clattered pots and pans disapprovingly in the adjacent scullery.

All the windows were open and the bees buzzed industriously above the flowers in the garden beyond. A blackbird had embarked on his sunset song and it had occurred to him that the evening would be one of the last he would spend before his life changed irrevocably.

That night, the air in the house had been as stifling as it was now in the half-deck. As he had finished his pie Jenny had reappeared to clear it away.

'Why don't you go for a walk, Master Jim?' she asked.

'Don't call me that.'

'It's a lovely evening.'

He felt suddenly emboldened by her presence. He wanted to recall the charm of their past intimacy, to say thank you and goodbye. 'There's no one to walk with. Why don't you come with me?'

'Now you know that wouldn't be proper. Anyway I've things to do and you like your own company. You used to tell me so.'

'I used to tell you lots of things, Jenny . . .'

'Aye, well you were a little boy then.'

'Won't you come?'

'Oi've work to do,' she repeated. 'Anyway, things change . . .'

Her suggestion of impropriety, of it not being the kind of thing to do, made him as angry as his father's blind prejudice. To conceal his feelings he rose and left her. He was disconsolate, peevishly cross and frustrated, but

41

he had not left the glebe before he remembered that it was a Wednesday, and on Wednesdays Mrs Broom took what his mother had always euphemistically termed 'her bath'.

With a beating heart he turned back towards the house.

She was already in her room with a ewer of hot water and a large bowl. She had, perhaps deliberately, left the door unlatched and slightly ajar. It seemed the house gave every warning to her, its floorboards creaking alarmingly, despite his stealthy progress. He gained the upper floor uncertain of what his quest would yield and could hardly believe his luck when he arrived outside her room without discovery. He was in a high state of excitement as, with a tremulous hand, he cautiously pushed the door. It gave way a fraction and he saw her at once. She had her back to him, pouring the hot water over her soaped body as she stood in the large bowl.

The light from the setting sun came almost horizontally through the attic window giving marvellous form to her sturdiness. He stared at her thighs, saw the twist of her hips as she bent and reached down, scouring her upper legs with a flannel, saw the rich full curve of her breast gleaming with soap and water, catching the light with a strange detachment from the vigour of her scrubbing.

He was tumescent, constrained by his own clothes, shaking and half-strangled by lust. Clumsily his hand sought some release but instead inadvertently pushed the door wide open.

She turned and saw him. For an instant they stared at each other, mutually shocked and surprised. Then, quite slowly, as though he was the one not to be started from his embarrassment, she deliberately turned and faced him. He saw the part of her he most yearned for, and fumbled a moment with himself, half fearing she would shriek in outrage, but she moved her hands, cupping them under each breast.

He stood stock still, not quite believing it was happening. He was not sure what to do, his knees seemed suddenly weak. She was smiling at him when he thought he heard, far off, the hoot of a car. Sudden fear flooded him; irresolute he wilted immediately, crushed by the burden of overwhelming sinfulness. Shamed, he turned and fled.

Behind him, unknowingly, he left Jenny crying. She had known only the busses of a few country lads before the colonel's son tupped her and left her with child. Since then she had perforce lived like a nun, daily reminded by her surroundings of her delinquent pregnancy. James Dunbar, in his eager and priapic adolescence, had seemed to offer her a little happiness.

He, above all people, should have understood her acute loneliness.

He sighed for her now, raged silently at his loss, resolving never to let such an opportunity pass again. In the airless half-deck he released himself from the statuesque vision, and fell asleep thirty minutes before he was due on watch.

On the bridge at midnight he found the ship slipping through the continuing calm with only the hiss of the sea made by her passing and the faint rumble of her reciprocating engines to break the silent night.

In the wheelhouse, faintly illuminated by the glow of the binnacle light, Able Seaman Morgan, Williams's watch-mate, could be seen at the wheel. Mr Mitchell was in the chartroom, enjoying a second cup of tea and studying his charts. For a moment or two Dunbar indulged himself with the fantasy that the *Kohinoor* was his own to command. It suddenly struck him that such a possibility was the logical outcome of the path he had entered upon, that the accruing of sea time for those daunting certificates of competency that he had heard of disparagingly referred to as mere 'tickets', and the projected voyage in square-rig, all had the single purpose of making him a master mariner and setting him in the place of Captain Steele.

It occurred to him he might not want to follow in the captain's footsteps and he stood on the bridge-wing and stared into the darkness, wondering not only what he was doing there, in the Gulf of California, but whether he was really there at all. It seemed that his recent memory of his encounter with Jenny Broom had more of substance than the fact of his presence on the bridge of the *Kohinoor*. Suddenly his very existence seemed in doubt.

Above his head the sky was almost clear of cloud and the firmament blazed with the icy fire of a myriad stars. The moon had yet to rise, but the light of the stars and the planet Jupiter lay narrow, shimmering paths upon the ink-dark sea. Slowly a strange contentment seeped through him and then slipped away. His onanistic act with imagined Jenny made him long for more than just existing, however uncertainly. Then guilt quickly followed, and he found his mind diverted, sidetracked by self-justification for the discontent that had made him commit his lonely sin. He sank into regrets, remembering those events which had disillusioned him during the long passage.

After the incident of the fog-locker he had found himself christened 'Foggy', and in the end accepted it. It marked him as having established himself among these men. In any case the soubriquet was preferable to Jimmy, or plain Dunbar. Even Captain Steele condescended to use it in Mr Rayner's hearing, so that afterwards the mate had said, 'You're lucky Father's in so good a mood these days. I think he may have forgiven you your cheek.'

Notwithstanding this token of quasi-approval, Dunbar found many of the tasks he was set uncongenial. As the junior apprentice he was made to scrub out the half-deck, the wheelhouse and the chartroom. He was also responsible for maintaining a high shine on the brass fittings on the bridge, from the window handles to the binnacle, the ferrules on the telescopes and the dogs which rounded off the ends of the teak rails. There were other brass embellishments which fell within his ambit; the half-deck port-rims, the brass side navigation lamps, the whistle and siren atop the funnel. But it was the ship's bell that he grew to hate. It completed his inventory of polishing and symbolised his condition of servitude in the very perversity of the task. The bell was mounted upon the forecastle and exposed to frequent showers of salt-laden and oxidising spray whenever the deeply-laden steamer thrust her bow into a sea. It therefore rarely gleamed to the standard required.

Captain Steele was punctilious about cleanliness, of which this obsession with shining brasswork was the primary manifestation, and his chief mate was no less enthusiastic. Had the Reverend Dunbar been able to walk upon water and, as it were, paid a call upon the SS *Kohinoor* as she made her passage up the Pacific coast of Central America, he would not have recognised the begrimed recipient of coal that had lain beneath the staithe in Swansea docks.

The South Wales Steam Navigation Company had not yet joined that growing band of British shipowners who kept their employees short of paint and tar and grease, believing that profit was the only reason for existence. They effected their economies through the more subtle strategies of short-changing their crews of both pound and pint where their victuals were concerned, and ensuring their wages were maintained at a level of bleak subsistence. That their ships were fully manned proved the wisdom of this policy.

The vessels themselves they maintained well, believing that prospective shippers would view a well-found hull with more favour than one whose appearance planted any doubts about safe arrival. That the *Kohinoor* carried the conveyor system for the San Martin copper mines was justification for the latter course of action.

But such considerations passed over the inexperienced head of Foggy Dunbar. He found all the cleaning and polishing demeaning. At home such tasks were undertaken by Jenny, or one of the village girls his mother annually employed for the spring cleaning. Yet, he had to admit, he had had no objection to such labours aboard the *Eliza Maude*, and Skipper Hopton could, on occasions, play the autocrat with greater severity than Captain Steele.

What had changed? He was accustomed to being honest with himself and realised with some distaste that he already entertained pretensions of grandeur, was already subconsciously aspiring to the mantle of command which brought with it the privilege of relief from such tedious and mind-numbing labour. It only slowly dawned upon him, for no one thought to explain, that the system to which he had tacitly agreed to conform, ensured that all who one day trod the bridge as shipmasters had once laboured humbly and menially. Like learning of the great German shipmaster Robert Hilgendorf, like learning to splice a heavy mooring rope and like acquiring his nickname, the realisation came with the enfolding knowledge that he had become part of a strange brotherhood.

He acknowledged that not one of the *Kohinoor*'s polyglot crew had looked down upon him when he had been scrubbing a deck or polishing brass. No disapproval akin to his father's objection to the keeping of 'bad company' had reproached him; the very open honesty of his actions and the reactions of those about him struck him forcibly. The sea life, for all its hierarchical structure and arcane rituals, which were open enough and thus collectively condoned, appeared to offer him a life without the hypocrisy he so disliked. That he had almost succumbed to the kind of snobbery which he despised reminded him that he was, unavoidably, his father's son.

He was, now he had time to think about it, reconciled to his new life. It was not perfect, of course, and he was at that age when serenity is impossible, but he acknowledged many of his first regrets had been foolish. Take the matter of the clouds, for instance. He had supposed that the clouds in the tropics would have a different character to those of the wide Suffolk skies of his childhood. He had no idea where this ridiculous assumption had come from. What he could not deny was the almost overwhelming sense of disappointment in finding a cumulonimbus was the same the world over. On the other hand, he had seen the staggering, remote and forbidding beauty of the Patagonian cordilleras, and the chilling splendour of the Wyndham Glacier, just as Magellan, Pigafetta and Fitzroy had observed them. The thought moved him so much that he had sought to capture this wonder by attempting a landscape drawing.

Although this was frustratingly unsuccessful, he did not give up and found stimulation in the use of a pencil. Mr Mitchell took an interest in his work and, in conspiratorial secrecy, gave him two of the ship's precious stock of soft-leaded chart pencils, encouraging him to further endeavours.

'You have a natural aptitude,' remarked Mitchell a little ruefully. 'Have you done much before?'

'A little at school.'

Impressed, Mitchell had nodded while Dunbar, seizing this new-found diversion, had sought to assuage his deep longing in drawing from memory the naked Jenny. He had never succeeded, nor kept his work, fearful that Humphries would discover and ridicule it.

He had seen other wonders on their long voyage: schools of dolphins, flying fish, and once, in the green waters of the equatorial belt, a lone turtle. Along the shores of Magellan's Strait seals and sealions had been visible through the binoculars Colonel Scrope-Davies had given him. When running north in the Humboldt Current along the coast of Chile, they had come upon a dozen sperm whales, and only the day before he had seen the flukes of a grey 'desert' whale.

All in all, Dunbar realised, he had little to complain of and nothing to regret. As if in ratification of his conclusion, Mitchell called him from the chartroom door.

'Foggy.'

'Sir?'

'You had better come and help yourself to a cup of tea.'

CHAPTER TWO

Puerto San Martin

Dunbar woke with an alarming start and found himself looking up into Williams's face. He had risen from a deep, dream-laden slumber into sudden, brilliant sunlight, like the breaching desert whale he had seen the day before. The image came to him as the dream faded, and was confused with that of the great red ensign which still burned in his mind's eye, imperfectly hiding behind its tantalising silken folds the opalescent gleam of Jenny Broom's wet haunches.

Williams had wrenched back the scruffy curtains round the porthole. The sudden sunshine had set Dunbar's heart thumping uncomfortably.

'You'll be able to get rid of that in San Martin.'

'Uh? What?' Dunbar frowned and put his arm up across his eyes.

Williams stood over him, grinning like a satyr at Dunbar's tumescence and laughing at his flaming embarrassment.

'Nice girls in San Martin, Foggy. They'll soon have that thing shrivelled to nothing.'

Dunbar pulled the sheet over himself, speechless.

'Anyway,' Williams continued matter-of-factly, 'it's

gone eight bells and the third mate's wondering where the hell you are. Says the wheelhouse needs a scrub before we berth, and the telegraph, binnacle and bell want polishing.'

'Oh, God!' Dunbar exploded, angry at the humiliating exposure, aware that he had overslept, that his fellow apprentice, Humphries, had not called him and he might be in trouble. Williams continued laughing.

'Language, Foggy,' he chided, 'language . . .'

'Leave me alone!'

Williams left the half-deck chuckling. Dunbar was full of confusion and apprehension. The prospect of trouble drove him from his mattress, the sheet about his waist.

From the porthole the deck was white under the sun, and beyond the guardrail, set in a sparkling blue sea, a small brown island drew slowly astern, as though it slid past a motionless ship. It was white with guano and a cloud of boobies wheeled about its summit. Beyond the islet, the coast of Baja California lay like a bronze and sleeping dragon, undulating along the western horizon.

Dunbar dressed hurriedly, aware of a quickening excitement at the prospect of arrival at Puerto San Martin as much as fear of the third mate's wrath. Williams's words came back to him and he shrugged off his embarrassment. The sort of incident that would have begun a month of ridicule in the school dormitory was the matter of a moment's wry amusement now. Dunbar felt a sense of relief and gratitude for the liberty of his new existence. His sense of foolishness seemed unfounded. Williams, he thought perceptively, had led such a public existence that the sight of a young man's erection excited nothing more than a passing ribald comment.

As for the prospect of girls, he would have none of that. He had heard his father rail stridently on the subject

50

of harlotry and the thought of a woman who . . . He shuddered with repugnance and bridled at the thought of an excess of lasciviousness. There was no excitement in the peccant thought, only a violent revulsion. Besides, when he got home he was going to see Jenny again. There was an earthy satisfaction in the thoughts *she* raised and he was certain she would welcome him, just as she did in his lonely fantasies.

All morning they ghosted past the dun and diminutive islands which bordered the Sea of Cortez, each with its complement of boobies and brown pelicans. As if in welcome, dolphins sported about the ship, riding the pressure wave pushed before the *Kohinoor*'s blunt, work-manlike stem. About the decks different tasks occupied the ship's company, replacing the usual endless tedium of rust-chipping and red-leading, of soojeeing and painting. Steam was let into the deck pipes to the clattering winches. The topping lifts were hove down so that the derricks rose from their crutches and gave the ship a purposeful, spiked appearance, transforming her from a pelagic wanderer to an unmistakable, amphibian adjunct of industry. This work, though in Dunbar's eyes destroying the essential magic of the ship, was cheerfully undertaken by her crew as evidence of the end of the passage.

It never occured to Dunbar who, though he was only on his first voyage, had the privilege of an occasional look at a chart, that these men had only the sketchiest notion of where they were on the surface of the globe. Nor did they much care about such trifles; it was none of their concern, for they had all come from sail, where uncertainty of passage times was part of the sea life. It had been their consolation that another day meant another dollar in their pockets, and to predict an estimated time of arrival with some certainty in a steamship seemed one of the wonders of the age.

Other manifestations of an imminent change of state were evident. Shoregoing clothes festooned the ship. Even Captain Steele's starched white duck suit was hung out to air on the boat-deck, and Dunbar was curious about the ownership of some of the extravagant garb that was seen gracing extempore lines rigged fore and aft. These fluttering and irregular decorations spoilt the functional symmetry of the ship. Reacting to this change of state, Dunbar felt alternately joyous at their imminent arrival, and nervous that the end of their passage signalled some irrevocable alteration to himself. It was a prescient instinct.

When he had finished his scrubbing and polishing, Mr Rayner appeared and ordered him to join Humphries who was preparing the ship's jolly boat, a small pulling dinghy in which Captain Steele would be rowed ashore from an anchorage. It sported a blue gunwhale and blue and white oars, with the ship's name and port of registry, Cardiff, in brass letters.

'You can polish them for a start,' ordered Edgar Humphries.

'You didn't call me this morning,' Dunbar replied doggedly.

'Are you complaining?'

Dunbar, angry at yet more of the accursed and verdigrised alloy, said, 'Well, yes. I am. I mean, the third mate was pretty decent about my being late turning to—'

'Then stop moaning.'

'I'm not moaning.'

'Sounds like it to me. Anyway, you're on watch tonight. The mate says we'll go alongside.'

'If we go alongside, what do we want this boat for?'

Humphries breathed with massive and contemptuous tolerance. 'We don't *know* we're going alongside, do we, eh? We prepare for whatever happens. If we anchor outside the port, the Old Man will want to go ashore straight away.'

'What for?'

'To see the agent.'

'The agent?'

'The agent; the comprador, savvy?'

Dunbar did not savvy; then another thought struck him, more personal than considerations about Captain Steele.

'What do I have to do?'

'What?' Humphries frowned up at him.

'What do I have to do – on watch in port?'

'If they work cargo you have to help whichever of the mates is on duty. If they don't work cargo, you have to keep the deck yourself. The mates knock off; you look after the moorings and the gangway – all that sort of thing.' Humphries affected an air of bored superiority.

'Oh, I see. Sort of ship-keeping.'

Humphries shot him a quick look to see if he was being mocked. 'Yes.'

'What are we going to do? Alternate nights?'

'I don't know. Thought I might do the days and let you do the nights. I'm more experienced. You can go ashore in the afternoons, if you feel like it – if the mate doesn't want you for anything, that is.'

Humphries had turned away to fiddle with the boat's bottom boards which he had been scrubbing. Dunbar had the impression he was, in the phrase he had learned from Williams, 'head-working', pulling a confidence trick to give himself some advantage.

'Don't they all go to sleep in the afternoons? Have a *siesta*, or something?'

Humphries shrugged. 'Sometimes.'

'So I get to see a sleeping town and you get to go ashore at night, is that it?'

Humphries turned and squared up to him. 'Look, Foggy,' he began, in a tone of mischievously reasonable concern, 'I want to spare you the embarrassment. I mean, you're a vicar's son and, well, this place isn't what you're used to.'

'I didn't know you'd been here before.'

'I haven't, but I've been to lots of other places: Yokohama, Singapore, Hong Kong, Takoradi, Freetown . . . I know what to expect.'

'In what way?' Dunbar was remembering Williams's references to his priapic state and he thought again of Jenny Broom.

'Well, er, you know, jiggy-jig.' Humphries clenched his fist and made an obscene gesture.

'You mean – girls?'

It was unfortunate Dunbar chose the juvenile noun, for he had almost discomfited Humphries. The senior apprentice, trying to play the worldly man, was now able to pour scorn on his gauche young colleague.

'No, Foggy, I don't mean girls. I mean *women*.'

They had hoisted a stream of flags from their signal halliards and picked up their pilot an hour before sunset, flinging a rope ladder over the *Kohinoor*'s side to the small boat which bobbed alongside in response to the signal. A tall, dark mestizo climbed over the rail, exuding a strong and unfamiliar scent of sweat, garlic and cheap toilet-water.

They had taken the pilot boat in tow and later cast it off just short of the wharf. Its crew of four oarsmen looked even more villainous than the pilot in their loose, dirty trousers and shirts.

The pilot for his part wore a uniform of royal blue with gold epaulettes. Shaking hands with Captain Steele, he had announced himself as Capitan Juan Ignacio Valbuena, pilot and harbour master.

Steele was impressed at Valbuena's prompt appearance in a country where he had previously experienced delay, and said so with British forthrightness.

'All of the port is much welcome for you, Capitan,' Valbuena responded. 'The copper mines make San Martin rich.'

'Quite,' replied Steele, as if the delivery of the conveyor system was due to his personal philanthropy.

'We go full speed through the anchorage.'

'We have a ready berth on arrival?' Steele asked uncertainly.

'Of course,' said Valbuena. 'Please steer some more to port.'

Steele exchanged a triumphant grin with Rayner. 'Have the men stand by, Mr Rayner,' he said formally, 'and ring on the engines to full ahead.' The mate put the silver whistle to his lips as the bridge telegraph exchanged a clanging message with its twin in the engine room far below.

The *Kohinoor* swung in through the anchorage, passing, to Dunbar's delight, two large four-masted barques, lying to their anchors, awaiting the copper from the mines in the distant hills. Empty and flying light, their slab sides were streaked with rust, but lovely to the boy's eyes, touched as they were by the westering sun.

Looking ashore he could see the thin line of a railway

running almost dead straight from somewhere behind the collection of buildings that was taking form as Puerto San Martin, into the distant hills. But for the monolithic pile of a great church, it seemed an inconsequential place, an extension of the mines, connected by that umbilical thread that the conveyor system in their holds was to supplant. He could see in the purple shadows of the brown hills the dark scars of the workings. Distance lent these details a remote insubstantiality. He could almost believe they were unreal, inconsequential scratchings on the quiet vastness of the desert.

The SS *Kohinoor* edged her way in towards the wooden wharf, responding now to the command of 'dead slow ahead' on her gleaming brass wheelhouse telegraph. She made slow progress, measured against the land, but Dunbar, who was leaning over her black steel forecastle bulwark in attendance upon Mr Rayner at his harbour station amid the anchors and mooring ropes, could see she stemmed a rushing tide.

The rail beneath his sunburned forearms was still warm to the touch, despite the rapidly cooling evening air. The ship retained the burden of the day's heat. From the tall funnel a great shimmering column of distorted air rose into the sky. Indeed the whole surface of the deck wavered, giving a liquid look to the substance of the ship, as though she had finally been possessed by the ocean during her long, arduous travail from Europe, and was to be delivered in this aqueous fashion upon a foreign shore.

On either side of Dunbar the seamen leaned, their eyes feasting upon the dusty yellow stripe of wharfage, with its idling longshoremen standing only half expectantly in the lengthening shadows of a single godown. They would move when the *Kohinoor* was close enough for the throwing of the heaving lines, one of which Williams was carefully coiling. Someone spat and a restlessness passed along the waiting men, like a sudden breeze through dry grass.

Beyond the godown a row of pallid stucco buildings, now in shadow, formed the waterfront of Puerto San Martin. They grew in shabbiness as the ship drew closer. A flagstaff, from which the national colours of Mexico hung sullenly, announced the headquarters of Valbuena. Other buildings bore floridly illustrated advertisements, captioned in Spanish. One of these, Dunbar supposed from the gleaming teeth of the sultry beauty adorning it, recommended a tooth-powder. Above the gaudy street-level decorations, their first and second storeys bore open windows, whose shutters seemed to hide dark and mysterious interiors.

There was a break in this façade where a street led inland, at right angles to the dusty quay. Slowly the forward progress of the ship exposed this to view so that the prospect of a square came in sight. Its centre seemed dominated by a few low and gnarled trees from which the yellow gleam of oil lamps could already be seen. Behind these rose the west front of the candy-cake church whose belfry towered above all the buildings in the place. Even in the shadow of the westering sun its pink and white and yellow pargeting was conspicuous. To Dunbar's heretic eyes, familiar with the cold, grey churches of the north, it breathed popish idolatry, its very exoticism full of a hideous and pervasive animosity.

The presence of the massive, dominating church failed to excite any wonder in him that here, on this barren, distant and foreign ground, devout, determined Franciscans had, with the help of their Indian converts, faithfully wrought to establish Christianity in so concrete a form.

Instead, its looming presence confirmed the fact that the voyage of the *Kohinoor* had brought him to a land at once alien and strange, inhabited by people profoundly different to himself, but also to a land that was hostile to him at some barely comprehended personal level. He felt a sense of fear and shuddered, remembering his earlier vague disappointment at the end of the passage and feeling again a sense of foreboding. Quite suddenly, the shuttered windows of the waterfront concealed unnamed terrors.

'Grey geese over your grave, Foggy?' Williams asked, dividing the heaving line, a handful of coils in each fist.

'See if the lad can do it, Williams. He's been lounging on the rail like a proper lazy jack.' Mr Rayner, the mate, lifted his cap and scratched his head.

'Think you can manage?' Williams asked in a low voice.

Dunbar nodded and took half the rope with the heavy monkey's fist in his right hand, holding the balance of the coil in his left. He had done this for Skipper Hopton on the *Eliza Maude*, but no one here knew that.

'When you're ready then, Dunbar, but don't leave it too late or the Old Man will be hollering at us.'

Dunbar stared at the quay which was suddenly much nearer, with the flare of the bow hanging out over it. Dunbar thought of the view of pews from his father's pulpit.

A collective sigh seemed to pass among the men gathered on the *Kohinoor*'s forecastle and Dunbar was suddenly nervous that he would miss with his heaving line.

'There she blows, my lads, broad on the port beam . . .'

About him men whistled and chuckled. It was suddenly clear from the expressions on their faces that this was a simultaneous manifestation of contentment.

Dunbar looked up. They had altered the angle of the road and the square. The west front of the church had moved behind the frontage and the left-hand side of the short road that led from the wharf to the square was formed by a long building sliding across their line of sight.

Dunbar had no idea what it was, and was preoccupied by the need to acquit himself well at the line throwing. He concentrated on his task, drew back his arm and hurled the coils in his right hand across the quay. The heavy monkey's fist, worked round a nut from the engine room, flew through the air, drawing out the uncoiling rope behind it as Dunbar opened his grip and felt the rope draw out. He remembered to hold the end and was rewarded by a faint thwack as the stretched heaving line landed on the filthy wharf.

'Very good, son,' grunted the surprised Rayner approvingly.

Looking down, Dunbar saw a barefoot longshoreman in grey shirt and loose brown trousers, a sombrero slung on his back, amble towards the line, tread on it and languidly bend and pick it up with his foot. When he had transferred the line to his hands he spat noisily into the dust, signalling his readiness.

'There's a lovely bloody oyster,' someone joked as Williams took the end of the heaving line and bent it on to a heavy coir mooring rope.

'Send away the spring first, mister!' Captain Steele hollered from the port bridge-wing where he could be seen standing alongside the pilot.

'As if we didn't know,' a man muttered.

'Aye, aye, sir,' Rayner responded without repeating the order to his men.

The longshoreman dragged the heavy rope and threw

the eye in its end over a bollard. Two men threw lazy turns round the bitts and let the rope render.

'Check her!' bawled Steele, and they threw their weight against the rope which shuddered and drew round the bitts more slowly until all the forward motion was off the ship.

The act officially ended the passage of the SS *Kohinoor* from Swansea. In the log, against the time of this event in which Dunbar had played his small but significant part, Mr Rayner later wrote: *Ran lines to berth, vessel secured port-side-to, No 2 berth, Puerto San Martin.*

As the men were dismissed from their stations, they went off the forecastle in high good humour. Dunbar looked again at the building which had excited their comments. He could see it quite clearly now, though it lay in purpling shadow. It dominated the waterfront and across its stuccoed brickwork it announced its identity. HOTEL PARADISO, he read.

At midnight Dunbar was called by the second mate. He had turned in after dinner and fallen asleep immediately. Mr Mitchell, going off duty at a time when his body had become inured to waking up for the middle watch, was lightheaded and hearty.

'They're going to start working cargo in the morning,' he explained, without saying exactly who 'they' were. 'When they start coming aboard, give the mate a shout, otherwise keep a good eye on the gangway and the mooring ropes, there's a good rise and fall of tide here, high water's about two and . . .'

'It's all right, sir, I understand. I've looked after a fishing smack alongside.'

'Ahh . . . Good, well that's about it. Most of the crew

are ashore. They'll be back in dribs and drabs, mostly drunk. I should keep yourself out of the way, if I were you. Anyway, if you have any problems, put me on the shake, all right?'

'Yes, sir.'

'Oh, and Foggy . . .'

'Sir?'

'If you leave your cabin, even to walk to the other end of the ship, lock it.'

'Aye, aye, sir.'

'Humphries ashore?'

'With the rest of them, I expect.'

'Catching pox, if he isn't careful.'

'He seemed to know what he was doing, Mr Mitchell.'

'They all do,' Mitchell said with resignation, then paused. He looked at Dunbar from under his brows. 'You *do* know what the pox is, don't you?'

'Er, well, I . . .'

'Its proper name is syphilis, Foggy, and it's very nasty. The end of your member grows a sore like a little red cauliflower and then it passes away and twenty years later you go mad. In the meantime you destroy your own life and probably several other people's.' Mitchell let his words sink in; Dunbar's face was curiously unresponsive. 'You do understand what I'm saying, don't you?'

Dunbar nodded. 'Yes. You get it from lying with unclean women.'

For a moment the archaic phrasing took Mitchell aback, then he recalled Dunbar's parsonage background and he nodded. 'And the women become unclean, as you put it, from going with infected men. I'm the poor devil who usually has to deal with them, the men that is, when they find out what they've got to take home with their pay-off. That's why I'd rather you kept yourself to yourself. If you don't catch the pox here, you'll almost certainly cop the clap.'

Mitchell's lecture seemed to have run its course; he stood rather wretched and embarrassed, looking at the blinking boy.

'Anyway, d'you think you can stay awake until daylight?' Mitchell smiled his kindly, serious smile.

'I think so, yes.'

'Good. You might like the look of the church when the dawn light catches it. It's a barbarous place inside, but the exterior's pretty impressive.'

'You've been here before, sir?'

Mitchell nodded. 'Once, when I was your age, on a ship called the *Quebec*. She was a little composite full-rigger . . . Still, that's another story. Want to borrow my watercolours?'

'Your watercolours?'

'To paint the church at dawn.'

'Well, I don't know . . .'

'All right, don't worry. Another time; we're going to be here for a while. There's no hurry.' Mitchell smiled again. 'Good night, Foggy.'

'Good night, Mr Mitchell.'

Dunbar was assiduous in his watch-keeping that night. It was the first time he had been in sole charge of a ship of the *Kohinoor*'s size, for now he was alone, Skipper Hopton's smack no longer counted. He walked every inch of the *Kohinoor*'s upper deck, the features of which were picked out in monochrome by a full moon. He haunted the deep shadows, sustained in his lonely vigil by the fantasy of his own importance. Thinking himself unobserved, he strutted, then swiped and lunged with an imaginary sword as he had seen the village boys do with their single-sticks, warding off what spirits inhabited the steamer's winches and unopened hatches. Clambering over the forecastle breakwater, he might have been a redcoat storming the Heights of Abraham in the wake of young General Wolfe when he halted, recalling the name of Mitchell's first ship, and recognising the suggestibility of his own imagination.

He snorted a short, derisory laugh at himself. He had been behaving like a boy! Single-sticks indeed!

He checked the head ropes and forward backspring, the very rope he had helped to land. They were tight, but not straining and he eased them a foot, for the tide was still rising. He was sweating when he had finished and leaned for a moment upon the rail, which was cool now, and stared out over the darkened town. The wharf was deserted, except for a dog which loped along the godown, a grey, lupine shape which stopped several times to sniff, and once to urinate with a faint, drumming sound on the corrugated iron. From time to time a gust of wind came from nowhere, raised a scuttering dust-devil which twirled in the moonlight, and subsided. Their sudden, unpredictable manifestation worried him far more than the *Kohinoor*'s shadows.

He wondered why, and then realised that he felt safe on board and these strange impish displays belonged *ashore*. All unknowingly he had been imbued with the instinctive distrust of the true sailor: that all that lay beyond the confines of his ship was dangerous and threatening, no matter how exciting and seductive. Despite his isolation he drew comfort from the battlemented ship. From here, on the aptly named forecastle, he might have been a Trojan, watching the posturing Greeks on the plain of Troy, secure behind his city's ramparts.

A few oil lamps gleamed through the louvred shutters along the waterfront. People were awake there, despite the lateness of the hour. What were they doing? He thought of Mitchell's words, of Jenny Broom and of lying with women, clean and unclean. Then he turned and went aft, to slacken the ropes on the poop.

A handful of men remained on board. The Sudanese firemen, upon the eve of whose holy day the *Kohinoor* had arrived in port, squatted on the poop-deck, talking and smoking. They looked up incuriously at Dunbar's incursion into their part of the ship and nodded at him. He could not understand their speech, but he liked to hear them, recognising the lilting cadence in their talk, the harsh and soft sounds punctuated by laughter, and he wondered at their apparent cheerfulness, given their lowly status on board and the impoverishment of their toiling lives.

'No go shoreside?' the eldest of the group asked as he batted away the insects hovering around the hurricane lantern placed on a crude wooden table on which also lay the bowls of their rice supper.

'No. Not tonight. On duty.'

'Ahh, duty. Go shoreside tomorrow, eh?' asked one.

'Get nice girl. Go jig-a-jig,' added another.

Dunbar temporised, feeling like Peter denying the friendship of Christ. 'Maybe.'

'Very good.'

Dunbar smiled wanly and turned away to wander forward again. Everywhere, it seemed, the same subject filled the very air, as though radiating from the heated brains and bodies of these men. He wondered whether, if he and Jenny Broom had done the thing he knew about and yet knew nothing of, he would be less prurient, more content. Or whether the act was addictive, as seemed to be the case, judging by the attitude of his shipmates. Was this, he asked himself with a very real sense of shock, a hunger that was never satisfied?

He began to wander aimlessly now, preoccupied, ascending ladders and then descending them, lost in thought. He felt a powerful yearning for Jenny, even at this stupendous distance. The ridiculous, yet voluptuous sensation had nothing to do with what he had supposed should form his chief interest in the opposite sex: love.

Had he been someone else, someone like Humphries perhaps, he might have dismissed the notion. But he was not someone else, nor could he dismiss the subject as some form of deceit used to stop young men falling into evil ways and succumbing to those temptations of the world, the flesh and the devil he had so often heard his father prohibit to every poor benighted confirmation class. He had experienced something different, something which he knew to be special, unique and painful, but something that existed in the world. Whether or not he was himself special, set apart from these others, he dared not consider. His father was one such and he, in his small, adolescent and rebellious conceit, had supposed he was himself ordinary, like other men, identifying as he did with Skipper Hopton and his rough crew. Nevertheless, love was, Dunbar knew, a reality.

He had fallen in love quite unexpectedly. It had shocked him with its impact and its intensity. She had been staying at Clayton Hall, a house-guest during that last Christmas of his boyhood; a relative of Colonel Scrope-Davies, his mother had said. 'Julia Ravenham, a niece of the colonel's. Such a pretty girl,' she had remarked, unwittingly treading on her eldest son's innermost feelings but informing him of the young woman's identity. The mysterious Julia had seemed to Dunbar to have been full

65

of the light and happiness, the promise and the wonder that the birth of the Christ child was supposed to engender.

All he wished to do after that high matins, when the church had been crammed and the carols sung with thunderous enthusiasm to combat the moan of the gale outside, was to see her again. When his father announced the colonel had invited the rector and his family to the Hall on Boxing Day, Dunbar went eagerly and with a hammering heart.

Julia had been there; she had made polite conversation with his mother and a fuss of the twins, but apart from a brief, dismissive look in Dunbar's direction, she took no notice of him.

But this neglect could not stop him from lying awake that night thinking the world was full of her loveliness.

He had seen her once more that Christmas. She had called at the rectory and offered to take the twins for a walk. The gale had ceased overnight and they woke to a covering of snow six inches thick. Dunbar was already out, enchanted by the transformation wrought in the landscape, and saw her with his brothers from a distance. He had begun to run towards them, aware that he had the perfect opportunity to speak with her away from the social intimidation of the Hall.

But then he felt suddenly foolish; his haste and a lack of anything to say seemed at once presumptuous and gauche. Her partiality for the twins hurt him. He stopped in his tracks. One of the twins must have caught sight of him and made some remark, for Julia looked directly at him, hesitated in her stride and then, as he stood unmoving, she had tossed her head and walked on, bending solicitously over the twins who were blowing on their frozen hands after making snowballs.

Dunbar turned and walked away. Ten minutes later he

was defending himself against an attack by three boys from the village whose snowballs were launched with more malice than fun. The unpleasant little skirmish had compounded his hurt.

That night he had lain in bed and raged against his fate. Surely, he had argued with himself, so strong a feeling of attraction could not go unreturned?

For this to be possible was not only too painful to be contemplated, but ran contrary to all the laws of nature as he then understood them.

Remembering Julia on that first night in San Martin, Dunbar felt a hardening of his heart. He would always love her, of course; how could he not adore a creature of such beauty and perfection? But he felt again the sensation of being outcast, made solitary by the actions of others. Julia had repudiated him. It was not surprising; he had nothing to recommend him, the eldest son of an impoverished country clergyman, scruffily clad and boasting no prospects, let alone any looks. But while logic had nothing to do with his sense of personal damnation, he could not shake off the conviction that the passion raised in him by those brief encounters with Julia had shown him to be fitted for such a great and transcendental love.

He *did* feel special and set apart. He was not ordinary after all, and could not deny it to himself. He felt buoyed up by this conviction which had nothing to do with the squalid activities of his shipmates in the Hotel Paradiso. He could almost persuade himself that was what had led him to run from the naked Jenny.

Dunbar had not gone unobserved. From his forward-facing portholes beneath the bridge, Captain Steele had watched the young man go forward, swiping left and right like a boy slashing at nettles with a stick. The *Kohinoor*'s master soon lost interest. He was busy sinking half a bottle of Scotch whisky, for he drank little while his ship was at sea and was fond of saying 'even a seaman must have an occasional day off'. Those who kept his company at such moments and knew him well were supposed to rejoin 'even if it is only every two months'. But he was also celebrating and calculating; celebrating the release of his life from marriage and laying his plans for acquiring the girl of his dreams.

Insofar as both he and Dunbar were concerned, their thoughts simultaneously contained a large proportion of idealised desire. But their contiguity ended at that point with a sharp and significant divergence. Where James Dunbar thought life, through the agency of fate, would engineer some meeting between him and some ideal lover in circumstances wholly favourable to himself, Captain Arthur Steele knew such mechanisms did not exist outside the covers of novels, and that a measure of engineering and investment had to be accomplished by oneself.

Prickly with lust though he was, Steele had no intention of making a fool of himself by running down the gangway in the wake of his crew. The *Kohinoor* was going to be in Puerto San Martin for some time; there was no hurry. Besides he wanted the ship's business with the cargo agent and the mining company behind him; he wanted cool morning air, daylight and a long period for selection and negotiation to conclude his private affairs. In short, he wanted all the tactical advantages of surprise and overwhelming force.

So he settled in his cabin and worked out his opening gambit, the line his initial approach would take, the way he suspected the conversation would go and the progress by which he would reveal his hand financially.

He had already secured from Capitan Valbuena the name and address of San Martin's doctor and felt reassured knowing the man had the almost homely name of Reilly. The fact augured well.

Captain Steele finally went to bed satisfied that he had considered most, if not all eventualities. He rewarded himself by allowing his last remaining waking thoughts to be of the young woman he would shortly acquire.

Mr Mitchell proved accurate: the *Kohinoor*'s wayward crew members began to return shortly after midnight in small batches. They had all been drinking and their progress across the bare expanse of the moon-bleached wharf was unsteady, though not uncontrolled. Taking the second mate's advice, Dunbar watched from behind a ventilator, chuckling with amusement at the antics of men trying to appear sober as they approached the gangway, only to cast aside any pretence as they began the more serious business of ascent.

Secure aboard, they swayed contentedly as they regrouped, before drifting forward to their berths in the forecastle. Snippets of conversation drifted towards Dunbar.

'Tomorrow I'll take five dollars and make a night of it.'

'A short time's better; gets it out of your system so that you can clean up.'

'What about the one with the black hair?'

'Dey all had black bloody hair, for Chrissakes.'

'No they didn't! One was a blonde.'

'Not the bit I saw.'

Dunbar had only an imperfect understanding of the detail of this repartee; the substance of it seemed clear enough.

Half an hour later two seamen appeared round the

corner of the godown. Between them drooped a third figure Dunbar knew at once was Humphries. The falls jerked as the gangway reacted to the trio's ascent. The seamen pushed and pulled the stoned apprentice up to the level of the main deck.

'Foggy!' one of them roared as they let their burden slide groaning to the deck. Dunbar came out of hiding.

'Done our bit for Queen and country, lad. Get the bugger to bed and mind he don't puke all over you.'

Dunbar took three-quarters of an hour to get his shipmate to the half-deck, and spent another ten breathless minutes trying to lift the helpless Humphries into his bunk before giving up and leaving him on the deck, covered by a blanket. Just as Dunbar was leaving, the wretched boy gurgled and threw up copiously, filling the air with the sharp stink of vomit.

Filled with disgust, Dunbar escaped to the deck again and resumed his lonely vigil aware that his accommodation had now become untenable.

Williams came aboard alone, at about three in the morning. He seemed sober and, seeing him on his own walking purposefully towards the foot of the gangway, Dunbar disregarded Mitchell's advice and met him as he stepped down onto the deck.

'Good morning,' he said ingenuously, 'welcome back.'

Williams seemed to rear backwards, holding his head oddly, turning to stare at Dunbar with his whole body and arching his back so that he glared down his nose. Even in the gloom his face had the appearance of a mask, and Dunbar realised with a sudden chill that Williams was viciously drunk.

'What the *hell* d'you mean by that?' There was such venom in the seaman's voice that Dunbar drew backwards, appalled.

'N—nothing . . .'

'I bloody hope so,' replied Williams, lowering his gaze and picking his way along the deck. 'I bloody hope so.'

The encounter spoiled the night for Dunbar. He did not even spy on the remaining revellers as they returned to the ship, but hid himself away until the dawn washed into the eastern sky and he felt dopey with fatigue.

Leaning on the seaward rail he watched the sun rise, a brilliant vermilion ball which seemed to lift out of the haze lying along the eastern horizon. Suddenly the ship was transformed. Every mast and derrick seemed as purposeful as a lance, the plates glowed gold and the funnel gleamed as though varnished.

'Want a cup of tea, son?'

Dunbar turned to see McKillop, the third engineer, emerging into the daylight, wiping his hands on the seat of his grubby boiler suit.

'Oh, yes please.'

'Number Three's bringing a pot up now,' said McKillop settling himself on the dirty canvas tarpaulin on the hatch which lay just abaft the entrance to the engine room. 'Got the night duty, did you?'

'Yes.'

'Better than getting pissed up, I suppose,' the engineer said unconvincingly. 'Ah, here it comes.'

The Sudanese fireman known as Number Three appeared with an enamel teapot and two mugs.

'You give one to 'prentice boy, Three.'

'Yes, sah.'

'Thank you,' said Dunbar as the brown-skinned face smiled at him.

'I go bottomside and fetch one more.'

McKillop poured strong, sweet and milky tea into the ironware mug that Dunbar held out, then filled his own,

71

sipped it and stared at the sunrise. 'Best time of the day,' he said.

'Yes, yes I suppose it is.'

'No doubt about it.'

They sat there for a few moments and then Number Three joined them, pouring his own tea and sitting on the hatch beside Dunbar. He drank with an avid, noisy enthusiasm.

'You've been up all night, too?'

'Of course,' replied McKillop. 'You can't leave Scotch boilers to look after themselves, you know.'

'I thought . . .' Dunbar began, then decided not to reveal the extent of his ignorance.

'You thought that when the ship got alongside and we stopped the engines, we all went on our holidays, is that it?'

'Well, not exactly . . .'

'Not exactly, no, but more or less, eh?' There was a tone of wry amusement in McKillop's voice. 'Hey, Three, 'prentice boy think ship stop and we blow boilers down.'

Number Three's eyes glowed white with delight and glee and he shook his head with a beaming smile. 'Ooooh no sah. Engine room never sleep. Captain sleep, number one chief officer sleep, sailormans sleep, but engine room never sleep, always keep boiler working. Tomorrow want steam for cargo winch, maybe move ship . . .' He shrugged with a finality that embraced all possible eventualities, then tut-tutted, chuckled, shook his head and sucked again on his tea.

'Maybe boil fresh eggs,' McKillop added with a wink.

Dunbar felt discomfited. 'I didn't realise,' he began lamely.

'You didn't *think*, Foggy, that's all. Nobody thinks about what they can't see. There'd be a deal less trouble in the world if people considered before they spoke. So that's two lessons you've learned before the rest of the ship's company find out they've got hangovers.' McKillop paused and emptied the teapot into his own mug. 'Never take steam and hot water for granted when you're a captain, Foggy, walking up and down on your bridge like Lord Charles Beresford, eh?'

'No, no of course not.'

McKillop chuckled again. 'I expect you will. Out of sight, out of mind, that's the engineers' lot. Anyway, I reckon it's about time you called the cook and steward, or you'll upset more than Number Three and me.'

CHAPTER THREE

The Hotel Paradiso

Dunbar was woken at sunset by a Humphries devoid of all traces of debauch.

'Come on, Foggy, get up. You can go ashore tonight, they're working cargo and the mate wants us both on daywork tomorrow.'

He sat up in his bunk aware that, in some indefinable way, the ship was different. Then he realised the clattering noise which had filled his dreams was the rattle of the busy winches. Dragging on a pair of trousers, he went out on deck.

The ship was indeed different. In the first place it was inhabited by dark and, for the most part, moustachioed longshoremen. One stood by the winch nearest to the half-deck, dextrously manipulating the steam inlet valve with a strong brown fist, while a splayed foot operated the bandbrake. These alternate movements either sent the wire-laden drum spinning or juddered it to a halt as the wire runner depending from the derrick head far above drew taut, and hauled sling after sling out of number four 'tween-deck.

Secondly the derricks had been swung 'yard and stay' fashion, an archaic term to describe the arrangement

74

whereby one derrick plumbed the hatch, the other the quay, while their united wires combined into a 'union purchase', cleverly plucked each heavy load out of the open holds and deposited it on the wharf. The splay-toed longshoremen were dextrous at the manipulation of their winches which rattled first one way, then the other, with intermittent furious applications of the brakes.

Looking down into the open hatch square, so assiduously battened for their long ocean passage, Dunbar saw gangs of the winchman's compatriots tugging at the shiny steel lattices of the conveyor system. Each one-and-a-half-ton section was slung with strops before the gang's foreman waved the hook down to snatch at another load for discharging.

It struck Dunbar as odd that he had slept through a day which had wrought so profound a change upon the ship. The *Kohinoor* had again that disorganised appearance he had first encountered in the King's Dock, Swansea, for all the functionality of the arrangement and skill in operating it. The ship's untidy and indisciplined air reminded him of his mother seen first thing in the morning; a circumstance with a slight air of impropriety about it.

Still worse was the lost day, the hours of daylight he had slumbered through. Though he had earned his rest, he felt his father would not have approved. 'Never waste God's time, my boy,' the rector was fond of saying.

Was the night not God's time too?

He thought of the returning drunks, of his mammoth efforts in getting Humphries to bed, and was fairly sure that here, in Puerto San Martin, God went to sleep with the sun. The conviction was incontrovertible, born of a close association with the certainties of the converted. He turned back to the half-deck, to dress properly. Humphries had made a pot of tea.

'Are you going ashore tonight, then?' he asked.

'I don't know. I haven't got any money.'

'You've got ten bob, that's plenty!'

'How d'you know?'

'I've seen it.'

'How?' Dunbar felt a mild resentment at Humphries' invasion of his privacy and feared for the additional money that had been his father's last gift.

'Don't worry about it, the important thing is, are you going ashore? We can have a good time on ten bob . . .'

'We?'

'Yes, you and me.'

The reason for Humphries' abandonment of his position as guardian of Dunbar's moral welfare became clear. 'If you think I'm spending my money to get you into the same state you were in last night—'

'Oh, don't be such a starchy bugger, Dunbar. Have you never been tiddly?'

'No. And you weren't tiddly, you were drunk, dead drunk.'

'I wasn't.'

'You were. Who d'you think put you to bed?'

Humphries frowned. 'Well I came back with, er, Straw and Copson, I presume . . .'

'Straw and Copson dropped you like a sack of potatoes at the top of the gangway.'

'You mean . . . you got me in here?'

Dunbar nodded, adding while he had the advantage, 'I didn't think officers were supposed to drink with the crew.'

Humphries blinked at him for a moment as though dumbfounded at what Dunbar had said, then he looked desperately serious.

'Foggy,' he began with a condescending sincerity, 'we are not officers. Officers do not polish brass or scrub wheelhouses. You and I are apprentice boys, less than worms. One day, maybe one day, we will be stuck on the bridge with half a yard of gold lace round our cuffs if we're lucky and find ourselves in the P & O or the British India, but until then don't worry yourself about being a fucking officer because no one else does.' Humphries paused and laughed. 'And don't kid yourself you're a gentleman either. Only the *Royal* Navy has any gentlemen in it, as you'll find out if you ever bump into the buggers.'

Dunbar was not interested in Humphries' assertions about the Royal Navy, but instead suffered a sharp and painful reminder of the social difference between Julia Ravenham and himself. He must have appeared crestfallen, for Humphries was generous in his gratitude.

'Well, if you put me to bed last night, I'll do the same for you one day.'

Dunbar recalled the vomit. Humphries must have cleaned up the mess. 'I hope you won't have to.'

Humphries laughed. 'I'll bet I do,' he said as the peals of the steward's gong rang through the ship. Outside silence had fallen. The longshoremen had finished discharging for the day.

'Let's have dinner, then go ashore,' Humphries added with obvious relish. 'The whole town promenades after dark.'

The citizens of Puerto San Martin promenaded without Dunbar or Humphries. The two apprentices were caught after dinner by Mr Rayner who had been asked by the second engineer to strip the wire off the after starboard winch at number two hatch. The piston gland needed repacking and it was easier to test it with the drum empty of wire.

'I shan't need either of you two lads on watch tonight, so you can get that done right away.'

'Bloody mate doesn't want to turn the crew to,' Humphries grumbled obscurely.

It was a filthy task, for the wire was well greased and difficult to coil, unlike fibre rope, as Dunbar discovered. Both of them were liberally smeared when they had finished and handed the winch over to a grinning McKillop who, in common with all engineers, found the spectacle of those unfamiliar with oil hugely amusing when, like themselves, they were covered in it.

'Now you're learning the meaning of the word *work*, boys.'

'Cheeky bugger,' Humphries snarled as they returned to the half-deck, each with a pail of boiling water and a bar of yellow soap. Looking at the white tropical shirt discarded on his bunk after dinner, Dunbar ruminated on the eccentricities of his new life: Humphries was being proved correct in his assumptions as to their status.

'Let's get ashore. Old Rayner can't keep us on board forever.'

'If he knows you were drunk last—'

'Well, he won't know unless you tell him, will he?' said Humphries, plunging his hands into the water and throwing it into his soaped face.

Dunbar looked at his shipmate. Humphries' lean body bore some curious scratch marks Dunbar had not noticed before. He was about to ask if the wire had caused the blemishes when a darker suspicion crossed his mind.

'What are you staring at?' Humphries snapped, vigorously towelling himself. 'Haven't got cold feet, have you? Come on, don't stand there. You said you wanted to go ashore, well, now's your bloody chance.'

'Where are we going?' Dunbar asked.

Humphries stopped and stared open-mouthed at Dunbar. It was becoming a boring but pointedly patronising habit.

'Where are we going? *Where are we going?* Where the fuck d'you think we are going?'

'I don't know,' Dunbar said angrily. 'I wouldn't ask, would I? Earlier you said something about the town promenading—'

'We're too late for that,' said Humphries dismissively, choosing to ignore Dunbar's reaction. 'All the señoritas are locked up an hour after sunset, except . . .' Humphries drawled the word lasciviously, rolling his eyes and licking his lips.

'Go on,' prompted Dunbar who was not so easily mollified and sensed he had surprised Humphries, 'except *what*?' He continued dressing.

'Except for the *señoritas*', Humphries said, delaying his toilet while he laid great emphasis on the Spanish word as if the pronunciation of this enhanced his superior worldliness in a more subtle way, 'in the Hotel Paradiso.'

'You mean the harlots,' Dunbar retorted sharply. 'Then what are you waiting for. I'm ready.'

He had meant only to snipe at Humphries, whom he did not much like, but, as he waited for his companion to finish dressing, his heart quickened with excitement and dread.

Ten minutes later, scrubbed and dressed in duck trousers and cotton shirts, they dropped jauntily down the gangway and onto the dusty wharf.

*   *   *

Above them on the boat-deck, Captain Steele watched them go with a quiet chuckle and a self-satisfied smile. He had devoted the day to his ship's business and had progressed his personal affairs only so far as to ask the agent to make an appointment for him with Dr Reilly at ten o'clock the following morning.

'You want doctor?' the agent had asked. He was a small, simian man of middle years with a constant worried look; this added an illusory concern to his next question; 'You are sick, Capitan?'

Steele had affected a stomach complaint, tapped his belly with his fingers and nodded, at which the agent did likewise, giving Steele a tragically compassionate smile. 'Me also. Bad, bad . . .'

The agent's voice had faded, as though recalling his own discomfort brought on an attack of pain. The distraction made him revert to his native tongue. '*Estaré a su disposicion* – pardon, Capitan, I shall be at your service at any time.'

'*Gracias*', Steele had replied condescendingly as the agent had picked up his battered briefcase and tucked it under his arm. The grubbily rumpled white suit bore a permanent stain of tan under the left armpit.

'What is your name?' Steele had asked as the man was about to leave his cabin?

'Maldonado, Capitan, Jorge Maldonado. The customs clearance will be through tomorrow, but it will not delay your discharge.' He made to go, then swung round. 'Ah, and I will not forget the doctor.'

Twelve hours earlier he had watched Maldonado descend the gangway as he now watched the two apprentices. So lofty a viewpoint added to Captain Steele's detachment. He felt a surge of anticipation fill him. Unlike the two boys, he had control over his desires and would pursue them without the stimulus of alcohol. The thought, however, would not prevent him from taking a drop before turning in.

Dunbar recalled little of that brief walk across the wharf. What had been bare and dusty was now littered with the steel lattice-work of the conveyor sections which gleamed dully in the starlight, for the rising moon was hidden behind a cloud bank to the east. Dunbar was conscious of staggering and experiencing a feeling akin to drunkenness as the ground seemed unsteady beneath his feet. It was an uncanny and disturbing sensation which Humphries, walking slightly ahead, appeared not to notice or to suffer from. They were therefore climbing the wooden steps into the small foyer of the hotel before Dunbar took much notice of his surroundings. The blaze of light from numerous oil lamps, each fitted with Argand burners and silvered reflectors, compelled attention, illuminating a formidable trio of figures.

Two were men; very tall and piratical-looking men with the indelible mark of the enemy upon them. Dunbar had seen pictures of such men in a book illustrating the defeat of Sir Richard Grenville. Cruel, hook-nosed faces that lacked only the beards and the distinctive Spanish morions to suggest he had slipped a few centuries back in time.

'Sink me the ship, Master Gunner,' he found himself thinking. 'Sink her, split her in twain; fall into the hands of God, not into the hands of Spain.' The incantation seemed to work, for the man lounging at the foot of the wide stairs smiled. The other, sitting in a chair placed next to a table, sat up and opened sleepy eyes.

They muttered something which sounded like '*Ah,*

caballeros Inglesias'. But it was the third occupant of
the foyer who made the greatest impression. Behind the
heavily draped table sat a floridly handsome woman. Her
dress was of crimson velvet, somewhat stained, with a
low neckline that revealed the savage cleft between her
breasts, the sight of which made Dunbar's mouth run
dry. Her face was heavily powdered and rouged, her eyes
lined with mascara and her mouth with carmine. In the
lamplight he was struck with its paradox, for the make-up
could not entirely obliterate the ravages of smallpox and
yet, like the revelation of her breasts, he could not deny
it possessed a shamefully compulsive attraction.

He swallowed and felt sweat break out on his brow.
The woman looked up at Humphries who was slightly in
advance of Dunbar.

'You come back, eh, señor?, and you bring your
friend?'

Dunbar was aware of a double door opening to the left
of the foyer, beyond which came the loud noise of men
talking.

'Of course I come back,' Humphries said preco-
ciously, turning to Dunbar and whispering, 'she's the
madame.'

'Oh,' Dunbar replied, gathering from the use of the
definite article that the woman was a person of some
importance, like *the* mate of the *Kohinoor*. He had not
taken his eyes off her impressive person.

'You go upstairs tonight?' the woman asked Humphries.

'Perhaps,' replied Humphries with, Dunbar noticed, a
lessening of his cocksure air.

'Will your friend go upstairs?' She turned her attention
to Dunbar, smiling at him and adding, 'He is handsome
English gentleman, no?'

Humphries seemed irritated at this partiality and Dunbar

asked with a sudden impulsive initiative which surprised himself, 'Did he go upstairs last night, ma'am?'

'Why you—' Humphries protested.

'Him?' The woman jerked her head at Humphries without taking her eyes off Dunbar, who nodded. She laughed, a full-throated and not unpleasant laugh of genuine amusement, explaining to her two male companions what had passed between them. They joined in the laughter; Humphries blushed. Then the woman put her left elbow on the table and extended her little finger, drooping it in a slow and significant gesture. The men laughed louder.

'Come on, we'll get a drink,' snapped Humphries, tugging at Dunbar's shirtsleeve.

'You have a drink and when you want to go upstairs, I will make you *caballeros* a special price.' The wide red mouth dismissed them.

They passed inside the saloon, to the left of the foyer. It was rapidly filling with seamen. Most of the *Kohinoor*'s crew seemed to be there and the air was thick with tobacco smoke. Moving among the men, who either stood at the bar or had gravitated to the tables, were a number of ragged boys in grubby cotton breeches and loose shirts who waited at table.

Humphries was about to turn on Dunbar and exact a retribution for his humiliation when his companion said, 'You were pretty lucky not to get caught into going upstairs. I suppose that is where the harlots are, is it?'

'You know about this place?' Humphries frowned. His incredulity made him look stupid.

'I suppose so, yes. It isn't a hotel, it's a house of ill-repute.'

'Boys, boys, it does me good to see you both! Come, have a drink with me.' Idris Williams loomed towards them, pushing through a group of sailors from one of the anchored barques. 'These poor buggers want us to buy them drinks. They've been here so long, they've run out of money and now we've arrived and pushed the prices through the roof.'

Williams seemed to derive no outrage from being thus exploited by the proprietors of the Hotel Paradiso, but then he was already tipsy.

'What's the matter with you, Foggy?' he asked, shouldering his way back through the grumbling sailing-ship men and drawing the two apprentices after him.

'Nothing.'

'Look, I'm not a bloody fool. What's the matter with you?'

'It's his first time in a place like this, Idris,' Humphries offered.

'No, no, no. He's got the bloody hump against old Idris; I can tell, see.'

'You know why then, don't you,' said Dunbar, embold-ened. Williams, having reached the bar, called for glasses of beer.

'I upset him, see,' Williams said, confiding in Humphries in a loud voice which passed for a stage-whisper in the general hubbub. 'When I got back last night, see.'

'No you didn't,' Dunbar said, not liking the direction the conversation was taking.

'This'll make amends.'

The beer was warm and unpleasant tasting, unlike the Adnam's ale brewed at Southwold, not far from Clayton Dobbs, which in a surreptitious moment at a cricket match he had illegally sampled.

'Shall we sit down, boys?'

They found a vacant table in a corner and Dunbar stared around curiously.

'You're asking yourself a question, Foggy, aren't you, eh?' Williams's tone was edgily unpleasant, reminding him of the unequivocally hostile glare the able seaman had given him in the early hours of the morning. There was something about Williams, some hardness in him, that vaguely frightened Dunbar. He recalled discovering something of it in their intimacy during the outward passage. Alcohol, it seemed, exacerbated it.

'You are asking yourself where the girls are, aren't you?'

Dunbar had no time to reply. The double doors through which they had recently come had been banging back and forth as more seamen entered the saloon. Dunbar recalled there was another steamer ahead of them and two more had been anchored in the outer road, which accounted for the proliferation of revellers, but at that moment the doors opened with a noticeable simultaneity and the man who had lounged sleepily beside the madame in the foyer stalked in.

He had lost all trace of indolence and was greeted with universal cheers as the crowd of men dispersed from the bar and hurriedly occupied the remaining tables. In the corner opposite to Dunbar and his cronies, beneath the casing of the stairs leading up from the foyer, he produced a stool and a guitar. The room fell silent and the man waited until this was total. Even the scruffy waiters and the barmen grew still.

Then, in a moment filled with anticipation, the man struck his right hand downwards across the guitar-strings. The single chord crashed like an intruder into the room. It seemed to Dunbar every man held his breath as the echoes of sound reverberated until, just as they diminished, another followed, pitched a tone higher, as though raising the expectations of the assembled throng. Then, his long fingers rippling across the strings so that waves of sound filled the air, the guitarist began a complex and virtuoso performance which abruptly stopped, was followed by yet another crashing chord, before alternate chords and knocks on the guitar's soundbox announced the staccato theme of a dance.

At this point, the patience of his audience terminated. A heavy black curtain to the guitarist's left, hitherto unobserved by Dunbar, was rent aside, and a tall, voluptuous mestizo woman appeared. She had the profile of a hawk and a face as savage as those of the guitarist and his compatriot. Her hair was drawn tightly back from her forehead and seemed dressed with Stockholm tar. A long, clubbed horse-tail dropped below her shoulders from the crown of her head.

If the madame had confronted Dunbar with a paradox of sensual beauty, she was outdone by the dancer. Encased from shoulder to calf in a glossy fabric which Dunbar supposed to be silk, she possessed a figure of superb proportion. Her dress terminated in a short and fluted skirt which whirled mesmerically about her ankles, revealing occasional lascivious flashes of white flesh above black shoes. These she pounded in rhythmic coincidence with the guitarist's beat.

Dunbar had never seen anything like it. He did not even compare it with the May dances of his native country folk, though they too contained suggestions of sexual expression. To the young Dunbar, they had seemed soppy, indulged in by contented rustics, and though at the time the thought had made him feel uncomfortable to the point of shame, it had only reinforced his sense of being set apart from his peers.

What he was witnessing now was something astoundingly different. In the foyer he had felt the pricking of indiscriminate desire, recognised it as a fleshly temptation and rejected it. This rejection had manifested itself in his recognition of the true purpose of the Hotel Paradiso, and also in his congratulation of Humphries at his lucky escape from 'going upstairs'.

But *this* woman possessed something far greater in her appeal. Here was a grandeur, a nobility and a voluptuously exciting pride. Dunbar was unaware of the calculation behind her appearance. For him there was no possibility that she was degraded by dancing before this audience, or that she prostituted her skill for the mere *amusement* of these men.

Dunbar felt only the thrall of his own desire. He was spellbound by the magnificent spectacle of this woman, by her allure, her art and her assurance. He, in common with all the company, was enslaved by her. She defied them and became a challenge; their desires responded; she had aroused them all and herself touched none of them.

The Hotel Paradiso would do much business following her performance.

The dancer stamped her way to her climax at a final violent chord. She became immobile, one hand on her hip, the other upflung, her arm glistening with sweat in the lamplight, only her breasts rising and falling with the effort of her exertion. Dunbar, Humphries, Williams and the rest leapt to their feet clapping, whistling and cheering. As the noise subsided and the men sat down, the dancer had gone.

The guitarist struck up a slow and melancholy air which seemed to precede a song. Dunbar had learned to dread such entertainment at home. He had always found the transformation of his parents' homely friends into would-be divas an embarrassment, but no song followed. Instead a pallid and frothily theatrical apparition appeared, which it took Dunbar several seconds to identify as a woman encased in layers of gauze. She was about twenty, a sturdy creature with the features of a native Amerindian, not unattractive, but lacking the defiant splendour of the dancer and pathetically ridiculous in her extravagant, contrived costume. She did not confront the audience with the impossibility of unattainable desire, but the accessibility of immediate gratification.

Her audience, though no less attentive, were far less silent.

Jerkily peeling back the layers of gauze with a complete absence of finesse, she revealed her figure encased in ribbed and coral corsetry, and pink stockings. She walked with an awkward, yet provocative gait up and down the tiny stage so that hip jutted and thigh and buttock wobbled with every step. Murmurs of appreciation rose from the watchers; there was an animal stink in the air. Dunbar noticed the waiting boys were once again running silently between the tables and the bar, responding to the requests of men discarding caution and eagerly resuming their drinking.

The final moment of the performance came: the woman, whose face had borne an expression of apparent indifference throughout, turned full-face and confronted the leering mass. She stood with her legs apart, her pelvis thrust slightly forward and both arms crossed upon her breast.

Her lower body invited sexual intimacy, her upper looked like the carved image on a tomb. Then, exploiting the cunning of a falconer's knot which her audience of seafarers appreciated, she jerked the lacing of the corset. The stiff garment parted and fell behind her; she stood naked in her stockings amid universal cheers, before abruptly turning, bending to retrieve the discarded corset and disappearing behind the curtain. She left only an impression of her bronze back and the flash of her stockings.

All about Dunbar men leapt up and down, thumped the tables, called for more women, more drinks, bellowing their appreciation and appetite for excess. Humphries and Williams were beside themselves, clapping and cheering. Then Dunbar was aware of something else, something which destroyed what he considered his personal detachment. The saloon was being silently invaded by women.

They came in on bare feet, in ragged dresses, some of which still showed signs of former elegance. Few had any pretensions to beauty and many had been marked by smallpox; but, like the last performer, they had desirable bodies which were groped by the sitting men among whom they passed. All wore compliant smiles, and this shocked Dunbar almost as much as their sudden appearance.

One of these women approached their table, flicked a dismissive wrist at the grasping hands of Williams, pulled a face at Humphries, and stood squarely in front of Dunbar. Beside him Humphries looked abashed. Was this the woman whose passion had caused the scratches on Humphries's flanks and whom he had been too drunk to satisfy?

Facing him, she swiftly bestrode Dunbar's knees, took his head between her hands and drew it towards her breasts. He was aware of the strong smell of musk and then his face was buried in her soft flesh. His hands had gone unbidden to her buttocks and he was rigid. He was unaware of Humphries's jealous and embarrassed sniggering. It seemed the world had centred on his lonely and poignant desire. She was Jenny Broom, she was Julia Ravenham, she was every woman; he felt he was melting, that he was no longer embodied, but timeless.

She hoisted her skirt and wriggled on his tumescence, driving her hips at him. She pulled his face from her breast and turned it up towards her. Her red lips were full and flared; they struck Dunbar as being dangerously exotic in their shape; he caught sight of bad teeth and smelled stale breath as she asked: 'You like? What your name?'

It seemed important not to reveal his true identity, as if to prevent her from running and telling his father. The thought was illogical, but potent.

'Foggy,' he admitted and deftly added, 'what's your name?'

'Maria,' she replied, stressing the second vowel and bending her head back so that her neck stretched. Impulsively he kissed it, then bent and again dug his head in her breasts, moving his hands up her back. She wore nothing under her thin dress and he felt her spine, her shoulderblades.

She suddenly pulled back, threw one leg wide and clear of him so that he caught a glimpse of the whole of her inner thigh, and sat on a chair to the left of him. He had not been aware of the chair before, one of the boys must have placed it there. She leaned forward, elbows on the table so that he could see her breasts, and picked up his beer glass, draining the little left in the bottom.

'You buy me drink, *si*?'

'A lucky lad like you can buy us all a drink,' put in Williams.

A boy appeared, perhaps the one who had deftly placed the chair in position. Two more whores materialised on the laps of his companions. Flushed, discomfited, thinking incongruously of the touchy point of honour,

Dunbar fished in his pocket, found a florin and put it in the hand of the boy.

'Beer,' said Humphries.

'Mescal,' said Williams, 'with beer.'

The women remained silent. The boy stood still, the silver florin on his outstretched palm.

'He want more,' explained Maria. Dunbar went to rummage further in his pocket, but Williams snapped: 'Bugger off and get the drinks.'

The boy did as he was bid. Dunbar did not notice his return; Maria was massaging his thigh, working her way with breathtaking slowness towards his loins. Williams and Humphries were occupied, each oblivious to the others. All about him men and women were similarly engrossed.

Maria pouted at him. Emboldened, he slipped his left arm about her waist and tried to draw her back on his lap; what he had done once, he might do again. But he felt her resistance and instead, placed his right hand on her breast. This she appeared to accept; her ministrations increased and he faltered in his own as he felt the rise of the inevitable. Well versed in her craft, Maria stopped, left him hanging expectantly, wanting him upstairs, committed and divested of his money.

She smiled, reached for her glass, indifferently left him massaging her breast as she drained the tiny glass of sugar water with its *soupçon* of tequila. Then she pulled his hand gently away, retaining a hold on his wrist.

'You love me, *si*? I love you. We go.' She rose, drawing him after her, but he faltered. She had mentioned love.

'No.' He felt the first awakening of revulsion and hesitated.

'You cherry boy?'

'No,' he repeated, not understanding her question but

91

shaking his head. He wanted to run, to escape from this infamous place. He looked desperately around, aware of men and women leaving the saloon in a procession through the double doors. He caught sight, as they swung, of a couple going upstairs.

'Come . . . you like, me very good, best girl in Hotel Paradiso . . .'

'No!'

Williams and Humphries looked up. 'What's the matter, Foggy? Nice bit of muslin like that not to your taste?' Williams's tone lashed him with its sarcasm. He suddenly hated the man, and broke free of Maria's grip. He wanted only to reach the door and was surprised she did not hold onto him, but let him go with an oath.

It was only as he bumped into a sailor and his whore making for the door, that he thought of his reception in the foyer. The two men, the madame, what would they make of his panic-stricken eruption into their presence? He opened the doors with a cool deliberation he was far from feeling. The madame was remonstrating with a single girl and looked round, as though to deal with another happy pair retiring upstairs, saw it was a single boy and turned back to the girl.

Thus ignored, Dunbar slipped towards the street. As he stepped out onto the verandah, something made him look back.

The madame was smiling now and taking money from the seaman whom Dunbar had bumped into. As the pair retired upstairs, the madame rounded again upon the lone girl. Dunbar saw she was in fact constrained by the tall mestizo guard stationed at the foot of the stairs. The man had her arms pinioned behind her back. The women spat a torrent of words at each other.

If Dunbar had been aroused by the madame's over-ripe

voluptuousness or the dancer's erotic attraction; if he had been teased by the stripper's blatant sexuality or the raunchy wantonness of Maria who had brought him to the point of climax, he had never seen anyone as beautiful as the girl with the blazing eyes as she confronted her tormentor, and he winced as she was struck across the face by the madame. He made to go back, but the mestizo caught sight of him and pulled the girl away behind the staircase, while the madame swung towards him, her face flushed and angry.

'*¡Marcha!*' she exclaimed.

Dunbar hesitated, then turned and walked miserably back to the ship.

CHAPTER FOUR

Femmes Fatales

Sunrise struck the façade of the great church like a blow.
The tall campanile, white and pink and ochre, the arched
interior of its belfry shadowed in purple, struck even
the pragmatic Captain Steele with its momentary beauty.
He was up early enjoying one of the cheroots Señor
Maldonado had brought him as a sweetener, promenading
his boat-deck clad only in the garish *sarong* he affected
at night in tropical latitudes.

He regarded Puerto San Martin with a critical air. After
all, this was a significant day, not merely for him, but for
the port itself. It amused him to see the long shadow of
his ship, spiky with sampson posts, masts and derricks,
fall across the wharf and up the walls of the godown
on the waterfront. The image seemed a metaphor of
his intentions, producing a low chuckle in a man not
habitually imaginative.

Captain Steele turned and walked across the deck,
squinting against the glory of the sun. It was already
several degrees above the horizon and gained in radi-
ance as it climbed in altitude above the layers of dust
that surrounded the planet and muted its splendour.
A glittering path of orange transmuting to gold upon

the deep ultramarine of the sea. It was going to be a perfect day. Captain Steele sighed contentedly, pitched the cheroot stub overboard, spun on his slippered heel and disappeared into his cabin.

After the longshoremen had come aboard, Steele went ashore, following Maldonado's directions. His first call was to Dr Reilly, whose consulting rooms were over a barber's shop in a side alley behind the port offices. The barber was idle and smoking a cigarette, squatting on the coping stones which formed a threshold to his salon. He rose as the resplendent white figure approached and, in a mixture of pidgin and gesture, invited Captain Steele to be shaved and have his hair cut.

Steele made a dismissive gesture, whereupon the barber sank back onto his haunches, his eyes following Steele with a mixture of appeal and hatred. Only the thought of future custom kept him silent.

The stairs up which Steele made his way did not inspire confidence; the aromas of cooking and urine competed for dominance, but on a gloomy landing at the head of the first flight he found a door marked with the doctor's name. He knocked. Feet shuffled audibly towards him beyond the door: it swung open. A careworn half-caste woman peered blankly at him.

'Dr Reilly?'

The woman muttered something and held the door open, then shuffled back into a bare room which contained a high, bare wooden bed and a glass-fronted dresser containing bottles, flasks and an assortment of unpleasant-looking instruments which Steele thought had gynaecological purposes. A scrubbed wooden stool stood beside the bed. The woman disappeared through a farther door. Steele heard a mumbled conversation, the rustle of a discarded newspaper, and a small, neat man entered the consulting room. He was almost bald, and cleanshaven. He wore a dark waistcoat and trousers, the former adorned with a watch-chain and fob. A pearl pinned his black cravat, his striped shirt was starched. His cuffs were turned back on powerful wrists and forearms.

'Ah, Captain Steele, Señor Maldonado intimated you would be coming. Please, sit down. It is your stomach, no?' The wide, well-formed mouth enunciated the English with a hint of an accent that Steele could not quite place. They shook hands. Reilly smelled strongly of tobacco.

'No. I'm afraid I misinformed Mr Maldonado.'

'Ah,' Reilly said knowingly, 'you have a more intimate problem, a venereal disease?'

'No, no, not at all, not at all, though my purpose in visiting you today is not disconnected . . .'

'You smoke?'

'Not now, thank you.'

'You will have coffee, then, if it is advice you wish for; let us retire somewhere more comfortable. Come,' Reilly waved his visitor to follow and raised his voice. 'Ursula! Coffee, *por favor*!'

Steele followed the doctor through into the further room. It was of moderate size and lined with books. A large, gilt-framed portrait in oils hung above a writing desk. It showed a fiercely moustachioed soldier who wore a bell-topped shako and a bandoleer full of cartridges, and brandished a sabre. In the background a town burned furiously. Though the face was sallow, the eyes were piercingly blue and glared startlingly out of the canvas. Opposite, a smaller picture of a woman stared back. A small watercolour of what Steele took to be a Highland loch occupied a third space. The room was the den of a bachelor.

'My grandfather,' Reilly said, noting Steele's interest in the military portrait. 'He was a general of brigade, an Irishman and, of course, a Catholic. His first battle was at Castlebar . . .'

Reilly paused, as if the name should prompt some reaction from Steele. It failed, for Steele had just realised the hint of a brogue in the accent and had realised the watercolour was of an Irish lough. He felt foolish; the connection was obvious, given the doctor's name.

Reilly watched his visitor's face and resumed. 'I speak English, Irish, French and Spanish.'

'*Irish?*'

'Castlebar is in County Mayo, Captain, and County Mayo is in Ireland.'

'Oh.' Steele was confused.

'Ah. Ursula has brought coffee, please, sit down.' Reilly courteously gestured his guest to an empty arm-chair from which most of the stuffing had long ago migrated.

After coffee had been served, Reilly, whose brown eyes contrasted with those of his ancestor and attested to local blood, sat back, crossed his legs and regarded his visitor.

'And now, what can I do for you?'

Steele explained. He had rationalised the matter to himself in his frequent rehearsals so that it seemed a quite seemly, moderate and proper thing for two men of the world to discuss. Reilly reinforced this opinion, showing little surprise at the subject.

'You are not the first to do such a thing, Captain. It is like Shenandoah, is it not?' Reilly chuckled. 'The captain loved the Indian maiden, eh? Gave the chief the strong

97

firewater, and 'cross the river stole his daughter, except you would not be stealing anyone and there is no chief.'

'There is a madame, I understand.'

'You have not met her?'

'No, I was hoping for an introduction.'

'By me?' Reilly raised his eyebrows, put down his empty coffee cup and lit another cigarette.

'Yes. I am happy to pay . . .'

'Of course you are, Captain, you can buy anything. In Puerto San Martin you are a fabulously wealthy man. Only the manager of the mines is a greater. But a meeting with the madame, tch, tch, that is not so easy.'

'First, is there a suitable girl?'

'Of course there is a suitable girl for you, Captain. If she is not here now we can find one in a *pueblo* not far away.'

'Ah, can I go to a, a *pueblo* and get one myself? Must I go through this madame? I shall still wish you to certify . . .'

'Of course, I understand your desire and my part in this delicate matter, but it would not be proper to avoid . . . you know . . .'

'But why not? Is there a man, a pimp?'

Reilly laughed. '*Dios!* No! There is most certainly not a pimp! But it would be dangerous to negotiate without the help of the lady of the Hotel Paradiso.'

'How is it – dangerous?'

'It is, take my word. It may also be, er, inconvenient for your ship. The wharf-labourers may not be as helpful as you would wish, and when you come to leave . . .' Reilly shrugged and pulled the corners of his mouth down. 'You understand? The papers, the certificates and customs clearances.'

'She is a woman of influence?'

'Exactly. Most certainly. More to people here than the mining company.'

'What is her name?'

'She will tell you her name, if she wishes, when she meets you.'

'And you will arrange a meeting?'

'Of course, but I will have to make a small charge.'

'Yes, yes. And you will examine the girl?'

'That is a matter of routine. It is my dubious privilege to examine all the girls in the Hotel Paradiso, every week. A charming occupation, I assure you. Now, I wish for payment in pounds sterling. Five pounds for the introduction, ten for the examination and each subsequent examination until we find someone suitable.'

Steele gasped. 'How many times do you think it will be necessary?'

'That depends on your choice, Captain. If you wish for my advice you will look for a reasonable figure without making a fuss. Beauty, as you understand it, is not often to be found here, though some of the girls are exceptional. Select one no older than fifteen, and she will eat from your hand. What more could you ask? But be generous; be prepared to pay handsomely. An English gentleman will not be expected to – what is the word? Ah, yes, to haggle.'

Steele soberly digested this information. He had thought to be obtaining a bargain and was surprised at the degree of sophistication he had encountered in his first interview. Nevertheless the prospect was undiminished in its appeal and he nodded agreement.

'Very well, Dr Reilly. Thank you.' He stood and held out his hand. Reilly rose, grasped Steele's hand and waved him out.

'I will let Jorge know when I have secured an interview.

99

Be patient, you may be kept waiting a few days, but perhaps not. The lady is, like all her sex, subject to whim.'

'For ten pounds, I hope you will persuade her not to keep me waiting.'

Reilly chuckled. 'It will not be up to me, but I will see what I can do.'

'Very well.' Steele paused. 'The details of this matter are between ourselves, Doctor, and the lady. I do not want Mr Maldonado . . .'

'Oh, no, I assure you of our discretion. Good day to you, Captain. Enjoy your walk.'

In the street, Steele replaced his Panama hat, lit another of Maldonado's cheroots and strolled towards the square. He had committed himself to more expense than he had initially estimated, but he was not unhappy. He would take the doctor's advice and enjoy his walk. He had a notion of showing himself about the place, and the sun was not yet too high to be uncomfortable. He was gratified to see that he was noticed, felt the eyes of the townspeople upon him. He affected indifference to the Hotel Paradiso and crossed the road towards the great church, playing the savant, staring upwards at the height of the belfry and brushing aside the begging urchins who insisted on cleaning his shoes.

After the first day of discharging, Mr Rayner had discovered a problem. The loading of copper *boleos* using the railway was a simple task for the longshoremen of Puerto San Martin. It was crude, unhealthily dusty and hard work, but it required little skill and no finesse. Occasionally the longshoremen handled general cargo, but the place was poor and it did not import foreign goods in great quantity.

Most of this inward trade for domestic consumption consisted of ironmongery, crockery and timber from which local craftsmen made furniture. When items of quality arrived, they usually formed the personal effects of the manager of the mines and his staff of engineers. They came in packing cases, the removal of which was well supervised.

No heavy articles had arrived since the rails, trucks and locomotives of the railway itself brought the first ever steamship into the port. But railway lines were not as complex and delicate as the metal sections of the conveyor system. These steel lattices possessed flanges and angled joints whose machined faces were vulnerable to damage if, for instance, they were carelessly swung against the *Kohinoor*'s hatch coamings. It proved difficult to make this point to the gang foremen who nodded vigorously, said they *comprende*d and continued as before.

Moreover, the sections were piled up on the wharf. The concept of stacking had clearly not been found necessary at any previous point in the port's development, so damage occurred ashore, one or two of the longer, unsupported struts being bent.

When an engineer from the mine arrived, the several score of sections lying higgledy-piggledy sent him into instantaneous paroxysms of empurpled rage. Herr Pedersen's rages were apparently legendary and the longshoremen, assured of their incompetence in Pedersen's mixture of Spanish, German and Danish oaths, forthwith ceased work and squatted gratefully in the nearest available shade.

Señor Maldonado was summoned, Capitan Valbuena was summoned, and eventually even Dr Reilly (as the most fluent English speaker in San Martin) was summoned, to resolve the dilemma. They assembled in

Rayner's cabin and the mate ordered beer, signing the steward's chit OCS – on Company's service.

A plan for dealing with the problem was mooted while the impromptu committee sat back and enjoyed a second and then a third beer. Pedersen was chief engineer of the mine and had only just learned of the arrival of the eagerly awaited machinery that morning. He had ridden into town post-haste.

After three beers he did not think the damage was as serious as he had at first thought and decided that his skilled staff could rectify what little had occurred. Nevertheless, the remainder of the consignment would have to be taken out of the ship with more care.

Rayner bowed to the inevitable, agreed to slow the discharge and to have each sling supervised. He told Valbuena that as a consequence the ship would require the berth 'indefinitely'.

There then ensued a debate, largely between Valbuena and Reilly, as to the precise meaning of the word. A bottle of whisky was sent for to oil the mechanics of interpretation and negotiation.

The delay, however, now caused concern to Maldonado who was responsible for hiring in the labour. This seemed to represent an intractable problem since slower, supervised discharge meant employing fewer longshoremen. Moreover, the contractor, for whom Maldonado was merely a go-between, would be loathe to lose income on such a large labour force.

Rayner asked for the contractor to be present. All except Pedersen protested the impossibility of such a proposition. When Rayner asked why, Reilly explained that the company that ran the labour also ran the town, and was as influential as the priests. It left such matters to its agent, Señor Maldonado. The unfortunate Maldonado was sweating profusely from anxiety as much as heat; he refused more whisky and seemed uncertain as to how to proceed.

Eventually Rayner said, 'We will employ the same number of men over a longer period, say three times the period, but only a third of them need turn up for work every day.'

Reilly put this idea to his compatriots. 'But there are six gangs,' whined Maldonado.

'So much the better, one ashore, one aboard . . .' The matter was solved. They went on to discuss other things, in an amiable and unhurried atmosphere, as the whisky bottle gained in ullage.

Pedersen, it transpired, had acquired his nationality by accident, having been born in the Danish province of Holstein. When Holstein was seized by the army of the Kaiser after the battle of the Dybbol Hill, he found himself a German. He had been in the San Martin mine for twenty-six years and lived with a half-caste girl in a bungalow near the workings. He had only four more years to serve before going home.

'Who is the contractor for the labourers?' Rayner asked when the conversation had fallen silent. Half-drunk though they were, they did not rush to answer. Rayner, who still sipped cautiously at his first whisky, perceived this reticence. 'He is a big man in San Martin, eh?'

'You are clever, Mr Rayner, but not quite correct,' said Reilly. 'The person concerned is, as you put it, big, by which you mean influential, I assume?' Rayner nodded. 'Yes, well it is not a man, it is a woman.'

'Ahhh,' said Rayner. 'Behind everything there is a woman. Doesn't a woman own the Hotel Paradiso?'

'It is the same woman,' put in Valbuena. 'She own the waterfront.'

'She is English,' added Maldonado, as if relieved of a great burden.

Mr Rayner's contribution to the success of this *ad hoc* committee meeting was to increase the supervision of the cargo discharge by his own people, and whenever it was deemed necessary to find men for unusual tasks, it was traditional to call upon the apprentices. Not only were they bound by indenture to obey all lawful commands of the owner's representatives, but it was assumed that, as aspirant masters and mates, they possessed a modicum of interest and intelligence. While Rayner instructed Mitchell and Sanders as to the new arrangements, he passed orders that as long as the gangs were aboard, Humphries and Dunbar were each to occupy a 'tween-deck and ensure every steel section was properly manoeuvred under the derrick hooks, slung correctly and lifted carefully. Since the ship was to work a forward and an after hatch, this would occupy both apprentices for the entire working day.

'Who'll keep the ship during the night, Mr Rayner?' asked the second mate.

'I'll ask the bosun to find me his most reliable seaman, Mr Mitchell. Morgan's a good man.'

In this way, Mr Rayner's assiduity caused Humphries and Dunbar to be faced with the daily temptation to go ashore every evening.

Dunbar spent the day in agony. He had assumed his behaviour of the previous night had been embarrassingly conspicuous; oddly, it attracted no comment. His shipmates, working off the excesses of their binge, were preoccupied with their own physical well-being and, if they recalled the incident at all, dismissed it as too trivial to be noteworthy.

Only Humphries and Williams had seen what had happened and their knowledge was imperfect. Humphries, who had been unable to pay for his pleasure, had been kicked out and felt a retrospective relief, rather than resentment at the decamping of his banker. He had been humiliated the night before, and despite his bravado and claims of vast experience had no funds without going cap-in-hand to Captain Steele, with whom he currently had little credit. Dunbar's wealth had seemed more accessible. Humphries's retreat had therefore been somewhat similar to Dunbar's; he had no desire to have anyone else refer to it, and so kept his mouth shut.

For his part, Williams had given the behaviour of his two companions little thought. They were, after all, barely men. Besides, drink had dulled his recollection and the subsequent events of the night had been far more memorable. If he thought of Dunbar at all, it was with a little regret that their friendship had suffered. Shortly before the longshoremen broke for their noon meal and *siesta*, he sought out Dunbar in number five 'tween-deck.

'Ah, there you are, Foggy. How are you getting on?' Williams clambered down the hatch ladder, stepped into the 'tween-deck and looked at the longshoremen as they struggled round a long steel box of slender girders with its internal axles, grease-boxes and rollers.

'Oh,' Dunbar replied, displeased at this intrusion, 'not so bad.'

'Good?' The foreman pushed his face between them, pointed at the slings and angrily demanded permission to hook on to the wire runners.

105

'*Si, si,*' said Dunbar, 'good. Now lift carefully.'

'Leeft carefullee . . .' The foreman made a gesture of supreme contempt, waved, and the section rose on the derrick runners.

It seemed that this charade had been going on for hours.

'I see you speak the lingo,' jested Williams.

'Yes,' said Dunbar briefly.

'Enjoy yourself last night?'

'Oh, it was all right. Look,' he suddenly shouted as the lifting sling swung towards the coaming above, 'watch that bloody load!'

'What happened to you?' Williams went on as the sling oscillated just short of the ship's steelwork. 'When I left with Teresa you'd gone.'

'You know I didn't much like, er, Maria.'

'Oh yes, I'd forgotten.'

'Had you?'

Williams nodded. 'Look, Foggy, about the other night. I get a bit . . . funny, you know, offhand, when I've been drinking. I didn't mean anything. Nothing personal, see?'

'All right. If you say so.'

'No harm done, eh?'

'No.'

Williams held out his hand. 'Shake?'

'Yes, all right.' Dunbar reluctantly offered his hand.

'Maria was the girl Humpo couldn't make the night before. Brewer's droop, he had.' Williams laughed, ingratiating himself with Dunbar at Humphries's expense.

'I put him to bed,' said Dunbar.

'Did you? Well, well, you're getting the idea.' Williams chuckled. 'You didn't fancy Maria yourself, then? She looked like hot stuff to me.'

'Her breath smelt,' said Dunbar desperately.

'Did it? Oh, that can really put you off. Be your first time anyway, would it?'

'No, not really . . .'

Williams looked keenly at Dunbar and did not push his line of questioning; it was not necessary. 'Look, come with me tonight.'

'No.'

'Now listen, if you've got a few bob you can see an *exposicion*. It's safe as houses; see how you like it . . .'

'What on earth's an *exposicion*?'

'Wait and see. You'll enjoy it! No bad breath to bother you. What d'you say?'

The temptation to see again the girl with the blazing eyes was overwhelming. He longed to discover her identity and to rescue her from the brutality of the madame. He could not believe that she was a harlot, for her beauty far surpassed even the ravishing Julia Ravenham, and he knew she was being coerced by the monstrously striking woman who guarded the door of the Hotel Paradiso.

Above his head a neglected sling crashed into the steel coaming.

'For Christ's sake, be careful!' he bawled.

'You'll come then?' Williams asked, smiling.

'All right.'

Captain Steele stood in the vast and gloomy nave of the church of San Martin. The alien scent of incense, damp and confessed sin assailed him. He felt a mild distaste at the sight of the two side chapels, where ranks of guttering votive candles set before the images of the virgin and Saint Martin bespoke an incomprehensible and primitive faith. This was affirmed by the row of confessional boxes, from one of which a low whispering echoed. Outside them, in adjacent pews, a handful of old women waited patiently. Cynically, Steele supposed they understood every peccant word.

Despite his intellectual sneering, Steele was impressed by the size and majesty of the building; it had the massive dimensions of a cathedral. The reredos behind the high altar was a magnificent gilded concoction of fluted niches, saintly images and the risen Christ, from whose pre-eminent position, cascading down either side of the righteous, the damned tumbled to hell.

The sheer splendour of this carved and impressive monstrosity, lit even now by the candles glowing on the altar, gave Steele an idea. He advanced down the aisle, his shoregoing shoes clicking with a satisfying irreverence on the stone flags, until he stood at the entrance to the chancel and regarded the ornate pulpit, lectern and choir stalls.

The reredos ascended above him, tier after tier of the good, each in symbolic isolation with some evidence of the source of their martyrdom, virtue or blessedness, each transfigured, noble of expression, perfect of form, flanked by the falling and tortured bodies of the patently ordinary: the fat, the thin, the ill-proportioned, the ugly, the disfigured.

The upright holy were predominantly men, men in whom the eye soon lost interest; the damned were predominantly women, many gross, their voluptuous bodies run to sinful seed, the few men falling with them goat-like, or bloated to impotent excess.

The primitive inequity and heartless message of this vivid imagery revolted even the unphilosophic Steele, proving the superiority of his own atheistical brand of practical mercantilism. He stared at the gold crucifix on the altar and smiled. Notwithstanding all this flummery, he thought to himself, or because of it perhaps, the place seemed ideal for his purpose.

He was aware of a shadow moving, then a man in the dark cassock of a priest emerged from among the choir stalls.

For a moment their eyes met. Steele knew he was recognised as a heretic and a foreigner, saw the look of irritation at his presence cross the face of the other man. He turned, and with a studied and insolent gait, ambled back towards the great west door.

'We'll see about you, my lad,' he murmured to himself, 'all in good time.'

He emerged into a small plaza where the first zealous Christians had burned an occasional stubborn apostate. Beyond lay the oldest part of San Martin, a warren of narrow streets and tall, neglected buildings from whose stained grey walls shutters hung awry and washing was festooned on lines.

Steele turned and walked the length of the nave along its outer wall, back towards the main square, which proved a later addition, developed with the port itself. It lay east of the church, the rounded basilica of which jutted into it like a promontory.

Gnarled trees, upon the boles of which posters and news broadsheets were pasted, grew up through the paving stones of what was now the main plaza. Beneath the boughs and the leathery leaves that rustled in the light breeze, a few tables and chairs had been set out. A handful of these were occupied and Steele sat at one himself, nodding at those curious enough to look up from their conversations, letters or newspapers.

A waiter padded up to him; he ordered coffee and lit another of Maldonado's cheroots.

'Señor . . . señor . . .' A boy tugged at his sleeve. Captain Steele finally condescended to have his shoes polished.

For Dunbar the day dragged interminably. As the sun approached the zenith the ship's steel fabric soaked up the heat, transmitting it below to the dusty 'tween-deck. Sweat seeped from him continuously and he longed for the noon break and the hour of *siesta*.

Having agreed to go ashore, the prospect of seeing the girl again was the most refined kind of torture imaginable. He could not take his mind off her, her beauty, her condition, her fate. He understood everything now; why he had been abashed at finding Jenny Broom naked, why Julia Ravenham had not returned his love, even why he had come to sea in the *Kohinoor* . . .

The wind of fate had been blowing him inexorably towards this strange, exotic encounter with the girl with the blazing eyes. He felt his superiority of race, of wealth and of power. Poor as he was, here in San Martin he was comparatively wealthy; he could afford a woman, could buy *her* and rescue *her* from the evil clutches of the voluptuous madame.

It was clear she resisted the madame's attempts to turn her into a whore like Maria. God knew he did not judge Maria; the woman had to make a living where she could and, Jesu help him, he knew she had attracted the animal part of him. But the sight of the girl with the blazing eyes had, as it were, reined him in from his headlong flight to damnation. Dunbar had already invested the unknown girl with the qualities of an angel.

He thanked his stars that he had resisted the temptation of Maria's willing body and wondered how on earth he

110

could have felt the worm of lust persuading him that the madame herself was in the least sexually alluring. Her conduct with the girl had revealed her as a virago: he could see the girl now, proud and defiant, pinioned by the man with the moustaches whom he had noticed instantly as an enemy; a cruel and heartless agent of the wicked madame.

He snarled 'Take care,' at the gang foreman as yet another length of the conveyor jerked aloft.

Captain Steele finished his coffee, and was in the act of throwing a handful of small change onto the table as yet another small boy ran up to him. He was about to speak sharply, when the urchin held out a slip of paper. Steele took it and read: *Miss Hawkshawe will receive Captain Steele at eleven o'clock in the Hotel Paradiso.*

Hawkshawe; it sounded like a British name. After his encounter with Reilly, Steele wondered whether this was an advantage or a disadvantage. There would be no trouble communicating, but he would feel damned awkward discussing his requirements with a British woman. Perhaps she was of Irish descent, like the doctor. A degenerate lot, the Irish, he thought; they would do anything for a drink. Money would smooth all things his way.

He consulted his watch, saw it wanted five minutes to the hour, and rose. The boy barred his way, huge brown eyes staring up at the white gentleman. Steele dropped a silver threepenny piece into his hand, saw the smile and the smudge of dirty heels as the boy bore his prize off.

The draped foyer was tawdry in daylight. There was no sign of the madame, though a half-caste woman, identical to the doctor's housekeeper, Steele thought, languidly swept at the stairs.

She turned at the sound of Steele's boots on the floorboards.

'Miss Hawkshawe?' he asked.

The woman pointed up the stairs, drawing aside as Steele passed. He caught sight of the saloon, where the chairs were all upturned upon the tables and the floor was damp from recent swabbing. Such hygienic precautions impressed the captain. He was himself meticulous about such matters aboard ship, but did not expect to find them ashore, especially in a Mexican whorehouse.

At the top of the staircase Steele paused. A long passageway extended to the left and right. Several doors were open and he realised they were the bedrooms, or rooms of assignation. The echoes of a woman's laughter floated along the passage. It was not obvious which way he should proceed and he looked back at the woman with the brush.

'Miss Hawkshawe?' he repeated.

The woman nodded and pointed straight ahead. Steele turned and saw the door facing the head of the stairs. She nodded and motioned him to go in.

Steele felt suddenly, inexplicably nervous. Gingerly he pushed at the door. It opened onto a further stairway which in turn led to a darkened room which lay across the rear of the building. It was a narrow room with heavy drapes round the walls. It smelt of stale perfume and dust. At the far end he was aware of the pale covers of a large bed set before which was an upright chair and a table. A tall-chimneyed oil lamp stood upon the table.

'Ah, Captain Steele, pray step forward so that I may see you, and you may see me.'

Steele had not the faintest idea where the voice had

112

come from. His eyes had not yet fully adjusted from the glare of the street and he shuffled forward, his heart beating foolishly in his chest.

'Come, sir, don't hesitate, sit down, sit down!'

The imperious tone made him move faster. He could see the upright chair was unoccupied and was searching the coverlet of the bed in case his interlocutor was an invalid. Then, just as he reached the chair, she swung round. The high-backed, winged Windsor chair on the far side of the table was almost completely invisible against the black drapes. As she swung it round with a slight squeak of its castors he saw she was veiled, a black net hanging over her face from a coiled torque of jet silk wound about her head. She wore an old-fashioned, high-necked and buttoned bombazine dress and reminded Steele of lithographs of the late Queen-Empress.

'Miss Hawkshawe?' He paused in seating himself, and held out his hand.

'There is sherry on the table,' she said, not turning to face him, but remaining side-on. 'Please sit down and help yourself. It is not appropriate we shake hands. This is not a social visit. You have come to discuss a matter of business, Reilly tells me.'

'Yes, ma'am.'

'Well, what is it?'

'I, er, I, um . . .'

'You want to buy a young woman, a clean young woman, a virgin preferably, and for as little money as possible. Is that not so?'

'Well, I had thought . . .'

'Are you married, Captain Steele?'

'I am a widower, ma'am.' The honesty of this reply gave Steele a little confidence, enough to pour a glass of sherry.

'Am I to believe you?'

'That is a matter for you, ma'am, but you may verify it with any of my officers.'

'Are you unusual in your appetites, Captain?'

'I'm sorry, I don't . . .'

'I cater for every taste, Captain. Nothing surprises me. Do you, for instance, favour sodomy? Or enjoy being whipped?'

'Good Lord, no, ma'am, neither.'

'I am pleased to hear it. While I can see what is going on here, I can control it, but I will not knowingly send a girl into bondage.'

'Of course not,' replied Steele meekly.

'Of course there are no guarantees in this business.'

'No, I understand. I have asked the doctor to examine—'

'Yes, yes, I know that. It's a reasonable precaution, but I was meaning that you and your character are unknown qualities.'

Steele thought of his visit to the great church and the idea he had had. It was an inspiration. 'If she is what I want, Miss Hawkshawe, I intend to marry her.'

'They all say that, Captain,' Hawkshawe said wearily, 'but I have no proof they ever do.'

'No, no, you misunderstand me. I mean to marry her here, in the church of Saint Martin.'

For the first time since the conversation had begun, Steele felt he had the advantage. He watched her turn full-face, staring at him, her features a pale blur behind the black mesh.

'You are a Catholic?' There was a hint of distaste in the enunciation of the word.

'If it is necessary.'

Steele heard a low and sinister chuckle as she resumed her former position, her head in indistinct profile.

'Before we discuss terms, perhaps you will tell me something: the *Kohinoor* is your ship, is it not?'

'It is.'

'You have brought a new method of transporting the copper from the mines to the wharf, have you not?'

'Yes. It is a conveyor system.'

'How does it work?'

Steele explained, marvelling that the woman was interested and intrigued at her origins, for her command of English was perfect. Miss Hawkshawe was no remnant of European blood, but someone born in England, by the accent, though there was just a hint of something else.

'Well, how much are you prepared to pay for this girl of your dreams?'

'I should like to see someone first,' Steele riposted, 'before committing myself.'

'But you are prepared to pay the doctor five pounds for an introduction to me and ten pounds for each examination.'

By his exorbitant charges, Reilly had already set a level for the deal, Steele reflected angrily, but he concealed this and said, 'I will pay forty pounds for a clean fifteen-year-old.'

The woman remained silent for a long moment. Then she said, 'Come back tomorrow, Captain, double your offer and I shall find you something to your liking.'

'Miss Hawkshawe, forty pounds is a great sum of money. I have to pay for a wedding. You have almost made that a condition of my acceptance as a client.'

'You have heard my conditions, Captain. If the conveyor system works to increase the export of copper, I shall have more ships here, prices will rise and you will later kick yourself for not having accepted my offer.'

The Windsor chair squeaked again and turned its high back to him. He had no alternative but to leave.

Eighty pounds was a small fortune!

Only when he was back in the street did he remember he had brought goods to trade. But such was the dramatic effect of his meeting, the matter had been driven out of his mind.

'Damn the bitch!' he muttered, walking back towards his ship.

CHAPTER FIVE

Knights Errant

The heat of noon beat down upon Puerto San Martin. Nothing moved, not even in the purple shadows. Only the kites wheeled in the sky above the town, riding the rising air which bore the smell of carrion. The cafés were deserted, the streets empty. Most of the inhabitants enjoyed their *siesta* in their homes, but in the deathly chill of the great church a few penitent women remained, queuing to confess their sins.

The longshoremen had abandoned the *Kohinoor*, slunk away and vanished. The steel hull of the *Kohinoor* transmitted the sun's heat to the vessel's interior. In the 'tween-decks, holds and accommodation, the temperature became unbearable, rivalling that of the boiler room. The crew lounged about, fractious, indolent and yawning, awaiting the resumption of work, much of their indifferent midday meal uneaten.

Then one man moved in this stupefying atmosphere. Conspicuous in his white linen suit and Panama hat, Captain Steele walked out of the Hotel Paradiso, into the blinding and vacant street. He squinted against the glare and the heat clapped him across the shoulders like a hearty and insincere acquaintance. Bracing himself he strode back to the ship with a measured tread, ignoring the heat, conscious of his dignity, his mind seething.

He had mixed feelings about the morning's events. Reilly seemed reliable enough and, all things considered, his expense well worthwhile. The strange Miss Hawkshawe, on the other hand, was no more than a procuress and Steele damned her, as he damned anyone who took money for little effort. On the other hand, once her frank and businesslike approach had overcome any diffidence he might have felt about the nature of the proposed transaction, he felt happy negotiating with her. Though enigmatic in the extreme, she spoke the same idiomatic language as himself. Moreover, her forbidding appearance made one forget she was a woman.

Nevertheless, eighty pounds was a great sum of money.

He came out onto the wharf. The heat here was intense, palpable. Even the dust lay inert in the windless air. The steel sections of the conveyor system gleamed and shimmered, reflecting the heat. The ship towered over the quayside, but it was not until the captain had hoisted his perspiring body up the gangway and was enveloped by the familiar shipboard smells, that he found any shade.

For Dunbar and Humphries, the afternoon passed in the same stultifying manner as the morning, but eventually the hour of sunset approached, the discharge slowed, and then stopped, and the grinning longshoremen left the ship, each man claiming the metal token that indicated he had worked on board that day and was entitled to claim payment at the end of the week. He might also redeem these tokens in several establishments run by Miss Hawkshawe. These consisted of a *cantina*, a general store and a cheap brothel in the old part of the town. The common male inhabitants of Puerto San Martin were not welcome at the Hotel Paradiso.

Humphries had discovered the trading value of the tokens by dint of a long, convoluted and energetically gestured conversation with several of the men working in number five 'tween-deck. He had established the fact that he himself might come by several of these tokens in exchange for certain items he could acquire. A large bath-towel, of which there was a supply in the steward's store, was worth two tokens; a bar of soap, one; a tablecloth of white linen from which a wedding dress might be contrived, six. Humphries reserved this information, resolving to bring pencil and paper below the next morning in order to establish a league table of wants and prices.

The opportunity thus offered to rid himself of financial dependence on Foggy Dunbar, whose resources, Humphries surmised, were in any case limited, greatly appealed to him. However, he would have to work fast before others among the ship's company cashed in. On a ship as tightly run as the *Kohinoor*, there was a surplus of very little and Humphries realised he would have to steal what he required and stash it somewhere safe as soon as he could.

'I don't think I'll bother going ashore tonight, Foggy,' he said, yawning. 'I'm dog-tired and it's so bloody hot. You don't mind, do you?'

'No, of course not.'

'Don't let me stop you, though,' Humphries added with feigned concern, suddenly realising he had assumed he would be alone in the half-deck for an hour or two that evening.

'Williams wants me to go ashore with him,' Dunbar

119

said, looking at Humphries, wondering whether to confide in him. He was rather glad that Humphries was staying aboard. The rescue of the girl with the blazing eyes could not be a combined effort: knights errant were by definition solitary. He had agreed to accompany Williams only as a means to a private end. But there was another matter that bothered him. 'What do you think of Williams?' he asked.

Humphries, eager to encourage Dunbar to accompany the able seaman, took a solicitous interest in his younger companion.

'Williams? Oh, he's all right. He gets a bit ratty when he's been drinking, but his heart's in the right place. Now he's got drunk a couple of times and rogered that bint Teresa, he'll be all right.'

'What's an *exposicion*?' asked Dunbar, changing the subject.

Humphries frowned. 'I don't know, why?'

'Oh, nothing,' said Dunbar, disappointed. 'I just wondered.'

After dinner that evening, Dunbar dozed until Williams woke him.

'Off in half an hour, Foggy. Get yourself ready. We'll have a walk in the square first, give ourselves an appetite.'

The plaza lay in the shadow of the church which rose like a mountain against the sunset. Beneath the gnarled trees, whose leaves rustled in the growing breeze, the oil lamps glowed merrily, and disposed among the tables and chairs sat the idlers, mostly young and single men. All about them, in what at first seemed a random, but then, Dunbar realised, was a carefully contrived circular procession, the population of Puerto San Martin promenaded. This was the hour of the *paseo*.

Dunbar recognised several of the men who had been working in his hatch. In clean white shirts and black trousers they looked quite different, and each had his wife, and some their daughters on their arms.

The women also wore black-and-white long skirts and white blouses, and many veiled their faces beneath *mantillas*, the lace falling about their shoulders. But here and there a shawl or stole of a brilliant colour – scarlet or crimson, blue or russet – caught the light. Some of these women wore flowers in their hair, some carried posies, while others flirted with their fans, flicking them open and closed, winnowing them in front of their faces in conformity with some ritual whose significance was contrived and, to Dunbar, incomprehensibly arcane.

'They walk round and round, see,' Williams confided in a stage whisper, 'showing off their women before locking them up again.'

From time to time, Dunbar observed, the promenading groups paused and exchanged pleasantries with one of the lounging men at the tables. The young men stood and bowed. Occasionally one bent over a clasped hand. There was a twitching of veils, and bobbing and turning of heads. The young men smiled, or looked serious. This posturing was at once studied and formal, but it also hinted at suppressed passions lying just below the mannered surface.

Dunbar observed one young beau test the limits of convention as he made to move aside the *mantilla* over a daughter's face. The mother, a tall, well-made woman, tugged her husband's other elbow, detaching the family and moving on, leaving a snubbed and flaming suitor foolishly behind. Beside him Williams chuckled.

'Imagine having to meet women in this way all the time,' he said. 'No wonder they need places like the Hotel Paradiso.' He exaggerated his pronunciation of the name.

The light *terral* bore the scent of flowers and musk. Dunbar observed the features of the women, fascinated. He sought to study the faces beneath the veils and from time to time a combination of proximity to one of the hanging oil lamps and a trick of the shadows threw a face into relief. He caught the attention of one handsome matron who immediately flashed and fluttered a fan before her eyes, so that her husband turned to glare. Dunbar felt strangely elated by the reaction.

'Let's have a drink,' suggested Williams, and they sat at an empty table on the edge of the promenading mass.

Williams ordered something and Dunbar asked, 'If all the women are so well protected, where do those we met last night come from? Surely none of these go to the Hotel Paradiso?'

'No, no,' Williams laughed, 'these are the respectable townspeople. They're not rich or anything, you can see some of the tally clerks and the longshoresharks among them, but they'll be respectable people, see. The girls that get themselves into trouble, or young widows, or women whose men have buggered off and left them, they end up in the Hotel. They'll be Indian girls from the villages as well, and some parents will be so poor that they will sell their children.'

'Children? Oh, you mean those boys who wait at table.'

'That's not all they do,' Williams said ominously.

The Hotel Paradiso seemed infinite in its wickedness and Dunbar resolved that he *must* rescue the girl with the blazing eyes from such a dreadful place.

'Although some of these people are poor,' Williams went on, 'they can be very proud. Look at this lot now; more Spanish than Indian.'

They watched a family approach four abreast. The husband was tall and wore a Spanish hat. He contrived to carry a silver-topped cane, even though each arm supported a lady. On his right his large wife walked in perfect unison with her husband, measure for measure. On his left, two slender daughters, arm-in-arm, their backs like ramrods, aped their parents. Dunbar sensed a deference in the passers-by, a subtle but significant withdrawal as this family swept along with a distinct air of pre-eminence.

He had once, as a very small boy, seen an earl and countess in church. They had been visiting Clayton Hall and they walked and were deferred to in a similar manner.

'That'll be the *Alcaid* and his family,' Williams said knowingly.

'How d'you know all these things, Idris?' Dunbar suddenly asked.

'D'you think I should be ignorant, being a seaman, like?'

'No, no, of course not; but you're so well informed.'

'I was taught to read, like you.'

'Oh, I didn't mean to offend you.'

'It's all right. I'm not offended,' Williams said shortly, rising to his feet, but Dunbar knew that he had touched a nerve. 'Come, it will soon be time for the *exposicion*.'

'But what *is* an *exposicion*?'

Williams laughed and regarded his younger companion. 'Well, Foggy,' he gestured expansively round about them, 'it's a bit like this only much, much more enjoyable!'

*   *   *

There was no sign of the girl with the blazing eyes in the foyer of the Hotel Paradiso, but the madame and her two henchmen occupied their posts as before. Williams went up to the woman and said something to her in a low voice. He must have mentioned Dunbar who stood just behind him, for she peered round Williams and stared at Dunbar for a moment before he heard her say, 'No!'

Williams looked round, put up a placating hand towards Dunbar and said, 'Go and order two tequilas, Foggy. I'll join you in a moment.'

As Dunbar went into the saloon, he heard Williams plead, 'He's young, never had a jig-jig. He wants to do it, but he's scared . . . Warm him up, Señora! You'll profit in the end.'

With mixed feelings, Dunbar sought out an obscure corner table and ordered the two tequilas without thinking. The saloon was slowly filling. Several of *Kohinoor*'s crew grinned at him and he felt a foolish but undeniable pride to be accepted among them. Williams caught up with him as the waiter arrived.

'You owe me a quid, Foggy. Give it to me later. Now don't say a word to anyone else, right? You're very lucky to be doing this, so just keep quiet and do what I tell you.'

'But, I don't understand . . .'

'Oh ye of little faith. Just do what I say.'

Dunbar sipped at the tequila and choked. 'I can't drink this!'

'Get it inside you,' instructed Williams, ordering a second.

'No, no thanks.'

124

'Just do what I say,' Williams repeated, with an uncomfortably reminiscent edge to his voice.

If Dunbar thought Williams was going to get them both drunk, he was mistaken. After the second tequila, Williams did not order anything else. They sat through the performance of the dancer and the stripper and when the women came in, Williams caught sight of Teresa and beckoned her over. She sat on his knee and Dunbar saw her hitch her skirt so that Williams could slide his hand up her thigh. He feigned not to notice, but watched her face until their eyes met and she smiled at him.

'You like a girl? Maria busy tonight . . .'

'He doesn't like Maria,' Williams said and Dunbar froze at the rudeness of this statement, almost willing to protest its inaccuracy, but Teresa seemed to accept it with a shrug.

'What girl you like then? And I call her . . .'

Embarrassed, he was about to deny any interest in women when he recalled the principal purpose of this visit. Emboldened by the tequila he said, 'I would like the young girl who was here last night.'

Teresa frowned. 'Here?'

'No, no, not in here, but outside, arguing with the madame.'

Teresa seemed puzzled for a moment, making the word 'madame' with her lips. Then she smiled and laughed. 'Oh, oh, *si, si*, young girl outside. No, she is not for you, she is too difficult.'

'Difficult? Why is she difficult?'

Teresa frowned. 'She is problem.'

'Why is she a problem?'

Teresa shrugged.

'What is her name?' Dunbar persisted.

'She is Conchita. You see her last night, fighting with Señora Dolores?'

Dunbar nodded. 'Yes. Where is she now?'

Teresa shrugged again. 'I don't know.'

'Is she in the Hotel?'

'You ask too many questions.' She pulled a face. '¿Que? ¿Que? ¿Que? I don't know where she is.' Teresa turned away to kiss Williams and Dunbar knew she was lying.

'He's in love with this Conchita,' Williams said, winking.

'No I'm not,' Dunbar protested, feeling again like St Peter at cock-crow.

A squat, ugly woman approached him. She wore a plain thin cotton dress from which the arms had been removed. Her broad Indian face was suffused with hope. He shook his head. She seemed old enough to be his mother. She stood her ground, cupped each breast and jerked her pelvis at him, simultaneously licking her lips. The crudity of her action was repulsive. He looked away. He was St Jerome now, assailed by temptation, keeping in his mind's eye his own private and profane enough vision of heaven. As if to conform to his fantasy, the supplication drained from the woman's face and was replaced by an ugly fury. She swore at him in thin, voluble patois.

He watched her buttocks wobble away under the thin dress, to pick up a sailor from another table and, taking him by the hand, lead him from the saloon.

'Any port in a storm, eh?' said Williams over Teresa's shoulder, his hands roaming over her back.

Other couples were leaving now. Most would reappear in fifteen or twenty minutes, the brief and cheap transaction of the 'short time' completed.

Dunbar averted his eyes from the couple opposite. He

felt foolish, sitting alone as Williams rummaged Teresa's body. A boy appeared at the table. He said something in rapid Spanish and Dunbar caught the word '*exposicion*'. Williams disentangled himself.

'Hey!' expostulated Teresa. 'You not going to—'

Williams clapped a hand over her mouth. 'Shhh . . .' He nodded at Dunbar. 'For him,' he explained, pulling a knowing face.

Teresa sniffed. 'Only for him?' she asked doubtfully.

'Of course. Afterwards, I come back for you.'

'Maybe I not here.'

'If you not here, I not walk you in the plaza tomorrow evening.'

Teresa frowned, then her expression changed to incredulous delight. 'You walk me in the *paseo*? Tomorrow?'

Williams nodded. 'If you don't go with any other man tonight.'

'You tell true?'

'*Ciertamente*,' said Williams, 'certainly,' and Teresa rose, her face transported with happiness.

'I wait,' she said firmly, walking towards the door, 'I wait outside.'

'Good.' Williams turned to Dunbar. 'Just follow me casually, Foggy, as if you were going out to piss.'

They returned to the foyer and Dunbar was aware of perhaps a dozen men who began to mill about until one of the madame's satraps, whom Dunbar recognised as the accomplished guitarist, waved them to join him. The dozen men followed. Behind the staircase, where a door purported to lead down into a cellar, it opened on a second stairway situated cunningly behind the main one. The henchman prevented Dunbar from joining the party until Williams hissed something at him and jerked his head in the direction of the madame. Dunbar was allowed to pass.

The stairway was narrow, steep, quite dark and smelled of dust. They stumbled upwards, round several right-angled bends until, completely disorientated, they emerged into a narrow room, lit by a single oil lamp. Along one side stood a line of plain wooden chairs; they faced a curtained wall. Without a word, the men filed in and sat down, facing the drapes. Williams bent his mouth to Dunbar's ear as he sat.

'They're mostly older, married men,' Williams whispered and Dunbar recognised the *Kohinoor*'s second engineer, the chief steward and two of her staider sailors. 'This is specially for them, and it's expensive.'

The henchman-cum-guitarist put his finger to his lips. The men sat motionless and silent, staring at the curtains, waiting. Then the oil lamp was extinguished and with a slight rasp, the curtain was pulled aside.

Dunbar drew back. The sudden removal of the curtain created the illusion that they were falling forward; in front of them a lit boudoir of surprising elegance suddenly materialised. The room would not have disgraced a Parisian mansion and they stared into it from the level of the picture rail. Hardly had Dunbar grasped the one-way nature of the glass, than the door of the boudoir opened.

Dunbar recognised Maria at once, but a Maria transformed by an elegant peignoir and the artifice of cosmetics. She drew after her a tall, blond seaman who stared about him for a moment, grinning with delight and surprise. There was an exchange of words, then Maria drew the sailor towards her and kissed him.

There was an audible change in the breathing of the men about him, but Dunbar took scant notice, for it had just dawned on him what he was about to witness.

*   *   *

128

When it was over and the participants lay back sated upon their pillows, the men in the gallery shuffled uncomfortably, recalled from a private past into a shared present. They were aware of each other again, aware too that they formed a small, exclusive and shamefaced group. Most had reacted, and the act, individually detached but corporately inspired, gave their confraternity a sheepishly relieved air.

Williams, thinking of Teresa, had contained himself. So had Dunbar. Although he had been excited to a lubricious pitch, the *exposicion* had made him think of the girl with the blazing eyes whom he now knew as Conchita. If he wanted to subject her to a similar act himself, he suppressed the desire in the conviction that he must prevent her from being compelled to submit to such a degradation, with others.

Just as the curtain was drawn across the one-way glass, Dunbar caught sight of the madame, Señora Dolores, entering the room below them. He saw she was not wearing her gown.

When the light was relit the voyeurs rose and shuffled out.

'Who was the lucky bugger?' someone asked.

'He's off one of those German barques in the roads.'

'I think he's the mate on the *Dagmar Vinnen*.'

'Does he get paid for that?'

'No, he pays for it.'

'Does he know we're watching?'

'Christ, no. He just thinks he's got lucky with the boudoir. She knows, though. That Dolores has half-a-dozen favourites and gives one of 'em the French dressing-gown thing. They get a kick out of it.'

'I s'pose when you spend your whole life fucking, it makes a change to do it in public.'

They stumbled down the stairs and found themselves in the yard at the back of the hotel where the urinals stood beneath the stars.

Williams was chuckling. 'Bloody clever those stairs, aren't they? Anyway, d'you enjoy that? You could've taken a bishop to watch, never mind a vicar's son, eh?'

Dunbar shrugged, tried to say something and could find no words. He felt he had come through a trial unscathed and, at the same time, it fuelled his desire to free Conchita.

Now he desperately wanted to discover her where-abouts.

'Are you going back to Teresa?'

Williams nodded. 'I'm going to sneak up on the bitch and if she's with another bloke, well . . .' He left the sentence threateningly incomplete.

'But she promised . . .'

'She's a whore, for God's sake,' Williams snapped and led them back into the saloon.

But Teresa had remained true to her word. She sat at the bar smoking a thin cheroot and, seeing Williams approach, she smiled, slipped from the stool and confronted him.

'Are you ready for Teresa now?' she asked, rubbing Williams's crotch. He grunted, and pressed close to her. 'And how did *you* like Maria, eh?' she turned to Dunbar. 'Or do you still want Conchita?'

Dunbar nodded. 'Yes, I do.' He looked about him, at the press of humanity in the saloon. Conchita was nowhere to be seen.

'I think,' said Teresa, her voice suddenly tremulous amid the babble, 'I think you are in love with her, *si*?'

And so ravaged by raw emotion was he, that Dunbar nodded again.

'Well, we're off, Foggy,' Williams said, taking Teresa's hand. As they left, Dunbar heard him ask, 'Does Madame Dolores ever ask you to give the *exposicion*?'

The crowd had swallowed them up before Dunbar heard Teresa's reply.

'Please sit down, Captain, and help yourself to sherry. Thank you for coming so early, but it is coolest at this time of the day and most suitable for the conducting of business.'

'Indeed, ma'am.'

There seemed to Captain Steele to be a new-found warmth about Miss Hawkshawe, compared to her icy composure on their previous meeting. For his part, he felt a greater confidence. The room was as it had last been, dark and lugubrious. He noted the neatly made bed.

'You are clearly a regular early riser, ma'am, as I am.'

'Ah, the bed. No, sometimes I do not sleep well. Sometimes I do not sleep at all. As one gets old . . . It is the least used bed in the establishment.'

Steele delighted in this lowering of her guard and attempted to exploit it. 'Even in this light you do not appear old, ma'am. Were you never fond of a man?'

'I have had a man writhing between my legs, Captain,' she said with a quick and disarming hauteur, 'but I was not fond of him.' Hawkshawe's vehemence was accompanied by her rising abruptly to her feet with such vigour as to make Steele jerk backwards. 'I was never permitted the luxury of feeling anything beyond the imposition of his intrusion. Once he had inserted his ravening part into me, he assumed I must have been enslaved. *Fondness* is something I have never felt, so do not think you can worm your way into my favour by flattery!'

'I meant no such thing . . .'

'Well, Captain,' she went on quickly, 'are you prepared to meet my offer?' She leaned over him, both hands on the table in front of her. He noticed the veins that ran over their backs and the heavy rings that adorned her fingers. Looking up at her face he saw the veil hung away from it. Before she could stop him, he had raised it. She drew backwards with a harsh intake of breath as though his touch had seared her. Torn from his finger and thumb, the veil hid her face again, but not before he had seen the disfigurement.

She resumed her seat, her hands trembling. She swiftly withdrew them to her lap, composing herself.

He waited a moment then said, 'I can make you no offer, Miss Hawkshawe, until I have seen the merchandise. However, I do have a considerable number of items to trade with you and which you might like to consider including in the price. Now, I would like to meet those young women you have, as it were, on the shelf, and make my selection. Then we can instruct Dr Reilly to examine them and, if all is well, make arrangements for a marriage.'

'If you ever do that again,' she said, breaking in, 'I shall kill you.'

'I beg your pardon?'

Her right hand reappeared on the table holding a knife; at the press of her thumb, the gleaming blade sprung out.

'Good God!'

For a moment they were both silent, then she said, 'Now, will you pour me a glass of sherry?'

'Of course.' He did as he was bid. 'There.'

She drank and put the knife away. 'You know . . . did you see . . . ?'

'That you are scarred, ma'am, yes. I was made bold by your confidences, I considered you were being obscure. You are, after all, pressing me for a considerable sum of money. I presumed, perhaps, and am sorry, but you cannot really blame me for being curious under the circumstances.'

'It was a gross indecency, Captain!'

'Ma'am, we are in a brothel. I am in your bedroom.' Steele paused. 'I am sorry if I took a liberty.'

She seemed to consider the matter for a moment, then, clearing her throat, said, 'Very well, let us resume. You were saying you had goods for barter. What are they?' Steele felt the icy control of yesterday had returned.

'I have a quantity of dresses, some material, silk brocade, velvet, laces, some haberdashery, toilet-water . . .'

'Have it brought here. I will give you a good price. You will get your woman. Go into the plaza and order yourself breakfast at the cantina opposite the church. Come back in two hours.'

Steele rose and walked towards the door. She stopped him halfway.

'Captain, do you have a young boy on your ship? A cadet perhaps, tall and with dark hair?'

'Aye, ma'am, Apprentice Dunbar. What of it?'

'He was here last night and, I believe, the night before, in the company of a seaman named Wilkins.'

Steele shook his head. 'I've no one of that name on board, ma'am. You must have been mistaken.'

'But you have a dark apprentice?'

'Yes. Dunbar's *his* name. He's a bit innocent to be a customer of yours. He's a vicar's son.'

'What's that you say? A vicar's son?'

133

'Yes.'

'Two hours, Captain.'

Steele sat under the trees and enjoyed his coffee. They had been expecting him at the cantina and had served him an omelette, fresh bread and coffee almost before he had sat down. He was pondering the strange events of the morning which was not yet far advanced. The shadow of the buildings to the east, the rear of those forming the waterfront, still stretched halfway across the plaza, so he sat in cool shade and regarded the sunlight on the rearing mass of the church opposite.

He felt an intense excitement, yet did not want to arouse undue expectations and pondered instead the odd events of the last hour. He had no idea what motive had made him lift the woman's veil, beyond curiosity and a mild sense of affront at her wearing it, yet he knew he had been impelled by an uncharacteristic and impetuous boldness in actually carrying out the act.

A kind of pride welled up in him, as though he had rediscovered some lost and youthful skill. That was, he reflected, the very purpose of his intentions! He hummed as he drank his coffee, delighted to have discomfited the old baggage. She would have plenty of money to assuage her damaged self-esteem!

He wondered why she had been interested in Dunbar. Surely she was not considering taking the boy as a lover? No, that was impossible, but something had rattled the old hag during the night. She had not slept, and mentioned a man named Wilkins. His own bit of impertinence had added to her woes.

But Captain Steele was not a man given to puzzling

134

over the insoluble. He reverted to dreaming about acquiring a new bride and it never occurred to him what effect so horrible a scar might have had upon Miss Hawkshawe.

When he returned to the darkened room he found the Hawkshawe woman had company.

'Señora Maria Dolores Garcia deputises for me, Captain. I teach all my girls English so that they may perform their function of entertaining seamen, most of whom speak some English. But I fear I am too frightful a sight to sit outside and entice custom myself.'

Hawkshawe's voice was hard again, she now alluded to her disfigurement with a callous offhandedness. Steele was not subtle enough to recognise the compliment of a confidence, an admission to an inner circle. He was in any case distracted by the voluptuous figure of Señora Garcia who was, in conformity to her location, position and the early hour, *en déshabillé*.

He bowed; Señora Garcia nodded graciously over her magnificent, corseted bosom.

'Please sit down, Captain. Señora Garcia came here some time ago, then she married and sadly became a widow soon afterwards.'

Steele was uncomfortably sensible to the woman's very obvious charms. 'I am sorry to hear it. The señora is a most handsome woman.' He bowed again.

'I am not for sale, Captain. Not even for a night.' Señora Garcia smiled.

'A pity, ma'am,' Steele replied. Señora Garcia crossed her ample thighs with a sussuration of silk. The skirt of her negligé fell open and she drew it back to her lap with a slow deliberation.

'She will help us in the matter of your choice and in finalising arrangements,' Hawkshawe said. 'Now, we have two girls for you to see. Either would be a good

135

choice. Mostly my girls are resting at this time of the day, but after your enquiries, I made these two sweep out the saloon.'

Hawkshawe paused and Steele rose.

'Where are you going, Captain?'

'You wish me to have a drink in the saloon?'

'Not at all, please resume your seat. Dolores . . .'

Señora Garcia stood and walked to the wall. After a moment's fumbling she drew back a curtain and Steele found himself staring down into the saloon.

'Well, well—' He broke off abruptly. There were two young women in the saloon. The chairs were upturned on the tables as he remembered them from the previous day. Both girls were down on their hands and knees, scrubbing the deal floorboards, with their backs to the watchers.

'They both have nice arses, though Estella has thin legs,' said Señora Dolores.

'Slim legs, Dolores,' Hawkshawe corrected.

'Which one is . . . ?'

'Estella?' Garcia went on, ignoring the correction. 'She is to the left, ah, she is standing up.' The girl stood and wiped her long hair from her eyes, though she remained with her back to them. Her thin dress was damp with sweat and stuck to her back.

'How long has she been here?' asked Steele.

'About a month and a half.'

'Turn round,' he said, out loud.

'All will be revealed in the fullness of time, Captain.' Hawkshawe's voice was cool, oily with feigned solicitude. 'Please sit and enjoy the spectacle. How many times at sea do you dream of such things?'

The thought that the mutilated procuress relieved her sexual frustration by such voyeurism crossed Steele's mind, but the thought was fleeting, for at that moment the girl called Estella turned. She had shapely breasts and he could see her nipples. Lust prickled him sharply as she looked up and, almost for his delectation, stretched with a feline grace. Her face was pleasing, without being beautiful, hinting at Indian blood. Her dark eyes were arched with heavy eyebrows, echoing the tufts of hair in her armpits. She said something to the other girl who had stopped scrubbing and was looking round at her companion. The corner of a table obscured her face. Then she too rose to her feet. Her hair was long, but she had caught it in a loose knot and piled it on the crown of her head so that a slender neck and the fragile shape of her ears were clearly to be seen. Her skin was whiter than Estella's, and her back slenderer, tapering to a narrow waist which swelled pleasingly to her hips.

Seeing his eyes, Garcia said, 'That is Conchita. She *is* too thin.'

'Perhaps the Captain likes thin women,' put in Hawkshawe. 'Besides, she is not thin everywhere . . .'

At which point the girl turned and, for a brief moment, seemed to look up at them. Steele's breath rasped in his throat. The girl's face was beautiful beyond his imagining.

'She is worth one hundred pounds, Captain.' Hawkshawe's voice cut into his thoughts.

Her breasts were large and firm. 'How long has she worked here?'

'Only a month.'

'You like her?' asked Garcia, with an edge to her tone of voice.

'The Captain is smitten,' remarked Hawkshawe.

'*Tanto mejor*,' replied the madame, 'so much the better.'

'How much is the other?' Steele asked, aware that he had all but abandoned his bargaining position.

'I could drop the price a little for Estella, Captain,' replied Hawkshawe with infinite cunning, playing her prey. 'Perhaps sixty pounds.'

'*Lo barato es caro*,' added Señora Garcia.

'What? What is that you say?'

'It is a Spanish proverb, Captain. "Cheap goods are the most expensive,"' explained Hawkshawe. 'Conchita is not a virgin, but . . .' The old woman clicked her tongue.

'She is not co-operative, Captain,' offered Señora Garcia. 'She does not make a good whore.'

'I do not want a good whore,' Steele said.

'Do not be foolish, Captain,' said Garcia, 'every man wants a good whore.'

'But, she is, er, willing?'

Garcia laughed. 'Oh yes, Captain, she is very willing, when the mood and the man suit her.'

'Close the curtains and bring her up here, Dolores.'

When Garcia had bustled out, Hawkshawe turned to Steele and said, 'Bring your chair beside me, Captain, and conceal yourself a little. Do not move or let her see you until I say.'

He did as he was bid, settling himself in the shadow of the old woman's wingchair just in time. Señora Garcia led Conchita into the gloomy room.

Steele watched, transfixed; distance had lent no false enchantment to her. She was stunningly beautiful and he attributed Garcia's hostility as much to jealousy as to the rather charming intractability of the lovely Conchita to conform to the regime imposed by these two formidable women.

'Conchita,' asked Hawkshawe, 'how is your English?'

'English – not – good.' The girl's voice was pleasantly modulated and she enunciated each word as she remembered it.

'What is this?' Hawkshawe went on, holding up a sherry glass.

'The glass – have a drink, yes?'

'A glass, Conchita, not the glass. And this?'

'Lamp, er, a lamp.'

'Good. Now translate from Spanish into English.' Hawkshawe spoke with a slow patience which surprised Steele. '*No hay que enfardarse.*'

Conchita swallowed, then said slowly and without expression, 'You must not feel offended.'

'*Se hace trade.*'

'It is being late, señora.'

'Becoming late.'

'Ah, *si*.'

'*Para cada cosa hay un tiempo.*'

'There is a time for allthing.'

'Time for everything.'

'Everything, *si*.'

'Not *si*, and not señora, Conchita.'

'Yes – madame.'

'Good. Now, *?Que piensa*, Conchita?' Hawkshawe asked, moving her chair and exposing the entranced Steele. 'What do you think of this gentleman?'

Steele blushed as her large, intelligent eyes fell upon him. The abrupt manner of his introduction caught him unawares. He had been endeavouring to remain unobserved and in order not to promote this impression further, he now stood up and bowed.

The girl was not in the least intimidated and subjected him to a long scrutiny during which Steele, feeling ridiculous but aware of the import of Hawkshawe's question, managed a smile.

'*Creo que es hombre muy agradable.*'

'This is Captain Steele, Conchita, from the steamship,

139

the *buque vapor, Kohinoor*. He is English. Now answer my question in English.

'English, madame?' She paused, placed a hand upon her breast and said, 'I – think – he – is – nice.'

'That is very good, Conchita.' Hawkshawe turned to Steele and muttered quickly, 'Do you wish to say anything, Captain? Though I should not yet reveal what you have come here for.'

Steele nodded and cleared his throat. 'I should like to say how beautiful I think the señorita is and to ask her if she will permit me to buy her a new dress.'

A look of puzzlement crossed Conchita's face and her eyes darted from Steele to Hawkshawe, pleading some confirmation of what she thought he had said.

Hawkshawe said in Spanish, 'The Captain wishes to honour your beauty by making you a present of a dress and some clothes.'

Pure delight flashed for an instant upon her face, though it was quickly succeeded by suspicion. The girl frowned and fired a few words back.

Steele heard Hawkshawe say '*si*' several times and watched her nod. Conchita fell silent. Then the old woman said something else. The word '*Capitan*' was repeated several times and while the girl pouted and appeared to consider the matter, Hawkshawe said to Steele, 'She knows enough. I have said you wish to promenade with her. For these girls, otherwise denied so public a sign of respectability, such a mark of favour will have a marvellous effect.'

'I am in your hands, madame,' Steele murmured.

'Well, Conchita? The captain is nice; will you walk out with him?'

Conchita nodded. 'Yes, madame . . . yes, *Capitan*, thank – you.'

140

'¿*Esta noche?*' asked Steele eagerly.

'Oh, yes. Tonight.'

'¿*Todas las noches?*'

'Yes. In – nice – dress?'

'Yes, of course.'

'I will see to the dress,' put in Hawkshawe. 'Anything you give her will be quite unsuitable for the *paseo*. You may indulge her as much as you like after the wedding.'

'You think she will marry willingly?' Steele asked in a low voice, bending to Hawkshawe, but never taking his eyes off the girl.

'Hold back your lust, Captain. Treat her like a perfect lady and she will eat out of your hand. How would you feel if you were raised to the peerage before breakfast?'

Steele nodded gravely, his eyes following as Hawkshawe motioned to the silently watching Garcia, and Conchita was ushered out.

'I didn't know you spoke Spanish.' Hawkshawe poured two glasses of sherry.

'I didn't. "Tonight" and "every night" almost exhausted my vocabulary.' Steele's tone was frivolously light-hearted.

'No need to ask why you learned *those* phrases,' Hawkshawe remarked drily, responding to his euphoria.

'Your teaching your whores to tell their customers there is a time and place for everything and that they should not be offended, shows you to have a practical grasp of your business, Miss Hawkshawe.'

'One has to be practical, Captain. It is the first rule of survival. Now, are we agreed on one hundred pounds?'

It was on the tip of Steele's tongue to agree, for Conchita far exceeded his expectations and, like his wife's timely death, her appearance seemed to have a fated appropriateness. But a native caution born of

141

a lifetime's haggling stopped him short of immediate agreement.

'She is certainly attractive . . .'

'Captain, she is a beauty!' Garcia had come back and sniffed her disagreement. 'Ah, Dolores, you dislike her.'

'Why do you dislike her, Señora?' Steele asked quickly, exploiting the difference between the two women, hoping to recover a bargaining stance and, at the same distracting moment, admiring again Garcia's magnificent figure.

'She is jealous, Captain, and Conchita is not compliant.'

'Ah, yes, you said she had worked for you for a month, I believe.'

'She does not earn her board and lodging, Captain,' put in Garcia.

'Has she been, er, available, to my crew?' Steele asked.

Señora Garcia shook her head. 'No. For a week in every month the girls do not work . . .'

'I understand,' Steele said quickly.

'So, Captain, you wish to walk out with her tonight?' Hawkshawe put in abruptly. 'I will have the doctor examine her by this time tomorrow, so shall we agree on one hundred pounds?'

'Eighty. That is what we agreed.'

'Come, sir. Don't spoil the ship . . . I was willing to negotiate on Estella.'

'Eighty-five then.'

Hawkshawe raised her eyes to Garcia and the two women exchanged a contemptuous remark in Spanish.

'One hundred, Captain. Sterling. With the right schooling that girl would not disgrace the salons of Paris. She is worth twice as much and you know it.

'Less whatever we agree on my own goods.'

142

'No, I will trade your dresses and haberdashery for the dress she promenades in and her wedding gown.'

'Damn it, madame, a hundred sterling and all my trade goods and notions!'

'We could let you sample the goods, spend an evening with her,' said Hawkshawe.

'Touch her, Captain; perhaps, if she is willing and you have been good to her, you could . . .' Garcia made a ring with her left thumb and middle finger and penetrated it with the index finger of her right hand.

'Have you a room that you could provide me? Not one of those filthy boxes.'

'Yes, we have a room,' Hawkshawe said. 'Tonight you may promenade with her. Tomorrow you will deposit fifty pounds and then you may spend an evening with her. You will pay the balance after that. That is a good bargain, Captain. You see how we trust you?'

Steele sipped his sherry and finally he smiled. What was a hundred pounds after all? 'And you will arrange for a marriage?'

'If you wish,' Hawkshawe said.

Steele stood and took Hawkshawe's hand, bending over it to kiss it.

'I agree,' he said.

'Very well. Then the matter is settled.'

'I will have my trade goods sent over.'

'Thank you. Now, if you will excuse me, there are arangements to make and I have a business to run.'

'Of course, madame.'

'Wait upon me at sunset.'

'It will be a pleasure.'

Captain Steele left the Hotel Paradiso walking on air.

CHAPTER SIX

The Promenade

Of all the *Kohinoor*'s company only Captain Steele enjoyed the luxury of pursuing his desires during the working day. For most, their recovery from the previous night's debauch was worked out in the multiple duties of shipboard life. A forenoon of recovery and the relief of the noon *siesta*, was followed by several hours of keen anticipation for the coming evening.

For a few, like Mr Rayner, the attractions of the shore had no permitted appeal. Not that the mate was not tempted, but he possessed that spirit of self-discipline some admire and others ridicule. Mr Rayner placed his duty above all other considerations, for he had a wife and four children whom he loved and in his work he found the means of exhausting himself, to the dessication of his coarser desires. Mr Rayner spent his life awaiting the domestic pleasures of tomorrow.

Some of Rayner's shipmates flirted with the distractions of the Hotel Paradiso, like the married men who had witnessed the *exposicion*; the second mate, Mr Mitchell, whose syphilophobia kept him on a miserably straight and narrow path of moral rectitude, remained obdurately on board. Privately, Mitchell acknowledged his conduct

144

was not due to innate virtue, but to his morbid and vivid fear. Nor did this exempt him from a corrosive jealousy of those who chose to indulge their senses fully. He was, he privately concluded, a coward, and could never make his mind up as to whether those men who, as it were, drained the cup of life to the lees, were recklessly foolish, or somehow admirably, if not heroically, contemptuous of the possible consequences.

As for the ship herself, though subject to the rise and fall of the tide, she nevertheless rode higher and higher out of the water as the steel sections of the conveyor system were gradually taken from her capacious holds and deposited on the wharf. By the time Captain Steele returned from his second visit to Miss Hawkshawe, Mr Pedersen had mobilised transport by hiring every available cart in the town and its environs capable of bearing even a single section of the conveyor's framework. The wharf became littered with small, flyblown *burros* who patiently stood between the shafts of this requisitioned transport, dropping their ochre turds into the dust until stirred to action by their owners.

Eventually, out of number two hold, a magnificent maroon and black steam lorry emerged which, once fired up, was capable of bearing no less than four sections out of the town to the location selected by an energetic Pedersen, who rode his cob up and down the steady stream of carts and supervised the gangs of casual labour he had rounded up. These gangs unloaded each steel lattice section at the prescribed spot where, in due process, it would be set in place and bolted to its neighbours in readiness to receive the immensely long, heavy-duty canvas belting that would bear the *boleos* of copper ore in a smooth, unremitting stream to the waiting ships. Pedersen's assistant engineers, together with their native helpers (all employees of the mining company), were erecting the vertical supports to which the sections would be bolted in one continuous structure from berth to mine.

No one in Puerto San Martin or the outlying villages could fail to be aware of the arrival of this modern wonder nor, in one way or another, to participate in its transfer from the black hull of the SS *Kohinoor* to form a silver thread running across the dun landscape. It was a marvel to realise how much had been contained in the black hull of the British tramp ship.

Dunbar was largely unaware of this. His perspective of the event was somewhat limited, since he was obliged to remain overseeing the longshoremen, though they now extracted the steel lattices with a care born of practice. His lack of a proper role allowed him to pace the cleared space of the 'tween-deck or to drowse somnolently, inhabiting his fantasies. He vacillated between planning the release of Conchita from her hideous bondage, to imagining the blissful future they would enjoy together. He switched from one to the other when the world of reality hinted bliss might be an impractical goal: if he once sprang her from the clutches of the seductive but evil Señora Dolores, what did he do then? He would have to abduct her, stow her away in a lifeboat and maintain her secretly until they reached home. Eventually he would have to confront the authorities, and he recalled enough of the dismal aspect of Swansea to realise they might not be as smitten with Conchita's loveliness as to allow her into Britain. Perhaps he could marry her . . .

And then, he would think with a shudder of shock, of his father.

The lonely and tedious duty of remaining below in the hot and dusty holds for hour after hour was an atmosphere in which to incubate such a jumble of fantastic thoughts. Dunbar's pure idealism was shot through with erotic images of Maria and the German seaman, and countered with the corporate guilt of the watchers of which he had formed a part. This depressing but insistent anti-climax only fostered a greater desire to help Conchita and to be liberated himself from these earthly lusts, for underlying all this was the incontrovertible loveliness of the dark beauty with the flashing eyes. In gaining her love, he subconsciously concluded, he could transmute the dross of his desire to a transcendent passion.

His mind's eye was constantly tormented by her image. He wanted to see her again and was driven to such a pitch of frustration that he stuffed sheets of paper into his shirt and, retreating into the cooler recesses of the emptying 'tween-deck, tried to recreate her from memory.

His drawings were a dismal failure, increasing the spiral of his desire and longing. Exasperated, he attempted to divert himself, flirting with representations of Maria: Maria alone, Maria with the German sailor, Maria doing the things he had seen her doing . . .

But he had little knowledge of anatomy, and this deficiency further irritated him, so that the cathartic effect of drawing was also denied him.

No matter how tedious the passage of time, it passes, and the westering sun finally released Dunbar and Humphries from their bondage aboard the *Kohinoor*. Humphries had, by a judicious plundering of the steward's store, amassed a stock of tokens in exchange for bars of Sunlight soap, muttoncloth, dustpans and brushes and a galvanised bucket. There was clearly scope for further exploitation.

'Going ashore then?' he asked brightly.

'I don't know. Maybe. Later.' Dunbar yawned. It was unfeigned, though his evasion was deliberate. Earlier, Williams had again asked Dunbar to join him and Teresa in the *paseo*.

'Why d'you want me there?' Dunbar had asked.

'Teresa will appreciate two *caballeros*,' Williams had answered and left Dunbar puzzling whether his motives were as solicitous as they seemed. 'Will you go back to the Hotel Paradiso?'

'Of course,' replied Williams cheerfully, his eyes sparkling with anticipation. 'Where else would I go?'

'Yes, all right. I'll join you.' Until Dunbar located Conchita, he needed the support of Williams to gain ready access to the Hotel Paradiso.

'I knew you would.' Williams grinned.

'Did you? How?'

'You want one of the girls,' Williams said simply, aware of Dunbar's youth. Dunbar grunted abstractedly.

Williams noted the wistful look and said, 'Well, buy her, get her out of your system. I suppose with your upbringing it's difficult. You'll believe in true love, I shouldn't wonder.'

'Well I . . .' Dunbar blushed uncomfortably. Williams was striking close to the mark.

'Look, Foggy, believe me I've known a few blokes find true love, but it never lasted. Too much is expected of it. Just fuck 'em and forget 'em before they forget you, man. Don't believe all what they tell you about disease and your nose falling off; that's all bullshit to keep you in your place, see, like your papa telling you to be a good boy so that you go to heaven and not to hellfire. I've heard them Bethesdas and Ebenezers ranting fit to scare the bollocks off any young lad. Didn't stop them doing what comes

148

naturally though, it just makes them feel bloody guilty afterwards so that if the girl gets caught, like, you know, with a bun in the oven, they was up the aisle all neat and tidy.

'It was meant to be enjoyed, like Maria and that German, like me and Teresa. You get yourself ashore tonight with a few quid in your pocket.'

'All right,' Dunbar had answered, intent on something other than what Williams suggested, but eager to be rid of the tempter pouring venom into his ears. 'All right, I will.'

Now he wished to avoid Humphries and, it seemed, Humphries wanted the same. 'Don't worry. I'm quite happy on my own,' Dunbar said to his fellow apprentice.

'I expect you'll find some of the crew at the Hotel.' Humphries was unwilling to share the proceeds of his theft.

'Yes, I expect so. Well, don't get drunk.'

'Don't preach,' said Humphries grinning. 'Don't you.'

'I might go for a walk,' replied Dunbar. It was not a lie, but it concealed a greater sin, all the worse for being meditated.

Dunbar raked all his money together and again slipped ashore with Williams. The able seaman was immaculate in scrubbed dungarees, a clean shirt with a coloured scarf tied at his throat and his hair neatly combed. His cheerfulness reminded Dunbar of the man he had first met and, intent on his private purpose, he matched Williams's high spirits with his own.

This evening, he had resolved, he would buy the favours of Conchita. Not, he hurriedly told himself, for any crude, carnal purpose, but to introduce himself, make her aware of his existence and wait for her to respond in kind.

Dunbar's mood on leaving the ship was thus one of immature expectation, based on a corrupted belief in the power of faith, the power and purpose of predestined love, and an aggressive determination to seize the moment. This dangerous combination led him to embrace Williams's plan, for the exhilaration of the *paseo* would raise his spirits and fill in the time he knew he would have to wait before he could reasonably demand Conchita. He had no wish to bolster his courage with tequila, any more than he wished to squander his money on the stuff; nor did he wish for his passion to be diminished by the dancer or the stripper. He saw his conduct in the Hotel Paradiso now as a kind of passage of arms: he had passed through the valley of the shadow of death and wanted only the reward of the girl whom he felt in his bones to be his soulmate.

Dunbar recalled the hero of Captain Marryat's book *Mr Midshipman Easy*, and how Jack had claimed there was only one young woman for every young man. Jack Easy had found his Agnes, a Catholic girl, and carried her off against all the odds. The recollection and the parallel in the story seemed to bolster his sense of purpose.

Teresa was waiting at the Hotel and descended the steps, smiling, to meet them. She linked her arms with both of her beaux and drew them against her. Dunbar felt the heat of her body and smelled the scent of her. As she swaggered into the square he felt the rub of her hip, enjoyed the soft sussuration of her petticoats and shared her exuberance, happy to be associated with her, all the while knowing she was Williams's girl, awaiting his own moment.

He saw other promenaders looking at them and enjoyed

the mixture of emotions that they displayed, each according to their individual social status: disdain, contempt, amusement, even, he thought, jealousy. He felt within himself that dangerous arrogance that smites foreigners in an unfamiliar culture, and rubs native noses in the wreckage of whatever conventions are being rudely broken. For Teresa this flouting of custom was a public revenge for the degradation of her private trade; she enjoyed every minute of her brief flamboyance.

Somewhere in the press of people, Captain Steele promenaded with Conchita. His progress was more dignified, more consonant, and although his person was unfamiliar, it was quickly identified by the curious. The beauty on his arm was not well known as an inmate of the Englishwoman's whorehouse and while there were those that guessed or assumed the worst, whispers of projected marriage and of the honourable conduct of the *Capitan* of the English *buque vapor*, set aside any condemnation.

'He is a widower,' it was whispered. 'He is rich . . . he owns the ship . . . she is named after a famous diamond . . . He made money at the diamond mines . . . the gold mines . . .' In rumour above all things, necessity is the mother of invention.

Few in Puerto San Martin were unfamiliar with a degree of poverty and the eternal struggle to make ends meet. Who could blame the parents of such a lovely creature, they muttered, nudging each other confidentially, for selling her? Who was she and where did she come from? people wanted to know. The girl in her white blouse and black mantilla looked like an angel . . . the Madonna.

Conchita was as flattered by the English captain's attention as she was terrified of the watching promenaders. She conducted herself with a wooden propriety on which

151

her natural grace conferred an enviable elegance. Those citizens who witnessed only one of these two strange parties were moved to comment, at the time and later; those who sat at the tables outside the cantinas and watched both, added to their observations the spice of contrast.

By this, Captain Steele's conduct acquired a measure of romantic approval and Conchita a degree of sympathy, whereas Teresa's *ménage à trois* achieved mere notoriety, though it was all she wanted of it, for she was as unaware of Captain Steele's stately progress as he was of hers. So packed was the plaza that neither party confronted the other, and so eager was Captain Steele to have Conchita to himself, that he cut short his promenade, releasing Conchita to return to the Hotel Paradiso, promising to follow in a few moments.

'I have something to do,' he said, excusing himself from so obvious a retreat and raising her hand to his lips.

'*¿Que?* You – say – we – go – eat.'

'*Si*. A moment. I have business. I will be very quick.' They were outside the entrance to the Hotel and Steele let go of her hand and gallantly bowed. 'Señorita, a moment only . . .'

Confused and disappointed at this abrupt termination, privately humiliated by what appeared to be a public abandonment, but mindful of Señorita Hawkshawe's instructions to behave inscrutably, Conchita gathered up her skirts and did as she was bid. Those few who saw the captain's hurried detachment made of it what the liveliness of their imaginations could devise. As for Conchita, she displayed a natural dignity in maintaining a proud and stately step until she passed beneath the garish portals of the Hotel Paradiso where she was met by Señora Garcia who whisked her swiftly away from the men lingering in the foyer. Once in the boudoir, Garcia swiftly explained Captain Steele would soon rejoin her. Señora Garcia had guessed where Captain Steele had gone and knew he would not tarry long.

Conchita stared about her, unaware of the prime function of the bedroom, which she had never seen before. It was not gossiped about by the inmates of the hotel. Those who performed there earned extra money and the fewer they were, the more they earned.

Curious but hungry, Conchita protested the captain had talked of food, at which Garcia grew angry and told her to wait. Conchita, confused by her experience in the plaza, and now in surroundings of such luxury as she had never guessed at, suffered a sense of sudden anti-climax at Garcia's response. Aware, from the events of the day, which had included a painful and humiliating examination by Dr Reilly, that she had been singled out for some purpose, and aware of Garcia's hostility, she stamped her foot, swore and pouted. Garcia struck her savagely across the face and left her to fling herself across the bed.

Captain Steele called upon Dr Reilly, setting his foot on the dark and evil-smelling stairs with a similar mixture of elation and anti-climax as Conchita was experiencing not far away. Reilly's shuffling housekeeper met him and showed him into the waiting room, but no further. After sitting impatiently for several minutes Steele stood up, then realised there was insufficient space to pace up and down as he wished, and sat down again.

At this point, the inner door was suddenly flung open and Dr Reilly, a cigar clamped between his lips and rolling his sleeves down, bustled into the room. Steele leaped back to his feet.

'My dear Captain, I had not expected you.' The cigar bobbed up and down as Reilly fussed with his cuffs.

'Have you conducted your examination?' Steele asked eagerly.

'My, my, you are impatient! Yes, yes, I have conducted my examination.'

'And?'

Reilly fastened his cufflinks with so maddening a deliberation, Steele feared the worst. The doctor took the cigar from his mouth. Coils of accumulated smoke emerged from his half-open mouth and drifted up in front of his face so that Steele was reminded of an Oriental idol behind a screen of joss fumes. Then Reilly blew the fog away and shrugged.

'There are no guarantees, of course, but she appears to be . . .' he paused, regarding the captain and drawing on his cigar again, 'uncontaminated,' he concluded on a blue exhalation.

'You mean she is free of disease?'

'Yes, yes, Captain. She is as free of all communicable disease as modern science can verify.'

'But there are no guarantees?'

'Few things are certain in this life, Captain, as I am sure you know. Beyond death, that is, and the passage of time.'

Steele was puzzled by Reilly's mood. 'I expected something a little more reassuring.'

'Captain, you are not dead yet,' Reilly cut in brusquely, 'go and enjoy yourself. You may pay me tomorrow, I have work to do now.' He turned away, swinging round in the doorway to his apartment to add: 'And try and treat her well. Not many men are as fortunate as you.'

154

This Parthian shot struck home. In an instant Steele's mood of happy anticipation was re-established: perhaps Reilly was jealous!

He regained the street with the same aplomb as he had borne during the *paseo*. He was conscious of achieving his ambition and conferring a great favour upon a fellow human being less fortunate than himself.

'Conchita? *You* want Conchita?'

Señora Garcia stared up at Dunbar, a smile hovering on her wide red mouth. One of her henchmen straightened up from where he lounged by the door and took a half-step towards the table at which she sat. She made a small negative motion with her left index finger and the man subsided. Dunbar's heart was hammering and his breathing was rapid. The madame's cleavage emboldened him.

'*Si*. I can pay. How much do you want?'

She was about to laugh, when a malicious thought, a whole series of malicious thoughts occurred to her and she compressed her red lips in an expression Dunbar interpreted as accession to his request. The mood of arrogance had not left him and he misjudged the madame's motives, assuming that she was to be bought with his money. He felt vindicated by her nod. Conchita should be rescued from this mercenary bitch!

'Short time, or all night?' Garcia asked, her large dark eyes staring at him. He was a handsome youth, she thought, and the directness of her gaze held his so that he felt the worm of lust start in his belly.

'All night.' He answered boldly, feeling this choice admitted him into this world where all, even the bodies of other people, might be bought for a price.

155

'You pay in sterling pounds.'

'Of course.'

'How much you have?'

'Oh, come on . . .' Dunbar met her eyes, felt her weighing him, matching his panting eagerness against his purse as she must have done with so many men.

'How much you pay for this Conchita, eh, *caballero*?'

Dunbar swallowed and thought fast. He dared not offer all he had, it deprived him of any chance of further manoeuvre; at the same time he wanted to overcome this woman's evil cupidity, to stun her with his largesse.

'Two pounds,' he said.

The woman sighed and sat back, looking at him again with disarming candour.

'*Caballero*, for Conchita two pounds will not get you a short time.' The woman paused and Dunbar felt confused. 'She already have a grand gentleman for tonight. He come soon. He is paying much money. If you want short time . . .' She shrugged, her eyes never leaving him.

A wave of bitterness swept over Dunbar. He felt pathetic, humbled, his great sense of longing, of love, of purpose, brought to nothing by the vindictive cruelties of the world. For a moment tears threatened to well in his eyes and then he thought of his resolve, of his image of adventure books, of the heroes of his childhood.

The hero was always tested by adversity; his heroism lay in accepting and overcoming such a challenge. A short time would allow him an opportunity to confront Conchita! He must not miss such a chance. He might pluck her out of this filthy place before her grand gentleman turned up and at least he would see her, and she him! Anything was better than retreat!

'Does she speak English – as well as you, madame?' He added the last clause confidently and was gratified to see the little compliment strike home. They were so proud, these people.

'Of course, señor, all my girls speak English.' She smiled and Dunbar could not help smiling back. 'Five pounds, señor?'

'Three.'

'Four.' He nodded.

It was all he had. It was destiny. She took the gold sovereigns and dropped them, one by one, between her breasts.

It was Señora Garcia herself who conducted her young customer to the bedroom where Conchita disconsolately awaited her middle-aged lover. Dunbar was too innocent to realise the irregularity of being thus favoured as he followed the swirling skirts and flashing ankles of the madame up the stairs.

The truth was that since Conchita had been sold to the brothel she had been unco-operative. It was not true to say she had not serviced a few customers – the *Alcaid* for instance, liked to sample the most beautiful of the new recruits – but she had formed too high an idea of her own worth. This form of vanity argued in favour of trading her to the English captain, but it had also made Señora Garcia's life difficult. Normally, when she had trouble with one of the girls, either Esteban or Juan, her bouncers, broke them to her will.

But Hawkshawe had been unusually protective towards Conchita, for some reason best known to her obscure self. Garcia knew better than to argue with the Englishwoman, to whom she owed her life, but she was not above taking a private revenge upon the hussy. It amused her to think of this young English boy-virgin slaking his lust before the little vixen was sold to his captain.

Dunbar followed Garcia until she stopped outside a door and opened it. He made to enter and halted on the threshold.

'Good luck,' he heard her say encouragingly.

It took him a moment to realise where he was. By the light of the single oil lamp Dunbar saw the room in which he and the others had watched Maria and the German seaman. He did not at first see Conchita lying across the bed, though she had raised her head and was staring at him.

'No,' he hissed, staring up at the mirror mounted in the ceiling. He confronted Señora Garcia. 'No, not here!'

She stared back. 'You have twenty minutes, *caballero*. There is no one watching.'

'But I can't—'

'There is no one watching,' she repeated softly, gently pushing him into the room. 'You are fortunate: this is the best room.'

She withdrew, shutting the door; he heard the dull thud of a bolt. At the same instant the girl sat up on the bed.

'Who – you?'

'Conchita?'

He advanced towards the bed so that the light fell upon her face. She had torn off the *mantilla* and her carefully groomed hair had released a stray lock which hung like a curled and oiled spring below the lobe of her left ear. Her cheek still bore the inflamed imprint of Garcia's hand, her red lips were slightly parted and her dark eyes glittered with tears of rage.

'My name is James,' he said slowly. He was ravished by her beauty; it was inconceivable that she was a prostitute. She was far too lovely and innocent to be the fallen woman of his father's sermons. 'James,' he repeated, smiling.

'James?' she said, frowning. 'Why you come here?'

'To see you, to talk to you. To take you away.'

'You come Captain Steele?'

Dunbar understood neither the question nor the allusion to Captain Steele.

'I don't under— No comprendee,' he said.

'Captain Steele speak you?' Conchita pointed at him and then herself, 'Take me to *buque vapor*?'

Dunbar's confusion was plain. '*Buque vapor*?' He frowned. Time was passing. He must make his point quickly and succinctly. He stepped towards her holding out both hands.

'I come to take you away. You cannot stay here. I can make your life different . . .' He summoned all his courage and added, 'I love you.'

It seemed for a moment that the veil of misunderstanding lifted, for her face cleared and she almost smiled.

'*You*,' she said with sudden vehemence, '*you* want to love me?' The smile set into a mask.

'Yes,' he said huskily, reaching towards her.

Just as his fingers touched her wrists she twisted away and put the width of the bed between them, shrieking a torrent of Spanish invective.

Dunbar stood foolishly, protesting, trying to calm her, to explain what he wanted for both of them. She was again the girl with the blazing eyes, defying an assault on her honour, only now, instead of the wicked madame, she was flinging her insults at him.

'Conchita!' he cried and moved round towards her, his hands extended in supplication. 'Conchita, please! You do not understand. I love you, I want to liberate you from a life of misery and sin—'

She pawed at his approach. He was a boy, penniless, a common seaman! Garcia was at the root of this humiliation!

Thwarted and increasingly angry, frantic that his noble intentions were being misunderstood, frustrated that time was not on his side, that his entire fortune had been expended in this futile confrontation, he caught her wrists and tried to draw her towards him. He saw briefly the swell of her breasts, smelled the scent of her and then she had twisted free and he felt the searing rake of her nails down his cheek and all the while the torrent of Spanish abuse poured from her lips.

He stepped back, unaware that behind him the door had opened until the tall guitar-playing henchman had expertly pinioned him. He was dragged protesting into the passage.

Señora Garcia was there too. She addressed a few sharp words to the guitarist and disappeared into the bedroom, closing the door behind her.

The guitarist's grip on him relaxed. 'Plenty blood.'

'It's all right. I have a handkerchief.'

'Ah.' The guitarist looked with some curiosity at the young man. 'Conchita very bad. Not so easy to fuck, eh?' He grinned, complicitly. 'You get your money back. Now you come.'

'No, no, it's all right . . .'

'No, no, I must take you someplace now.' The man's hand gripped his elbow firmly. Dunbar had begun to tremble in reaction. He submitted to being led away. He supposed it had something to do with a refund and barely noticed where they were going, or the curious stares of the sailors and their whores as they passed each other in the alleyway.

* * *

160

It had been Williams's intention to return to the Hotel Paradiso with Teresa, but she had other ideas. There had been talk of marriage among the girls when they assembled, as they always did after the *siesta*, for the meal that they ate under Hawkshawe's roof and which was both part of their pay and part of the price they paid for their employment.

Marriage and escape from the brothel was what most of them aspired to and Teresa had fixed on Williams as her most likely opportunity. She had a married sister living in the poor quarter of the town and, by prior arrangement, had secured a room for the night to which she now carried off Idris Williams.

He had no objection. The sister, whose name was Isabella, had prepared a dish of spiced mutton and a bottle of cheap wine for them. They sat on the edge of the bed, flirting happily, fondling each other with such eagerness that meat juice and grease smeared their bodies and their clothes. Giggling, they fell onto the palliasse that lay on the floor behind them.

Esteban, the guitarist, conducted Dunbar through a door at the head of the main staircase and up another flight. Slightly confused, he thought at first he was about to be taken to the room with the one-way window, for this dark chamber was similarly narrow and draped with heavy sable curtains. At the far end a single light burned.

'You stay,' Esteban whispered, as though he were a sidesman in church conducting a late parishioner to a pew among the hushed congregation. Then he disappeared.

Dunbar stood stock still, suddenly apprehensive. He had blundered into a world he did not understand, had been confronted by a lovely young woman he sought only to help, and now felt he awaited the judgement of execution. There was something almost dreamlike in the sequence of events.

He could see the elongated chamber was set below the rafters. Was this some temple of idolatry? Of devil worship and – God forbid! – satanic rites?

The trembling that had begun as a reaction to Conchita's outburst began again. Then there was a squeak. Something at the far end of the room moved and a voice, enunciating the words in perfect English, commanded:

'Step forward to where I can see you!'

He did as he was bid, his heart again hammering in his chest. The squeak had come from a high-backed Windsor chair which contained the figure of a veiled woman.

'Step forward,' she repeated, though her tone was less imperious.

He edged forward cautiously, as though the floor beneath him was about to give way.

'Closer,' she breathed and, as he approached the table beside her chair upon which stood the oil lamp, she rose with a dry creak of corsetry and, picking up the lamp, illuminated his face. He was conscious of the encrustation of congealing blood on his cheek.

'You are the son of a clergyman,' she breathed almost wondrously, ignoring his wound.

'How do you know?' he asked.

'It is true then.' Her hand, a flash of ivory in the umbral darkness, flew to her breast. 'What is your name?'

'James. James Dunbar.'

'And your father?'

'My father is the rector of Clayton Dobbs, in Suffolk.'

'Dear God . . .' She sank back into her chair, her voice suddenly querulous. 'Who was the man with whom you came on your first visit? He was a seaman of some sort.'

'You mean Williams? He is an able seaman.'

'You are sure of his name? He does not call himself Wilkins?'

'No.' Dunbar was overcoming his surprise. This woman was elderly; he began to feel ashamed of his initial fear. He wanted his money back, but for the moment confined himself to answering the old woman's questions. 'His name is Williams.'

'And why did you come here tonight?'

The question caught him unawares. 'I . . . I wanted Conchita,' he said, then added, 'I wanted Conchita to take her away from here.'

'To make a good English wife of her?' The woman's voice rose to a pitch of contempt which provoked Dunbar.

'Yes, perhaps. Who are you?'

'All in good time . . .'

She seemed about to say more but the door opened and Señora Garcia appeared at the head of the stairway. She had left the door open and a shaft of light lit her indecently from below. She had shed her dress and was attired as Dunbar had seen her attending Maria and the German officer. Her white and ample thighs swelled above her stockings and her hips were constrained by black garters.

She exchanged glances with the old woman and, with a dry rustle of black bombazine, the mysterious lady moved round the table. She placed her hand upon Dunbar's arm.

'Come,' she said, leading Dunbar towards Garcia, then past her, to the corner of her room beyond the stair. Tamely, Dunbar followed. One of the curtains with which the entire place was hung was drawn aside; he found himself in the gallery from which he had watched the *exposicion*.

163

'Look, my young friend . . .'

Garcia had joined them; he stood between these two women feeling a sharp and indecent propinquity, both imprisoned and yet on the threshold of some incomprehensible freedom. Señora Garcia drew back yet another drape and they stared down into the bedroom from which he had so lately tried to save Conchita.

The beautiful young woman lay on her back on the bed, propping herself up on her elbows, her knees bent, her legs apart. Her shoulders were bare and she had drawn her skirts up around her waist. She stared at Captain Steele who stood red-faced in his shirt tails at the foot of the bed, rigid with desire. Horrified, Dunbar watched as Steele moved forward to place his hands upon Conchita's knees.

Dunbar felt himself touched; Señora Garcia's breath was warm on his face.

'*Caballero*,' she whispered, 'watch . . .'

He was filled with the desire to escape. Twisting free of the women he found the exit by which he had left on his last visit. Stumbling blindly down the rickety stairs, he emerged into the stinking yard containing the urinals. Scrambling over a fence he dropped into an alley behind the hotel and took to his heels.

PART TWO

Mutiny

CHAPTER SEVEN

Sanctuary

Dunbar ran through the darkness in a furious oblivion, unaware of his surroundings. He recalled little of the direction he took, beyond a vague recollection of sheering off from a distant prospect of the *Kohinoor*'s deck lights. In the strenuous physical effort of flight, his mind blanked out all the images of the past hours, as though he sought temporary amnesia in a tremendous output of physical energy. This sustained his pounding legs and heaving lungs until at last, defeated by rising ground and exhaustion, he collapsed, winded, sobbing for breath and drenched in sweat, onto a tussock of dry, rustling grass that rose out of the night.

He drifted into complete unconsciousness, his entire being numbed and demanding the veil and benison of sleep. When some time later he awoke stiff and cold, he was quite unaware of where he was or how he had got there.

Shivering and aching, he raised himself, then clambered onto his feet, swaying as his head spun. A bitter, frosty chill filled the air and the sweat of his exertion had long ago dried upon him. He cast shakily about and thought he was dreaming, for what looked like a distant town,

167

pinpricks of occasional light, lay below him, a dark smudge on a grey landscape lit by a moon which rose over the Sea of Cortez. He turned; above him reared a low cliff which formed the foot of a broken *mesa*. Slowly it dawned upon him that the bright spots which marked the sharp line dividing the land and the sea were the *Kohinoor*'s deck lights.

'That's the wharf,' he murmured to himself in a kind of uncomprehending wonder, thinking he had been sleep-walking; then a spasm of shuddering shook him suddenly into full, shame-laden wakefulness.

He recalled everything, from the arrogant enjoyment of the *paseo* to the final moment of prickling disillusion as he had stood between the sinister black figure of the veiled lady and the profane and voluptuously erotic form of Señora Garcia.

A rising gorge compelled him to void himself in a con-vulsive eructation of horror and loathing. Paradoxically, despite the cold, he felt sweat break out on his clammy skin, before he fell to shivering again. He had never felt so unwell; he crouched in the lee of the grass tussock, knees drawn up, like a wounded animal quietly awaiting death.

He remained in this passive state for above an hour. At first his conscious mind shunned a further repetition of the disturbing images, but they sneaked back into his mind's eyes like dirty gossip. He saw Conchita's beautiful face, her lustrous eyes and the curl of her black hair against the curve of her neck; he saw the swell of her breasts and then above them the scorn on her face. He saw too her parted thighs, the naked belly of Captain Steele and the rigid cock that sprang from the tangle of hair in his groin.

He remembered, too, the softer flesh of Señora Garcia and the black, creaking, fusty stiffness of the old woman, felt his own stark lust, compressed between them. He thought he would burst with the agony of its insistence and the defeat of his most honourable instincts as Captain Steele slithered into an uncomplaining Conchita.

It was the cold, and the instinct of the young to survive, that brought the images back. Each time the sequence ran, it was more vivid, and yet somehow less terrible. It had shocked him but, he slowly acknowledged to himself, only insofar as he had been confronted with the lust of others. What truly confused him was not so much the sight of Captain Steele rampant, or Conchita compliant, nor even the motives of the two women watching with, he thought, a voracity equal to that of the men whose company he had so recently kept, but the confusion arising in himself from the dichotomy of his sense of honour and his own desire.

What emerged from this gradual process of acceptance was at first a deep and tragic sense of disappointment over his failure to make any impression upon Conchita. Then it occurred to him that it was impossible to communicate the strength and idealism of his love for her; and finally there prevailed a gloomy realisation that he had made a fool of himself.

The shame of this gradually faded; he was unaware that this detachment was due to the onset of hypothermia. The desperation of his condition was borne in upon him by an urgent impulse that he must move or perish. His romantic dream fell away from him like scales from his eyes. His noble impulse had reduced him to this catatonic state, and the impulse of a burgeoning anger sent a tremor through him; he moved, transmitting a cracking and painful stimulus to his turgid circulation. He forced himself head-down, into a kneeling posture, drawing his legs up in preparation for standing. Pins and needles seared him as life danced back into his half-dead limbs.

He raised his head again and struggled to his feet. He

felt a growing compulsion to move, to hasten the return of blood to his extremities and end the pain of its advance the quicker. He staggered forward, downhill. His legs folded under him and he fell headlong. Slowly, he repeated the process and raised himself to his feet again. The air he drew into his lungs rasped icily down his windpipe. The muscles in his legs felt like lead. Slowly he turned and began the easier task of walking uphill, feeling the additional sensation of a panic that he was heading away from the ship, but that he must, of necessity, ascend, until he possessed sufficient control over himself to attempt going downhill. Occupied in this way, he came out on the little cliff that had overhung the path and the tussock of grass upon which he had collapsed earlier.

The broken *mesa* formed an outcrop on the edge of the rising slope that, somewhere to the west of him, turned into the mountain range forming the spine of Baja California into which bored the shafts of the copper mine.

He turned once more to stare out over the port and the Sea of Cortez. He had collapsed on the road between Puerto San Martin and the mine. The track was lined with telegraph poles linking the distant town with the copper workings. Dully in the moonlight he could just discern, lower down the slope, moonlight catching the twin threads of the railway line and, beside the track, the broken and disjointed gleam on the steel sections of the conveyor system where they lay in readiness.

It took his bruised and troubled mind a few moments to process this information and realise he had run several miles and was now exposed to the rigours of the desert night. It occurred now to his full consciousness that the chill he felt might be fatal and with the thought came another, hard on its heels: that despite his feelings of rejection, he had no wish to die.

On the contrary, he wished to live, not merely to crawl back to the ship with his tail between his legs, a gauche and humbled first-trip apprentice, but with some credibility even if this was so private as to be imperceptible to others.

Then, with a sudden fury, he thought of his lost money and forgot his despair; the memory, spawned from his sense of foolishness, acted like a catalyst and summoned from his battered ego a sharp prickle of another desire, that for revenge. He glared down at the sleeping town and blasphemously thought of Christ taken by the Tempter to the rock above Jerusalem. An irrational but powerful sense of omnipotence flooded him. He thought of his father preaching, of how near he had been to the wages of sin. He thought of the money, a precious fragment of his father's inadequate stipend which he had pressed into his departing son's hand in a rare moment of intimacy on the Swansea dockside. He thought of how, in his innocence, he had intended to use that money as an honourable ransom to release the most beautiful young woman he had ever laid eyes upon from a form of unspeakable bondage.

Now the owner of the Hotel Paradiso possessed it.

Within moments he had began to descend in the direction of the town.

Despite the resolution of its beginning, it was not a triumphant progress. The nearer he drew the more uncertain he became. The feeling of omnipotence evaporated as Puerto San Martin ceased to be a few beads of light at his feet and took on a more substantial form.

What could he *really* do? He felt he should make some dramatic impact on the town. It occurred to him that setting fire to the Hotel Paradiso might be a satisfyingly biblical conclusion to the night, but he might thereby destroy innocent people as well as the disgusting satyr that was Captain Steele and the wanton and shameless harlot that Conchita had turned out to be.

A dog barked as he made his way through the empty streets and narrow alleyways, his footsteps ever more purposeless.

What *could* he do?

He found himself in the old plaza at the west end of the great church, where once zealous missionaries had burnt intransigent Indians. The moon, now riding high, filled it with an ethereal light and glistened on the saints clinging to their niches on the west front. The effect was breathtaking and deceptive; the alien stucco façade was grey in the moonlight. It might have been a northern cathedral; he was suddenly, poignantly reminded of his father's church and impulsively crossed the square to lean against the great wooden door and grasp the huge, polished iron ring.

He thought of the ancient rite of sanctuary and, as he twisted the cold metal and the door opened noiselessly on oiled hinges, he passed inside, half hoping to see the great red flag, pallid in the moonlight.

He regretted his action instantly. The vast, cavernous darkness was filled with an unfamiliar smell. He associated the stale and lingering scent of incense and old wax with idolatry and popery. The glow of the sacristy lamp seemed tiny, emphasising the immensity of the enclosed darkness. Dunbar stood stock still in the oppressive air. He could detect no feeling of the divine presence. The cavern seemed filled with a vast and silent screech, as if all the souls who in life had passed through the great church, railed against his intrusion.

And yet he killed the impulse to run, as if realising that to do so yet again and from such a place, would be

172

a final defeat from which nothing good could arise and in which he must abandon his self-esteem. He quelled the panic that rose like bile in his gorge and, out of some childish obligation to his parents' faith, out of some last, faint hope that the romantic honour of his intentions to rescue Conchita should yet have an echo, he dropped to one knee.

He tried to murmur the Lord's prayer before realising that here, in this place, it was called the Paternoster and would be chanted in Latin. He did not know how to invoke a saint, nor whether one would listen to him. He was an alien, an interloper, himself lost to whatever redemption this huge and cold place could offer.

The enormity of his misjudgement seized his heart. This was a place conceived and built by a terrible faith, a faith that burned those who doubted one iota of its teaching. It hated the offspring of enlightenment, and hated even more those that yearned for a greater, individual freedom.

He rose to his feet and then, unbidden, a bleaker and more terrifying conviction seized him; long afterwards he had no idea why the thought entered his mind at that particular time or place, only that it did and it at once filled him with a great dread and a great solace.

In his desire to draw and paint, in his embryonic and scarcely acknowledged compulsion to create artistically, he espoused an even greater apostasy than that of mere Protestantism. The thought ran through him like an electric shock. The urge to run evaporated; he had nowhere to run to. He was confronted by the core of his existence, the spring of all his motivations. In his youthful confusion, he did not know how fortunate he was, only how lonely he felt.

As he walked slowly back towards the great door, he subconsciously processed, as he had been taught to do when bearing his server's candle behind the crucifer at the high eucharist. But this was no act of witness; it was not even the time-serving, form-following test he had so often endured for the sake of filial duty and family harmony. This was an act of abandonment, the laying up of the imperfect faith of the church into which he had been born, like an old, redundant regimental colour. It was also the acknowledgement of his own unique existence.

Long afterwards he called it his real coming of age and the moment he knew for a certainty that while formal religion was a sham, something purposeful stalked through the cosmos.

The first hint of dawn was leaching into the sky as he emerged and turned along the length of the nave, to arrive in the new plaza where only a few hours earlier he had promenaded on the unholy arm of Teresa. A greyness filtered between the buildings leading to the wharf, one of which was the Hotel Paradiso.

The door remained open and the entrance hall was lit by a single oil lamp. He could not fail to compare it to the tiny flame burning faithfully in the darkness of the huge church. This lamp caught the scarlet plush of a curtain, and the dark crimson wool of the blanket draped on the table over which Señora Garcia had presided a lifetime ago. Now Esteban, his head on his folded arms, dozed upon it.

Dunbar stood in the entrance. Fate had driven him down from the road to the mine and the elevation of the broken *mesa*. Frightened, he had sought the spiritual sanctuary of the church and while it had rejected him, he had found within its terrible silence a new strength, greater and more durable than the nervous terror which had impelled him pell-mell onto the lower slope of the mountains.

He stepped forward; Esteban remained motionless. At the foot of the stairs he gave the supine guardian a last look, then began to climb, his footfall silent on the carpet. For the first time he noticed that whoever had established this opulent house had spared no expense in its fittings. They rivalled the few baroque folderols he had seen at Clayton Hall, and must have been brought to this curious place from Europe or the eastern seaboard of the United States.

At the top of the stairs he paused. The passageways leading left and right contained the whores' chambers. No sound came from them, for this was the hour of repletion, when served and serviced slept oblivious. He suddenly understood the geography of the place and how, from the floor above under the roof, the one-way mirror-glass allowed the strange old woman to stare down presidentially upon her establishment. Except, that is, for the one place where, if desired, access to others might be permitted and from where he had watched first Maria and the German and then, last night, Captain Arthur Steele and Conchita, the girl with the blazing eyes whom he had so hopelessly fallen in love with. The thought that they lay sleeping in each other's arms only a few yards away, spurred him on. Almost without thinking, he pushed open the door at the head of the stairs and began to climb the second flight beyond it.

'I hoped you would come back.'

The voice startled him. She sat at the table where he had first seen her, forbiddingly veiled, side-lit by the oil lamp, a pen in her hand, a ledger open before her. All about her the black curtains were let down. She might have been in a castle lined with Arras tapestries.

'Come and sit down.'

It was strange, Dunbar thought to himself; he felt no nervousness now, no fear as to who or what she might be, and approached the woman almost as an equal. He sat opposite her as he had been bidden. His eyes, cheated of her face by the veil, fell upon her hands as they lay on the ledger with its inscribed columns.

'I have come for my money,' he said in a quiet voice that sounded distant, as though belonging to someone else.

'I hoped so much you would not say that. It is not worthy of you.'

'What do you mean? I have very little money and I was cheated—'

'You came to buy a girl.'

'I came to take Conchita . . .' he paused, drew strength from her silence and went on, 'I came to buy her and take her away from you.'

'To rescue her from my clutches?' she asked ironically.

'Well . . . Yes, yes that's what I intended to do.'

'And she would not come with you?'

He sighed and looked down. 'No, she wouldn't. She didn't understand.'

'Dolores – Señora Garcia promised you Conchita, I presume?'

'Yes.'

'Did you really think she would come with you?'

'Yes.' He felt suddenly emboldened, proud to state his case in this den of iniquity and vice. 'Yes. I thought she would realise I loved her. I thought my love might prevail.'

A faint hiss that might have been a mere exhalation or a quiet wheeze of incredulity escaped from Hawkshawe.

'Don Quixote,' she murmured, using the Spanish pronunciation so that he failed to understand. 'You were disappointed then. Young men who try to be honourable or heroic usually make fools of themselves,' she added.

'That isn't fair.'

She barked a short, dry laugh, like a fox, he thought. 'You expect fairness in a world such as this? Only an Englishman would make a remark like that. No,' she softened suddenly, '*that* isn't fair. To be fair I would have to say only an English gentleman would make a remark like that.'

Dunbar felt mollified by her ironic compliment.

'Wouldn't you really rather have value for your money?' she went on, watching him frown and adding, 'oh, I don't mean with Conchita, but another girl?'

'No!' he retorted sharply.

She barked again, though more softly. 'You are a romantic. That is very dangerous. One day you will have a woman and wonder what all the fuss is about. But I forgot you are the son of a priest. Your father is a rector, isn't he?'

'Yes.'

'And your name is James, is it not?'

'Yes, it is, but—'

She ignored him and went on, 'I will give you your money back, James, in due course.'

'How – ?'

'How do you know? Is that what you were about to ask? You do not think you can trust me, is that it?'

'Well, I . . .' He fought down an emerging awkwardness and brazened the thing out. 'It did occur to me, yes.'

'Like you, I have my own notions of honour, James. *Just* like you in fact.'

'So you are English yourself.'

She broke into her dry, barking laugh. 'My dear James, never assume the English have a monopoly on honour, and

177

certainly not in a place where Spanish blood runs thicker than treacle; but, yes, I am English. Moreover, like you, my father was a cleric, though not a rector. I think he came home in expectation of a bishopric.'

'Ma'am?'

'You don't believe me? Well 'tis true.'

'What . . . what is your name?'

It seemed the only thing he could ask, but she brushed the question aside with one of her own.

'What is the name of the man with whom you first came here?'

'Williams,' he replied, 'you have already asked me this question.'

'Are you sure?' He could not see her expression behind her veil, but the note in her voice expressed a doubt he felt was accompanied by a frown.

'Of course I'm sure.'

She fell silent for a moment, shifted stiffly in her seat and said, 'My name is Hawkshawe, Richenda Hawkshawe. I am unmarried.' Her name, enunciated with a certain dignity, seemed in perfect consonance with her age and the creaking black bombazine. He had never heard her Christian name used by a living person, but there was a gravestone in the churchyard at Clayton Dobbs which bore it. The coincidence, on this strange night, struck him as being significant. 'It is an unusual name, you'll allow, James?'

'Indeed, Miss Hawkshawe.'

'There never was a Bishop Hawkshawe,' she said wistfully.

'Er, no. Certainly I never heard of one. I mean I never heard my father mention a bishop by such a name.'

'It was a long time ago. You are wondering whether I am telling the truth, are you not?'

178

'Well, I . . .'

'Just as you imagined Conchita to be an innocent virgin, like Andromeda awaiting rescue by Perseus, you see before you a senile old crone who runs a brothel on a Mexican waterfront and claims to be the daughter of a priest. You would say that my trade had made me forgetful, perhaps mad; that I was consumed by vice, with delusions of grandeur and that this . . .' she flicked impatiently at the veil and fell momentarily silent. Her tone of wistful longing suddenly curled back and struck Dunbar like a whiplash: 'Conceals the ravages of syphilis!'

Hawkshawe almost jumped to her feet, rising so quickly that she jerked the cloth and carelessly overset the ink bottle into which she had been dipping her pen. Dunbar, startled, sought to redeem himself by righting the capsized bottle, but not before the ink had run over the page. He dabbed at the black pool with a wad of blotting paper, his eyes seeing the names of the girls forming the left-hand column on the page, the amounts they had earned, the right. He read Maria's name and beneath it the first syllable of Conchita's, though it afterwards occurred to him it might have been that of a Consuela.

The ink had obliterated their earnings.

'I'm sorry,' he murmured, apologising illogically, guiltily.

He watched her hands trembling on the edge of the table. They were old, roped with blue veins and the foxing of age, but they were undeniably what his mother would have called 'lady's hands'. She stood over him as he sat, still holding the blotting paper. The veil had fallen away from her slightly, and he saw the line of her chin as she leaned on her fists and stared straight ahead, over his head, as if seeing something terrible in the shadows.

Apart from her hands, her whole body trembled; then she sniffed and looked down. Suddenly she shifted her weight, put her right hand upon his head and gently stroked his hair. He did not resist her touch; there was a surprising tenderness in her caress and he felt no repulsion as her hand slid down his scabbed cheek and under his chin, lifting his face.

'We are all many people,' she said quietly, as if reading his thoughts, 'and we become the person life makes of us.'

She sat, her hand trailing away until only her fingers, and then a final rasp of manicured nail, touched him. He felt overwhelmingly weary, yet her physical contact had left him with a strange longing.

'You are very tired and very lonely, are you not?'

He nodded dumbly, unable to speak, feeling a lump in his throat. She reached to the left of the lamp, where the light gleamed on a decanter, and poured him a glass of sherry.

'Here, drink this.' She paused, watching him sip the wine. 'You are extraordinarily like him,' she said in a low voice.

'Like who?'

She ignored his question. 'This man you call Williams, do you know his Christian name?'

'Yes, of course; it's Idris.'

The sharp intake of her breath surprised him, then she muttered something inaudible and sat slowly, with a great deliberation, the veil rustling as she nodded, agreeing with some inward thought.

'You are Bobs, aren't you? Bobs come back, as I knew you would one day.'

He had no idea what she was talking about. 'Who is Bobs? I have already told you, my name is James Dunbar . . .'

'Idris,' she murmured. 'You are certain of that? Yes, yes, of course you are and I knew it anyway.'

He looked at her, thinking her half-mad, before a thought occurred to him. 'You think Williams is someone else . . .'

'No!' she broke in sharply, 'I may wish *you* to be someone else, but not Idris. I know Idris.'

'Well, who is Bobs?'

'Bobs was my brother, my younger brother.' Her voice had subsided again. She seemed to have sunk into a reverie, she spoke so slowly and quietly, almost as though she did not wish him to hear. 'Robert was his name, though we called him Bobs. He was only six when they killed him.'

'Killed him? Who killed him? I don't understand.'

Again she affected not to hear him. Then she began to speak, telling her awful tale with a quiet and dignified eloquence.

'It was just before Christmas, midsummer in Australia, when the ship *Macassar* left Melbourne and stood out to sea from Port Phillip Bay. We picked up a westerly gale as soon as we cleared the land and Captain Hunter set a course across the Bass Strait to pass into the Pacific Ocean to the south of Clarke Island, through the Banks Strait.

'My father, retiring from a fruitless mission to the goldminers of Ballarat and unable to establish himself in a Melbourne parish, had decided to return home. He assured my mother he had high hopes of the Bishop of Bath and Wells with whom, many years earlier, he had been at Oxford.

'I was fourteen, and had been born a week before my parents left England. My father had seen that I was properly educated, largely by himself, despite the squalor of our surroundings in the goldfields. It was he

181

who, having consulted Captain Hunter, explained all the details of our passage. I think I have remembered them correctly – I can visualise my father earnestly tracing the track of the *Macassar* across the chart he had borrowed from the master.

'Captain Hunter was a kindly man despite his fierce expression, high colour and flame-red hair and whiskers. He wore a black frock coat and a top hat in port, and I at first thought him a bishop, for in my ignorance the only people of consequence I had been nurtured to regard were ecclesiastics. My father soon disabused me of this misconception.

'But I liked Hunter and was flattered by his attentions. He was a lonely man who did not mind talking to a child of fourteen. Today I might regard his attentions less charitably, but he never did me any harm and, at the end, did what he could to protect us.'

Dunbar thought better than to interrupt at this juncture and watched in fascinated silence as she drew a second glass towards her and filled it. Her hand shook as she replaced the stopper in the decanter and raised the sherry to her lips. Soon Hawkshawe resumed her story.

'As saloon passengers, the *Macassar* carried my family and a married couple whose name I never knew. The husband was a military officer and I remember he wore undress uniform during the day, and a mess jacket at dinner. His wife was rather frail and I remember distinctly thinking she must once have been pretty. I remember too, my mother saying she was "quite washed out", and the phrase exactly described her appearance, so that I thought she must have actually been subjected to a flood or something similar. What silly fancies children have.

'The major, or whatever he was, was rather vain and preened his moustaches continually. I was fascinated by his long legs and his striped overalls, but my mother declared him to be "no good". I took these judgements as final and therefore did not much like him either.

'Captain Hunter had three officers to assist him, but I only recall the second because of the way he died. One of them was always on duty, but the others would take dinner with us passengers and the captain. We all sat round a big table in the saloon from which our cabins led off; they were not very big and the bunks were deep, like coffins, to prevent one from rolling out in bad weather.

'It was uncomfortable, because the saloon was at the back of the ship, under the poop-deck, and once or twice we had water pour through the skylight above our heads.

'The captain said it was nothing, which delighted Bobs and me, but I think the major's wife was frightened. I remember now, she was called Felicity. Her husband used to call her that in a superior kind of way which made mother disapprove. Anyway, my father said we were better off than Jonah. He meant it as a joke, but he was so serious a man that it was difficult to tell and no one laughed. I felt sad for my father, and perhaps a little ashamed.

'Apart from us passengers, the ship was laden with a cargo of wool. Bales and bales of it lay below hatches in her between-decks and holds. It has a funny smell, wool; oily and greasy. The ship also carried a quantity of gold in what I later learned was called her lazarette. There was quite a lot of gold dust . . . Quite a lot.

'Captain Hunter had had trouble with his crew. When the *Macassar* arrived at Melbourne, many of them had deserted for the rich and easy pickings of the goldfields around Ballarat. Even I, at fourteen, could have told them the pickings were neither rich nor easy, but no one would have listened to a girl, never mind the daughter of a preacher, for we were hated, hated as only the voice of reason and morality can be in a world given over entirely to the acquisition of wealth, hopeless though that quest was.

'Oh, there was gold there, all right, but few found it and the fighting and the slaughter that went on amidst drunkenness and brawling was nobody's business. I saw little of this for myself, but I overheard my father telling my mother what he had heard happened at the diggings. Sometimes Father would attend a man condemned for murder and witness the hanging. Occasionally we would get a poor battered girl to patch up who would be no better than she ought to be and no worse than men made her, as my mother used to declaim as she cleaned them up. They were the first prostitutes I knew. Some were sad little mice, others women of great spirit and greater misfortune. The most brazen never required my mother's attentions.

'That was where most of Captain Hunter's crew went when the *Macassar* had arrived at Melbourne in the southern spring. When he came to sail three months later he had great difficulty in manning his ship. The dregs of the port were engaged; the police turned the petty criminals, the drunks and waterfront pickpockets, the half-wits, pimps and ponces out of the jail. They were mostly unsuccessful prospectors whose means had run out and who had turned their hands to whatever means they could earn a living by. Almost all of them had arrived as seamen and therefore could be shipped out as such. It was these men who made up the crew of the good ship *Macassar*, Captain Theobald Hunter commanding.

'We passengers knew nothing of all this, of course; the ship looked spruce enough; the sails were set and braced, or whatever was done to make them carry us out of Port Phillip Bay, and at first all went well. Whatever deficiencies were complained of, Captain Hunter explained away with some remark such as, "We've been in port too long, ma'am, the men get rusty."

'But the gale into which we ran and which bore us swiftly into the Tasman Sea towards New Zealand and the Southern Ocean beyond, did not abate. I remember one night, several sails blew away and the whole ship shook with the tattered canvas tearing off in the night. There was some shouting and it was clear all was not well. No one slept and we were all in the saloon with Father and the major popping in and out trying to help, and trying to find out what was going on. I think now they only added to poor Captain Hunter's burden.

'It seems to me your Captain Steele in his steamship has an easy time of it nowadays.'

Hawkshawe paused and drained her glass, then she refilled it and continued. 'I think perhaps I knew more of what was going on than my father. Bobs used to run about, apparently unaffected by the weather and the dreadful motion of the ship. He overheard bits and pieces and came back to tell me men were swearing as they had done on the goldfields, and saying things might be bad, but would get worse before they got better. I think, poor lamb, he thought it all a great adventure. After all, he had lived his short life on the edge of hell, and survived. What was a ship in the great Southern Sea, compared with the foul mud, disease and greed of the diggings?

'Oh, I know what you are thinking, James Dunbar; you are thinking I am the worst kind of hypocrite to be the owner of a brothel and to condemn that cesspit of foulness.

'But hear me out before you make your judgement . . .'

Dunbar made no move to comment, nor to contradict her, so vividly did Hawkshawe conjure up the past and so ably did her telling of the tale portend disaster.

He was impatient for her to go on, and held his tongue. Hawkshawe's voice, the sherry and his own exhaustion had transported him into a world in which reality seemed to recede and the image of the full-rigged ship *Macassar*, bound from Melbourne to Liverpool, tramping through the dark blue combers of the Southern Ocean, filled his mind's eye.

He quite forgot the dawn of the new day and the demands of the *Kohinoor*. He unwittingly abandoned the obligations of the mundane present, seduced by the plight of the young Richenda Hawkshawe, and the excitement of his own imagination suddenly caught up in a true adventure.

Without causing any interruption in her words or exciting any protest, Dunbar abstractedly drew the ink-blotted ledger towards him, turned the page and took up Hawkshawe's pen. He began drawing, dipping his nib in the residual ink and limning in with quick, ecstatic marks, the tossing seas, and the painted ports of the *Macassar*'s hurrying hull. The pyramids of the ship's sails took form, superimposed upon the faint blue and red ruled lines.

All about him he felt the wind and the sibilant hiss of the sea.

CHAPTER EIGHT

The Macassar

'I have told no one of this, of what happened aboard the *Macassar*. Not even Dolores. Afterwards I tried to forget those terrible events and to make something of my life in all its altered circumstances. I was driven by the compulsion to survive, as if, in my continued existence, eventually in this remote spot, I would find enough of revenge to leave true retribution to Almighty God.'

Richenda Hawkshawe gave a low and hollow laugh which shook her sinister veil. Dunbar sensed he was being scrutinised, though all he could see of her eyes were two vague dark shadows where he supposed them to be.

'Then Idris Wilkins walked in here,' she went on, 'as large as life and bold as brass. I recognised him at once, and he brought *you* with him! I never thought to see you this side of heaven, Bobs, but here you are . . .' She paused, fretfully. 'It troubles me you are with him, though . . . this Idris . . .' She hissed the name intensely.

Hawkshawe was quite lost to reality. She sat, rigidly upright, only the veil trembling from her speech. Her voice and the scratching of Dunbar's pen as it sought to illustrate her words were the only sounds in the lugubrious room. Below, the Hotel Paradiso lay quiescent.

But there was a third person in the room: Dolores Garcia, waking alone in the large bed she usually shared with Richenda Hawkshawe, lay and listened. Raising her head she saw the young *caballero*, Dunbar, who had excited her friend's interest, his handsome head propped on his elbow, his right hand drawing swiftly and confidently. Dolores Garcia smiled over his embarrassment of the previous evening; it was an unimportant event in such a place as the Hotel Paradiso, and she thought little of it. Instead she saw him as a young and handsome man, as yet untainted by the world. And he awoke in her a strong and poignant longing.

Dolores Garcia understood enough English to follow Hawkshawe's words and though she had long ago heard some of her employer's history and guessed more, she had never heard the whole, dreadful tale. It was clear Hawkshawe had forgotten her and that the *caballero* Dunbar was oblivious to her presence. An expectant thrill of presentient excitement kept her quietly abed.

Hawkshawe had drawn her unresisting audience after her, deep into the past.

'I never knew exactly what happened, or exactly when, for the vividness of the events of that morning have eclipsed the things that happened just before them. I am robbed of all but my last terrible memories of my family . . .'

Her voice was quite level now, almost emotionally expressionless and objective, as though she stood outside herself, watching her recollection unfold. This detachment lent her story a powerful credibility.

'We must have been a week into the new year, perhaps ten days, when the storm reached its height. All I can remember is the noise below deck where we lay in our berths, dozing when we could, but mostly terrified at the thunder of the waves sweeping over us. Such fear was as nothing compared with what was to come, but at the time was real enough. Water swirled about us, slopping from one side of the cabin to the other and our clothes, papers, books, and bits and pieces of our belongings floated about in it. It seemed at times that the *Macassar* must have driven bodily under the surface of the sea and the roaring thunder of the storm and its effect upon the straining ship was indescribable.

'From time to time Captain Hunter would come down below and speak to us, reassuring us that all was well, despite what we in our ignorance took to be evidence to the contrary. Would that that storm had raged for a month and driven us fast across the bottom of the world. Once the captain spoke to Father, asking him to do his duty among us as a man of God, so poor Father got up and went to see the major and his wife; I can see him now, wading through the water, clutching for a hand-hold as the ship lurched and trembled, bearing the dimmed glim of his faith.

'Then, I cannot tell exactly when, but it was daylight, we were pooped. I understood this later, when I heard it talked about. A great wave, running faster than the ship, came up behind and reared above the ship, just at the point of its breaking. The giant comber crashed down upon us, sweeping away anyone exposed on the deck and cascading below so that it seemed the whole Southern Ocean was pouring into the inundated hull. We were up to our waists in water and this extra weight made the *Macassar* more prone to the next attack.

'The two men at the wheel were swept overboard and, I learned afterwards, Captain Hunter ordered more sail set, so the ship could outrun the waves. The men refused to obey. Hunter, with great forbearance, explained why it must be done and the mate led them aloft, an unusual act, but one signifying the importance of Captain Hunter's order. While they were loosing the sail, part of it blew back over the yard and flung another man into the sea; a fourth was lost as he came below, swept from the rail just as he was climbing out of the shrouds onto the deck.

'These losses were attributed to what the men later called the captain's foolhardy and unlawful order.'

Hawkshawe paused, as though her audience needed a period of silence to digest the stupidity of this assumption and to imagine the wild and elemental horror of what she had narrated. Then she sighed, and took up her sad tale again.

'As if satisfied with those four lives, the gale began to abate. Although the sea still ran high the following day, it had lost its venom, and thereafter slowly subsided. Water no longer came below and by nightfall the clang of the wash-ports had ceased, telling us the sea no longer poured over the rail. Gradually the water was pumped out of the ship and confidence returned. We managed a meal in the saloon in more or less normal circumstances and we looked forward to a reasonable night's sleep, notwithstanding the damp state of our bedding.

'The next morning the major paid us a visit. He was sallow and hollow-eyed, but he managed a smile.

'"Everything's going to be all right now, isn't it, Major?" Mother said with a forced cheerfulness she must have been far from feeling.

'"Of course, Mrs Hawkshawe," he replied, but I will never forget the major's expression, for his eyes lied and I thought at first he was not very brave as he asked my father if he could have "a private word".

'"May we go up on deck and take the air?" Mother asked, anxious for us. You were being particularly fractious, Bobs, at your prolonged confinement. D'you remember?'

Dunbar stopped drawing and shook his head.

'It was a long time ago . . .' The old woman paused for a moment and then went on.

'"Not yet, Mrs Hawkshawe," the major said, leading Father out of earshot.

'I don't know what exactly passed between the two men, but I imagine it was a discussion about the mood of the crew, for the major was a busybody and father came back looking anxious, saying nothing to answer my mother's query. In view of what happened in the next two hours I can only think that this was the substance of what had been said.

'You tried to follow the two men on deck, Bobs, but Mother must have sensed something amiss, and stopped you, commanding you to get back into your sodden bunk, but you wouldn't remember that.

'I heard afterwards that the crew came aft in a body at about noon, demanding to speak to Captain Hunter. The poor man was still fast asleep in his bunk for the first time for almost a fortnight, and the mate, who had gone aloft to lead the men in setting sail at the height of the storm, refused to wake him, saying they could see the Old Man later.

'"Our shipmates are asleep in the ocean,' their spokesman cried, "get the bugger up!"

'It was then we heard the sound of raised voices, and a moment later the major's wife Felicity rushed into our cabin. She was plainly terrified. Her husband had warned her "things might not be too pleasant for a while". So we sat and waited, half-fearful of what was happening, but not really knowing, the women wondering where their husbands were and why it was so important that we remained below. Then both Father and the major stumbled down the steps into the saloon, and came to us in our cabin.

'I knew at once something dreadful had occurred, it was plain in the faces of both the men. The major's wife clung to him and he pushed her aside and drew a pistol.

'Father was remonstrating as to the foolishness of producing the thing when, a moment later, there were more steps on the ladder and down tumbled the seamen. My father called out a single word – and my whole life was shattered:

'"Mutiny!" he cried.

'I remember looking at you, Bobs. For some time, before the weather got really bad and confined us below completely, you had told me of the man called Thirle. Our life near the diggings had made us aware of the vagaries of human character and you had told me this man had tried being friendly, but you had confided to me you thought Thirle to be what was called a "bad-fella".

'You had pointed Thirle out to me. He was not old, not thirty in fact, with a thin, pale face, red-gold hair and a wiry figure. He was typical of a digger, except that he seemed never to smile. His eyes were blue, but cold as ice. As I looked at him, coiling down a rope in the waist, he caught my gaze and stared back. He radiated a kind of suspicion, as though in some way he could be a threat.

'It was Thirle who appeared at the head of the seamen a few seconds after my father had uttered the terrible word.

'I now know that Thirle had meditated what he did for some time, and that the loss of the men overboard gave him the excuse he needed to put his evil design into practice. Maybe it was not an excuse; maybe Thirle himself sent a shipmate off the end of the yard in that storm. God knows he was capable of it. He had a handful of conspirators already, but the loss of the seamen overboard now made all the disaffected crew his confederates. Those who remained loyal . . . Well, enough of that now, let me tell it in its place. I did not know it, but Captain Hunter was already dead. Or perhaps he wasn't, but floated astern, in the wake of his ship, watching our masts disappear as he drowned. Thirle himself had flung Hunter overboard. The stunned shock of that single act gave him the moment he wanted to secure the mate, who was still on deck, and then the two junior officers who were below at the time. We were his next port of call.

'The major levelled his gun at Thirle as he forced his way among us all crowded into our cabin. Thirle's arm flashed out and he had grabbed my father as a hostage, pinning him with a forearm across his windpipe and a switchblade knife pointing upwards at his heart. Thirle was a past master at the art of brawling.

' "Don't be a bloody fool," he snarled at the major, "drop your gun."

'I have always wished my father had died at that moment, stabbed by Thirle as the major shot the mutineer. I suspect my father may have wished it too, supposing the major could have hit Thirle in that heaving ship; but Father could not speak and the major tossed his gun onto the deck, where it joined the sodden debris still lying there.

'Thirle thrust my father forward and he fell on his knees, gasping for breath while Thirle coolly bent and picked up the pistol. Then he told us to assemble in the saloon.'

She had lost herself in her story now, had forgotten Dunbar and her own fiction that he was her brother, forgotten that she had explained some of the details before . . .

'The saloon was a pleasant, panelled room situated in

the centre of the poop under a large skylight. The officers' and passengers' quarters led off it forward. The master's stateroom was behind it. The room was principally a mess and was dominated by the dining table; and tied to their chairs were the three officers. Several of the mutinous sailors, their knives in their hands, were also there. One of them swung a bunch of keys on his right index finger, a look of triumph on his face. His name was Partridge.

'I will never forget their smiles as they watched us come in.'

Hawkshawe paused; Dunbar had stopped drawing, spellbound. He was scarcely aware of her unstoppering the decanter and refilling her glass. His mind's eye was filled with the suspended images of victims and mutineers, and the picture of a young and beautiful Richenda, a fantasy aided by her veil. He was filled with the ominous horror of what he felt was about to happen.

'You shall know *exactly* what these men did,' Hawkshawe said.

'Thirle made my father and the major sit alongside the officers. We three women and Bobs were made to occupy the seats opposite. Then Thirle walked round behind the men as his followers quickly tied their hands behind their backs with lanyards I recognised as the gaskets most sailing-ship men carried in their pockets for odd jobs about the deck.

'I don't think I heard the first gunshot. There was suddenly a mess across the polished mahogany of the table, followed by a curious smell. But I heard the second and third. The reports echoed round and round the saloon and the mess of blood and brains and shattered bones littered the table and spattered us, as smoke and the stink of gun-cotton filled the stale air.

'I wished to faint, like the major's wife, but my heart

beat too hard and I was merely sick. Thirle had shot the major, the chief mate and the third, who was about twenty-one. They still sat in their bonds, but their heads had fallen forward on their breasts. Their faces were mercifully hidden from our full view, for the impact of the bullets had broken their necks. All we could see, sitting opposite, were red and dangling tatters. The major's moustaches ran with blood which, in the sudden silence, dribbled noisily. Such a very *ordinary* noise . . .

'And then Felicity began screaming, sitting quite still and upright, but screaming, screaming, screaming, and I knew she did it to blot out everything, to fill the whole world with a noise of her own making, a noise so real, everything else had not happened. Thirle slapped her hard across the face and a second silence, more awesome than the first, descended upon us.

The second mate and my father were spared and I can see them now, rigid with shock, bracing themselves for their turn – which never came, not then. Thirle required a navigator; what he required my father for remained to be seen.

'The dead men were lucky, though; they died quickly, without knowing much. Thirle was almost humane in the way he dealt with them, compared with what, in due course, he was to do with the rest of us.

'Then Felicity began to whimper and Thirle began to give his orders.

'I have asked myself since why men are capable of such acts as Thirle was to perpetrate in the succeeding days, acts of such extreme cruelty as to excite a disgusted horror, but also a curiosity. People are capable of heartlessness amounting to cruelty, but these are usually acts of omission: neglect, indifference, those things which we ought to have done . . .

'But those things which we ought not to have done, those things can be very terrible.

'People are frequently cruel in their struggle to survive, for in this struggle, they often take horrible and unnecessary advantage of others. Men and women fought over inconsequential things in the diggings, not because they were essential to survival, but because by achieving them, they enhanced their sense of well-being, their importance and thus their chance of weathering whatever assault fate next made upon them. These things too, I can understand.

'But Thirle was wantonly cruel, and in what he did next there is only one explanation. He derived a potent satisfaction from it, the sort of satisfaction normal people find in spending themselves; no, more than that, for Thirle not only enjoyed what he did for the sensation it caused, but because he gained by it. It was a means of both attaining and retaining – *power*.

'He was wickedly clever, in his way, for by encouraging his men to excess, he led them beyond the pale of lawful conduct, binding their crime of mutiny as an accessory to his of murder.

'"Get rid of these first, boys," he said, oh, so matter-of-factly to his men, pointing the major's pistol at the slumped bodies. And then, waving the gun at us, added, "And you women, clean this shit up!"

'My mother, Felicity and I, gagging and sobbing, found the steward's mop, bucket and swabs and began to clean up the foul remains.

'While we did this, the mutineers hauled the dead up on deck, then Thirle said, "Lock the second mate in his own cabin and this God-botherer in the third's." My mother stopped for a moment to reach out and touch my father's sleeve as he was dragged past while the major's wife repeated over and over, "These were his lips, these were his lips." But it did not stop her from ridding the saloon of the mess that had been her husband's lips and the lips and cheeks and brains of two other men.

'And, oh, God, I remember the eagerness with which we cleaned that table-top as so . . . so shameful . . .'

Hawkshawe hung her head, as though in an act of contrition for a guilt comprehensible only to her. Staring at her, Dunbar wanted to ask, 'What of Bobs; what of the little brother you mistook me for?'

'When they had restored order to the saloon and confined their two prisoners, the rest of the crew who had thrown in their lot with the mutineers, crowded in. I did not know then, that in addition to the murdered Captain Hunter and his mates, the other mutineers under the leadership of Thirle's close friend, the man named Partridge, had been disposing of the bosun and sailmaker, and would have killed the cook, had not he been as necessary as the second mate. I think some other loyal seamen had been knifed and tossed overboard.

'They must have left one or two of their number at the helm, but the rest all gathered about us. There were faces among them with whom we had passed the time of day and exchanged smiles. My mother tried to appeal to their good nature, but just as a few began to squirm and look guilty, a little impish boy jumped out of the crowd and put out his tongue at her. The men laughed and the child pulled faces at her and jumped around Bobs like a monkey.

'My mother fell silent, as much for Bobs's sake, as for herself. In the face of such foolish capering, she had lost the initiative: the men's laughter was harsh and mirthless. I think that was the moment most of them truly passed beyond redemption.

'That little boy's name was Idris Wilkins.'

Dunbar felt a cold chill along his spine and the hair crawled on his neck. This revelation both surprised him and yet seemed to have something fore-ordained about it. The old woman's identification with him as a reincarnation of her long-dead brother had seemed like a brief lapse into senility, the mental aberration of a moment or two, based perhaps on some facial resemblance or the similarity of his domestic origins. But if Idris Williams was indeed formerly known as Idris Wilkins, then he, James Dunbar, had become a small part of this appalling story.

Hawkshawe did not mark the naming of the impish boy by a pause in her narration. She was steadily working her way to a recounting of the greatest of her ordeals, and she spared nothing of its horrific details.

'Then Thirle spoke. "Well, my boys, we have the ship, we have her cargo and a few odds and sods to pick over . . ."

'We three women and my little brother were the odds and sods.

'I have only a vague idea what happened in the succeeding hours, for the four of us, my mother, Bobs, Felicity and myself, were locked in Captain Hunter's cabin. I remember it smelled of the man's tobacco and a stale mustiness, and I remember, too, my mother trying to console the major's widow and little Bobs crouched in a corner, his knees drawn up, shivering like a hurt animal.

'Some time, in the evening it must have been, Thirle came back with Partridge. While Partridge stood and watched us, Thirle opened the captain's safe, discovered more keys and, pulling back the rug that covered the floor, exposed a small, padlocked hatch. When he had opened it, he took one of the oil lamps from a bracket above the captain's bunk, lit it and disappeared below.

'A few minutes later he emerged, gave Partridge a grin,

at which Partridge looked overjoyed, locked the hatch and pocketed all the keys. He flicked back the carpet, straightened up and regarded us with an expression of fierce pride.

'It was the face of utterly corrupted power; he had become a primaeval creature beyond all decency. I had thought such men inhabited only the pages of history or perhaps the remotest parts of the world, yet to receive the benefits of civilisation. Not even the degradation of the diggings, with which we had a passing familiarity, had led me to suppose anyone was so utterly beyond redemption. But it was not into a decline that Thirle had sunk, such as I had seen overcome drunks and the poor whores in Ballarat. Thirle was a man uplifted by what he had achieved, a devil incarnate.

'God help the world if such men become legion.

'"Well, Curly," this unholy creature said, using Partridge's nickname, "I'm having the girl. Do you want the major's missus, or Mrs Hawkshawe?"

'Fear seized us all at that moment. I took the contagion as much from the reaction of my mother and the major's wife, as from fear for myself, though I was not entirely ignorant of what it was Thirle meant, or what was likely to happen.

'"The others'll want something, Nick," Partridge replied, rubbing his chin.

'"Well, make your bloody mind up. Some of them'll go crazy for that boy."

'That was the point at which my mother protested. She ranted at Thirle and flung herself at him, but he just laughed! Laughed and grabbed both wrists before her nails could rake his face, twisted her viciously about and pressed her so hard up against the wall that her head cracked.

' "Cool down, Mrs Hawkshawe. D'you want me to kill the lad?"

' "Take *me*, take *me*, but leave the boy, I beseech you!" she cried. "Not that, not that!" My mother was beside herself and she looked from me to Bobs and then to Felicity. "Felicity, help me," she cried, but the major's wife seemed paralysed.

' "What is it they want to do, Mama?" Bobs asked. He seemed to come out of his trance and stood up, advancing on Thirle and saying, "Leave my mother alone, d'you hear? Leave her alone."

'Partridge caught him by the ear and pulled him to one side with a cruel wrench.

' "Have pity, sir, have pity! He is no more than a child," my mother sobbed.

' "Get him out!" Thirle snarled. "Lock him in the mate's cabin."

' "For God's sake!" my mother went on pleading.

' "Shut it!" Thirle shifted one hand to her throat and I heard her head crack back against the wall again, where he held her until her eyes began to bulge.

' "Hit him, hit him," sobbed Felicity feebly, and I suppose she meant my mother to strike him in the groin with her knee, but I recall Thirle was too clever and had my mother so pressed against the wall she could not move. I think that Felicity's lack of courage, the removal of Bobs and what I thought was the strangling of my mother, made me realise I must do something. What held us from acting in concert I cannot now tell, except that the effect of Thirle's presence upon us struck terror into our hearts and one felt immobilised and powerless. Had we three women attacked Thirle and Partridge in those first moments, we might have reversed events, but we reacted piecemeal, selfishly . . .

200

'Behind, but never joining me and coming to my support, crouched Felicity, screaming her advice.

'"His balls, his balls," was all she could say, and in a second it was all over. I was conscious of my mother sliding to the floor and then Thirle struck me with such force that I felt my neck crack and saw a bright flash of light.

'When I awoke it was dark. I was quite alone, lying in the captain's bunk. My head and neck ached intolerably and I felt sick when I tried rising from the pillow. I could hear the familiar noise of the ship rushing through the water and the faint groan of the rudder, noticeable from the captain's cabin which was almost above it. Then, and perhaps it was what had woken me, I heard a scream.

'It was like no other sound I have ever heard, but it pierced me like a knife blade. I was certain it was Bobs, for there was a deathly silence afterwards and I never saw my young brother again.

'Food was brought to me next morning by the steward. He refused to answer my questions, or even to meet my eyes. He was a rather weak little man and quite incapable of helping me, or anyone else for that matter, when under the influence of so terrible a character as Thirle.

'I told him I didn't want any food, and all he said was, "Please eat, miss. You must keep your strength up."

'I'm sure he meant it kindly, and a youthful hunger would probably have overcome all in due course, but I wish that I had starved myself to death.

'I do not know how many days I was kept locked away. I lay for the most part on the captain's bed, rising only to use the commode which the steward emptied from time to time. Periodically I heard footsteps on the companionway that led up on deck, and the sound of voices, men's voices of course. Occasionally the door would open and, instead of the little steward, Nicholas Thirle would come in. He never said a word, just stood, his body swaying with the motion of the ship, his face a mask, staring at me with those ice-cold eyes.

'Only once did he do anything different. I asked him what had become of my mother and brother. He raised a finger to his lips.

'He wanted me kept in silence, as though I no longer existed, or at least to dissuade the rest of his foul crew from remembering me. He was so very, very clever.

'I seemed to slip into a sort of trance. The reality of being imprisoned on a ship, or having witnessed murder and my mother being assaulted, seemed part of a gross and horrible dream. Instead I was back in Australia, walking the streets of Melbourne with my mother and Bobs, as I once did, on what was probably the happiest day of my life. We had been invited to a ball and my father had insisted both Mother and I had proper gowns. I have no idea why he wished to act in so generous and uncharacteristic a fashion; we were usually scrimping and saving, and he disapproved of frivolity. But I have lived that afternoon a hundred times in retrospect, so I cannot in truth recall the event itself with any clarity. It became for me a gateway into the happy past, into a life which lost all its faults and inconveniences, and seemed concentrated in that single afternoon. Only in the last few years have I been able to remember much else properly. The rape of my memory is a part of what Thirle did to me.

'One morning I awoke to the roar of the anchor cable going out and realised the ship was still, upright, no longer moving. We had arrived somewhere, civilisation must be near, retribution and release were to hand . . .

'How naive I was!

'Thirle had ruled his crew with a rod of iron, allowing

them just enough of what they craved to keep them driving the ship, and promising them an orgy of delights when the *Macassar* reached a safe haven. I did not know it then, but we had anchored in a remote and narrow passage, hidden between great mountains, somewhere in the Chilean archipelago. It was here that Thirle was to play out his great crime.'

CHAPTER NINE

The Mocking of God

'The ship grew silent at anchor and then I heard the footsteps of many men as they assembled in the saloon laughing. There was the chink of bottles, and I knew they were about to get drunk.

'I rose and dressed. I think I thought the more clothes I wore, the safer I would be. I was shaking fearfully, terrified of what was going to happen. I thought I was to be dragged out among them, and quailed when I heard Thirle's voice command them to silence. I heard him ask them if they all had a drink, and when the noise of their arranging this had subsided, I heard him tell them to bring 'the God-botherer' in.

'At this mention of my father I kneeled at the keyhole to the door. I could see nothing beyond the backs of two men and a stretch of the saloon table. Even that was now loaded with the foulest of memories . . .

'They brought my mother in next. They must have kept her in an almost perpetual state of intoxication, for she giggled and I heard my father call her name. Then Thirle called upon my father to prove there was a God. He asked what they meant, and Thirle said he was a priest and should work a miracle. Father protested they were intending blasphemy. Thirle responded that they intended something far *more amusing* than blasphemy. There was a lot of noise; I heard my father protesting, my mother giggling, then crying, after which my father shouted in anguish.

'I do not know how many men raped my mother before my father's eyes. I only know that Thirle did not. He sat calmly looking on, where I could see him through the keyhole, and I think he knew I was watching.

'When they had finished, they pushed Father about and left him insensible. Thirle afterwards told me he had mocked God with impunity and proved He did not exist. No miracle had occurred.

'It was one more step in the debasing of his men, which further bound those of them who survived to silence. It was not yet the worst thing he could do. He could make them condone crimes such as mutiny and rape by their confederacy. Murder was a more subtle matter in which they were only accessories. Drunk, and satiated on the bodies of my mother and the major's wife, he now reminded them of the reasons they had mutinied, of the infamy of Captain Hunter as a representative of all those who had held authority over them in their miserable lives, inciting God knew what demons from their unholy pasts.

'I will say this for him; Nicholas Thirle possessed a gift for rabble rousing. He employed it now to work his followers into a frenzy. They became frantic, aroused with a new desire to revenge themselves upon someone they conceived to be among those elevated in station above them.

'I was reminded of the cruel excesses of the Jacobins and their reign of terror in Paris, sixty years earlier.

'The second mate was no more than twenty-five years of age, a short, active man of powerful build, though no match for these monsters. I could see him as they stretched him upon the table, his mouth gagged. I think they all struck at him with their knives in an orgy of blood-letting which made them complicit in this most foul and deliberate of murders. At first he turned his head this way and that, but finally he seemed to stare straight at me, as if death enabled him to see me crouched behind the door to the captain's cabin. As if to warn me it was my turn next.

'I have no idea why I was exempt, unless they were either too exhausted, or too frightened of Thirle to challenge him. Although I was not molested, I was left for a further night of waking nightmare, terrified of making a sound, yet wanting to scream and scream as Felicity had done, to lose myself in the noise of my own outrage.

'I was finally released the following morning. I emerged into a charnel house. The bloody carcase of the second mate lay where they had left it and there were several other bodies, their throats systematically cut, strewn about the place. They were the corpses of mutinous sailors murdered in their drunken sleep. The foul reek of blood hung in the air and the carpet was sticky with it. My flesh crawled as I averted my eyes. My wrists were bound and tied to a line, the other end of which was given to Idris Wilkins. He was told to exercise me on deck and I was walked about like a dog.

' "Come and take a peek in the fo'c's'le," the little devil said, opening the door to where, in bunks and on benches, sprawled everywhere it seemed, lay the dead, slain with chilling efficiency. It was clear to even my benumbed brain that Thirle had killed all those accomplices who were superfluous to his plans.

'I jerked my tormentor away and he tied me to a pinrail.

For a moment I stood stupefied, resting my head upon the cold harshness of a wire stay. I think it was at this time that it gradually dawned upon me that all that had happened was real and not a terrible dream from which I might awake. For some reason I was preserved, and there was a future hideous with terrifying possibilities.

'I remember the cold striking me, and my shivering uncontrollably. Looking up and over the ship's rail I saw the silver waters of the inlet and the black and grey scree at the foot of a great cliff. The sky seemed limited to a narrow slit far above the tops of the mountains, a hard silver streak, the same colour as the merciless water upon which the *Macassar* lay at anchor. There was no civilisation – nothing.

'Wilkins came skipping back to me at that moment, intent on torment, thrusting his hand up my skirt until I kicked him away. I bit him when he tried fondling my breasts, but I could do nothing when he spat in my face. God knows what else he might have done had Thirle not called him to perform some errand. It was clear the boy went in fear and dread of the man. Thirle came forward, checked my halter and then touched my face. It was the first intimacy.

'God help me, but it occurred to me then, and I can remember the thought now, that if I made him fond of me, he might be kind to me.

'This of the man who had destroyed my family!

'How quickly we are reduced to nothing . . .'

Hawkshawe paused. The intense pain of this reminiscence seemed to Dunbar to be worse than the horrors she had witnessed.

'It was the worst moment?' he asked.

In the darkness, Dolores Garcia held her breath at the presumption of the question. She was weeping silently and she watched astounded. Dunbar reached out a hand and touched Richenda Hawkshawe.

'Yes, oh yes,' breathed the old woman, 'he had debased me so far without laying a finger upon me.'

Dunbar refilled the sherry glass. 'Go on,' he said quietly.

'They had prepared a boat; provisioned and equipped the best of those carried on the skids above the main-deck. It was already over the side with its mast fitted. By way of a rope ladder, Partridge and a couple of hands were making the final preparations for departure: our departure. Just before dark I was led back to the saloon. It had been cleared of the dead and the table was set out for dinner.

'"You must all eat well tonight," Thirle commanded. My mother and Felicity sat down with Thirle and his cronies. Turning to us he added, "You women will be allowed half an hour to pack your clothes. You may take one of those ditty-bags each." He indicated a selection of the small canvas kitbags sailors have. Each bore the initials of its previous owner. I do not remember what we ate, only that we ate it in silence, my mother, Felicity, Thirle, Partridge, the two men whom I only ever knew as Nobby and Sands, Idris Wilkins and I.

'My mother, who with Felicity had cooked the meal, looked terrible; I hardly recognised her. She avoided my eyes, never once acknowledging my presence. I think she thought me already debauched and, because of my comparatively unruffled appearance, thought I had been seduced by it.

'I thought of her as already dead. I had heard her giggling stupidly and the thought of her ordeal disgusted me. I could think of nothing to say. There was no sign of my father.

'My mother drank immoderately, as did Felicity. Thirle

208

kept their glasses full. He would only allow me one. When the meal was over, he made us drink a toast to the success of our continuing voyage. My mother was drunk. One of the men, Sands, I think, ostentatiously squeezed her breast. Then Thirle and the two men Sands and Nobby left us and we sat in silence while Partridge cleared some papers in the captain's cabin and Wilkins kept guard on us. Once again, we did nothing. About twenty minutes later we were allowed to pack our belongings. I took warm clothing and some blankets. I remember telling my mother to do the same; she moved like a ghost, her face blank.

'We were forced over the ship's side, down the Jacob's ladder into the waiting boat. We women were manhandled and mauled by our new protectors. It was growing dark and a keen wind was blowing. After a while there was a shout from above, and with some difficulty Thirle lowered three small but obviously heavy iron-bound boxes over the side. Partridge grinned and took possession of them. They contained the gold which had been among the *Macassar*'s cargo and which had fomented the outrageous conduct of Thirle and his gang.

'Thirle soon came down the ship's side and we cast off, pulling clear of the ship under a pair of oars. When we were about two hundred yards distant, the oars were taken in and preparations made to hoist sail on the single mast.

'"Where's my husband?" I suddenly heard my mother say, looking round her, as though only now she realised we were leaving the shelter of the ship.

'"We left him behind with the others, Mrs Hawkshawe. Thought they'd like a preacher-man to see them on their way."

'"But he's not dead . . . I haven't seen his body! Where is he?" her voice rose to a scream and the scream ended as Thirle leaned forward and hit her.

209

'And then our attention was drawn back to the ship as a crackling roar shook the gloom. The fire seemed to explode from the waist where Thirle had clearly assembled all manner of combustibles, the paint and canvas and oil and so forth which every ship carries by way of chandlery.

'The fire spread quickly, so that the details of the *Macassar* were lost and the ship became a great black shape nurturing the fierce blaze that sent crackling flames leaping up into the twilight.

'It already seemed quite dark, such was the glare of the fire. From time to time small explosions went off as the heat reached tinned provisions or cans of varnish. There was a memorable period when it seemed that the outline of the ship's rigging was represented by fire, like a cunning display of pyrotechnics, and then the mainmast fell and sparks flew upwards, and the heat wafted down upon us like the breath of hell itself reeking of wool.

'My mother was sobbing uncontrollably. I heard her calling my father's name and I realised he had been left aboard, alive, locked in a cabin, the flesh cooking upon his bones.

' "Dear God . . . dear God, have mercy upon us all," my mother said lucidly.

' "There is no God, Mrs Hawkshawe," Thirle declaimed, "there is no God. Man is alone on the planet, Mrs Hawkshawe, quite, quite alone!"

'And with that we watched the *Macassar* burn to the waterline and finally sink.

'Partridge spat a good-riddance over the side and the cold of the black night enfolded us. The sail was hoisted and we began our long voyage northwards. Settling down for what sleep we could get on the bottom-boards of the leaking boat, I took my mother in my arms.'

Hawkshawe sat in silence for several minutes before resuming. The silent patience of her listeners was a testimony to the power of her narration and the horror of her personal ordeal. Only Dunbar's pen made a noise, scratching a representation of the *Macassar* at anchor, the *Macassar* on fire, and the boat sailing away from an empty anchorage. It was no more than his imagination giving form to the old woman's revelations.

Below them the Hotel Paradiso came slowly to life. Esteban drank coffee preparatory to evicting the customers. What muted sounds reached the heavily draped room went unheard.

'Many years lie between these events and today, and still the story is not ended. Idris Wilkins has come back . . .

'I do not know how many days we sailed north, there is so much of this in which time and feelings seemed to be destroyed, warped by events, as though perception shrank and dulled itself to everything. And it is now so long ago. Mercifully my mother did not survive the voyage in the boat. Her spirit had been broken by the violation of her body and she can never have forgiven herself for her drunkenness, enforced though it was, for she had held it the worst thing that beset the diggings and brought so many of the women there to ruin. I think she half-believed she had contributed to what they did to her.

'I think her death spoiled Thirle's plan, so perhaps she wrought some vengeance upon her persecutors.

'Felicity lived longer, much longer, proving of tougher, more selfish metal than I would have thought, and perhaps thereby taught me a lesson; to bend like the reed and not break like the oak. I wished to die a thousand times, but need not tell you of all this. Thirle was clever to the end. Sands and Nobby fought over Felicity and Thirle refused

211

them any chance of taking me, though they tried. He kept me always close to him after we had landed, which we did somewhere south of Valdivia. The lifeboat, carefully prepared, was left to drift ashore on Chiloé Island, giving the impression that the *Macassar* had foundered with all hands.

'Hiding in a cave, we melted down the gold and poured it into crude moulds made in the sand by the impression of buttons. Thus we made hundreds of gold discs, and all of us sewed them into our clothing to distribute the weight, to make us accomplices to the theft and believe we had some stake in the success of the enterprise.

'Although I had no vested interest in the matter, I was weakening, for I had no reason to live beyond a perverse desire to survive. So reduced was I in body and spirit that, at this time, I had no thought of revenge. The weak enjoy no such luxuries.

'And Thirle, God rot him, wooed me for his first time, never taking me with the crude force Sands and Nobby constantly used as they bickered over Felicity. In the end *she* mastered them, lifting her skirt and enduring it as though she did no more than pass water. As for me,' Hawkshawe shrugged, 'I was a girl, and Thirle knew how to pleasure a girl. My pleasure robbed me of protest; afterwards it increased my guilt. That is how I know how my mother felt at the end.

'Despite the discs we had sewn into our garments we were unable to accommodate all the gold and the men carried the balance in the ditty-bags upon their backs. We women and Wilkins carried the remainder of our equipment and the gold we had managed to sew into our clothes. It was dreadfully hard going and our feet were bleeding badly within hours.

'Three days after we had landed, while we were making

212

our way north, travelling mainly by night, Sands knifed Nobby in one of their interminable arguments. Thirle made no attempt to intervene and I believe he was not displeased when Nobby bled to death. Sands was made to dig the grave and Nobby's gold was given to Wilkins to carry. This was Thirle's first mistake, for it admitted Wilkins to what he conceived to be the company of men.

'Thereafter Felicity belonged to Sands in theory, but Wilkins, I noticed, who was as lustful as any young man, began to ogle both Felicity and me. We hardly ever spoke and I think she was already half out of her mind.

'A few nights before we reached Valdivia, Wilkins forced himself on her. We had camped in a gully and Sands had gone off to relieve himself. Thirle made no attempt to stop them; he remained, as he always did, aloof, watching and waiting for the weaknesses of others to deliver them into his hands. He prevented me when I went to stop Wilkins and held me so that I was compelled to watch. Wilkins was only a child, he cannot have been more than eleven or twelve, but he had caught the infection of power from Thirle's example. He was precocious and excited to a high and shameless degree.

'Felicity let the boy spend himself and then gathered him into her arms and held him, crying as if he were her own child. As for me . . . *you* know what effect it has, watching others do it; Thirle was inside me when Sands came back. He chased Wilkins out of the gully and then returned to Felicity.

'Do you know what that name means? It means happiness. God! what an irony . . .

'He made her suck him as a punishment; stood there and made her kneel in front of him and suck him. I turned away and Thirle laughed.

'"You'll do that for me, one day," he said.

'Next morning Thirle woke me before the others and cut my hair short. Then he made me dress in men's clothing. Most of it was Nobby's. I unpicked the gold discs from my clothes before we burned them. As the others woke, Thirle said we would have to split up at Valdivia. Sands asked what he would do and Thirle said, "Whatever you like, you're a man of substance, but never, ever mention where your money came from. The same goes for the ship, her captain or what happened."

'"But she'll blab," Sands replied, indicating Felicity.

'"Then you know what to do," my lover replied, adding, as he kicked Wilkins to his feet, "we're going on, good luck."

'Sands had jumped to his feet protesting. The shock of being left alone struck him. He was a man without personal resources and had followed Thirle with the blind and foolish obedience of a dog. I think they had known each other for a long time. As Thirle began to walk away a spark of intelligence kindled in Sands's mind.

'"Hey," he called, "this ain't fair, Nick, you've got all Nobby's gold."

'Thirle turned and asked, "What are you going to do about it?"

'"I'll bloody show you," shouted Sands, picking up his knife and running towards us. Thirle shot him. He told me afterwards he had only one bullet left in the major's pistol and thought it a good shot. He was quite without pity or remorse. The noise of the shot echoed round and round the gully so that I thought the whole world would discover us, but only the crows rose up in protest, and they soon subsided again.

'"I'd let the vultures have the bastard," Thirle said sighing, "if he didn't have all that bullion on him." We returned to the camp, stoked up the fire and buried Sands

214

close under a rock. Then we made strips of cloth from his duds into which we sewed the balance of the gold.

'Towards evening, Thirle announced he was leaving Wilkins in charge of us for a few hours. He gave Wilkins the pistol and told him to shoot us if either of us tried to escape. I did not know the gun's chamber was empty. I was compelled to submit to Wilkins fondling me, but he did not try to force me further. I told him Thirle would be angry, which frightened him, and he turned to Felicity. She accommodated him readily. She was completely broken, a perfect drab. I do not think she was capable of escape, even supposing there had been somewhere to escape to. Thirle had returned by midnight. Behind him on a halter was a small donkey.

'We left the gully the following morning and the four of us marched on towards Valdivia.

'Thirle had stolen as much money as he could find aboard the *Macassar* and could thus put us up at a kind of inn without arousing suspicion. He pleaded no understanding of Spanish but, with a mixture of pidgin and mime, made us out to be English prospectors. At the sight of Thirle's sovereigns, the proprietor was incurious. Thirle had Wilkins and I lodged in the same room, since I was masquerading as a young man, and left us with the most dreadful imprecations; he took Felicity as his trollop, giving the innkeeper knowing winks and appealing to the universal freemasonry of the philandering male. She, poor creature, looked the part. He locked her in her room and sat up half the night in a complicated conversation with the proprietor by which he learned a ship would be sailing for Valparaiso in two days.

'As for me . . .

'Wilkins left me alone the first night; on the second he attempted to get into my bed. As he had been charged with guaranteeing my silence when we arrived at Valdivia and had threatened me with his knife, I do not know by what attraction he now thought he could seduce me. But Thirle, maintaining the fiction of being a mining engineer and a hard-drinking man, took no notice of us, and, having locked us into our room, departed for another convivial evening with his host. Wilkins must have relied upon our being left alone, or on Thirle not suspecting his lust.

'He was so young, yet so strong, and in his irresponsible hands the keen blade of the knife . . .

'He made me undress and kneel at his feet. When I refused to do what he wanted, he hit me with the knife's pommel and when I bit him he did this . . .'

Hawkshawe lifted her veil; the scar seamed her face from her left cheek to her eyebrow and still showed the coarse puckering of crudely inserted sutures. Her left eye socket was empty; it wept perpetually.

'Oh, God,' whispered Dunbar.

She left the veil folded back over her head, and moved the lamp so that its shadow threw the scar into furrowed relief.

'Look at it, Bobs,' she said, confused in her reasoning, 'look what your friend did to your sister.

'Thirle stitched me up and beat Wilkins senseless. At the first opportunity the boy ran away. I think he soon afterwards shipped out; it was not difficult, for no questions were asked in places like Valdivia if you palmed a few pieces of gold. He didn't get away with much. Thirle said Wilkins posed no threat. The boy had done too much to blab, and if he did it would be his word against Thirle's. Thirle knew the workings of men's minds.

'We missed the first ship, and the second. In Valdivia, Thirle could not get rid of me as he had so many other inconvenient people. He was compelled to maintain the

216

fiction of my false sex and to say I was very ill. I was still useful to him, now that Wilkins had run away, but I knew he would not keep me long, disfigured as I was. He found an abortionist in the town, explaining he required the man's services for Felicity, then had the fellow remove my eye, the mess of which threatened to putrefy. I was in a fever for a month, but by now there was no ship to hand and Thirle still could not abandon us without leaving most of the gold, which he kept in the panniers the donkey had been carrying. The bags looked like his mining samples.

'I was still feverish when we finally sailed for Valparaiso. We looked almost respectable. Thirle had bought clothes and three large portmanteaux, so that, despite my bandages, we seemed to be an engineer, his loose and drunken mistress and his assistant. What authorities there were then could be bribed and Felicity, reduced to a state of incoherence most of the time, was a subject for which the Chilean gallant felt a certain chivalric sympathy no matter how reprehensible her liaison with Thirle appeared to be.

'Many of Captain Hunter's sovereigns, and perhaps many of the major's and my father's, greased palms to ease our way northwards. No word was heard of the *Macassar*, no enquiry followed the finding of the boat, no suspicions were aroused that outlived the payment of back-handers.

'Thirle made certain Felicity passed her time in a drunken stupor. As for me, well, he talked to me, and once he took me to our cabin and made love as men do to each other, because he could not look at my face. I knew then what had happened to Bobs . . .

'I guessed Thirle was going to dispose of me at Valparaiso. He booked us into an obscure hotel which was half brothel, half waterfront saloon and began drinking. It was a foolish thing for him to do. His second mistake.

I knew my days were numbered and that he would find some way of disposing of the gold safely, now we were in so large and cosmopolitan a port. The rest in Valdivia had encouraged me to think a little of the future; it rekindled a bleak hope. Now Thirle got drunk; perhaps he was human after all.

'We were all in the same room, the three of us, and I lay awake, unable to sleep. Felicity had passed out hours earlier. I tried to decide how to escape and if I did so, where I would go and what I would do. In the night I smothered Thirle with his pillow. When he was dead I forced open his mouth and made myself sick. It was not difficult. Felicity did not wake. I left the empty whisky bottle beside him.

'Then I took some money, a portmanteau, paid my bill and left, saying he was a bastard to work for and was always drunk. The old porter who kept the door asked me what had happened to my face and I told him it had been an accident when we were prospecting in the mountains. A piece of rock had cut me when we had been blasting. My life spent near the diggings at Ballarat had given me sufficient knowledge to lie convincingly, as gold prospecting had for Thirle. When the old man asked what we had been looking for I answered silver. Like at Potosi, he said laughing, yes, I replied, like at Potosi. Well a woman has silver between her legs, he said. But a man has to work, I riposted, and we laughed.

'How I had changed in those short weeks since the *Macassar* had left Melbourne; what a dissembler I had become; how well I invented lies; how well I was capable of looking after myself!

'I could hardly carry the portmanteau, it was so heavy, but I left enough gold with Thirle to divert any suspicions he had been robbed.

'I booked myself into a similar establishment a few

doors away. When I had settled in my room, there was a knock at the door and a girl came in asking if she could be of any use to me. I knew by now what that meant. I invited her in and she obligingly undressed.

'She was golden-skinned like Dolores, with soft breasts. When she saw I was a woman she was surprised, but not revolted. She spoke a little English and I told her my wound was because of a man, that I had dressed in man's clothing in order to find him and revenge myself upon him, but I had had no luck yet. She told me men were no good. She had been deceived and made pregnant, then abandoned. Men only wanted a woman for one thing and for joy and comfort a woman needed to be loved by a woman.

'I confess that I lay in her arms that night and felt my pain a little less.

'In the morning she found me some clothes. I walked out of the place as a woman and have worn a veil from that day to this. There was little fuss made when an English mining engineer was found dead, choked on his own vomit. His "wife" was rumoured to have been quite mad. No mention was made of the gold, or of a young assistant. I think my moderation meant no one spoke of me and no hue and cry was raised. I hope the old porter found Thirle and discovered he no longer had to work, though I expect the owners of the place kept most of the money; them and the police.

'My new friend helped me find employment in Valparaiso; she was a good Catholic and I became housekeeper to a priest. He was not a bad man and from time to time he would come to me for a little consolation. The first time he came to my room a little drunk, I recognised the look in his eyes.

'"You wish to have something to confess, *padre*?" I

asked, and let him into my bed. I had picked up a little Spanish and every day learned more. I think he felt his fornication was vitiated by my disfigurement; perhaps he thought he conferred upon me a great honour. At least he allowed me a few years of stability and never asked about my baggage. When I conceived once, he knew of someone who could dispose of the inconvenience.

'The joint sin made us confederates. Little by little, with Father Ignacio's help, I was able to invest the gold. When he fell ill of a cancer, I nursed him until his death. Then I took passage to Antofagasta, Callao and Guayaquil. In Ecuador I bought a small dressmaker's business. I might have been there still, but some five years later one of my customers told me the day's news was the arrival of a small brig which had been dismasted in a squall and had reached port with difficulty. The brig belonged to a distant relative of hers and he was also the master. Now he faced ruin, and the family could not afford to help. It was such a pity, for the brig was making a passage in ballast to Panama where she had been chartered by a mining company. They had had some equipment brought overland to Panama and wanted it shipped to an old Franciscan mission town on the coast of Baja California where a copper mine was being opened up. The brig's owner had only the promise of the charter; all was forfeit if he did not reach Panama in time. This sad tale did not dissuade my customer from buying an expensive dress, nor did I try and stop her. Instead, I arranged to meet the brig's owner.

'I was restless and ready to move on. From utter dependence upon the unspeakable Thirle, I had moved to the protection of Father Ignacio and learned the Spanish of the west coast. I had proved I was capable of running a business and had had time to think of what I could do with my life. I had lost my family; I could not go back to

England. I knew no one except Felicity and Wilkins had survived from the *Macassar*.

'Wilkins had gone. Felicity was half-witted with grief, drink and debauchery. I had asked Father Ignacio to find her and settle her in the care of an order of nuns, the Sisters of Saint Vincent de Paul. I left some money to keep her. She will have died a long time ago.

'Father Ignacio asked few questions and kept my secrets as I kept his.

'When the dismasted brig limped into port, it occurred to me I could become more than a back-streets seamstress, and the gold had bought me more than a little quiet security. It had bought me power; and I was of a mind now to exercise this new-found power. I had no thought then of revenge on Wilkins and cared only for myself, for self-preservation, for independence. I could not bear to think of Thirle and how he had tricked me, of my own submission to his violations, of his demand for satisfaction once I had admitted his presumptuous part.'

Hawkshawe's voice became anguished and her clenched fist banged the table. 'Oh, how I suffered the mortification of the victimised, conscious of my own guilty compliance, ever dreaming of it, of how, if I had acted differently, things might have turned out some other, happier way. I even despised myself for vomiting into Thirle's foul and gaping mouth, yet it had been a clever deception and proved my own inner resource.

'But I had regained something of my own good opinion of myself in the independence of my little shop in Guayaquil, even though it did not reflect the state of my secret wealth. My fortune irked me. It was too much a reminder of the past, and I wished to bury it in some business proposition fitting its origin and the means by which I came by it. I asked myself what satisfactions

221

I could seek in a ruined life. A husband and children were beyond me; Thirle and Father Ignacio had seen to that.

'But I knew what satisfactions debased men sought; even men of God like Father Ignacio could be brought low, to slaver like dogs after the bitch. I had been brought up in the Christian faith and in expectation of human goodness. I was not made of the stuff of martyrs; few of us are.'

Hawkshawe's passionate outburst subsided. She resumed her story in her former, matter-of-fact tone.

'Captain Rodrigo Carlos Valbuena thought me the answer to his prayers. I thought him the answer to mine. I made over my business in Guayaquil to my chief seamstress, of whom I was fond, and bought a half-share in the brig. When she was repaired I sailed in her to Panama. There we loaded for the place which has since become Puerto San Martin. I was twenty-eight years old. I have been here ever since.

'When we had unloaded our cargo, I sent Captain Valbuena north for timber. He made ten voyages on charter to me. I began to build the Hotel Paradiso. Later, in a bigger ship, Valbuena brought me other materials, carpets, lamps, curtains, dresses for my girls, the rococo fittings, the special mirrors.

'He was a kind and gallant man and offered to marry me.

'His son is now the harbour master.'

Richenda Hawkshawe finished her story with these almost gossipy details. The pathos had become mundane; the drama, mere ordinary commercial opportunism. Dunbar felt a lessening of interest and was at once ashamed of this. Only Richenda heard the regret in the last sentences.

Dunbar had never heard such a catalogue of horrors, nor been so riveted as by their fascination. He felt something of the complexities of her guilt as the details of this sorry biography had touched the darker parts of him. As with the voyeurism, he had been aroused as well as appalled, mixing disgust and pity with a shameful, prurient interest.

Why had she told him all this? Was it because she thought him to be the reincarnation of her brother, or because she was senile, as half-mad as the deserted Felicity? Why had she chosen *him* to unburden herself to? Because he was like Bobs? Because he too was a priest's son? Because he too had arrived in a ship with parts for the mine?

Or just because he had arrived with the man she believed to be Wilkins?

Moreover, she had confessed to murder!

The knowledge laid upon him a moral burden. Had she confessed before? Perhaps to the priest in Valparaiso, Father Ignacio? In which case she might be forgiven by God, if she believed in God.

Earlier that very night he had thought that the God of priests and of churches, those institutions subsumed by the state, was not omnipotent, perhaps did not exist. Was it possible this God was a mere demiurge, a jealous, subordinate deity who, as maker of the world and of man, in some way connived at the way his creation functioned?

Had he discovered in his moment of revelation a transcendent authority, a greater ordering of all things, of the universe itself?

His eyes fell on the table before him. He had drawn Richenda Hawkshawe's mutilated face in savage *chiaroscuro*, his pen cross-hatching savagely. He had been quite unaware of doing it and looked up now, to see if she disapproved.

Tears poured from her right eye and from the shrivelled socket of the left. She was sobbing, her shoulders shuddering as the reaction wracked her.

'Please – please don't cry.' Dunbar made to rise, but cramp and a sudden onset of painful pins and needles immobilised him. He winced and screwed up his eyes for a moment as his head reeled.

From the bed, Dolores Garcia saw the heave of Hawkshawe's body and swept aside the bedsheets. In an instant she was beside the older woman, had embraced the disfigured head and held it against her breasts.

'Oh, *Dios*,' she murmured pityingly, 'my love, my love . . .'

The rustling manifestation of Garcia and the sound of her voice astonished Dunbar. Garcia's naked body seemed to fuse with the stiff, fusty and upright figure of Hawkshawe, a powerful image of physical compassion. The thin peignoir fell from Garcia's shoulders like a heliotrope banner and her great brown eyes, filled with tears, stared over Hawkshawe's head. She saw the ink drawing.

Dunbar sat almost terrified in anticipation of anger. None came. Garcia's gaze transferred to him and she made a small, commanding gesture with her head, summoning him to come closer.

Shakily, Dunbar rose and edged round the table. His heart hammered as he approached the two women and Garcia reached out and took his arm, drawing him closer. Then he felt himself embraced; Garcia's arm, warm-smelling of scent and sleep, was about his shoulders and he stared into the woman's face over Hawkshawe's grey head and its stiff, dusty veil. Moved by some impulse, he put his own arms about the two women and felt Hawkshawe respond, her hands rising to clasp the forearms of her two comforters.

It seemed to Dunbar that they remained thus for about a minute, and then Hawkshawe heaved a great sigh, as though recovering her self-command. Both Garcia and Dunbar drew back spontaneously.

'Thank you,' the old woman breathed, 'thank you.' She looked up at Dunbar. 'Sit down again,' she said, and when he had done so, added, 'you are not Bobs, are you?'

'No, Miss Hawkshawe.'

'I didn't think you were. It was nice to hope . . .'

'I understand.'

'Do you?'

'I think so.'

'You have drawn me, I see.'

'I'm sorry, I didn't know I had done it. It seemed to just . . . happen.'

'I am very ugly.'

'No . . .'

'Don't be gallant. You have tried that once tonight.'

'Yes, I have. I'm sorry. It seems a long time ago.'

'Will you bring Wilkins to me, tonight?'

Dunbar thought of his friend, his sea-daddy, and remembered the streak of viciousness in him. 'Do you wish me to?'

'Yes.'

'What will you do to him?'

'I wish to speak with him.'

'You won't – ?'

'You think I might kill him?' Her smile twisted her face horribly.

'No, but . . .' A thought suddenly occurred to Dunbar. 'What is the time? Should I not have been back on board by now?'

'Don't worry. I think I have enough influence to protect you.'

'How? I mean, thank you, but why should you do this for me?'

'Because you came here for something tonight.'

'My money? Oh, I had forgotten about that.'

'No, not your money, though you shall have that returned to you.' Hawkshawe turned and beckoned over her shoulder. 'Dolores . . .'

'Yes, I shall give the *caballero* his money.'

Dunbar looked up at Dolores Garcia as she stood beside her employer, the peignoir wrapped around her, her arms crossed under her breasts.

'Would you like to draw Dolores?' Hawkshawe asked. 'I would like you to do that for me. You need not go back to your ship today.'

'But, ma'am, I must.'

'I told you, Captain Valbuena's son is the harbour master.'

'It is not necessary,' whispered Garcia, reaching forward and plucking at Dunbar's sleeve as Miss Hawkshawe rose slowly to her feet.

'But I must,' Dunbar protested feebly.

'Come,' said Garcia.

'Go with her,' commanded the old woman as she walked stiffly to the head of the stairs, 'let her teach you something worth knowing, and afterwards you may draw her.'

The call of duty faded as Dolores Garcia slipped the wrap from her shoulders and stood before him, lit by the dim lamp on the table. Her ivory splendour glowed against the black background and then his advancing shadow fell across it.

Breathlessly he reached out towards her.

'*Caballero*,' she whispered. '*¡Acercate!* Come near me!'

CHAPTER TEN

Absent Without Leave

'What d'you mean, he's gone?'

'I mean he's not on board, sir; he's absent without leave.' There was a meanness in Humphries's report. He had had a riotous night, financed by his tokens and petty theft; but *he* had been back on board by cock-crow. Butter would not have melted in his mouth.

'Are you sure he went ashore last night?' Mr Rayner, more inclined to be *in loco parentis* than Captain Steele, thought of knifings in dark alleys, of drunken boys falling from gangways into the narrow gut of water betwixt the ship and the wharf; he had seen, or heard of, it all before.

'Yes, sir. He went ashore with Williams, to the Hotel Paradiso, I think.'

'Oh, bloody hell. Have you seen Williams this morning?'

'Yes, he was with the bosun and lamp-trimmer topping the derricks on the foredeck.'

'Oh, yes, they've finished the sections there,' Rayner ruminated, ever thinking of his precious cargo. 'They're opening the forrard lower holds this morning.' Humphries shuffled and coughed. Rayner was recalled to the present crisis. 'Have you searched the ship?'

'Yes, Mr Rayner, and I've asked everyone on board.'

'Everyone?' Rayner frowned.

'Well, pretty well everyone, sir.'

'Then if he isn't drowned, he's still ashore.'

'Williams said there was a girl he fancied, sir,' Humphries put in, an edge of malice to his voice.

'Oh, God, not some tawdry trollop at the Paradiso?'

'I don't know, sir.'

'I hope you haven't been dipping *your* wick?'

'No sir, I have not!' Humphries's mock indignation failed to fool Rayner, but he thought nothing of it and dismissed the apprentice as Jorge Maldonado appeared in the cabin doorway.

'*Buenas dias*, Meester Mate.'

'*Buenas dias*, señor. Come in and sit down.'

'Thank you. I hear one of your apprentices is missing.'

'Yes, yes the lad called Dunbar. How do you know?'

'A friend of mine, one of the tally clerks, recognised him, saw him running out of town towards the road to the mine late last night. My friend was a little drunk at the time, but I hear from your second officer just now when I come aboard, that this apprentice is not here on board.'

'No. What the devil would he run out of town for?'

Maldonado pulled the corners of his sad mouth down and shrugged, at which point Mitchell appeared.

'Well, any news of Dunbar?' Rayner asked.

'He's not on board.'

'I have asked Hernandez,' Maldonado went on, 'that is the name of my friend, to come up and tell us what he saw.'

Rayner explained what part the tally-clerk Hernandez played in this mystery. With the explanation scarcely finished, Hernandez arrived. Maldonado pulled himself up in his chair and fired a volley of questions at the tally-clerk. At the end, Maldonado turned to Rayner and summarised by way of translation. 'It is as I said. Señor Hernandez was going home after a few hours in his favourite cantina, when your apprentice, Dun—?'

'Dunbar.'

'*Si*, Dunbar, ran past, very . . . *rapido* . . .'

'Very fast?'

'*Si*, very fast. On the road going to the mine.'

'Was he being chased?' asked Mitchell.

Maldonado passed the question on and returned Hernandez's reply. 'No . . .'

Hernandez added something and Maldonado translated, his face wearing a lugubrious smile. 'He says, "except maybe by the devil!".'

'All things are possible here,' breathed Rayner, half to himself.

'If he ran out of town in the direction of the mine,' said Mitchell, 'perhaps we might enlist Pedersen's help. He is on the wharf now.'

Rayner nodded. 'Yes, very well. If he's been out in that desert all night, he'll be half dead by now. You go and do that, Mr Mitchell. I'll let the Old Man know what's happened.'

'He's not on board either, sir,' said Mitchell from the doorway, 'he went ashore about half an hour ago. Had his tiger carrying two huge bales of gunny. Poor old Chang looked like a coolie!'

'Bloody hell!' Uncharacteristically, Rayner swore for the second time in less than an hour.

'Look, Mister Mate, they're getting careless again, see what they've done with that flange.' Pedersen pointed indignantly at a lattice section and Mitchell stared at the slight distortion.

'I think a little heat and some brute force will get it to align sufficiently,' the second mate said, eager to press on to the matter of Dunbar.

'Oh you do, do you? A little heat and a toffee hammer, I suppose . . .'

'Mr Pedersen, one of our two apprentices has gone missing. He was last seen running away out of town in the direction of the mine. Did you see any sign of him this morning when you rode into town?'

'No, I have seen nothing unusual this morning, but I was not looking for a runaway boy. Perhaps you should treat him properly, not like you treat your cargo.'

'What hatch did this come out of?' Mitchell asked sharply.

Pedersen looked up at the deck of the freighter. 'Number five.'

Mitchell gave an exasperated sigh. 'That is where Apprentice Dunbar should have been this morning,' he said, turning back towards the gangway.

'What about my cargo?' Pedersen called after him.

'I am doing my best!' flared Mitchell over his shoulder.

They were just about to lift a sling out of the square at number five hatch when Mitchell peered over the coaming. With a clatter the winch revolved, taking up the slack of the derrick runners. The long steel section snapped its slings tight and rose jerkily. The gang foreman, looking up and seeing Mitchell staring down, shouted at the winchman. The winchman took no notice and began to reverse the winch barrel controlling the port derrick runner, dragging the load towards the side of the ship adjacent to the wharf.

Had he lifted the load high enough, nothing untoward

would have happened. As it was, the lattice swung violently. Fortunately the delicately engineered flange swung clear, above the coaming, and only the lower longitudinal angle bars struck the coaming with a screech, scraping the paint and causing a shower of sparks.

'For Christ's sake, be more careful!' Mitchell roared at the winchdriver. The man snarled at him and mouthed an obscenity. Mitchell turned to the foreman.

'Hey foreman! Tell this bloody winchman he's sacked. Off the ship! Now! ¡Vamos! ¡Presto!'

But the foreman, sensing trouble, had hidden from sight in the wing of the hatch, under the deck. Mitchell swung his legs over the coaming and descended the ladder in hot pursuit.

The 'tween-deck was almost empty. No more than a dozen of the lattice structures now lay awaiting discharge and they had to be dragged out of the extremities of the space. The foreman and his gang clustered around these remnants in the under-deck gloom. It was clear that they were drunk. Two men held half-empty bottles and another empty one rolled slowly amid the dust and debris littering the plating of the deck. Mitchell bent and picked up the loose bottle. It was an obscure brand of Scotch whisky, familiar only to those used to ship's stores.

'Where did you get this?' he asked. They regarded him in resentful silence. He repeated his question, advancing on them.

'I buy,' the foreman said.

'Where? On the ship?'

The man nodded. 'Si, on ship.'

It could have been anyone, Mitchell knew, anyone among the crew with access to the steward's stores. Even, perhaps, the chief steward himself. He pointed upwards and then swept both hands, palms downwards in an outward, horizontal gesture as he said: 'Winchman, finish, *finito*!'

They fell to jabbering among themselves. One or two shouted after him as he made for the ladder to the open deck above. He knew he was being cursed. As he regained the deck, he saw Rayner and Maldonado.

'Señor!' he called, stopping the two men as they walked round the deck. 'Señor, that man,' Mitchell pointed at the winchman, 'take him off the ship, he is drunk and all the men working in this hatch are drunk!'

'What's that?' said Rayner.

'It is not possible,' expostulated Maldonado, leaning over the coaming and yelling below.

The foreman appeared and a staccato conversation took place. At the end Maldonado shrugged. 'The foreman he say the whisky came from the ship. It was a present from one of your officers . . .'

It was Rayner's turn to protest. 'A present from one of the officers? Rubbish!'

Maldonado, having received further information from the foreman, added, 'It was one of the apprentices; the missing apprentice maybe?'

'Dunbar?' Rayner was incredulous.

'No, he wouldn't do that,' added Mitchell, 'and the bugger told me they bought it. No one gives whisky away.'

'Be that as it may, Dunbar's not here, is he?' Rayner said suspiciously. 'And I don't know where the devil he's got to.'

'I'm sure there's a reasonable explanation.'

'I hope to God you're right, but it looks as if the little toe-rag's got mutinous.'

'Oh, that's a bit strong.'

'Well, cunt-struck then. Whatever you want to call his

conduct, it puts us in a damn difficult position now.'
Rayner turned to the agent. 'Señor Maldonado, tell the
winchman to go home and come back tomorrow. Get
another one for today.'

'Meester Mate this man will lose a day's pay.'

'I don't care, he shouldn't be drunk. He might kill
someone.'

'But one of your officers—'

'Give him a bloody token, then, but don't try the trick
twice. I won't stand for it. And tell them to surrender all
the bottles they've still got.'

Maldonado addressed the winchman, and that worthy,
having exchanged a few observations on the parentage of
officers of the British mercantile marine, climbed down
from his winch and lurched past them in the direction of
the gangway. As he shoved passed Mitchell, he raised a
cautionary finger and wagged it under Mitchell's nose.

'You no-good man! You bastard!'

'Shut—'

'Steady Mitchell,' cautioned Rayner, 'let him pass.'

'We should have sacked the bugger,' snapped Mitchell.
'Now all you've done is condoned the matter.'

'Mind your manners, Mitchell!' Rayner snapped.

'I'll bet it was that mealy-mouthed little tyke Humphries,'
Mitchell added defiantly.

'What the hell's the delay?' Pedersen's voice hailed
from the quay.

'Just coming, Pedersen!' shouted Rayner. 'Discharging
a ship isn't like tipping copper ore out of a bloody hopper,
you know.'

'You wouldn't know that by looking at the condition of
some of these flanges, Rayner,' Pedersen retorted.

'Get the last sections out of the 'tween-deck, so we
can open these after lower holds, for heaven's sake, Mr

Mitchell,' Rayner said sharply, turning on his heel.

'Aye, aye, sir,' snapped the second mate, leaning over the hatch again. He made an urgent, sweeping gesture with his arm. 'Come on! Get on with it! Fast! *¡Pronto!*'

'*Si, si, pronto, pronto,*' the foreman grinned up at the second mate. 'I not have a winchman.'

'Good morning, Captain. I trust you enjoyed your evening.'

'I did ma'am, but . . .'

'Then you will not object to our settling the affair at once.'

Captain Steele was surprised to find Miss Hawkshawe seated in the entrance foyer and was irritated not to be taken upstairs to conclude his business with her privately. Her presumption that he would conduct his affairs in semi-public irritated him. This feeling was compounded in the knowledge she had spoiled his high good humour.

He had left Conchita asleep at about one in the morning and strolled back to the ship, smoking a cheroot, full of well-being. He had no wish to appear at dawn, like his seamen, sheepishly joining a queue of men drained of lust. There was a pleasing propriety about his conduct which augmented the physical satisfaction of the evening. If he was observed, he would be seen returning after a thoroughly enjoyable run ashore. Moreover, he would be found next morning in his proper bed-place, and thus escape any suggestion of dubious conduct.

Dubious conduct, indeed! The thought had made Steele chuckle to himself. Conchita had been superb. Her sinuous body with its ample breasts and lovely face had roused him to a peak of passion which he had thought age had robbed him of; and he, aided by former experience, had brought her to her own throbbing and liqueous climax; there had been no pretence in her quivering ecstasy!

Oh, he had been satisfied with his lot earlier in the morning; now he was not quite so sure. He felt Hawkshawe should, for decency's sake, lend the present proceedings a little dignity, and said so.

'Dignity, Captain; how so?'

Steele's Chinese steward lumbered incongruously into the plush foyer in his wake, bearing the bales of trade goods. It was Steele, rather than Hawkshawe, who seemed deficient in dignity.

'You received me most courteously earlier, ma'am. Now you make me feel like a travelling vendor.'

'May I remind you, Captain, you acted impertinently when I treated you like a gentleman. On that occasion you suggested that being in my bedroom, and in a brothel withal, allowed you to be presumptuous. As for being a travelling vendor, that, Captain, is precisely what you are.'

'Very well, ma'am,' Steele said indignantly, 'I will instruct Chang here to return directly to the ship with these bales.'

'And I will charge you one hundred and twenty pounds for Conchita.'

'You wouldn't!'

'I would. And if you renege on the deal, I shall charge you twenty-five pounds for lying with her last night.'

'That is monstrous!'

'It is business, Captain, and you know it. She pleased you very much and you, I am delighted to say, appear to have made a good impression on her. Now, do you wish me to contact Father Xavier, or will you pay me twenty-five pounds and abandon the poor girl?'

Steele sighed. He had been outmanoeuvred; but so

what? He felt his indignation dissolve. He was being petty; he had got what he had come for. 'Arrange the wedding, Miss Hawkshawe,' he concluded.

'Very well. First, you have the money?'

Steele turned to his patient tiger. 'All finish, Chang. Go back ship, tell *Dafoo* Captain come back bimeby.'

'Yes, Captain. Chang go back, tell *Dafoo* Rayner, Captain stay shoreside more time, come back bimeby.'

When the Chinese steward had gone, Steele counted out the sovereigns.

'Thank you. Now, will you marry in uniform? If so, I will have Valbuena give away the bride.'

'I think not, Miss Hawkshawe. Captain Valbuena's uniform has a certain air of, er . . .'

'You would be penny-plain to his tuppence-coloured, I assume?'

'You have it exactly. Can you suggest anyone? Would Dr Reilly be willing?'

'There would be a degree of ironic satisfaction in such an arrangement, I suppose,' observed Hawkshawe drily.

'Do you think it would be obvious?' queried a concerned Steele.

'While you do not want to be an object of ridicule, Captain, only those who know you for a fastidious man would guess.'

'Very well. Would he do it?'

'Why don't you ask him?'

'Then the matter is settled saving only a date.'

'Tomorrow? To wait longer might be a mistake.'

'Yes, yes, that would be fine.'

'I think it would be best if you do not see your bride until then. Anticipation, Captain, will sweeten her attractions, which you know to be delectable.'

'It appears I am entirely in your hands, ma'am.' Steele

236

strove to recover his dignity. He made to put on his hat, then hesitated and added, 'You would not permit another man to . . .'

'To mount your mare, Captain? Good heavens, no! She is being kept in a gilded cage, like the heir to the Grand Turk.'

'Very well. Good day to you. You will send word of the final arrangements?'

'By letter. Father Xavier will require payment, as will his servers and choir.'

'No matter, ma'am, please do what is necessary.' Steele knew there was little he could do about such costs.

'Father Xavier will know you are not a Catholic.'

'I am sure, ma'am, you of all people will persuade him of a way to evade any technical obstacles. He may consider me a Catholic for the day.'

'At a very moderate fee, Captain, I am sure I can arrange matters.'

'Good, then I shall see you in church at what, ten in the morning?'

'Very well. Oh, by the way, Captain, I have one of your boys here, young Dunbar, the lad I asked about. He is sleeping off a severe headache. If you permit me to use him as a messenger, it will make things so much easier.'

Steele had paused on the threshold, frowning. 'Dunbar? The boy is here? Good Lord, I would not have thought he had it in him . . .'

'Oh no, Captain, you misunderstand. He hasn't been with any of the, er, girls. He just got rather drunk and I felt sorry for him. You wouldn't grudge an old woman's whim, would you?'

'Of course not, ma'am,' Steele smiled.

'And he won't get into any trouble when he returns?'

'He'll run a greater risk of that in here, Miss Hawk-shawe!' Steele laughed. 'Don't forget my bundles. Good day to you.'

Mr Mitchell was out of sorts and angry. Rayner should have insisted that Maldonado dismiss the drunken winch-man, and the rest of the gang. Humphries had put the ship in a difficult position and if he had been stealing stores, he would be in real trouble. He was equally upset about Dunbar. The lad had real potential and Mitchell was a generous enough spirit to see a latent artistic talent there. If he was wrecking his health in the notorious brothel it was more than a pity; it was a tragedy.

Mitchell stumped forward where the lower holds were already disgorging more steel sections and, from number two, black diamonds: coal. Already clouds of fine sable dust had begun to rise on the hot air.

Mitchell stood and cursed volubly.

'What's amiss, Mr Mitchell?' Rayner, free of the agent, arrived to stare down into the gaping hold. His mood was conciliatory.

'Bloody coal dust, bloody Port San Martin, and bloody apprentices, that's what's the matter, Mr Rayner. You know it was probably Humphries who sold that whisky?'

'Well nobody gave it to them, that's for certain. But not Humphries, surely. I thought the chief steward—'

Mitchell shook his head. 'No, Mac wouldn't do such a stupid thing.'

'I must admit I didn't give it much thought just now; I was more concerned about keeping the discharge going, what with Pedersen blathering from the wharf. Did you see the damage?'

'Yes, it's minimal. They'll loose-bolt it and then draw it all together. You know what engineers are like.'

'Aye, pernickety lot.' Rayner sniffed and said: 'Well, if you think it is Humphries, you'd better go and get him. He reported Dunbar missing, you know.'

'Yes, but then he would, wouldn't he?'

Mitchell went in search of Humphries, leaving a rather puzzled Rayner behind. A large wicker basket of coal swayed out of the adjacent hold, surrounded by a cloud of acrid black dust which fell upon the mate's immaculate white ducks.

'Oh, damn and blast it!'

Dr Reilly's staircase smelled slightly less of urine, Steele thought as he mounted it, and the brass furniture on his front door had been newly polished. The shuffling house-keeper acknowledged his arrival with a nod, and showed him into the anteroom. It was full of waiting invalids, who looked up at the smartly dressed English gentleman.

'Oh, I, er, I had not wished to inconvenience . . .'

The shuffling woman stared at him uncomprehending. The patients watched with dull, incurious eyes. Steele backed out.

'I will return at a more suitable moment.'

'*Cosa de ver*,' someone said as the door closed again behind the retreating Englishman. A murmur of agreement rippled through the waiting room. It had indeed been a thing worth seeing.

Steele felt oddly discomfited by the encounter as though, following the well-being generated by the *paseo* of the previous evening, he had just discovered the underbelly of the town. The odd sense that his actions of the night had forfeit the inhabitants' unmitigated approval left him twinged with guilt. At the foot of the stairs he paused, recovering his composure.

'Ah, señor, pleez you come my shop.' The barber, unemployed as usual, snipped his scissors invitingly. Steele was about to dismiss the man, when it occurred to him he must look his best for the forthcoming marriage ceremony.

'Very well,' he snapped pompously, 'you may cut my hair and trim my moustache.'

'*Si, señor, al paso.*'

Steele sat while the barber executed a *veronica* with a near-white cotton cape, tucked it about his neck and arranged it with some art over his knees. Then the man clipped and capered about the chair, chattering in Spanish all the while, a professional patter concerning the town's news and scandal, quite unconcerned that his patron could not understand a word. It was probably just as well. The captain, perforce, ignored this meaningless drivel and stared at himself in the mirror. He was not at all bad looking, for his age, and what did age matter when he could . . . ?

He allowed himself to think of Conchita, of the velvet scabbard he had found for his sword. He had confessed to the phrase as he entered her and was erotically proud of it. He hoped she had understood it, for it lost none of its imagery by daylight. He drowsed with reminiscence as the barber smoothed down his hair with rosewater and comb, the stroking almost sensual in its intensity. Steele basked in contentment and anticipation.

When he had finished Steele's hair and was about to embark on the delicate operation of trimming the lower fringe of his customer's luxuriant moustache, the barber paused, went to a door and called, 'Maria!'

A plump, handsome woman appeared and the barber addressed a few words to her, before resuming his ministrations. Bent before his customer, his expression serious and his lips unmoving for this final, delicate act, the barber snipped with singular concentration, his scissors rigidly horizontal. Ten minutes later Steele submitted to the ritual of the mirrors. He was allowed strange views of his head from behind, and invited to admire his nape's smooth transition from hirsuteness to a rough, pink hide.

When he nodded satisfaction, the barber swept the cotton save-all from him in an elegant flourish. A brush was applied to Steele's shoulders before he stood and reached into his pocket.

'No, no, señor, *por favor*.' The barber indicated a pair of rickety cane chairs beside a low table on which a newspaper lay. At this point the woman Maria returned, bearing a pot of coffee, a cup and a saucer.

Steele had no particular reason to return to the ship, indeed he could drag his heels for a while in order to call upon Reilly when the doctor was less busy. Already he had observed several people leave the surgery above. He inclined his head in assent and sat down. He was gratified at the fuss being made of him and admired Maria as she bent and poured his coffee.

'*Gracias*,' he said. 'Do you have any cigars?' He made a vee with his fingers and mimed the act of smoking.

'Ah, *si, si*.' Maria and the barber exchanged a brief word and she disappeared for a moment, shortly returning with a cigar and a lucifer. Steele bit the end from the cigar and accepted the match.

Utterly contented again, he sat back and enjoyed the aromas of tobacco and coffee.

An hour later Reilly himself, his morning surgery over, clumped down the stairs and stepped into the street.

'Ah, Doctor!' Steele called, leaping to his feet, 'Dr Reilly, may I detain you a moment? Better still, may I buy you something to eat?'

241

Reilly stopped and looked round. 'Captain Steele, that is very kind of you.' He pulled out his watch, looked at it and returned it to his waistcoat. 'I heard you had visited me this morning. I gather your night was pleasant?'

Steele winked. 'Magnificent, Doctor.'

'Good. I have an appointment in half an hour . . .'

'Will you take something with me? A glass of wine, perhaps?'

The doctor caught the barber's eye. The man was hovering anxiously, concerned that his rich patron was going to leave without paying.

'Rodrigo will get us some wine, Captain. Let us have a glass here.' He addressed a few words to the barber, who looked relieved and almost ran to give Maria the order.

Steele and Reilly sat down. The doctor brushed his knees, glanced at the newspaper and then placed his elbows on the chair arms and touched the tips of his fingers together. He stared at Steele.

'So, all is working out well, then?'

'Very well indeed. Miss Hawkshawe drives a hard bargain, but she is fair.'

'She is English, Captain,' Reilly remarked drily, 'what else would you expect? Tell me, how is the girl Conchita? You did not overdo things, I hope?'

Steele leant forward and lowered his voice. 'Between us, Doctor, as men of the world, I had almost expected her to be cold towards me. Not a bit of it! She was eager and willing, and,' he hesitated, then threw caution to the winds. 'She was like a velvet scabbard. D'you understand, Doctor?'

Triumph shone in Steele's face and Reilly suppressed his wry grin with difficulty.

'I understand perfectly, Captain.' Reilly broke off as Maria brought a bottle of wine and glasses. '*Buenas dias,*

Maria,' he said, moving the newpaper for her and pouring the wine. 'So you are a happy man?'

'Why should I not be?'

'Long may it continue, Captain,' said Reilly raising his glass in a toast.

'Thank you.'

'But you did not call on me to tell me all this, did you?'

'No, of course not, I called on you to request a favour.'

'Which is?'

'That you do me, you do us, the honour of giving away the bride. We are to be married tomorrow.'

'Ah.' Reilly sighed, took a deep draught of his wine and put the glass back on the table. Steele leant forward and refilled it. 'I am afraid, Captain,' Reilly said slowly, 'I must decline the honour. It is very kind of you to ask me, but,' he shrugged, 'it is not possible.'

'Miss Hawkshawe seemed to suggest . . .'

'Miss Hawkshawe is a remarkable woman in many ways, Captain Steele. Nor is she as old as she appears; chronic gonorrhoeal arthritis has aged her, but she has a keen mind. She enjoys more power in this town than is good even for an Englishwoman. Unfortunately her wealth permits her to have her own way most of the time and she is apt to consider a thing done when she makes up her mind it shall be done. I am sorry, but in this instance I must prove her wrong. She has misled you.'

'Oh.' Steele looked crestfallen. 'May I ask why you refuse?'

Reilly sighed again. 'Captain Steele, when you arrive home with your beautiful bride she will be an *exotique*, a trophy of your travels, of your manhood. Here, when people ask after the bride, it will become common knowl- edge she was an inmate of the Hotel Paradiso and was, forgive me, a common whore.'

A bubble of pride burst in Steele's heart and was replaced by a quavering misgiving. 'But Miss Hawkshawe assured me Conchita had hardly had any customers and was not a compliant enough type to make a good—'

Reilly put his hand up to stop Steele. 'I am sure the señorita told you nothing that was not true, but it is not good for me, as a doctor, to become associated, in anything other than a professional sense, with the women from the Hotel Paradiso.' Reilly paused to swallow the wine remaining in his glass.

'Consider, Captain, Puerto San Martin is not Paris or London. I have my own life, my own circle of friends, which includes women of a certain social class. They do not ask who are my other patients. You have seen where I live. In order to allow me to help the poor of this place, I must keep my wealthier patrons. They do not want to be reminded they have a pox-doctor for a physician. Do you see? You cannot buy everything, Captain. I am sorry, but there the matter must rest.'

'Very well, Doctor, I understand.' Steele gloomily shared the rest of the wine. 'Can you recommend anyone who might . . . ?'

Reilly stared into the distance. 'Have her given away by Esteban, the guitarist and *majordomo* of the place, and have his wife, the dancer Gloria and the beautiful Dolores Garcia attend her. *That* should create what you would, I think, call a stir, yes?'

'The Madame Garcia,' said Steele musingly. 'I suppose it would be rather fitting.'

'Now, Captain, there is a woman worth both ears and the tail.'

'Yes, indeed.'

'But not even *your* money would have purchased her.'

244

'How so?' Steele frowned.

'If she ever has a man again, he will be a most fortunate individual. Her . . . what did you say? Ah, yes, her velvet scabbard will be most consoling. But alas, she is inclined to be a Sapphic.'

'Ah. I see. But she was married once?'

'Yes. Her husband . . . oh, it is of no consequence. The wine has made me talkative.' Reilly drained his glass and took out his watch. 'Pardon, I must go! Thank you for the drink. I am sorry not to oblige you.'

Steele half-rose. 'No matter.'

Reilly nodded to Rodrigo, the barber, and left. 'No matter,' repeated Steele ruminatively. He thought for a moment, then called the barber. 'Rodrigo!'

'Señor?'

'Do you have pen and paper?' He mimed the act of writing. '*Comprendez*?'

'*Si, si.*' Rodrigo raised his voice. 'Maria!'

Five minutes later Captain Steele had despatched a note by the barber to the Hotel Paradiso asking for the arrangements to be made as Reilly had suggested. Then he strolled back to the ship. It was dinner time and he felt weary. He would indulge himself with a *siesta* today, to keep up his strength for tomorrow.

Dunbar woke alone in the bed and stretched himself langorously. For a moment he was confused as to his whereabouts, then he hurriedly sat up.

'Ah, you are awake. Good.' Richenda Hawkshawe turned from her desk, pen in hand, and looked at him over a pair of *pince-nez*. She was unveiled and the shocking sight of her brought everything back to him.

'What is the time?' Dunbar asked throwing his legs out

of the bed and feeling about for his clothes.

'Do not concern yourself with the time. I have made your peace for you with Captain Steele, he was here this morning on business. I said you had a hangover.'

'Oh, I did not know he had business with you.'

'Well he does. I have many interests and deal in many things. He brought me some dresses and haberdashery, but you are not interested in those kind of things, are you?'

Dunbar smiled. 'No, not very. I did some drawings last night, didn't I?'

'They are in my ledger here, come and look.'

'I cannot find my trousers . . .'

'I should not worry.'

He suddenly found he did not care and leaped from the bed to stand behind the old woman and look over her shoulder. He saw the *Macassar* under full sail, then shortened down in the gale. Where had he learned what sails she would have carried? Then he remembered seeing the *Potosi* in the south Atlantic and recalled Miss Hawkshawe using the same name to describe somewhere in her story. She turned the pages; the mutiny unfolded and the *Macassar* burned in the southern fiord, the mighty cordilleras, just as he had himself seen them, dwarfing her.

'It was all true,' he murmured.

'It was all true,' she echoed. She turned and looked at him. He saw again the terrible mutilation and she noticed his revulsion. 'We are all mutilated, one way or another,' she said.

'Yes, but . . .'

'Bring Wilkins to me.'

'Yes, yes I will try. Where is Dolores? You asked me to draw her and I would like to see her again.' He paused and smiled. 'But I only have your pen and—'

'And I am using it, yes.'

'I have pencils on the ship. I wish I had some paints. I really want to paint a proper picture of her.'

'She is very beautiful and you are very talented. When I was a girl my mother taught me to paint in watercolours, but they went when . . .' Hawkshawe sighed. 'It does no good to dwell on the past.' She paused for a moment and then said: 'I want Wilkins here all the same. As for you, you are a good-looking young man. You have made Dolores very happy and she, I think, has made something of you. Are you in love with her?'

'I don't know. I want to . . .'

'That is understandable.' She looked down and laughed. 'But Dolores might not want to again, so prepare yourself for disappointment.' She barked her harsh vixen-laugh, and Dunbar covered himself, embarrassed.

'Your clothes are on the far side of the bed, on that chair.'

He found them and dressed with his back to her. When he turned round, she was standing beside the table, leaning on a stick, holding out two letters to him.

'Come back tonight with Wilkins. There is a note here for Captain Steele, but on your way to the ship, oblige me by going to the church and asking for Father Xavier. This other letter is for him.' Seeing Dunbar frown, she added, 'As a personal favour to me. I shall see you tonight.'

It was a command. He took the letters from her. 'Humour an old woman and kiss me,' she added.

He felt a surge of affection and pity for her. Gone forever was the gauche inhibition that had kept him from Jenny Broom or stopped him pressing his attentions upon Julia Ravenham; gone too was the self-delusion, the mistaken assumptions about another human being.

With great deliberation he put his lips to her scored

cheek and felt the deep furrow of her savage mutilation.

As he straightened up she swept the veil back over her face. But not before he had seen the tears start in both her eyes.

'Well, Humphries,' said Mr Rayner, 'if you didn't give the longshoremen whisky, who did? Dunbar?'

'I don't know, sir, I suppose it's possible.'

'I suppose it is possible, Humphries,' Rayner said slowly, 'but as he isn't here to answer for himself, I will give you one more chance to tell the truth.' Rayner's tone was tired. He did not want this sordid little trial of wits and wills. If Humphries had stolen from the ship's stores, it was a very serious offence, particularly when an apprentice was concerned.

'You went ashore last night, didn't you?'

Humphries havered a moment, clearly debating with himself the advantages of coming clean with this particular morsel of truth. Rayner's tone was languid, bored; at least, so Humphries judged. He had obviously forgotten the detail of their earlier conversation. Mr Rayner was an old woman. He fussed continuously over the ship and the cargo. Humphries made up his mind.

'Er, yes, sir, I did go ashore last night. I believe I told you so this morning.'

'And when you were ashore, what did you do?'

'Well, I had a few drinks . . .'

'Even though, under the terms of your indentures, you are forbidden to enter taverns and alehouses?'

'This was a cantina, sir.'

'A cantina? Ah, I see. It makes such a difference, doesn't it? And then what did you do?'

'I came back to the ship, sir.'

'You didn't go off and have what I believe is called a jig-a-jig?'

'No, sir.'

'Then who was the young woman you were seen with at about eleven o'clock last night?' Rayner watched at this sprat of a lie, to see if a mackerel would go for it.

'I, er . . .'

'Was it perhaps your sister?'

'No, of course not, sir, I, er . . .'

'Well?'

'Well, it was a young lady I had met.'

'A young lady?' Rayner's tone was incredulous. The mackerel had taken the bait nicely. All it wanted now was for him to barb his prey. He frowned. 'A young lady? In a place like that?'

Rayner had been thinking of the Hotel Paradiso. He had no idea of the low brothel Humphries had resorted to in order to exchange his tokens for the favours of a whore. Humphries, on the other hand, recalled the place only too well. He was already having second thoughts about the wisdom of his foolhardy adventure.

'Who saw me, sir?'

'I saw you, Humphries,' Rayner lied, 'and I think you had better own up to it. You could well need salvarsan before we get home.'

A sudden, awful fear gripped Humphries's stomach and made him feel sick. He hung his head. 'Yes, sir.'

'You misbehaved last night, didn't you?'

'Yes, sir.'

'And you lied to me this morning, didn't you, when you said you had not been with a woman?'

'Well, I, er, yes, I did, sir.'

'And I put it to you, you are lying over this business of the whisky. Who else would think that game worth a candle, except an apprentice with no money?'

'I'm sorry, sir.'

'I wonder what your father would say.'

'For God's sake don't tell him, sir, please.'

'I should report this matter to Captain Steele. He'd have your indentures cancelled at once.'

'Please, sir . . .' Humphries was deadly pale and sweat caused an unpleasant sheen to stand out upon his face.

'You're a real little shit, Humphries!' Rayner said, with a vehement passion that took the apprentice aback; 'a contemptible little turd! Get the hell out of my sight!'

The west door of the church stood open and the cool of the interior was welcome after the heat of the plaza. It scarcely seemed to be the same place Dunbar had visited hours earlier, nor did he seem the same person as he had been then. And yet he was; his metamorphosis had been well advanced by the time he reached the false sanctuary of the church.

Its alien oppression was still omnipresent, but he felt it less urgently now. He wondered if it was merely the daylight which made the difference, and then decided that it was not. He had rejected a formal concept of God here, in the small hours of the same day, and come to his bleak and lonely conclusion.

Since that excoriating moment, thanks to Dolores Garcia, he had also become at one with his corporal self.

He thought of the church at home and how its holy chill always seemed deathly. He thought too of his father, and wondered what the rector would say if he knew his son had lain with a woman twice his age. But the burden of sin was almost joyfully borne and Dunbar felt no trepidation in enquiring for Father Xavier.

PART THREE

The Blue Peter

CHAPTER ELEVEN

The Red Bedspread

It was the hour of high and torrid noon when Dunbar regained the shade of the *Kohinoor*. There was something odd about the ship, he thought, as he approached the foot of the gangway, and then he smelled the pungent coal dust, and saw the stuff lying on the wharf alongside number two hatch. Much had been done in his absence, he thought guiltily.

'Where the bloody hell have you been?' Mitchell confronted him on the boat-deck.

'It's all right, Mr Mitchell, Captain Steele knows all about it.'

'Does he? Well that makes it all fine and dandy then! Damn it, Foggy, some of us have actually been worried about you.'

'That's very decent of you, sir.'

'Where have you been, anyway?'

'In the Hotel Paradiso.'

'Oh, Foggy, for God's sake.'

'It's not what you think, Mr Mitchell, honestly . . .' Dunbar was genuinely touched by Mitchell's concern, but he desperately wanted to change the subject. 'Have you any oil paints on board, sir?'

'Oil paints?'

'Yes, sir, I had an idea you had mentioned oil paints, you know, with linseed oil and turpentine, a chap had them at school. I borrowed them sometimes.'

'I do know what oil paints are.'

'Sorry, sir, of course you do.'

'What d'you want them for?'

'I want to do a portrait of someone,' Dunbar said, his eyes alight with enthusiasm, 'I really do. I feel this compulsion to, to, oh, I don't know . . . Anyway, if you haven't got any there's no point in getting excited about the idea. Sorry, sir.'

'Wait a minute. You're right; I do have a small box actually. My mother bought them for me, but I've never tried to use them, they take too damned long to dry and are very impractical, especially on board ship.' He looked at the young man and realised that his earlier instinct about Dunbar's talent had been correct: the lad burned with the fire of creative energy. 'Look, why don't you have them, they're no good to me, I shall never use them.'

'Oh, I couldn't, sir, not if they were a present from your mother.'

'Shut up and obey the last order.'

'That's tremendously kind of you, Mr Mitchell.'

'I know,' said Mitchell sarcastically, 'I'm like that. Come along to my cabin.'

As Mitchell was on the point of handing the black japanned tin box over to Dunbar he hesitated and said, 'There is one thing, Dunbar, I had almost forgotten in your mad enthusiasm.'

'Sir?'

'You didn't get hold of any whisky out of the ship's stores and pass it on to any of the native gangs, did you?'

'Good Lord, no, sir! Why should I want to do a thing like that?'

'I don't know why anybody should want to do a thing like that, but someone did. Here, take the paints. The lamp-trimmer's got some canvas in his store, or you can cut a panel out of the boxes the bolts for the steel sections came in. Herr Bloody Pedersen's broken a couple of them open on the wharf this morning; I should help yourself.'

'Thank you, Mr Mitchell, thank you very much!'

Excited though he was by Mitchell's generosity, Dunbar first had to declare his errand to Captain Steele, and excused himself. He found Steele asleep in a chair in his cabin and, since it seemed improper to wake his commander, Dunbar left Miss Hawkshawe's letter propped prominently up on the captain's desk.

Having collected the paintbox from Mr Mitchell, Dunbar bore it off in triumph to the half-deck. Here he found Humphries, also lying down, but with his eyes open, staring at the deckhead, miserable and preoccupied.

Mindful of his promise to Miss Hawkshawe concerning the man she knew as Wilkins, he decided to catch Williams before work resumed. Humphries seemed introspective and disinclined to chat, so Dunbar paid him little attention. He found Williams lounging outside the seamen's accommodation, leaning on the rail.

'So there you are!' Williams said, when he caught sight of Dunbar. 'The whole ship's been searched for you this morning,' he added, lowering his voice. 'I didn't let on I had a fair idea where you were!' Williams laughed and Dunbar leaned on the rail beside him. 'You started all sorts of rumours flying.'

'Did you get on all right with Teresa?' Dunbar asked.

'Yes, of course I did.'

'Aren't you getting a bit old for that sort of thing?'

'Many a fine tune is played on an old fiddle, Foggy.'

'You know you said you shipped out of Liverpool on the *Earl of Balcarres*,' Dunbar said.

'Yes.'

'Where did you leave her?'

'Why d'you want to know?' There was an edge of suspicion in Williams's voice.

Dunbar shrugged. 'Oh I don't know, I'm just interested.'

'Well I'm interested in how you got on with that bint, Conchita. Did you . . . ?'

'No, I didn't.'

'Ah, that's why you're jealous of me and Teresa, is it? Are you going to tell me what happened?'

'Not if you don't tell me where you left the *Earl of Balcarres*. Was it in Australia?'

'Look, what the fuck is this? The bloody inquisition? What's it to you?'

'Have you ever heard of a ship called the *Macassar*?'

'The *Macassar*?' Williams straightened up, visibly startled, but swiftly regained his composure. 'Why are you asking me all these questions?'

Dunbar, realising Williams might turn unpleasant, temporised. 'Oh, I heard she'd gone missing. I read it somewhere and wondered if it might have happened at about the same time you arrived in Australia on the *Earl of Balcarres*.' Dunbar's disingenuous air gave Williams the lifeline he sought; it never occurred to him to enquire where Dunbar had learned of the *Macassar* going missing. He frowned in mock concentration.

'She might have been at Circular Quay when we got there.'

256

'That's Sydney, isn't it?' Dunbar asked. 'I thought she sailed from Melbourne.'

'Well it might have been Port Phillip Bay, I don't bloody well know. What's it to you?' Williams stared at Dunbar.

'Nothing. I was just curious. Look, d'you fancy the *exposicion* tonight?'

'No,' Williams said shortly.

'Come and have a drink with me at the Hotel Paradiso, then.'

'Why? You've become a right little nosey parker. No. Anyway I'm meeting Teresa in the square this evening.'

'So you won't come with me?'

'No. Now sod off.'

Reluctantly Dunbar returned to the half-deck, conscious of having failed Miss Hawkshawe. He was not yet ready to give up, and after only a moment's consideration he had hatched a plan to trap Williams.

As the longshoremen reappeared after their *siesta*, Dunbar slipped ashore again. The door of the Hotel was closed and he knocked upon it vigorously. It was eventually opened by Esteban.

'Señorita Hawkshawe,' Dunbar said.

'She sleep,' said Esteban, 'everybody sleep. You go back ship.'

'This is important. Tell her she must keep Teresa here tonight. She must not let Teresa go to the *paseo*. Do you understand? *Comprendez*?'

Esteban looked at Dunbar. He had heard how the young Englishman was of some interest to his employer. Esteban knew it was not wise to cross the old woman. Besides, he needed the security of her house to maintain his wife and himself. He nodded. 'Teresa not go with your friend tonight, eh? She stay here?'

Dunbar nodded emphatically. 'Yes. *Si*. Teresa want to go with my friend, but it important she stay here. You keep Teresa here.' Dunbar cast about for some more imperative phrase. 'Señorita Hawkshawe tell me to tell you.' He used his index finger to great effect.

'Okay.' Esteban grinned in wolfish anticipation. 'I keep her here, sure.'

'And tell—'

'Okay, okay, I savvy, Meester Englishman. Now you go. All girls sleep. Conchita sleep. She very busy girl, okay?' Esteban grinned again. Dunbar felt suddenly sorry for involving Teresa, but Williams gave him no choice and she would be out of the way.

It was only when he was halfway back to the ship for the second time, he realised he had almost forgotten about Conchita.

Captain Steele woke when the winches clattered into life. He rang for his steward, and as he did so he caught sight of the letter addressed to him and propped conspicuously on his desk.

When Chang arrived he ordered tea and told his tiger he wished to see *Dafoo* Rayner. Then he re-read Miss Hawkshawe's note. The arrangements with the priest seemed to be in hand, Esteban and his party would 'give away' the bride and, as a generous and unexpected post-script, she offered a small wedding breakfast at the Hotel Paradiso after the service. Steele smiled to himself. Clearly Miss Hawkshawe had had second thoughts about her unseemly welcome to him that morning. The question was, having purchased the girl from the old procuress, did he want to return his new wife to the scene of her past life? He thought not.

'You sent for me, Captain,' Rayner said, rubbing sleep from his eyes.

'I did, Mr Rayner. There are one or two things I wish you to do.'

'I wanted a word with you anyway, sir.'

'Very well. How's the discharging going?'

'Pretty well, apart from a hitch this morning . . .'

'Good,' cut in Steele. 'I want you to call a halt tomorrow.'

'A halt? I was under the impression you wanted—'

'Surely my meaning is plain? I want a break tomorrow, Mr Rayner.'

'May I ask why?'

'For the very good reason I am getting married.'

'*Married?* Good God, what for?'

'Oh, the usual reasons, Mr Rayner,' Steele said pointedly. 'Even you must be familiar with them.'

'May I ask who the fortunate lady is?' Rayner asked, trading the sarcasm.

'No one you'd know.'

'I didn't suppose it was, sir,' the mate replied wearily. 'I'll tell Maldonado.'

'She's of good family and very handsome,' added Steele hurriedly, ignoring the mate. 'Now I want you to tell Maldonado – you may invite him to the wedding, by the way, and I want the church decorated. Use the usual bunting, national flags, that sort of thing. And at nine forty-five in the morning I want all the officers and apprentices in uniform and in church.'

'I don't think any are Catholics, especially not young Dunbar; his father's an Anglican cleric.'

'I don't give a damn if they're bloody Quakers and Dissenting Methodists, just get them into church. Oh, and I want you to be best man.'

'Me, sir?' Rayner was astonished.

'Well who the devil else is there? You're supposed to be my right-hand man.'

'Well, I didn't sign on for this.'

'You signed on to do what you're bloody well told.'

'D'you have a ring, sir?'

'Of course. I'll give it to you in the morning.'

'You came prepared then, Captain,' Rayner observed drily.

'Oh, yes, certainly.'

'And where were you intending to spend your honeymoon? In the Hotel Paradiso?'

'Don't be impertinent, damn you,' Steele said, giving the mate a sharp, quizzical look, wondering what tittle-tattle and scuttlebutt he had heard, but already Rayner was thinking of his beloved ship. 'Oh, and one other thing, when you pass the word for the officers to wear uniform tomorrow, I don't want a lot of gossip about my impending marriage. Just tell them I want them in church, tell them it's a local holiday or something, they'll think nothing of that in a Catholic country.'

'You're keeping it a surprise, are you, sir?'

'I just don't want the whole bloody ship nattering about it,' snapped Steele, irritated. 'It's a simple enough matter, surely?'

'Perfectly, sir,' said Rayner. 'I shall not mention it to anyone. Now to another matter if I might . . .' He explained the affair of Humpries and the whisky, concluding with the remark, 'It's a pretty serious business, sir.'

Steele considered for a moment and then said, 'Youthful high spirits, Mr Rayner, I'd say, though I intended no pun. You can work the backside off the young thief when we're homeward bound.'

'You're not going to cancel his indentures, sir?'

'He's got time to reform himself, see the error of his ways and all that. Perhaps we should send him to confession and make a good Catholic of him before tomorrow,' Steele jested, most inappropriately, Rayner thought.

'But it's a serious offence, Captain, and one which should not be condoned.'

'Oh, do as you see fit, I've other things on my mind at the moment.'

Sensing himself dismissed, Rayner withdrew. 'Aye, aye, sir.'

'Oh, by the way,' Steele called after him.

'Yes, Captain?' Rayner reappeared.

'I want young Dunbar available to run errands, so consider him free to come and go.'

'All right. Does he know what's going on?'

'Certainly not!' Steele paused, then asked, 'And will you have a drink with me later?'

'If you wish.'

'You are to be my groomsman, Mr Rayner.'

'I hadn't forgotten, Captain Steele.'

Humphries was summoned by Rayner shortly before the mess-room steward sounded the dinner gong throughout the ship.

'Captain Steele wishes me to tell you he is disgusted by your conduct, Humphries.'

'Sir.' The apprentice stood shamefaced.

'But as there is some sort of a religious festival tomorrow your first act of penance is to attend the church at eight o'clock tomorrow morning to decorate it.'

'To decorate it, sir?'

'It seems Captain Steele has volunteered us for the

261

decoration of the church. I imagine it has something to do with keeping the locals happy. There is to be some sort of, er, celebration.'

Rayner explained what was to be done and then dismissed the young man. Then he sat down and considered the turn events had taken. Mr Rayner liked a smooth, predictable, well-oiled life. Good, he had observed, seldom grew out of surprises, and whilst there might conceivably be exceptions, he knew surprises to be generated by plain chance, whim and fancy. In Mr Rayner's book, whim and fancy were most unreliable progenitors of anything worthwhile. Particularly when they originated with Captain Arthur Steele.

Able Seaman Williams sat in the mess-room and toyed with his food. The reference to the *Macassar* had rattled him; he had assumed the business long dead. But Foggy Dunbar had dug the information from somewhere, though he could have known nothing of substance: it was mere coincidence. The young bugger read too much, that was all.

On the other hand, it would do no harm to be cautious. He thought of a future in Puerto San Martin. The engineer, Pedersen, or whatever his name was, would need men used to taking orders to oversee the construction of the conveyor system. If he made a good impression, permanent employment at the mine might follow. And he had found in Teresa a young and devoted woman.

He was getting old; he might not have another such opportunity. What had Britain to offer him? More of the same: a small pay-off, a few days of wild living in Liverpool, then, when his credit had run out, he would sign on another ship like the *Kohinoor* for another voyage. The cycle would go on until he died.

Whereas here, with Teresa . . .

He had jumped ship before, as Dunbar had so nearly found out! If he went tonight, they would have time to find him. He would have to leave just before the *Kohinoor* sailed, when they hoisted the blue peter at the foremasthead as the signal the ship would depart in twenty-four hours. He could sound Teresa out tonight and he would begin to salt his gear ashore, in case he had to act hurriedly, and to make his final departure inconspicuous. To that end, Williams decided, rising from the mess-room table, he would keep all his money hidden about his person. It reminded him of the old days when that bastard Nick Thirle led them to Valdivia, on a donkey, just like the pictures of Jesus Christ he had seen when they tried to make a Christian child of him!

Dunbar did not bother with dinner. He went in search of the bosun and some canvas, stretching and tacking a sheet of the stuff over a piece of board he found in the carpenter's workshop. He had no idea of priming the rough surface, but a few experimental strokes with the chippy's pencil showed up the difficulty of marking it.

Mitchell put in an appearance in the half-deck after dinner. 'You need charcoal for that,' he advised, and threw a packet of Rowney's best willow sticks to the delighted Dunbar. Then he turned to Humphries who lay on his bunk. 'What's the matter with you?'

Humphries looked sullenly at the second mate, then got up and walked out on deck, ignoring both Mitchell and Dunbar.

'He's upset about something. He hasn't said a word

to me since I got back. It's to do with that whisky, isn't it?'

'He hasn't mentioned it to you, then?' Mitchell asked and Dunbar shook his head.

'Not a word.'

'Well, he's certainly in disgrace.' Mitchell was about to leave, when he added, 'Oh, I almost forgot, the Old Man was asking for you at dinner. You seem to be in favour at the moment. He wants you to take a message to the Hotel Paradiso. Something to do with business; a private trade deal, I expect. I just hope your chum hasn't sold all the whisky,' Mitchell chuckled as he left.

Dunbar reported to the captain's cabin where Steele sat in his shirtsleeves and braces, scribbling a letter. 'Ah, Dunbar, take this to Miss Hawkshawe, there's a good fellow. There's no answer expected, so you needn't loiter about in that place. I don't want you hungover tomorrow. I want you here on the boat-deck in full uniform at nine o'clock. D'you understand?'

'Yes, sir.'

'Full whites, number ten rig, all right? You have got number tens?'

'Yes, sir.'

'Good. Consider yourself on church parade, you and Humphries, that is. You don't object to going to a Catholic church, do you?'

'Not particularly, sir. May I ask why, sir?'

'We're all going to a wedding,' said Steele, sealing the letter and handing it to Dunbar. 'Now you cut along and stop asking questions.'

The last thing Captain Steele wanted was a ship boiling with rumour.

As Dunbar ran back to the half-deck and picked up his

paints and canvas, Mitchell completed his rounds of the deck and returned to the officers' alleyway where Rayner called him into his cabin.

'You'd better give your best uniform an airing, Mr Mitchell, we're all commanded to church in the morning. Ten o'clock. Father's orders, atheism is no excuse.'

'Don't tell me the old bugger's got religion.'

'Nothing would surprise me. Be so kind as to pass the word on, will you. The chief engineer and so on.'

'What about the cargo?'

'We're declaring a *fiesta* or something of the sort. It's a confounded nuisance, and I've got to let Maldonado know.'

'Shouldn't we tell Pedersen?'

'I suppose we should, but frankly, I'm not trekking out to that bloody mine. Anyway, he's got enough of those sections on the wharf to keep him busy tomorrow, and the next day's Sunday, so, if we resume the discharge then, we should catch up.'

'D'you want me to send word to Maldonado?' Mitchell asked.

Rayner nodded. 'If you would. Though I don't see how he's going to stop all those bloody longshore sharks turning up in the morning.'

'I should let him figure that one out.'

'Yes, good idea.'

'I'll see to it then?'

'If you would, Sid.'

Dolores Garcia was at her post behind the plush-draped table as Dunbar walked in.

'Señora,' he said, smiling and inclining his head in a half-bow, 'I have brought my paints, my colours.' He held out the box and the rectangle of canvas. It was rather unprepossessing.

She returned his smile and spoke in her low vibrant voice. 'It is early, *caballero*.'

'I have a message for Miss Hawkshawe.'

'Go to her.'

'Will I see you . . . ?'

'Later. Yes.'

He smiled with lascivious anticipation and ascended the stairs and as he did so it crossed his mind to wonder where Conchita was. He would like to paint her portrait too, but felt he lacked the mastery of his materials to do her justice. Whatever she was, and despite her rejection of himself, she was still beautiful. It was a relief, he thought as he tapped on Miss Hawkshawe's door, to be able to think of her in this detached way. Without that cruel confrontation he might have nursed his passion unrequited for a long time.

Had he loved her? Or had he been obsessed? He was left no time to debate the difference, for he heard Richenda Hawkshawe calling him to enter.

She was not at her desk, but sewing. Her lap was covered by a white dress which seemed brilliant in the gloomy room.

'Ah, it's you, and you've brought a missive from Captain Steele, no doubt.' She swept the veil back off her face and cocked her head to read the letter he handed her.

'Is that a wedding dress?' he asked.

'Yes,' Hawkshawe replied, reading the letter. When she had finished she asked, 'How did you know?'

'Captain Steele mentioned something about a wedding.'

'Did he say whose it was?'

'No.' Dunbar cast about the room for some method of extemporising an easel.

'You delivered my letter to Father Xavier, did you?'
Hawkshawe asked.

'Yes, I did. Did you get my message to detain Teresa?
I spoke to Esteban.'

'Yes, she is here. I tried not to raise her suspicions.'

'I want to set this canvas up,' Dunbar ran on eagerly,
'and get on with my painting. I hope Dolores will not
be long.'

He began to look around the room as Hawkshawe bent
to her task again.

'Who is marrying then?' he asked absently.

'One of my girls,' Hawkshawe said evasively.

'Oh. Look, may I use this chair?'

'Do as you wish.'

Williams arrived in the plaza at the rendezvous he had
arranged with Teresa, beneath one of the lamp-lit trees.
Already the square was filling with promenading couples
and the cafés were overflowing with idlers. Originally he
had found her insistence to participate in the *paseo* an
amusement; it appealed to his own self-esteem as much as
to hers. But Dunbar's probing questions, innocent though
they might be, were unsettling reminders of his guilty
past. His new-found determination to break his articles and
desert the ship made him less desirous of flaunting himself
in public. Teresa's simple, flamboyant pleasure became
suddenly irksome and filled with a shadowy danger.

Williams's irritation increased when he failed to find
her waiting for him. He hung about for a while, thinking
her merely late. Then he assumed she had selected the
wrong tree, and walked round the square searching under
the others. When, unsuccessful in his quest, he returned
to the rendezvous to find there was still no sign of her,

he wondered if she might have arrived in his absence and left again.

This cycle of anxiety was a measure of the effect Dunbar's queries had had on Williams. For some time he stood irresolute. The plaza filled and it seemed to Williams that he was the centre of a slowly encircling and hostile crowd. It was a ridiculous fantasy, he told himself, but the need to escape combined with the realisation that he had been made a fool of. Teresa had another client, a younger man. She was even now at the brothel, in the very act of making her proposition.

Forcing his way through the affronted crowd, Williams hurried towards the Hotel Paradiso.

He stormed into the foyer flushed and angry, casting only a quick glance at the woman behind the table. It was not Señora Garcia, but the tall dancer, though he took scant notice of the fact and made directly for the saloon, convinced he would find Teresa there.

The stripper was waddling off stage, her pink corsetry clasped to her, her plain face expressionless. The room was already filling with the Hotel's drabs. Casting about, he could see no sign of Teresa.

'Surely she hasn't already . . .' he was muttering to himself, shoving other patrons aside.

'Hey, watch it!' someone called after him.

Williams elbowed himself to the bar and ordered a drink. He needed a moment to think. He could not believe she would two-time him, not after what had passed between them the previous night. The old fear of being made subservient, a victim, always at the whim of others, returned to him and spawned an angry determination to enforce his will.

Downing the tequila, he began to fight his way back through the press of bodies to the door.

* * *

As the sun dropped behind the distant mountains and threw them into deep purple silhouette against a scarlet sky, Mr Rayner joined Captain Steele for a quiet pre-nuptial drink.

'I daresay it came as a bit of a shock to you, my announcing my marriage, eh?'

'Well, Captain, I have to admit it was the last thing I expected.'

'You're a married man; you understand.'

'I understand the natural impulses, but, er, aren't you, well, we're neither of us young men, Captain Steele. It strikes me that one ought . . .'

'You're going to tell me to grow old with dignity, aren't you?'

Rayner shrugged. 'Well, yes, sir, I was.'

'Well, may I remind you that I'm not as old as you.'

'True, not quite as old.'

'And you know that we seafarers hardly get our fair share of the fluff and muslin, despite what people think about us as degenerates.'

'Yes, I'll agree with that.'

'So, all I wish to do is catch up a little. My wife passed away and left me a free man. I decided to remarry. I decided to remarry a younger woman of my own particular choice, if you see what I mean.'

'I think I do.'

'And I think, when you see her, you'll agree she's a peach.' Steele refilled their glasses with the same brand of Scotch whisky Mitchell had discovered in number five 'tween-deck.

'Cheers,' said Rayner. 'I assume your bride will honey-moon on board and travel home with us?'

'Of course. D'you foresee a problem?'

Rayner shook his head. He could imagine several potential problems, but to voice them would, under the circumstances, appear neurotic. Anyway, he was not a malicious man and wished Steele well, whatever his thoughts of the possibility of a *mésalliance*.

He raised his glass. 'May I offer you my congratulations, Captain Steele, and wish you every happiness.'

'Thank you.'

They sat for a moment in silence, then Steele remarked, 'Well, we've had no trouble with the men. If you remember, you were worried about it.'

'Yes, I was.'

'And I proved you wrong.'

'Yes, but in a way I'd rather have had a few drunken firemen and ABs to worry about, than to find an apprentice selling stores.'

'You worry too much, Mr Rayner. We'll deal with him later. We've got something to celebrate tonight. Have another drink . . .'

'He's here!'

Hawkshawe's voice cut through the stuffy air of the upper room, wrecking Dunbar's concentration as he raspingly limned in Dolores Garcia's head on the coarse, unprimed canvas. As for his model, she jerked awkwardly and could not resist rising and staring down through the glass into the crowded saloon below.

'Damn it!' Dunbar muttered, crossing the room to join the two women. For a second it occurred to him how much had changed since he had last stood with them, confused and ashamed, staring down into the boudoir. It was doubly odd how easily they had accepted him and how he had

270

adapted to being with them. It transcended having been Garcia's lover, and had something to do with the odd way he had integrated with their own relationship. Dunbar did not fully understand the nature of this, beyond realising they were intimate friends; but he was not a person who sought to exclude the complexities of a relationship of long standing, because he had been afforded the privilege of a night in Garcia's bed. He felt it a privilege; even, in a curious, old-fashioned sense, an honour, and while he did not understand himself at a conscious level, supposing he had thought about it, this tolerance enabled him to observe and in due course comment through the medium of brush and paint.

By a strange and fateful sequence of events James Dunbar had, within the space of forty-eight hours or so, been detached from the deadweight of his past, and set upon the lonely path of artistic achievement. But he knew none of this as he sought out and located Williams, drinking at the bar.

'It *is* him,' Hawkshawe hissed, and almost as if Williams heard this positive identification, he rose and made for the door of the saloon. As he did so, Hawkshawe moved with surprising swiftness to ring a handbell. A few moments later there was a rapid crescendo of footsteps on the wooden stairs and Esteban appeared in the doorway.

'Señora?'

Hawkshawe snapped instructions at him in Spanish: 'You know the man I want. Bring him here!'

Esteban's footfalls thundered back downstairs.

Life had cheated Williams of much, but to his natural intelligence it had added cunning. He possessed a slum-bred, feral instinct; the effrontery of a confidence trickster when

271

it was needed. Esteban's wife, not entirely unused to her current front-of-house duties, saw a lone English seaman who had shortly before entered the Hotel Paradiso, quit the place with a look of dissatisfaction. She was not in fact the cool elegant creature she appeared when dancing. A lost customer was an affront to her, a threat to her way of life, an opportunity missed. She made a rude and insulting gesture at Williams's back.

When, a moment later, her husband ran down the stairs asking for 'the bad Englishman', she pointed to the street. Esteban ran out onto the porch, looked left and right, shrugged his shoulders and returned inside to exchange a few words with his wife. It was not until he heard the bell ring imperiously a second time that he reascended the stairs to tell a now furious Hawkshawe that Williams had escaped her.

'Damnation!' Hawkshawe swore, turning to Dunbar. 'It hasn't worked!'

Dunbar felt the accusation as palpably as if she had struck him; he had let her down badly.

'Where is Teresa?' he asked.

'She is here, in the Hotel.'

'Yes I know, but where, where exactly?'

'She is with . . .' Hawkshawe began, turning on her heel and, leaning on her walking stick, stumped the length of the room, passing the door and flinging aside the curtain into the long gallery at the far end.

'She is with Conchita!' Garcia said, suddenly comprehending and following her friend. Dunbar in his turn brought up the rear. As he reached the entrance to the secret observation gallery, he heard the rasp of more curtains as Hawkshawe drew them back and exposed the ornate boudoir.

The room was not as brilliantly lit as it had been for

the *exposicion*, but Conchita and Teresa could be clearly seen sitting side by side on the edge of the bed with their backs to the observers above them. They too were sewing, though the relevance of a white train escaped Dunbar. He was eager to begin the portrait in which he sensed a great challenge, but was captivated by the curl of dark hair that hung down the nape of Conchita's neck, and felt his heart lurch at the sight of it.

It was clear, too, that both young women were happy, for they were laughing together and Teresa nudged conchita, instantaneously convincing Dunbar it was she who was to be married.

Beside him Hawkshawe sighed with relief, but it was premature, for at this same moment the door opened and Williams entered, his finger to his lips. Teresa's hand went to her mouth. She was at once astonished and apologetic. It was easy to see she had lost all track of time and this apparent distraction further convinced Dunbar of her forthcoming marriage. This realisation complicated Williams's situation as far as Dunbar was concerned and he wondered what Hawkshawe intended towards Williams. Did she mean him to marry Teresa and expiate his sin against Richenda Hawkshawe by working for her in some fashion?

Confused, he was visualising his own part in brokering this satisfactory conclusion, when Hawkshawe commanded: 'Ring the bell again! Quickly!'

Dunbar ran back across the upper floor and rang the handbell, again summoning Esteban. By the time he returned to the window, Miss Hawkshawe was banging her stick on the wooden floor and Señora Garcia was remonstrating with this noisy evidence of impatience. The reason for this outburst was clear: Teresa and Williams had fled, and Conchita stared after them, an expression of bemusement on her half-turned face.

Dunbar shrugged; for him this sequence of events seemed increasingly remote; it was the end of an ancient mutiny and the destiny of the strange protagonists who were playing out the last act in its residual drama. His attention had become diverted. As he had peered into the elaborate boudoir with its three occupants, he suddenly saw the effects of light on solid masses, of the natural balance of composition and of its disruption and reconstitution by movement. He saw the energy latent in line, the impact of colour and the transmission of passion without its noise and consequences.

In an instant he had forgotten Williams and Teresa as lovers, forgotten Conchita as an object of intense desire, forgotten Hawkshawe and the tragedy of her life, and Garcia as the receptor of his seed. His heart had not skipped at the sight of the errant curl of Conchita's hair out of a longing for sexual intimacy, but at the impact of inspiration.

Long afterwards he knew it was the scarlet bedcover which had acted as a catalyst. It came from one of Captain Steele's bales; fate had brought it from England and confronted Dunbar at this intense moment of crisis with a reminder of the great red flag in his father's church. This splash of brilliance had attracted his eye to the acute aesthetical aspect of what he had been observing. He felt transformed by this, excited that what he had sought so blindly for so long had finally been revealed to him. The crucial importance of expressing what he saw in terms of how he felt and reacted to it, hit him with almost physical force. The flag had awakened his young mind to something only dimly perceptible, confused it with the impositions of religion, of patriotism and of duty. His solitary nature had recoiled and developed a pardonable belief in the purity and inevitability of the fusion of spiritual and physical love as the expression of his existence.

Then the Hotel Paradiso had proved the folly of this noble but hopelessly idealistic and unworldly aspiration; instead it had initiated him into an earthier and more terrifying existence; one he sensed as more honest, though, more capable of interpretation and of self-fulfilment. It had also shown him what he, uniquely, must do.

But the personal revelation of an artistic future was incongruous with the extremity of Richenda Hawkshawe's anguish. As Dunbar stood dumbstruck, Esteban had reappeared and been sent packing again in pursuit of the runaway lovers; the furious procuress next turned on Dunbar:

'Get after him!' she railed. 'You know I want him here!' The walking stick thumped as Dunbar was cruelly dragged back into the present. His conclusions about Hawkshawe's motives in summoning Williams were clearly wrong. 'Here!' she repeated and the stick struck him across the shoulders.

But the effort caused her to stumble and he caught her, felt the trembling rage in her before she thrust him away.

Dolores Garcia hurriedly brought her a glass of sherry while Dunbar stood and rubbed his bruised shoulder. Had she not struck him, he might have joined Esteban in a fruitless search of the unsavoury alleys of Puerto San Martin. But the blow made him stubborn, made him resent being dragged into this ancient vendetta.

And Dolores, as she led Hawkshawe unsteadily back to her upright chair, murmured to him, '*No hay que enfardarse*, do not be offended.'

When she had settled the old woman in her chair, Garcia looked up and nodded. Then she sat and composed herself, her head held high.

Dunbar stepped forward to resume work, stared at her and smiled back.

'Good,' he said, picking up the stick of willow charcoal. 'Very good.' And the absorption of the portrait embraced him completely.

CHAPTER TWELVE

The Villain Unmasked

Dunbar was caught up by the compulsion to create. So, it seemed, was Dolores Garcia, who sat immobile while Dunbar worked on. After a few moments Richenda Hawkshawe rose from her chair and came and stood beside Dunbar, watching him work.

'I suppose it is unjust of me to expect you to do more than you have,' she remarked, passing no opinion on his work, but referring to the escape of Williams.

'Miss Hawkshawe, I'm sorry. I want to do this painting very much, as much for me as for you,' Dunbar replied, 'but I am very nervous. I've never had a live model, never painted in oils and only hope I can do Dolores justice.'

Hawkshawe conveyed the sense of Dunbar's words to his sitter, who smiled. As he tried to mix his first flesh tint, Hawkshawe moved slowly away.

'He will be back, I'm sure,' she said quietly. 'I am sorry I struck you.'

Hawkshawe sat again, plying needle and thread. Dunbar felt nothing towards Williams, though he could not have pursued his former sea-daddy, for Williams had brought this indifference largely upon himself by his arbitrary and occasional hostility. Dunbar was in the grip of the self-centred drive possessing most artists, and was discovering the strange power of the desire to convey something beyond the mere ordinary in a representation of the familiar. This was a complex compound of Garcia's powerful attraction and the experiences of the past forty-eight hours, to which had to be added the pure, fulfilling delight of manipulating the soft and lustrous black charcoal, and the rich consistency of undiluted oil colour, as he picked out the features of his beautiful mistress sitting in the half-light.

He was oblivious of the time, forgetful of Williams, dividing his attention between his canvas and his subject. Once only was Dunbar reminded of the present, of events beyond his work, when Esteban returned to report he had found no trace of Williams but concluded that he had earlier re-entered the Hotel over the fence into the yard containing the urinals. He had a fleeting memory of going over the same fence in the opposite direction. Otherwise his whole being was absorbed by his intense aspiration to create a true work of art. Only when Garcia's eyelids drooped and her head fell forward so that she broke the pose, did he concern himself about her. She had sunk into a reverie and now jerked awake with a start.

'*Se hace tarde*,' she said apologetically. 'It is getting late.'

'I am sorry, I have given you no rest.' Dunbar stepped forward and helped her to her feet and she winced as circulation restored itself, giving a nervous laugh and leaning on him. Impulsively he kissed her cheek and led her to look at the canvas.

He had drawn the outline of her head unerringly and painted the creamy tone of her skin with considerable skill, building up the modelling of her proud head with umbral shadows and picking up the sharp highlights on forehead and nose. The lips were still unformed and it was clear he was having trouble, for false starts had been scraped clean.

He felt her arm encircle his waist as they stood in silence looking at the canvas, and he sensed approval; and then she turned away, catching his wrists and drawing him towards the bed.

Richenda Hawkshawe took no notice, but continued to sit at her work where, long after the lovers had fallen silent behind her, after the saloon had emptied and the last bedroom door had closed on its temporary occupants, she too fell asleep.

'Señorita! Señorita!'

Esteban burst wild-eyed into the upper room, tucking his shirt into his breeches.

Hawkshawe woke with a start and Dunbar sat up in bed with Dolores stirring beside him. He had no idea of the time, but he seemed to have slept for several hours, and judged it was already morning. Hawkshawe was trying to comprehend the import of Esteban's intrusion. Dunbar heard the names 'Teresa' and 'Williams' pass between them, then Hawkshawe was on her feet and sweeping aside the curtain which obscured the window into the saloon.

'What the devil has he done now?' Hawkshawe exclaimed and her tone alarmed Dunbar. He swung his legs out of bed and reached for his trousers. A moment later he was beside the old woman staring down at Williams as, with a rough tenderness, he laid an unconscious Teresa on one of the saloon tables. The shutters were still up and the saloon was lit by the early daylight seeping through the open door.

'I'll go and see,' Dunbar said, hurrying past her and down the stairs.

'Take her into the bedchamber,' Hawkshawe called after him.

The spilled beer on the floorboards of the saloon was sticky on the soles of his bare feet.

'What in heaven's name's the matter?' he asked Williams as the seaman looked up, alarmed at his intrusion.

'Thank God it's you, Foggy,' Williams was sobbing and gasping for breath. Tears gleamed on his face and he tried to hold Teresa's head up with one hand and wipe his face with the other.

'What's happened?' Dunbar asked.

'I don't know, I don't know,' Williams repeated, bemused. 'I didn't mean to do it, but I woke up and found she'd gone and taken all my stuff, see? All my clothes, all my money . . . I thought she'd done a bunk.'

Dunbar bent over Teresa; she still breathed, but her skin felt cold and clammy to his fingers.

'What have you done then? You haven't knifed her, have you?'

Williams looked panic-stricken: 'No! No! Nothing like that . . .' He gulped a great breath of air as Dunbar, leaning over Teresa, saw the contusion on her opposite cheek.

'You hit her!'

'I thought she'd stolen everything!' Williams said, seeking to justify his actions.

'Help me lift her,' Dunbar commanded as the figure of Señora Garcia loomed in the doorway. Between them, the two men carried the unconscious woman and followed Garcia as she twisted through the stairways and short passages that brought them to the boudoir. She had snatched up a lamp which still burned in the foyer and lit them into the darkened room. Williams and Dunbar stumbled to the scarlet-covered bed and eased their burden down alongside Conchita. The shuffling disturbance and sudden occupation of the bed woke the sleeping girl. She gave a short, surprised screech, silenced by a sharp word from Dolores Garcia, and withdrew herself from the bed, wrapping her arms about her cotton shift.

'Dr Reilly will come soon; Esteban go to find him,' Garcia said, lighting more lamps. 'What you do to her?' she asked Williams, who was standing abject and trembling, as much from his exertions as from remorse.

'She took my money and my clothes; I woke up and she was gone, gone with everything. What would you think, eh? Your clothes, your money, *all* your money gone. Stolen!'

'If she'd stolen it how did you find her?' Dunbar asked.

But Williams was not listening. He was again giving vent to his justification for what had happened, confessing to the three of them who stood aghast, trying to make sense of the sequence of events.

'I pulled a bedsheet round me and ran out, down into the street. I waited behind one of the columns wondering what to do, see, and after a moment I could see her walking back down the street. I hid behind the column; she didn't see me, but I caught her . . .' He paused, then ran on. 'I didn't see the basket. When she fell over, she dropped it. My shirt, my trousers, my money . . .'

'You did hit her, then,' Dunbar said, trying to make sense out of this cascade of words.

'Of course I hit her! I knocked her flat! She'd stolen my money, my clothes—'

'But they were in the basket. Is that right?'

'Yes, yes.'

281

'And she was coming back to you?'

'Yes, yes she was coming back to me. But she'd taken the money.'

'For safe-keeping I suppose, along with your clothes.'

'She had washed and ironed them . . . dried them in the bakehouse across the road.'

Dunbar frowned uncomprehendingly. 'Didn't you guess she was going to do something like that? I mean, if she's going to marry you, she's not going to run off with your money, is she?'

'How d'you know she's going to marry me?'

'Oh, Idris, you bloody fool! I guessed; this place is full of . . . Oh, hell it doesn't matter. You're in real trouble now.'

'They'll hide me here, won't they? I mean I've been a good customer and I'll keep my head down until the ship sails. I don't want the magistrate issuing a warrant to arrest me. I'll pay whatever it costs to hush the matter up . . .'

'What about the doctor? Will you pay for him as well?' Dunbar asked contemptuously as he joined Garcia beside Teresa. Across the bed from them he was aware of Conchita, her beautiful dark eyes full of anxiety for her companion. As Dolores stroked Teresa's face, faint groans escaped from her swollen mouth. Garcia turned and raising her fingers, touched Dunbar's face, running them along his jawline and stopping at the angle of his lower mandible.

'Broken,' she murmured.

'You're in bigger trouble than you know.' Dunbar rounded on Williams. He cast a look at the mirror on the opposite wall; the faintest suggestion of a shadow showed behind its reflective surface.

'You take this man to Señorita Hawkshawe,' Dolores muttered. 'I'll stay with Teresa and wait for the doctor.'

282

'You'd better follow me.'

Dunbar led Williams back to the foyer and up the flights of stairs.

'Will they hide me up here?' Williams asked, and Dunbar felt disgust at his shipmate's ready detachment from the consequences of his rash act and the fate of its victim. His eagerness to save his own skin at whatever cost was contemptible.

'How d'you know they'll . . . I mean, how d'you know where to go?' Williams was almost laughing, the relief was so clear in his voice. 'You're a real friend, Foggy, a real friend.'

Dunbar stood aside as they reached the upper room. Miss Hawkshawe sat as when he had first seen her, bolt upright in her high-winged armchair, her veil lowered. She spoke as soon as she saw the two men.

'Close the door behind you, James.' Her tone and the use of his Christian name left him in no doubt he was to guard it. 'Come here, Mr Williams.'

Dunbar leaned back against the door and watched Williams shuffle forward. Hesitation and misgiving were in every step, his new-found confidence rattled by the strange woman in front of him.

'Sit down.'

Williams complied obediently.

'What have you done to Teresa?'

Dunbar saw Williams's shoulders rise and fall. 'It was an accident. I thought she'd stolen my money, see.'

'I asked what you have done to her, not why you had done it.'

'I hit her.'

'D'you often abuse women?'

'Me? No. I've been a good customer of yours since the *Kohinoor* berthed—'

'The last time we met, you were abusing women.'

Williams shook his head violently. 'No, no, not me, ma'am. You're making a mistake, I've never been here before.'

Listening, Dunbar wondered if Williams was lying. He had certainly conveyed the impression of having visited Puerto San Martin before, when they had spoken of the place while splicing the mooring ropes.

'I didn't say you had,' Hawkshawe said. 'I said the last time we met, you were abusing women.'

'Then you're making a mistake; you must be confusing me with someone else . . .'

'There's no mistaking you, Idris Wilkins.'

There was a moment's silence, then Williams seemed to press back into his chair, his head shaking from side to side, the denials so vehement that they could only be untrue.

'No! No! My name is Williams, Daffyd Idris Williams.'

'You're a liar! Your name is Wilkins and you were aboard the *Macassar*!'

The silence following this accusation hung in the morbid room until the shock of it had begun to ebb. Williams turned slowly in his seat and looked at Dunbar.

'You knew this, didn't you? That's why you mentioned the *Macassar*.'

'I asked you if you had heard of such a ship, yes.'

'Why didn't you tell me?' Williams gave up this line of questioning as another thought crossed his mind; he spun round on Hawkshawe, rising to his feet. 'Who are you?'

She tore the veil from her head. 'Remember me? The girl you wanted to rape?'

Williams recoiled. 'Hawkshawe,' he breathed.

'You are condemned out of your own mouth!'

Triumph and vindication was clear in Hawkshawe's

every syllable. A feeling almost akin to relief, but compounded with pity, filled Dunbar, for he was not unconscious of the fact that he had, in a way, betrayed Williams. The seaman's admission relieved him.

Again shock stunned Williams. He stepped back and the chair upon which he had been sitting overset. Then he turned and began to run towards Dunbar who flattened himself against the door.

'You little bastard,' Williams snarled, but he made no attempt to contest the passage of the door with Dunbar; instead he passed him and clawed at the drapery at the far end of the room, quickly revealing the entrance to the long gallery overlooking the boudoir.

'Stop him!' Hawkshawe's warning came too late to galvanise the astonished Dunbar. He had been anticipating an assault, expecting the same fate as Teresa as he was knocked clear of the door to the stairs. But Williams was quick-witted enough to know that the gallery from which they had watched the *exposicion* lay on the same level as Hawkshawe's quarters, and had unerringly located the communicating passage.

Even as Dunbar darted forward to follow, Williams caught up one of the chairs lining the wall and, with a tremendous blow, smashed the one-way mirror. The crash of the breaking glass mixed with the screams of Conchita and Dolores. As the silver fragments tinkled on the floor below, Williams leaped through the jagged hole. Dunbar saw he had fallen half across Teresa's legs, with the bulk of his body clear, bouncing on the scarlet coverlet. The bellow of rage from a man sitting on the bed identified Dr Reilly. Then Williams rolled over, clear of the bed, and was about to make for the door when it burst open and Esteban stood there with a rifle.

Beside him Dunbar heard the harsh, vixen-laugh of Richenda Hawkshawe.

'Stay where you are!' she commanded. 'I am coming down.' And to Dunbar she said, 'Give me your arm, James. I have waited a long time for this moment.'

But before they could move, before Dunbar had even proferred his arm to the old woman, Williams had seized the astonished Conchita.

Dunbar saw the flash of steel appear at her throat.

Hawkshawe leaned heavily on Dunbar as the pair descended the dark stairs. Her feet and stick thumped the urgency of her progress, and her breathing rasped with pain and effort.

'He must not – must not do anything to her . . .'

Dunbar did not know Hawkshawe's anxiety was not entirely for the pure welfare of Conchita as a person. He was still unaware of her existence as purchased, promised merchandise.

They reached the lower passageway and Esteban drew aside to allow them a view of the room. Teresa had recovered consciousness and lay on her back. Dr Reilly was calmly completing his bandaging of the battered girl's jaw. Shards of broken glass glittered around him. Dolores Garcia, her heliotrope peignoir clasped about her, sat on the opposite side of the bed. Fright had robbed her of her voluptuous confidence as she watched Williams.

The British seaman had his left arm about Conchita's waist, encircling her arms. She wore only a plain cotton shift which was rucked and pulled tight across her belly, leaving her legs bare. Williams's right fist held the long blade of his deck-knife to her throat. Dunbar knew the edge to be as keen as a razor, for he had seen how easily it sliced manila fibres. Under the slight prick of the knife blade, Conchita had pulled her head back upon her captor's shoulder. Her eyes were huge with terror.

'Ah, Foggy,' Williams said as he caught sight of Dunbar and Hawkshawe in the doorway, '*you* won't want me to hurt this little chicken, will you?' He jerked Conchita with a vicious twist that lifted her feet from the ground; she gave a short screech. 'Teresa's not dead. So tell that bastard with the moustache to fuck off and take his gun with him. I'm going to walk out of here with Conchita and I'll only let her go when I get back to the ship if you guarantee that Miss Hawkshawe won't take any action against me.

'I was only a kid when I got involved in that business aboard the *Macassar*. The whole ship had gone mad. You ask her. I wanted to live as much as she did; if I hadn't gone along with Thirle, he'd have killed me. I don't know why he didn't. Christ, I was only twelve!

'What chance did I ever have in life, eh? I ran away to sea to escape being beaten by my ma's pimp; I ran away from the *Balcarres* to escape buggery by the ship's cook. Then, when I shipped aboard the *Macassar* I was caught up in a bloody mutiny! D'you think I wanted that? Eh?'

Williams's tone was strident with reproach and injustice. 'The only thing *I* did wrong was not to tell anyone when I got back to Liverpool. But who'd listen to a guttersnipe like me?'

'You told no one because you were guilty,' Hawkshawe broke in.

'That's a lie! You went along with Thirle; I watched you let him fuck you. You didn't scream "rape!", did you?' He turned to Dunbar again. 'She's a clergyman's daughter, Foggy, a Christian, just like you. Ask her to forgive me. I didn't mean to hurt Teresa. If I'd known what she was doing, d'you think I'd have hit her? You know me well enough . . . you know how I feel about her!'

'Striking a woman is an odd way of demonstrating affection,' said Reilly, rising and repacking his bag. 'I should stop what you are doing before anyone else is hurt.'

'You keep out of this!' snapped Williams, a note of desperation in his voice. 'Foggy, promise me?'

'What are you going to do?' Hawkshawe whispered to Dunbar. 'Are you going to prove a true gallant, or do we have to let him have his way again?' Dunbar looked round at her. The scar was hideous against the pallor of her skin; Williams's accusation had struck home. 'Here,' she said, 'take this.'

She pressed her stick into his hand. 'Twist the top,' she added. He realised she had given him a swordstick.

'Foggy? Are you letting that conniving bitch turn you against a mate?'

'Let Conchita go, Idris,' Dunbar said, edging into the room, the swordstick behind his back. 'You don't want to get into more trouble, and you don't want to hurt her. She's nothing to do with all this.'

'She hasn't told you all about the *Macassar*?'

'Miss Hawkshawe has told me everything about the *Macassar*, Idris, everything. She's even told me about the power Thirle gained over people and how he could compel them to his bidding. I don't even think she wants to hurt you.'

'Then what does she want, eh?' Williams cried, his voice rising in a screech of wild desperation. 'What's the point of her making all this fuss?'

'Look, there's no reason to hurt Conchita.'

But Williams was beyond reasoned argument. '*She* kept Teresa here last night to get me to come and find her, didn't she? What did you have to do with that, eh? You wanted me to come here when you knew I was going to meet Teresa at the *paseo*.'

'Look, I, er . . .'

'No, you look. You're just the same as the rest of them, you won't give a man a chance.'

'You didn't give Teresa a chance,' broke in Reilly, closing his bag with a conclusive snap. 'Let us have no more of this nonsense. Send for Captain Steele and the *Alcaid*.'

Conchita gave a strangled scream as Williams gave her another convulsive jerk. 'Foggy!'

'Let her go, Idris.'

'No!'

'Look, we can't stand here all day . . .'

'What's that behind your back?'

Dunbar hesitated as he realised he could conceal the weapon no longer and silently cursed Hawkshawe for pressing the thing on him.

Now she said: 'If you don't let Conchita go, Wilkins, Esteban will blow first Teresa's brains out and then yours.'

'I don't care!' Williams yelled. 'I don't fucking care! That fucking ship fucked both our lives up. Either we go our different ways or you can kill me. If you do I'll take this little baggage with me!'

Whether he intended to or not, Williams left no time for anyone to respond. He was engulfed by a mounting feeling of despair, of never communicating with others and of having lost touch with those he had trusted. Incapable at that moment of seeing in his own behaviour anything which had contributed to his rupture with Dunbar, he felt the apprentice's betrayal as keenly as if the knife had been at his own throat. He was overwhelmed with darkness, and struck where he hoped to hurt most.

The knife made no sound as it opened Conchita's throat; air bubbled bloodily out of her collapsing lungs and as Williams let her go, her head fell backwards. The severed

289

carotid pumped great gouts of scarlet into the air as pain and reaction flared momentarily in her eyes before they grew dull.

Garcia screamed; Esteban discharged the rifle; Teresa raised her bound head and roared through clenched teeth. Dunbar whipped the swordstick up and lunged at Williams. Esteban's shot had winged the seaman's left shoulder as he jumped clear of his victim. Conchita slithered to the floor, foul with her own lifeblood. Williams jumped forward, hacking with his knife at Dunbar's blade; he caught the foible with his knife and slashed left and then right, knocking the slender steel aside. The return swipe rasped across Dunbar's breast as, still barefoot, he slithered in Conchita's gore.

He felt the incision of the knife, felt the nick of it against his ribs, but no pain, only the sudden furious desire to strike back before it was too late. He twisted and thrust hard just as Williams stepped past him, trying to reach Esteban before the *mestizo* could again fire the reloaded rifle.

The swordstick was a weapon of defence, possessing only a point and a few inches of sharpened blade, but it drove in under Williams's left armpit and pierced his body so deeply that his forward movement wrenched it free of Dunbar's failing grasp. Bleeding copiously, and losing consciousness as the searing pain of Williams's knife wound finally struck him, Dunbar fell across Conchita's body.

The sound of Esteban's second shot filled the room. Williams was flung backwards, bent double as the bullet passed through his belly.

CHAPTER THIRTEEN

The Blue Peter

'Well, Doctor?'

In the confusion following the events of the dawn, Dunbar had been brought to the upper room where, pale, bloody and unconscious, he lay in Hawkshawe's bed. She stood watching Reilly as the doctor finished his suturing. Reilly drew the needle through Dunbar's breast, tied the final ligature and looked up at Richenda Hawkshawe.

'He is a strong young man. The left *pectoralis major* is lacerated, cut to the bone in places, but he will recover. It was lucky I was here.'

Reilly swabbed the mess clean.

'And the other?' Hawkshawe asked.

'Both wounds are mortal. That sword blade of yours pierced the lung, and a gunshot at that range,' Reilly shrugged, 'well, you saw the mess it made. By night-fall, I should think.' He rinsed his hands in the bowl of water provided and dried them on a towel. 'D'you care?' he asked, looking up at the straight, black-clad and veiled figure.

Hawkshawe sighed. 'To be truthful, I feel a trifle cheated. I had a score to level with him.'

'So I gathered. Was it an old score?'

'A very old score. He tried to rape me when I was a young woman.'

Reilly looked doubtful. 'Rape? He must have been almost a child,' he remarked.

'D'you doubt me?'

Reilly shrugged. 'Why should I doubt you? What others consider extraordinary, I have found not to be so. He was one of the men who . . . ?' He let the question hang as Hawkshawe nodded.

'Yes, yes,' she broke in. 'I cannot always believe it happened. Sometimes it seems no more than a bad dream, but seeing him again –' she broke off and sniffed, collecting herself. When she spoke again, her voice was harsh. 'He was a vicious youth whose close association with men of such evil dispositions as beggar description had utterly corrupted him.'

'And how would you have gained your revenge?'

Hawkshawe paused, as though uncertain, then said, 'I wanted to mark him as he had marked me.'

'Ah,' Reilly nodded, understanding, 'he was the one who disfigured you.'

'Yes.'

Reilly completed dressing Dunbar's wound. 'This one will come round soon and find breathing painful. Dolores Garcia seems fond of him.'

'They had become lovers.'

'¡Dios!' Reilly looked up sharply, 'I am jealous! I thought . . .' he shrugged, then resumed packing his bag.

'Sometimes,' Hawkshawe shrugged, 'she needs a man. I did not know you found Dolores attractive. I had thought you would not countenance a whore for your bed.'

'Perhaps not,' Reilly said, shaking his head. 'The man of science in me would have denied what the man of passion desired.' He gave a short, self-deprecatory laugh. 'Are we not all composed of contradictions? It is what prevents us from attaining happiness.'

'Are you suggesting revenge would have been wrong?'

'No. I confess I was thinking of myself.' Reilly closed his bag with a snap. 'But that is something I think you already know the answer to, do you not?'

He looked at her, aware that her one eye, hidden behind the veil, had turned inward. He could not know of her self-disgust at vomiting over Thirle, of how that simple, even sensible act, had robbed her of any satisfaction; that in her need for dissimulation, she had made of a justifiable homicide nothing more than a murder. This self-recrimination had for years dripped like acid on her soul, linking her forever with the foul and guilty acts of 'love' and thus her own implicit condoning of what had happened.

'This young man saved you the trouble of committing a mortal sin. He has done it for you, an agent of your own desire, a proxy.' Reilly half-guessed her state of mind.

'D'you believe in fate, Doctor?'

'No, not rationally; but . . .' Reilly shrugged and smiled, standing up and touching Hawkshawe gently on the arm.

'You don't know, do you? You harbour doubts.'

'We all harbour doubts. The world is full of incomprehensible mysteries. We should accept them until science unlocks them. I have already admitted to my own contradictions.' He smiled again, ruefully. 'Señorita, you know some of us are fortunate, others not so fortunate. A few people are very lucky, more are very unlucky. How can we judge these things? They are relative and fluid. In your life you may have been among the most unfortunate, yet here, in Puerto San Martin, fate has endowed you to a degree. Is that not so?'

293

'You patronise me, Doctor!'

Reilly shrugged. 'Of course. That is my function as a doctor.'

She sighed. 'But you are right.' She paused a moment, then added, 'Sometimes, though, you can see people who are marked out, one way or the other. Wilkins was marked; he was bound to come to a bad end. I think I knew that all those years ago . . .'

'Yes. It is possible one can have an instinct for such things.'

'I thought this boy was my brother Bobs,' Hawkshawe said, putting her hand out towards Dunbar. 'It was a foolish fantasy, but served to enmesh him in events here.'

Reilly demurred. 'That was circumstantial. He came here like most men, young or old, looking for a dream. Conchita perhaps.'

'*She* was ill-fated,' Hawkshawe interjected with a sudden vehemence, 'but he is lucky, I think.'

'I doubt he would agree with you just at the moment,' Reilly remarked drily, in an attempt to drive the old woman from her morbid train of thought. 'Though you may be right.'

They both looked at Dunbar who stirred uneasily, his eyelids fluttering.

'Why don't you go home to England in his ship?'

'What for? As you said, one's standing is relative.'

Reilly grunted. 'Well,' he said, 'I suppose I must go and inform Captain Steele what has happened to his intended bride.'

'It is fortunate you witnessed what took place.'

'Yes.' Reilly said, relinquishing the intimacy of the conversation, 'You will want me to swear an affidavit before the *Alcaid*. I presume also you want me to keep your connection with this man Wilkins out of the affair?'

'Of course. I have my house to run; you have your practice. The man ran amok and seized Conchita as a hostage.'

'And Esteban shot him after he had assaulted another customer.' Reilly looked down at Dunbar.

'No, not a customer, Dr Reilly. He was an artist, commissioned to execute a portrait. Come and judge for yourself.'

Dunbar's unfinished painting still stood on its extemporised easel. He had attempted the mouth again, and this time caught the line of Dolores's lips, though he had yet to encarmine them fully.

Reilly nodded his head appreciatively. 'He did this?' he enquired, a hint of incredulity in his voice. 'It is good, it is very good. The boy has talent, real talent.'

'You think so?'

'I am certain of it. He has passion too.' He reflected a moment, then turning to her said, 'You are right; he is one of the lucky ones.'

They stood for a moment in silence, then Reilly sighed and said, 'I must get on, Señorita. I will return later. The other will bleed slowly to death. As for him,' he jerked his head at Dunbar, 'have Dolores keep an eye on him. That should prove a powerful specific.'

Rayner was shaving with extra care when Chang summoned him to attend Steele. 'Captain say you come quick, sir. He very upset man.'

'What's the matter, Chang?'

'I no savvy. He just speak: "Quick! *Dafoo* come quick!"'

Rayner hurriedly wiped his face and walked along the alleyway to the master's cabin.

'Come in, come in,' Steele was still in his dressing-gown, though his hair was brushed and his cheeks were glossily smooth. He indicated a rather dishevelled, exhausted-looking stranger who sat in the chair Rayner had occupied the previous evening. Both men were drinking whisky. 'This is Dr Reilly; my chief officer, Doctor, Mr Rayner.'

'How d'you do?' The two men exchanged formal greetings.

'The doctor speaks excellent English and has some very bad news.'

'Oh. May I ask . . . ?'

'My *fiancée* has been killed. Apparently she was seized as a hostage by Williams, one of our able seamen, who, by all acounts, went berserk in that damned brothel you warned me of. He was too confoundedly handy with his knife and wounded young Dunbar who went to the aid of . . . of my young woman . . .'

'Dunbar will be all right, gentlemen, I assure you. Your seaman, however, though he is still living, has sustained a mortal wound himself.'

'How did that happen?'

'He was shot,' explained Reilly, deliberately avoiding any reference to Dunbar's part in Williams's death, 'by one of the pimps.'

'The doctor happened to be present, Mr Rayner; he was attending a woman whom Señorita Conchita, the young woman I intended to wed this morning, was visiting.'

'The woman I was attending,' Reilly expatiated, 'had also been injured by your Williams.'

Steele was visibly affected by the news and Rayner was putting the facts together and reaching a rather different conclusion.

'You witnessed everything?' Rayner asked, addressing Reilly.

'Yes, I did.' Reilly sought to distance himself. 'It was reminiscent of the last act of *Hamlet*.'

'I see.' Rayner paused, then asked, 'D'you want me to pass word that the officers won't be required in church this morning?'

'Yes, of course, Rayner, of course.'

'I must go too, Captain.' Reilly drained his glass and stood up. 'Please accept my sincere condolences.'

Both men left Steele alone and walked out onto the boat-deck. 'I am almost sorry for him,' Reilly said, when they reached the top of the ladder to the main-deck.

'You knew all about this marriage, did you?'

'I was consulted, yes.'

'This Señorita Conchita, she was a whore, I presume?'

'Yes. But an extremely beautiful one.'

'I thought as much.'

'You should not judge him too harshly.'

'I don't judge him at all,' said Rayner bitterly, 'it's not my job. Getting the cargo out of this hooker is my job; that and looking after the apprentices, one of whom is a thief and the other's lying wounded after a brawl in a brothel. From what Captain Steele said to me of Dunbar's recent activities, his trafficking with the Hotel was on Steele's account and had something to do with this so-called marriage.'

Reilly paused as they reached the top of the gangway. 'I know nothing of that, Mr Rayner, but your Dunbar will be back. He'll need rest for quite a while, but you should look after him. He's a very talented artist.'

'An artist!' Rayner exploded incredulously. 'An artist! What in hell and damnation does that mean?'

'It means he has a talent. Good day to you.' Reilly put

on his Panama hat and descended the gangway. Rayner watched the strange doctor disappear and returned to his incomplete shave, muttering imprecations about art and artists. He was stropping his razor when Maldonado and Pedersen entered his cabin with a singular want of the usual courtesies.

'Is this true, Rayner?' Pedersen asked abruptly.

'Is what true?' asked an exasperated Rayner.

'Why, that you are not working cargo this morning?'

Maldonado tried to interpose himself between the angry engineer and the lathered Rayner. 'I tell him, Señor Mitchell come last night and say no cargo work today. There is plenty of cargo to shift off the wharf and maybe we have to stop to clear more space—'

'*Teufel*, that is nonsense—'

'Gentlemen! For God's sake stop your prattling. We will work cargo as normal. I am sorry, Señor Maldonado, I have changed my mind; Pedersen, you can stop worrying.'

'But you said—' Maldonado began to protest.

'I know what I said, but something has happened and we will work cargo!'

'Thank God for that,' observed Pedersen, and as if in recognition of his blasphemy, the bells of the great church began to ring.

Dunbar felt the knife wound every time he breathed. The pain gradually intruded into his consciousness, waking him with its sharp insistence as it tugged like a rope across his chest and he panted in short, shallow gasps. He opened his eyes and groaned, attracting Dolores, who moved across the room and looked down upon him. She looked older, devoid of rouge and carmine, her skin sallow, her large eyes hollowed, dark with the bruises of sleeplessness.

He felt no disgust at this revelation, and wondered fleetingly why he should. Then he entertained two simultaneous thoughts, as though his consciousness presented him with two options. One was that even this careworn, unguarded and revealed face possessed an elusive and haunting beauty; the other was that she seemed to show him the image of the under-painting he had striven so hard to achieve, the colourless modelling of her face's form, her flesh upon her bone.

And though it was this image of her that would persist to inform and guide him in every subsequent portrait he afterwards attempted, it was the first that touched his heart. He reached out and raised a shaking hand to her cheek, at which tears spilled from her lustrous eyes.

'Don't cry,' he murmured.

'You are young. You will go soon. Your ship finish cargo.' She held his hand against her face and screwed up her eyes. Crow's feet ran out, seaming her skin, and passion stirred in him, along with the marvel that he could so affect her and she so affect him.

'Dolores,' he whispered insistently.

He awoke again later to find Mr Mitchell in the room. He must have groaned again, for Mitchell, who had been standing staring at the incomplete portrait, turned towards him with a start.

'Ah, you are awake, Foggy. I was quite lost in admiration, particularly as I have just met the subject.'

'You like it then?' Dunbar asked.

'Like it? I think it is superb. But I think you have misled me. This is not a beginner's work. You've done something of the sort before.'

Dunbar shook his head. 'No. I've tried a few sketches

299

from memory, but nothing more, and nothing with real oil paints.'

'Good Lord.' Mitchell paused; he was at once jealous of the boy's precocious talent and as quickly ashamed of his envy, drowning it in the realisation that Dunbar was no longer an inexperienced and callow boy.

'They tell me she's the madame.'

'Yes. She is.'

'Is she the one you . . . ?'

'Yes. Yes she is.' He felt a kind of liberation in being able to own up to his actions without feeling them sinful. Perhaps they were, perhaps they would seem so in the old rectory, but what had passed between him and Dolores earlier, whatever it was, and he knew it had not been the thing he had thought of as love, it had not been sinful.

Whatever one chose to call it, it had been compounded of an irresistible passion, of pity and joy, of understanding and compassion. He had felt all differences of age and culture dissolved in a transitory moment of communion after which a sad poignancy infused him. He had felt himself older and if not wiser, then certainly less special, less apart. He was at once liberated and at the same time enthralled. He understood why the firemen aboard the *Kohinoor* had, along with every other man jack of her libidinous company, thought of nothing else but the haunting preoccupation of lust.

He watched Mitchell as the second mate stared again at the painting, and pitied him.

In the next few days Dunbar endured a succession of visitors. Rayner and Sanders, Teresa with her jaw bandaged, McKillop the third engineer, even Captain Steele. Then Reilly came back, not in his capacity as a doctor, but to translate for the *Alcaid* and the *Alcaid*'s clerk, who took his deposition down, reminding him of the death of Conchita.

He remembered how he had slithered and fallen upon her, how their bodies had, in the end, commingled blood as he stabbed his former friend with a desperate fury in that frantic moment. He recalled how the passage of time had slowed, and how his perception picked up and retained details. He could see the flash of light upon the knife blade, saw it draw the beads of scarlet blood, and then reveal the hissing pipework of Conchita's once lovely neck as sliced and horrid meat.

And now he felt his falling out of love with her a cruel and heartless betrayal. It did not matter she had rejected his mad, impulsive appeal to her. He had dropped her with a suddenness he scarcely understood.

He pondered this enigma.

He could not dispute her beauty and found he could still dream about it as he lay unsleeping in the stifling darkness, but he could not understand his swift yet irreversible change of heart and mind.

Sometime in the small hours Hawkshawe came, lamp in hand, and stood over him. It seemed she never slept and he apologised for monopolising her bed.

'It is no matter. You cannot sleep?'

'No. I was lying here thinking of Conchita.'

'Her end was terrible.'

'Yes. And so unjust.'

'Many things are unjust. Justice is merely a word signifying a grand aspiration. It does not exist, like day or night, nor like good or evil, or winning or losing. She was fortunate in that she died quickly. Many take years to die.'

Dunbar realised the insensitivity of his remark, set against this woman's wrecked life.

'I'm sorry, that was inexcusable of me,' he said doggedly, 'but I was not thinking of her death. I came here to release her. I thought myself in love with her and yet it seems I did not truly love her.'

'You were infatuated with an idea which she embodied,' Hawkshawe explained. 'Had not Dolores rescued you from your folly, you might have expected too much of every woman, all of whom would have ultimately disappointed you. Conchita, all unwittingly, rejected you. She was cruel, but ultimately did you a service.'

'Perhaps,' mused Dunbar, 'but at the time her vehemence was rather shocking.'

'Of course it was. You were a threat to her future.'

'I was a threat? How? I intended to offer her what I thought was a better future.'

Hawkshawe gave her low, vixen-laugh. 'Did you really think you could carry it off? You would not have got her aboard that ship of yours.'

'I might have been able to smuggle her on board.'

'Captain Steele would not have let you.'

'He might not have known, until we had sailed, at least.'

'He would not have sailed, my lad. He would have turned Puerto San Martin upside down if she had gone missing.'

'Why?' Dunbar frowned.

'He had arranged to buy her out of my employment and marry her himself.'

'Marry her?'

Outrage made Dunbar sit up; the pain and nausea which accompanied this sudden movement made him gasp and he subsided again, muttering, 'It isn't possible.'

'It very nearly happened. He should have been honeymooning.'

302

'I never thought . . .' Realisation struck him. 'It was Conchita's wedding you were preparing for, not Teresa's! I remember Captain Steele mentioned something about a wedding. It never occurred to me it was to be his own!'

'Why should you? You were too busy deluding yourself.'

'Yes, I was, wasn't I?' Dunbar said. 'And now . . .'

'You think yourself one hell of a man, is that it?' She was looking sharply at him from her one good eye.

He shook his head. 'No. You and Dolores have been very kind to me. I am not an ingrate. You know what has passed between Dolores and myself. I am as good as naked before you both.'

'What a damnably queer turn of phrase you have.'

'But it is how I feel. And I'm not ashamed of it. I am not in love with Dolores, yet I feel infinitely tender towards her.'

'Even though she is old enough to be your mother?'

'I cannot think of her like that. Anyway, she doesn't love me. I think she is more fond of you.'

'Maybe, but she will cry when your ship sails.' There was a pause, then Hawkshawe asked, 'Did you know you could paint?'

'No. Well, yes, I think I sort of knew inside. When I began to draw, when the *Kohinoor* was outward bound, I mean, I sensed an urge which I was continually failing to satisfy. Everything I tried to record fell short of my expectations. It was maddening. Then the second officer, Mr Mitchell, he came here earlier, gave me those oil paints and suddenly I felt the quality of the paints themselves seemed to liberate me from the constrictions of just using a pencil. And, of course, I was painting Dolores.'

'Yes. Yes, you were.'

'The two things coincided.'

'Three things coincided, I suggest,' said Hawkshawe brusquely. 'Consider yourself extremely fortunate to have been introduced to the art of love in such circumstances. Set them against my own, for instance.'

'Yes. I'm sorry.'

'I have never liked men, since Thirle. Had I not thought you to have been my brother, I might not have confided in you.'

'Do you regret making that mistake?'

'About your identity?'

'Yes, and confiding in me.'

Hawkshawe considered the matter. Then shook her head. 'After what happened aboard the *Macassar* I lost any faith in God. I became too busy fighting for survival. Age had fuddled my wits when you arrived, just as it will fuddle them when you are gone, but had you not come here, you could not have discovered yourself. Besides, neither of us can say with certainty whether you might not have inherited the soul of my brother Bobs.'

'Do you believe in the soul?'

Hawkshawe sniffed and looked away from him. He was reminded of a gun-dog pointing, as though at some distant and elusive game.

'I think', she said cautiously, 'I believe in some small centre of our being that is entirely physical. I do not think it lives beyond the span of our bodily life, yet I sense it has some purpose beyond our mere mortal existence. Beyond that I would not dare to speculate.'

'Please sit down, Captain.'

The veiled Hawkshawe gestured to the chair opposite her own. Steele fidgeted and tried to look beyond her.

'Dunbar is asleep. He has been up today and Reilly

agrees he will be able to attend tomorrow. Perhaps you would be kind enough to ask your steward to bring his uniform here.'

'Yes, yes, of course,' Steele said, his manner agitated.

'All the arrangements have been made. Father Xavier—'

'Miss Hawkshawe,' Steel broke in, 'I will come straight to the point . . .'

'You want your money back.'

'Well, yes,' Steele was sweating. 'Unless . . .'

'Not another girl, Captain?'

'I wondered . . . the young woman I saw that first time, the one with Conchita, I forget her name . . .'

Hawkshawe shook her head. 'Reilly reported her poxed, Captain. She is not for you.'

'Oh! No, no, of course not. What a pity.'

'However, I could arrange for Teresa . . .'

'Teresa?'

'The girl with the broken jaw, the one your Seaman Williams struck. It would be an act of magnanimous compassion . . .'

'No! No! That's not what I had in mind at all.' Steele waved a hand dismissively.

'What a pity,' Hawkshawe observed drily. 'In that case, Captain, you shall have your money back in full. I shall arrange for Jorge Maldonado to bring it aboard before you sail.' Hawkshawe rose with a creaking of her ancient stays. 'I think that concludes our business,' she said, dismissing Steele from her presence.

When he had gone, she smiled in the gloom. The money was irrelevant. There were always losers; the trick was never to become one, no matter what the circumstances.

Dunbar recalled little of the requiem mass beyond the

swirling incense, the splendour of the choir and organ, and the red ensigns and tricolours which draped the church. Hoisted for the wedding, they had been thought equally fitting for the twin funeral service over the bodies of Conchita and Williams, symbolic of the two nationalities brought together by untimely death.

The sinned against and sinning lay side by side at the entrance to the chancel. The sordid circumstances surounding their deaths were submerged beneath the purchased choral liturgy of the Roman Catholic church; the formal splendour of Captain Steele and his officers in uniform; the desire of the citizens of Puerto San Martin for any solemn undertaking which broke the formal monotony of their lives, and the exploitation of this desire by the *Alcaid*, the harbour master, the apparatus of government, and the mercantile interests of the port.

Conchita was eulogised as a latter-day Magdalen, a young and promising woman of exceptional beauty and God-given loveliness; Williams a passion-torn foreigner whose lost soul had finally found peace in the infinite mercy of Almighty God.

As the large congregation spilled out into the old plaza, then drifted along the outer wall into the newer square, Father Xavier led the *cortège* to the cemetery. Captain Steele, his hat tucked under his left elbow, followed the coffins. The gold lace on the cuffs of his frock coat caught the sunshine and his officers, similarly attired, trailed uncertainly behind him in diminishing rank. Rayner, knowing the captain mourned the loss of his dreams, dutifully prayed for the friendless Williams, while Dunbar walked a little unsteadily between Miss Hawkshawe and Señora Garcia, as though between two sabled aunts. Few of his shipmates could have guessed the strange relationship which had burgeoned between them, though Mitchell watched the swing of Garcia's hips with an unbecoming and inappropriate envy.

'What a confounded waste of time,' muttered Herr Pedersen irritably.

'Such rituals are very necessary,' remarked Reilly who, with the engineer, brought up the rear of the solemn little procession.

'Only to the ignorant and superstitious,' Pedersen retorted.

Reilly nodded. 'Perhaps you are right, but you will never eradicate ignorance and superstition, my friend, not with all the engineering in the world.'

Dunbar returned to his ship a week after the funeral. Reilly took out his sutures that morning and pronounced him fit enough. Dunbar saw Richenda Hawkshawe only once more before the *Kohinoor* sailed. When he had left the Hotel in the company of the two women, Hawkshawe had tactfully insisted that, since he had finished the painting, it would be better if he did not come back to the Paradiso. He recognised the finality and the wisdom of her suggestion. Garcia had visited him the night before the funeral and both knew it had been for the last time.

The ship was loading five thousand tons of copper *boleos*, one of the last cargoes to be brought from the mine to the wharf by railway. Hampered by his wound, Dunbar had been placed on light duties and was conveying documents to Señor Maldonado's as the loading neared completion. He found Richenda Hawkshawe ensconced in the agent's office. She had clearly been expecting him, for she handed him an instantly recognisable parcel, wrapped in crushed brown paper.

'I understand the *Kohinoor* sails tomorrow,' she began.

307

'Jorge tells me you hoisted the blue peter this morning.'

He nodded. 'Yes, that's right, ma'am.'

'You must take the portrait with you.' She handed it to him.

'But it was done for you,' he said.

'It was a whim; I meant nothing by it at the time. It may mean much to you. Not now, but later, and besides . . .' She looked at Maldonado who coughed awkwardly, rose and left. 'Besides, the matter in which I confided. I would be obliged if the sorry tale of the *Macassar* died with me. I want you to promise me you will say nothing about it. It can be of no interest to you. Will you promise me that?'

'Yes, if you wish.'

'I hope the painting will remind you of your promise, and of what you can become.' She paused, rising to her feet as he reluctantly accepted the wrapped canvas, adding, 'It will also remind you of Dolores.'

'I shall never forget either of you, Miss Hawkshawe. Please give my sincere . . .' He could find no words to express himself. He knew he could not speak of love, yet his vocabulary seemed bereft of an expression deep enough to convey the strength of his feelings.

'I will tell her.'

She held out her hand; he took it and then raised it to his lips.

'The paint was quite dry,' she remarked, her voice quavering, 'when we wrapped it.' She withdrew her hand and made to pass him. Impulsively he put the picture on Maldonado's desk and seized her in a boyish hug. The stiff old woman shook silently in his embrace. When he let her go, she stumbled out of the room and left him foolishly contemplating himself in a mirror.

'What would Father say,' he muttered to himself, pulling a wry face, 'if he knew I felt affection for an old procuress?'

When he returned to the ship he unwrapped the brown paper. The thicker layers of paint were still soft to the touch, and slipped inside the wrapping was a sheet of paper upon which Hawkshawe, in the beautiful copper-plate hand he recognised from the ledger, had written: *Beautiful women will always torture you, so learn to resist them. You will be stronger for it.*

'What've you got there?' Humphries asked, coming in to the half-deck at that moment.

'Nothing,' snapped Dunbar, bundling the rough canvas in his locker, 'nothing at all.'

Dunbar had occupied the forward station when they had arrived at Puerto San Martin. When they left he was allocated the poop, in company with Mr Mitchell.

Both men stared astern as, with a faint jangling of bridge and engine-room telegraphs, the *Kohinoor*'s propeller increased its revolutions and the ship's speed. Below the docking bridge, the seamen completed coiling away the heavy mooring ropes. Dunbar thought of Williams as Mitchell dismissed them from their harbour stations. The port dropped astern as the ship passed through the anchorage. One of the German barques was preparing to move alongside into the berth vacated by the British tramp ship.

Dunbar felt Mitchell touch him on the shoulder. 'I'll leave you to say your farewells then, Foggy.'

'Aye, aye, sir.'

The sky had clouded over towards evening and the buildings along the waterfront seemed to merge and float like a grey island above the dull, calm sheen of the sea. Only the great belfry of the church was recognisable, a hard edge set against the far, dim line of the mountains. It seemed improbable that the fading smudge contained the Hotel Paradiso and its inmates and associates: Richenda Hawkshawe, Dolores Garcia, Esteban and Gloria, and the still bruised Teresa; Reilly, Valbuena, Maldonado and the impatient Pedersen.

It was still more inconceivable that Conchita and Williams had once existed in the full vigour of life, and now lay dead. Or that the place held the secret of the terrible mutiny aboard the *Macassar*.

A secret he had vowed to take to the grave. He straightened up and reached for the ensign halliards, slowly lowering the grubby red bunting. The movement made him wince as the knitting muscles of his breast protested.

How would he explain the scar?

EPILOGUE

The desire to enter the church before the rectory was compelling. He had the driver unload his sea-chest and, having paid the man off, negligently left his traps beside the road and entered the churchyard.

It was a grey, nondescript day, set between summer and autumn. The leaves on the trees were no longer a lush green, but were rustling with a nascent dryness in the east wind that blew off the North Sea. As he pushed open the door, he felt the wind rush past him to stir the long silken folds of the huge red ensign.

The movement reminded him of the flags hanging in the church of San Martin, and then the image faded, as though nothing more than a dream, an insubstantial figment of his imagination. The church of San Martin did not exist; the funeral had never taken place; Conchita had never existed. He himself had never existed beyond this place. The *Kohinoor*, the voyage, all were part of an elaborate fantasy.

But for the scar. It itched with an irritating insistency at such moments.

The church was as empty as the road outside and he turned and walked out. Despite the chill wind, sharp on the body of one just returned from the tropics, the graveyard seemed warmer; even, he thought blasphemously, friendlier.

He smiled to himself. Somewhere over in the north-west corner was the headstone marked with the name Richenda, and in his baggage there was a tyro portrait of a woman called Dolores . . .

Jenny Broom opened the rectory door to him.

'Master James!' Her surprise turned to a wide, welcoming smile. He followed her into the hall as she explained that his mother and father had gone to Ipswich.

'Why didn't you send word you was coming home?' Jenny asked, putting tea in the teapot and taking the old black kettle from the hob.

'I wanted it to be a surprise.'

'Oh, it's that all right,' Jenny laughed. 'My, how you've changed!'

'Have I?' He grinned back.

'It's so good to see you! Why only last week your ma was wondering where you were. Said so right there, where you'm standing, and now here you are, large as life!'

'And you're looking lovely, Jenny,' he said boldly, moving forward as she poured the tea, to stand beside her.

She looked up at him and he could smell her warm breath. 'Oh, you've changed, Master James!'

They hugged and he kissed her hair and felt himself stir. She pulled back laughing. 'Oh, none of that, Master James, not now I'm spoken for.'

'Spoken for? What's this?'

'Life don't stand still just 'cause you'm not here,' she prattled happily, handing him a cup of tea. 'Alfred Slater's proposed to me. We're to marry in the new year.'

'That's wonderful, Jenny,' he said, wondering if he meant it. He could not recall Alfred Slater, though he knew the surname well.

'His older brother was batman to the colonel's son.'

312

'Ah, yes.' Dunbar remembered the Boer War hero of Clayton Dobbs.

'Alfred says he's quite happy if I continue to work here and your ma and pa say that's all right . . .'

He listened to her recount the events he had missed by his absence: two deaths from old age, a boy drowned in summer floods, four christenings, six confirmations and the expected dissolution of an unhappy marriage. He watched her broad, freckled and open face as it animatedly catalogued these village tragedies and triumphs. Clearly Alfred Slater was good for her. Then a thought occurred to him.

'Jenny, may I ask if you'd do me a favour?'

'Long as it's decent, Master James,' she shot back, eyes twinkling.

'I'd like to paint a portrait of you.'

'A portrait?' She frowned, uncertain of his meaning. 'You mean . . . like those ones they've got up at the hall?'

'Not as good as those, but something like them, yes.'

'But they'm all ladies. Why don't you go up and ask Miss Julia? She'm staying up at the hall.'

'She'd probably say no, Jenny. Anyway I want to paint you. It wouldn't take long.'

'Well, I . . . what would your ma and pa say?'

There was the noise of footfalls on gravel. Dunbar remembered the trunk and ditty-bag left beside the gate. He heard his mother's voice call out, 'It must be him!' and the noise amplified as she opened the front-door.

'I don't care what they think, Jenny,' Dunbar said hurriedly, smiling.

'All right,' Jenny consented as the kitchen door flew open.

'James! It *is* you! Oh, I'm so sorry we weren't here to welcome you!'

He embraced his mother and over her shoulder saw his father standing in the doorway. The rector's sober garb and motionless appraisal thrust a sudden poignant memory of Richenda Hawkshawe into Dunbar's mind.

'Father,' he said.

'Welcome home, James.'

The rector's voice was unemotional and his eyes seemed cautious; almost, Dunbar felt, to the point of suspicion. His mother had released him and was staring up at him, her eyes wet with tears.

'Oh dear, you're so grown up,' she said, 'and as brown as a berry.'

His father stepped into the kitchen and advanced with hand extended, his heel irons clicking on the flagstones.

'How are you, my boy?'

'Very well, Father. And you?'

'Oh, no complaints, no complaints. We'd better haul your effects in from the road. It looks like rain.'

'Is that tea hot, Jenny?' Dunbar heard his mother ask.

'I'll make a fresh pot,' Jenny replied as the two men went out into the hall.

'Good voyage?'

'Yes, very.'

'Good.'

They passed into the garden and the rector said, 'Old Skipper Hopton died shortly after you left.'

'Oh, I'm sorry to hear that.' Jenny had not mentioned Hopton.

'Died at sea,' the rector added. 'Heart failed.'

They picked up the trunk and manhandled it back into the house.

'The twins are well,' his father grunted as they manoeuvred the trunk through the front door into the gloomy hall.

314

'Oh, good. They're at school, I suppose.'

'Yes. Your mother misses them, of course. Why don't you unpack this thing here, save us taking it upstairs.'

'Yes, of course.'

'The evenings are beginning to draw in.'

'Yes.'

'Colonel Scrope-Davies has asked your mother and me to dine on Saturday. Would you like me to mention that you're home? Young Julia Ravenham's staying at the moment. D'you remember her?'

'Yes, but I doubt if she remembers me.'

'Well, I expect she'd rather have someone of her own age to talk to.'

'Very well.'

'I'm seeing the colonel tomorrow; he's bound to ask you. She's on her own rather, unhappy love affair or something. Your mother will tell you the details. I'm sure she knows them by now. It's all different these days with you youngsters gallivanting about the world. Let's join your mother for some tea, eh?'

'Good idea,' said Dunbar, stepping round the trunk. 'I've some nick-nacks for you.'

'Oh, they can wait until later. We'll see if there's anything with a passing resemblance to a fatted calf to kill for dinner and you can indulge us over a glass of sherry.'

The rector seemed to mellow and, opening the kitchen door, gently thrust his son inside.

The lights were already lit and burning brightly as Jenny poured tea into the cheery blue and white cups while Anne Dunbar laid macaroons on an elaborate cake stand.

'Good to have the prodigal return, eh, my dear?' the rector said expansively, patting his son on the shoulder.

☐ An Eye of the Fleet	Richard Woodman	£4.99
☐ A King's Cutter	Richard Woodman	£4.99
☐ A Brig of War	Richard Woodman	£4.99
☐ The Bomb Vessel	Richard Woodman	£4.99
☐ Flying Squadron	Richard Woodman	£4.99
☐ Under False Colours	Richard Woodman	£5.99
☐ The Darkening Sky	Richard Woodman	£4.99
☐ Endangered Species	Richard Woodman	£4.99

Warner Books now offers an exciting range of quality titles by both established and new authors which can be ordered from the following address:

Little, Brown and Company (UK),
P.O. Box 11,
Falmouth,
Cornwall TR10 9EN.

Alternatively you may fax your order to the above address.
Fax No: 01326 317444
Telephone No: 01326 317200
E-mail: books@barni.avel.co.uk

Payments can be made as follows: cheque, postal order (payable to Little, Brown and Company) or by credit cards, Visa/Access. Do not send cash or currency. UK customers and B.F.P.O. please allow £1.00 for postage and packing for the first book, plus 50p for the second book, plus 30p for each additional book up to a maximum charge of £3.00 (7 books plus).

Overseas customers including Ireland, please allow £2.00 for the first book plus £1.00 for the second book, plus 50p for each additional book.

NAME (Block Letters) ....

....

ADDRESS ....

....

....

☐ I enclose my remittance for ....
☐ I wish to pay by Access/Visa Card

Number ☐☐☐☐☐☐☐☐☐☐☐☐☐☐☐☐

Card Expiry Date ☐☐☐☐